(continued from back

The Venus Henry _____ in *Clash by Night* and _____ ons to appear in *Astound* _____ test years of that magazin _____ rld with two novels as colorful and imaginative as the originals.

SURFACE ACTION

Johnnie Gordon was born to wealth and privilege in the Keeps, but his whole life has been dedicated to becoming a warrior of the Free Companies like his uncle. Now his chance has come—a deadly struggle through hellish jungle to steal the enemy's most powerful battleship. If Johnnie succeeds, then one more duty awaits him: a duty that will haunt his nightmares forever. But if he fails, Venus will die as surely as the atom-blasted Earth died; and Mankind will die also.

THE JUNGLE

Brainard's torpedoboat was in the wrong place at the wrong time when a salvo of shells flung him and his crew ashore in their wrecked vessel. Without a radio, they're as good as dead—unless they can cross the island through a jungle where every animal is a danger and the plants are even worse.

Brainard and his fellow Free Companions are hard men who've faced death in battle, but now their enemy is a green Hell that wants not only to defeat but to devour them . . . as it will some day devour all of Mankind—unless Brainard and his crew survive, and they can turn the lessons they've learned in the jungle against the even greater enemy that lurks in the Keeps themselves!

Hard-edged politics and combat written by a man who's seen both personally, displayed in a lush setting created by two of the finest SF writers of all time!

AND A BONUS!

The author's travelogue of ten days among the real jungles, reefs and ancient temples of Belize, told with the sharpness of observation and anecdote which have made his fiction so vividly memorable.

SEAS OF
VENUS

DAVID DRAKE

SEAS OF VENUS

Copyright © 2002 by David Drake. *Surface Action* copyright © 1990 by David Drake, *The Jungle* copyright © 1991 by David Drake.

A Baen Books Original Omnibus

Baen Publishing Enterprises
P.O. Box 1403
Riverdale, NY 10471
www.baen.com

ISBN: 0-7434-7192-X

Cover art by Bob Eggleton

First mass market paperback printing, March 2004

Library of Congress Cataloging-in-Publication Number 2002026278

Distributed by Simon & Schuster
1230 Avenue of the Americas
New York, NY 10020

Production by Windhaven Press, Auburn, NH
Printed in the United States of America

Contents

Introduction
-1-

Surface Action
-5-

The Jungle
-249-

The Real Jungle:
Belize 2001
-451-

Introduction:
SEA STORIES

For my thirteenth birthday, my parents gave me a collection of SF (bought from a guy who was entering the Navy) which included *The Astounding Science Fiction Anthology*. Among many other great stories in the volume—it was John Campbell's own distillation of Golden Age SF, after all—was *Clash by Night* by Lawrence O'Donnell.

It was years before I learned that Lawrence O'Donnell was a pseudonym of C.L. Moore and her husband, Henry Kuttner. Most O'Donnell stories were written primarily by Moore, but this one seems to have been Kuttner's work in large measure. (After Kuttner's death, Moore renewed the copyright in Kuttner's name alone.)

Details of authorship didn't matter to me when I was thirteen, and they don't matter a great deal now: *Clash by Night* really blew me away. A writer is what he reads, and this story marked me to a greater degree than I could've imagined at the time. (Well, at the time I couldn't have imagined that I was going to be a professional writer. Even after twenty-odd years it seems pretty strange.)

Kuttner and Moore wrote about mercenary soldiers of the future, basing the concept on the Condottieri of Renaissance Italy. These bands were more romantic than most mercenaries (in part because they didn't do a lot of hard fighting), and many writers, Kuttner and Moore included, have emphasized the romantic aspect.

But the Condottieri were also businessmen—the name means contractor and is the same word you'd use if you were hiring someone to build your house or to carry your goods from Venice to Rome. In recognizing the business aspect of mercenary soldiering, *Clash by Night* from 1943 is an order of magnitude ahead of most stories about mercenaries written either before or after it.

I jumped at the opportunity to get *Clash by Night* reprinted when Marty Greenberg suggested I do a sequel to it for a series of double novels he was packaging. I wrote *Surface Action* as a thematic sequel which could've been published in *Astounding* in 1943. In Kuttner and Moore's story, a young soldier who thinks he wants to be a civilian comes to a realization about himself and his world. In mine, a young civilian who thinks he wants to be a soldier reaches a similar insight.

Surface Action didn't appear in the double series (the details are on my website for those who want them) and was instead published separately. Because it didn't appear with *Clash by Night* I made minor changes to the terminology, but it remains a direct response—and homage—to the original. I then wrote *The Jungle* in order to get *Clash by Night* back in print.

Surface Action has a simple plot and a structure that would have fit in with the fiction *Astounding* was publishing in the 1939-43 period (which I and many others consider the Golden Age of Science Fiction).

I don't like to repeat myself, so for *The Jungle*, I went to multiple viewpoints and paired each segment of consecutive narrative with a flashback from the same viewpoint but set at widely varying periods of the past. The structure is more complex even than what I used on the much longer *Northworld Trilogy*. I'm happy with the way the experiment worked out, but I've never tried to do anything like it again.

Writing a story always has an element of puzzle in it. These two novels had more than the usual, because I was writing in someone else's universe and using assumptions current in 1940. I doubt that Kuttner and Moore really believed in an ocean-covered Venus, but they could set their story on one without explanation (and indeed, Isaac Asimov could do the same in 1955). Before I could get on with my story, I needed to throw in terraforming and evolutionary developments which are more colorful than probable.

My story is about people; about the way people feel and think and interact under stress. That's the same subject that Kuttner and Moore addressed, and it's the focus of most of the fiction that interests me.

The novels gave me scope for writing about the natural world—which in their case was mostly my backyard writ large. I've never subscribed to the suburban dream of neatly manicured lawns. Our present house is in the middle of a 15-acre meadow which we bushhog once or twice a year to keep trees from taking over. At the time I wrote *Surface Action* and *The Jungle* we were on a half-acre lot, but we'd deliberately allowed the back—where I wrote outdoors, using laptop computers—to go feral if not exactly wild. This setting added immediacy to the descriptions of hostile blackberries and honeysuckle. Once I had to wait before copying because a jumping spider had crawled into the floppy drive and I didn't want a tragic accident.

As a whim—mine and Jim Baen's both—this volume also includes an account of my family vacation in the rain forest of Belize. It's not my first experience of real jungles—that came in War Zone C in 1970—but it's by far the more pleasant. Those of you who aren't interested in non-fiction can ignore the travelogue, but those who read it will be able to recognize echoes in future fiction of mine that touches in any way on jungles or lost cities. Based on my stories to date, that'll be a pretty high percentage of my output.

My main consideration in writing both *Surface Action* and *The Jungle* was to get more people to read *Clash by Night*. If you like what you read here, look for the original; I've reprinted it a couple times myself, and I believe there's an on-line version available for a modest charge.

Having said that, these novels gave me great pleasure to write. I hope that some of the fun I had will translate to pleasure for the readers.

Dave Drake
david-drake.com

SURFACE ACTION

For Mark L. Van Name
Who has made my life easier
as well as more interesting.

PROLOGUE

And we are here as on a darkling plain
Swept with confused alarms of struggle
*   and flight*
Where ignorant armies clash by night.
                                    —Matthew Arnold

Five hundred years before the first colony ship landed on Venus, an asteroid which had been expanded into a fat nickel-iron balloon impacted with the upper Venerian atmosphere. There it spread its filling of tailored bacteria to graze among the roiling hydrocarbons.

That was the start of the terraforming process.

Thousands of asteroid casings followed the first. All the early ones were loaded with bacteria which broke down the poisons, forming free water through biochemical processes and creating mulch as they died and their bodies drifted toward the surface.

The upper layers of the atmosphere cleared and no longer trapped the sun's heat. The blankets of bacteria moved lower, following the hellish temperatures and poisonous hydrocarbons in which alone they could exist.

Rain fell—and vaporized again, long before the huge lashing drops had reached the surface. Furnace-hot

layers of air cooled and cleared, and the rain continued to fall.

Even before the Venerian highlands rose above the
remaining strata of hydrocarbon haze, asteroids spewed
seeds, spores, and Earth-standard one-celled life into
the atmosphere. The new cargoes spread and fell with
the rain; and mostly died, but not quite all.

Men sent more asteroids filled with more life, and
the life flourished.

The sheen of water-vapor clouds reflected the dangerous majority of sunlight from the reformed planet,
but the short, higher-energy end of the spectrum
penetrated the clouds most easily. The actinic rays
aided mutation, and the virgin surface of the planet
permitted adaptive radiation on a scale never imagin-
able on Earth.

Asteroids strewed eggs; at first invertebrates,
then those of backboned life forms, though none so
advanced that the young required parental care.

The colony ships arrived.

In a degree, the planners who seeded Venus with
life had been too successful. Land and sea both teemed
with a savage parody of "Nature red in fang and claw."

The seas proved easier to colonize—"at first," the
planners said, though the temporary expedient quickly
hardened to permanence. Domed cities sprang up on
continental shelves a few thousand feet down—beneath
the sunlight and the light-driven violence of the surface layers, but well above the scarcely less fierce
competition in the deep trenches where all organic
matter at last settled.

Seven days, four hours, and thirty-four minutes after
the last colony ship landed on Venus, Earth's final war
triggered a fusion reaction in her oceans. By astronomical standards, the resulting star was both small and
short-lived; but it would smolder for thousands of years,

and its first milliseconds had been enough to cleanse the planet of life.

Mankind survived in the domes of Venus.

Only in the domes of Venus.

The individual cities were independent and fiercely competitive, though the causes of their conflicts had no more logic to those not involved than did the causes of men's wars through the previous ages. Earth's blazing death throes imposed order of a kind on the wars of Venus, but not even that warning trauma could bring peace.

Nuclear power and weapons were banned, as guns had been banned in Japan during the Shogunate. The ban was enforced with absolute ruthlessness. Domed cities were vulnerable to conventional weapons of the simplest sort. A dome which was believed to harbor nuclear experiments was cracked so that water pressure crushed its inhabitants into the ooze before they could drown.

Apart from that, war on Venus was fought on the surface, and by warriors.

Independent contractors, like the condottieri of Renaissance Italy, built bases and fleets with private funding and staffed them with volunteers. They fought one another for hire, and in the interim they fought the jungles for their very lives.

Domes went to war according to set rules. When battle and mercenaries' blood had decided the point at issue, the losing city ransomed itself to penury. The winning dome recouped the cost of the fleet it hired, and the winning military entrepreneurs collected a comfortable victory bonus.

The losing mercenaries had the amount of their original hire and whatever they had managed to save from the wrack of defeat. That might be enough for them to go on to lesser contracts, desperately trying to rebuild their fortunes; or they might be forced to merge with another company on unfavorable terms.

Sometimes they merged with the fleet which had just defeated them. Business was business.

The fleets seemed a romantic alternative to life in the climate-controlled safety of the domed cities. Civilians aped the dress and manners of the mercenaries or scorned them, but no one in the domes could ignore fleet personnel in their uniforms and their dark-tanned skins.

There was no shortage of volunteers to take up the reality of the romantic challenge. . . .

1

A taster of wine, with an eye for a maid,
Never too bold, and never afraid. . . .

—Bliss Carman

The crowd in Carnaval finery burst apart with a collective shriek.

The man forcing his way toward Johnnie through the revelers had a stubble beard and a wild look in his eyes. His left arm clamped a woman against his chest like the figurehead of a packet ship. Her domino mask hung from one ear. There were scratches on her collarbone, and the gauzy blouse had been shredded away from her breasts.

The man's right hand waved a butcher knife with an eight-inch blade.

"All right, you whore!" the man screamed. His dilated pupils weren't focused on anything in his present surroundings. "You want to spread it around, I'll *help* you spread it around!"

The knife slipped like a chord of light-struck ripple toward the woman's belly.

Johnnie's right hand dropped as he swung his hips to the left. The hem of his scarlet tunic had tiny weights in it, so that the ruffed flare stood out as his body moved—

Clearing the pistol holstered high on Johnnie's right hip.

The woman's body shielded all of the madman except his arms and the wedge of face including his staring, bloodshot eyes. The Carnaval crowd was a montage of silks and shrieks surrounding the event.

Johnnie's hand curved up with the pistol; faster than a snake striking, faster than the knife. For an instant that trembled like the sun on dew, the line of the pistol barrel joined Johnnie's eye and the madman's.

The muzzle lifted with a flash and a haze of clean-burning propellant. The sharp *crack*! of muzzle blast slapped through the screams. The madman's right eye socket was empty as his body spasmed backward in a tetanic arch. His arms lashed apart, flinging the woman to one side and the butcher knife to the other.

Johnnie took a deep breath and loaded a fresh magazine from the pouch on his left hip, where it balanced the weight of the pistol. The holographic ambiance faded, leaving behind a large room whose walls were gray with a covering of vitalon, a super-cooled liquid which absorbed bullet impacts within its dense interior.

A red light glowed on the wall above the door. Somebody was in the anteroom, watching the sequence through closed-circuit cameras.

The muscles of Johnnie's lean face set in a pattern scarcely recognizable as the visage of the good-looking youth of a moment before. He holstered his weapon and touched the door control.

"Well," he said as the armored door rotated and withdrew, "are you satisfied, Sena—"

The man in the anteroom wore a Blackhorse dress uniform, with the gold pips and braid of a commander.

His only similarity to Senator A. Rolfe Gordon was that both men were in their mid-forties—

And they'd been brothers-in-law before the Senator's wife ran off with a mercenary not long after she gave birth to Johnnie.

"Uncle Dan!" cried Johnnie. He started toward Commander Daniel Cooke with his arms wide . . . before he remembered that what was proper for a boy of nine should have been outgrown by nineteen. He drew back in embarrassment.

Uncle Dan gave him a devil-may-care grin and embraced Johnnie. "What's the matter?" he demanded. "Did I develop skin-rot since I last saw you?"

He stepped back and viewed the younger man critically. "Though I won't," he said, "offer to swing you up in the air any more."

"Gee it's good to . . . ," Johnnie said. "I wasn't expecting to see you."

"I have a meeting with the Senator this morning," Dan explained. "And I thought I'd come a little early to see my favorite nephew."

"Ah . . . shall we go somewhere comfortable?"

"If you don't mind," replied his uncle, "I'd like to watch you run through a sequence or two."

Dan's smile didn't change, but his voice was a hair too casual when he added, "The Senator comes to watch you frequently, then?"

"No," said Johnnie flatly. "Not often at all. But too often."

His face cleared. "But I'd love to show *you* the set-up, Uncle Dan. The screens in the anteroom—"

"I'd prefer to be in the simulator with you," Dan said. He lifted his saucer hat and ran his fingers through his black, curly hair. "Though I won't be shooting."

"There's some danger even with the—" Johnnie began until his uncle's brilliant grin stopped him.

*Right, explain the danger of ricochets to Commander
Daniel Cooke, whose ship took nine major-caliber hits
three months ago while blasting her opponent in Squadron Monteleone to wreckage.*

"Sorry, Uncle Dan."

"Never apologize for offering information that might
save somebody's life," Dan said. "Got a jungle sequence
in this system?"

"This system's got about *everything*!" Johnnie
answered with pride as the gray walls dissolved into
a mass of stems, leaves, and dim green terror. As the
holographic simulation appeared, the climate control
raised sharply the temperature and humidity of the air
it pumped into the environment.

They were on the edge of a clearing, a dimpled
expanse of yellow-brown mud. The surface was too thin
to provide purchase for any plants save those which
crawled about slowly on feather-fringed roots. Creatures with armored hides had trampled a path around
the periphery of the clearing, through the brambles that
were now curling to reclaim the terrain.

A bubble rose from the mud and burst flatulently.

"The trouble with the simulator," Johnnie said in a
whisper, "is that you *know* there's something there in
the mud."

The air was still and as moist as a sponge.

"Which makes it exactly like the land anywhere on
Venus' surface," said his uncle, also speaking quietly.
"Go on, then."

Johnnie took a step forward. If he'd been expecting to run a jungle sequence, he'd have equipped
himself with a powered cutting-bar and a more powerful handgun. . . .

His left arm brushed aside a curtain of gray
tendrils, roots hanging from an air plant to absorb
water from the atmosphere—and entangle small

flying creatures whose juices would be absorbed to feed
the plant. The simulator couldn't duplicate the touch
of vegetation, but a jet of air stroked Johnnie's sleeve
to hint at the contact.

A swamp-chopper exploded toward them from the
oozing muck.

Johnnie drew and fired. His thumb rocked the grip's
feed-switch forward even as the first two rounds of
explosive bullets cracked out, shattering the creature's
stalked eyes.

Johnnie threw himself sideways. He fired the
remainder of the magazine as solids which could
penetrate the swamp-chopper's armored carapace while
the blinded monster thrashed in the vegetation where
Johnnie had been.

Genetically, the swamp-chopper was a crab, but
ionizing radiation and the purulent surface of Venus
had modified the creature's ancestors into man-sized
predators. They retained lesser arthropods' unwilling-
ness to die. Despite 18 rounds into its thorax, the
creature was still trying to claw through the bole of
the holographic tree with which it had collided in its
blind rush.

Johnnie slapped a fresh magazine into his pistol and
aimed.

Dan put a hand on his arm. "Forget it," he said.
"Don't worry about the ones that can't hurt you.
Let's—"

"Cooke?" boomed an amplified voice. "Cooke! What
are you doing here?"

Both men turned. The red light which glowed in the
heart of a thicket of holographic bamboo indicated that
someone was in the simulator's anteroom.

"Duty calls, lad," said Dan, rising to his feet. Johnnie
shut the system down, just as something green, circular,
and huge sailed toward them from the middle canopy.

Dan opened the door. Senator Gordon stood in the anteroom with his legs braced apart and his hands in the pockets of his frock coat. He neither stepped forward nor offered to shake hands.

Dan offered an ironic salute. "Good to see you again, Senator," he said.

"If I'd known you had nothing on your mind but playing foolish games with my son, Commander Cooke," Gordon said, "I wouldn't have bothered making time in my schedule to see you. Particularly at *this* juncture."

Dan ostentatiously shot his cuff to look at the bioelectrical watch imprinted onto the skin of his left wrist. He didn't bother to say that he was still twenty-three minutes early for his appointment because Gordon was already well aware of the fact.

"The games I've come to discuss aren't silly ones, Senator," Dan said coolly.

"For that matter—" he added with a raised eyebrow "—these simulations aren't silly either. Which is why I offered to buy Johnnie a membership to a commercial range."

"Yes, of course," the Senator said. When he was angry, as now, a flush crept up his jowls and across the hair-fringed expanse of his bare scalp. "You'd have had John spending all his time in the warehouse district. No thank you, Cooke. I can afford to accommodate my son's whims in a less destructive way."

"Right," said Johnnie in a brittle voice that sounded years younger than that in which he had been speaking to his uncle. "You got me the simulator, all right. *After* you knew Dan had already taken out a membership for me at Action Sports!"

"Something I've learned over the years," Dan said mildly, "is that the reasons don't matter so long as the job gets done."

He smiled at his nephew, but his face cleared to neutrality as he focused on Senator Gordon again. "But that's not what we're here to discuss . . . and I think your office would be a better location."

Johnnie nodded. "I'm really glad to see you again, Uncle Dan," he said. "Maybe if you have time—"

"No," said his uncle, "I'd like you to accompany us, Johnnie. You see—" and his face segued again from smile to armed truce as his eyes locked again with those of his ex-brother-in-law "—this concerns you as well as the Senator. And everyone else on Venus."

Gordon's face was just as hard as that of Commander Cooke. "Yes," he said after a moment. "All right."

As Johnnie followed the two older men into the elevator to the Senator's penthouse office, his heart was beating with a rush of excitement greater than that he'd felt minutes before in the simulator.

He didn't know what was going on.

But he knew that it wasn't a simulation.

2

There is a Hand that bends our deeds
To mightier issues than we planned:
Each son that triumphs, each that bleeds,
My country, serves Its dark command.
—Richard Hovey

Senator Gordon's office befitted the most powerful man in Wenceslas Dome—and mayhap in all of Venus. The penthouse windows commanded a sweeping vision, down across the city and up to the black ceramic dome.

In the center of the dome hung a ball of white light, framed in black swags: an image of Earth as she had become, and a warning to the generations of Venus why nuclear power had to be banned if Mankind were to survive in this her remaining refuge.

"Sit down, sit down," said the Senator as he stepped behind his broad, ostentatiously empty desk and seated himself.

Johnnie obeyed, his face expressionless. He'd only been in his father's office a dozen times during his life, and he'd *never* before been invited to sit.

The cushion sagged deeply beneath him. He looked

across the desk at the Senator and found that he was looking up.

Uncle Dan, moving as gracefully as a leopard, sat on the arm of his chair. The mercenary officer smiled frequently, but there was more humor than usual in his expression as he winked at Johnnie and then returned his attention to Senator Gordon.

The Senator spread his hands flat on the desktop in a pattern as precise as the growth of coral fronds. He didn't look at them. "I want to make it clear before we begin, Commander," he said, "that negotiations between Wenceslas Dome and the Blackhorse are conducted between the Military Committee and your commanding officer, Admiral Bergstrom. *Not* between me and you."

Dan raised an eyebrow. "And you can't speak for the Military Committee, Senator?" he said in false concern. "There's been a coup, then?"

The Senator became very still. "No, Commander," he said. "But there hasn't been a change of leadership in the Blackhorse either. Has there?"

"No, quite right," Dan said. He spoke easily but with no attempt to feign nonchalance. "Admiral Bergstrom talks about retirement, but I think it'll be years—unless he dies in harness."

The soft cushions made Johnnie feel as though he were cocooned and invisible. Neither of the older men seemed aware of his presence.

"Whereupon," the Senator continued, "he'll be succeeded by Captain Haynes . . . whom you hate rather more than you hate me, don't you, Commander?"

Dan shrugged and turned up his left hand in a gesture of dismissal. "Oh, I don't hate Captain Haynes, Senator," he said. "He's as good an administrative officer as a mercenary company could have . . . but a little too much of a traditionalist, I think, to become

Admiral of the Blackhorse at a time when Wenceslas
Dome is overturning so many traditions."

It was like watching a scorpion battle a centipede.
Uncle Dan feinted and backed, but his manner always
hinted of a lethal sting, waiting for the right moment.
The Senator drove on implacably, trusting in the
armor of his certainty; absolutely determined.

"Now, if you said Captain Haynes hated *me* more
than any other man on Venus . . . ," Dan added. "In
that, I think you might be correct."

The Senator sniffed. "A distinction without a
difference," he said. "And in any case, Blackhorse
internal politics are of no concern to me. All that
matters to Wenceslas—to the Federated Domes—is
that the Blackhorse stand ready to earn the retainer
we pay you. If there's a problem with your side of
the bargain, perhaps it's time for us to engage some
other fleet."

Dan pouted his lips in agreement and said, "Yeah,
that's the problem all right, Senator. That's just what
I came to talk to you about."

Nobody in the office breathed for ten long seconds.

The Senator checked a security read-out on the
corner of his desk; found it still a satisfactory green.
"Say what you came to say, Daniel," he said, speaking as flatly as if his words clicked out through the
mandibles of a centipede.

"Heidigger Dome has hired Flotilla Blanche," Dan
said. "Carolina's got the Warcocks. We could handle
either one of them without problems. If Blackhorse
alone faces both of them together, then that's all she
wrote. For us. And for you."

Johnnie expected Dan to undercut the weight of his
words with a shrug or a grin. Instead, the mercenary
officer's voice was as emotionless as that of the dome
politician a moment before.

"Yes," said the Senator, "of course. So you'll have to associate another fleet for the duration."

Senator Gordon's penthouse was designed to impress, but it was a working office as well. Johnnie flipped up the right armrest of his chair to expose the keypad there. His fingertips began to summon data while his eyes flicked back and forth between the older men.

"We *need* to associate another fleet," said Dan, the emphasis making clear there was more than agreement in the words. "But no other fleet will deal with us. Nobody I trust."

Holograms of the three fleets sprang to life in the air on either flank of the desk: Blackhorse to the Senator's right in blue symbols, Flotilla Blanche and the Warcocks to the left in red and orange respectively.

Senator Gordon looked startled. He glanced about the room for a moment before he noticed his son's hand on the keypad. Dan's eyes narrowed, but there was no other change in his expression.

The Senator's focus returned to the core of the discussion.

"That's not good enough," he said, slapping the words out like a poker player showing his hand a card at a time. "The retainer Wenceslas Dome has paid you over the past five years has made the Blackhorse the most powerful fleet on Venus . . . and the most profitable. If you're trying to cut corners *now*, you're going to regret it."

He pointed his index finger. It looked white and pudgy compared to the mercenary's sinews and mahogany tan, but there was no doubting the reality of the threat the gesture implied. "You will, Daniel. And Admiral Bergstrom. And every member of the Blackhorse."

"I didn't say the other fleets rejected the deals we

were offering, Arthur," Dan answered calmly. "I said they wouldn't deal with us at all."

For an instant, his lips curved into a grin as humorless as the edge of a fighting knife. "We of the Blackhorse have done very well from our association with Wenceslas, as you say. Unfortunately, others have noticed that and decided to . . . do something about the matter."

Dan pointed at the columns of blue ships. "Leaving us with that," he said. "And you with that as well, Arthur . . . because I don't think your idea of a Federation of Venus is any more popular among your peers than the Blackhorse is with ours."

There were eighteen dreadnoughts in the display's first blue column, but two of the symbols were carated: ships so seriously damaged in battle three months before that they were still out of service.

Across from the Blackhorse array were twelve red battleships and ten orange. One of the latter symbols was marked with a flashing carat, indicating it was doubtful. Because of the long association, Wenceslas Dome's data bank had much better information on the Blackhorse than on any of the other fleets.

In light forces, the disparity of strength was even more marked. Each of the three companies had a pair of the carriers which bore gliders and light surface vessels into the battle zone. The orange and red columns showed an advantage of two to one in cruisers and three to two in destroyers.

Only in submarines did the Blackhorse rise to near equality with its combined opponents. *Near equality* is a synonym for *inferiority*.

"Why hasn't Admiral Bergstrom told me this?" the Senator asked quietly. Before there could be an answer, he rephrased the question: "Why are *you* telling me this, Daniel?"

"Admiral Bergstrom doesn't like to bear bad news," Dan said. "He thinks there must be a way out, though he doesn't see one. Captain Haynes thinks there *is* a way out. Haynes was one of the founding members of the Angels, and he's convinced that he can bring Admiral Braun into an agreement with us."

Johnnie's fingers tapped the keypad.

"And *you* think?" the Senator prompted in a voice as dry as the sound of a rattlesnake sliding over leaves.

"I think there's a way to win, yes," said the mercenary. "But neither Bergstrom nor Haynes are going to find it."

The Angels' forces now hung in slate-gray holograms alongside those of the Blackhorse. The smaller company was lopsidedly weak in cruisers and destroyers, and they had no carriers at all. When the Angels operated alone, they had to depend instead on skimmers launched from their dreadnoughts to keep hostile hydrofoils and surface-effect torpedoboats at bay.

But the Angels *did* have five battleships; and the nine 18-inch guns mounted on the newest of them, the *Holy Trinity*, made her a match for any ship on the planet in a one-to-one slugfest.

The Senator, his eyes on the blue and gray columns of the display, said, "You don't believe your forces, strengthened by the Angels, can successfully engage the fleets hired by Heidigger and Carolina, Commander?"

The question mark curled in his voice like the popper of a bullwhip.

"I wouldn't believe Admiral Braun if he told me the sea was wet, Senator," Dan said. "Captain Haynes is a perfectly truthful man, making him—"

"Making him very different from you, Commander!" Senator Gordon's face was gorged with blood. Watching him, Johnnie suddenly realized that "shooting the messenger who brings bad tidings" had not always been an empty phrase.

"Making him unsuitable as a negotiator with Admiral Braun," the mercenary continued. "And making him an unsuitable choice for Admiral, in my opinion; but that's neither here nor there. The present problem is that whatever Haynes thinks, the Angels *won't* be supporting us when it comes to the crunch."

Uncle Dan's voice was calm only in the sense that an automatic weapon shows no emotion as it cycles through the contents of its feed tray.

"I see," said the Senator. "You believe that because Wenceslas Dome is pursuing a *practical* plan of confederation, the leaders of the other domes are concerned at their potential loss of power—"

"As you already knew, Arthur."

The Senator nodded. "As I already knew. And the fleets, equally concerned that a Venus united in peace will have no further need for them, are refusing to ally themselves with the Blackhorse. Making it impossible for the Blackhorse to engage the forces hired by Heidigger and Carolina."

"Not quite, Arthur," Dan said. "We'll engage Flotilla Blanche and the Warcocks, all right. And whichever additional companies join them—as I expect may happen."

Johnnie flinched to see the grin which suddenly distorted the mercenary's face.

"The thing is," Dan continued, "we'll lose. You'll lose. And Venus will lose, Arthur. Unless . . ."

"Go on," said Senator Gordon.

"Unless you let me take Johnnie here to the surface tomorrow as my aide," Dan said, and his grin became even more of a death's-head rictus.

3

When the stars threw down their spears
And watered heaven with their tears
Did he smile his work to see?
Did He, who made the Lamb, make thee?
— William Blake

The Senator began to laugh—honestly, full-throatedly.

When Johnnie *understood* what his uncle had just said, his whole being focused on what the Senator would do. He heard the peals of his father's laughter, but he still couldn't believe it. *Any* other reaction was more likely!

The Senator got up from his chair, wiped his eyes with the back of a pudgy hand, and walked to the windows. "Oh Daniel, Daniel," he said to the man behind him, "you had me worried there for a moment. You must really hate me, don't you?"

Even Uncle Dan seemed nonplussed. "Arthur, this isn't a joke," he said.

"No?" said the Senator, glancing over his shoulder. "Well, I suppose that's too innocent a word for it, yes."

His face changed into a mask of white fury. "Come here, Commander—and you too, John. Come and look. Come!"

Dan obeyed without expression. Johnnie followed him, silent but as nervous as if a portion of the floor had just given way. Too much was happening, too suddenly, and he didn't understand the rules. . . .

The array of warships distorted as Johnnie's body blocked portions of the projection heads, then reformed behind him.

The Senator pointed out the window. "Do you see those people, Commander?" he said. "Do you?"

There was nothing abnormal about the figures below. Parents chatted on benches in the Common as their children played; couples found nooks in the foliage, better shielded to passers-by than they were from above; on the varied strips of the powered walkways, shoppers and businessfolk sped or loitered as their whim determined.

"They depend on my decisions, Commander," the Senator explained. "Their children will depend on the decisions I make today."

"I see th—"

"They depend on *me*. And all *you* care about is destroying my family, piece by piece—first my wife, now my son. Because you never had either one!"

"Arthur, don't be a bigger fool than god made you," Dan said in a tone of quiet menace.

"I'm not such a fool that I—"

"Arthur, *shut up*," the mercenary ordered. His voice rose only a little, but it took on a preternatural clarity that could have been understood through muzzle blasts and the crash of rending metal.

Dan crossed his hands formally against the small of his back. He didn't step forward, but the pressure of his personality lifted the Senator's chin like a chop to the jaw. "Senator, I always argued with them when they said you didn't have any balls, but—"

The Senator blinked. "*Who* said—"

"Everybody! Everydamnbody!"

Dan raised his right hand and snapped his fingers dismissively. The Senator flinched; Johnnie edged back, wishing that he was anywhere else in the world.

"You joined the Blackhorse when I did," Dan continued. "but you didn't have the balls to stick with it. You—"

"If you think courage is just shooting—"

"You didn't have the balls to make your marriage work!" the mercenary snarled. "You didn't have the balls to be a father to your son! And I kept saying, 'Yeah, but he's putting his whole *life* into a dream, so the other things don't matter to him.'"

The Senator's face was blank and as pale as unpainted marble.

"Only now," Dan concluded, "it turns out that you don't have the balls to save your dream *either*. So they're right, you *don't*—"

"Get out of here," the Senator said. "Get out of Wenceslas Dome within an hour. Get out of—"

"Right, Senator," Dan said in a ham-fistedly ironic tone. "Right, you can dismiss me. But remember: when I go, so does the last real chance of uniting Venus before somebody decides it's better to use atomics than lose—"

He gestured with his thumb toward the glowing ball that hung above the Common, the reminder of Man's first home and its glowing death.

"—and Venus joins the Earth."

Johnnie sucked in his first breath for . . . he wasn't sure how long. "Senator," he said, "I'm an adult. If Uncle Dan wants—"

"John," said the mercenary in a voice as hard as

the click of a cannon's breech rotating home, "sit down."

"But—" Johnnie said in amazement.

"Is this a foreign language?" his uncle demanded. "Listen, *boy*, I could find a dozen officers who have your skills. I needed *you* because I need somebody I can trust implicitly—but if you think you can argue about orders, then you're no good to me and your father, and you're no good to *any* fleet!"

Johnnie backed to his chair, then stumbled into it over the right arm. It wouldn't have done him any good to look where he was going, because his eyes were glazed with shock.

"I think perhaps we'd all better sit down," said Senator Gordon. His expression had returned to normal: cold, distant; and, beneath the soft flesh, as hard as that of his former brother-in-law.

He sat calmly, then touched a switch. A pump whirred as it sucked fluid from the cushion beneath the Senator, dropping his eye level to that of the men across the desk from him. "Precisely what is it that you think my son can achieve for you, Daniel?" he asked.

"I can't tell you that, Arthur," Dan said.

His voice caught and he cleared his throat before he went on, "That's partly because I'm going to have to play the situation as it develops . . . and partly because it's not something that you need to know about. You have the political side to deal with. That's enough for any one man."

The Senator watched Dan without speaking.

"Arthur," the mercenary said, "I can tell you this: I'll be risking everything I have to save your plan of confederation."

"Your life, you mean," the Senator amplified.

"I've been risking my *life* for twenty-five years now, Senator," Dan said with the edge returning to his voice momentarily. "That's just my job. What I'm talking about is the chance—the certainty if I fail—of being cashiered from the Blackhorse and banned by all the other fleets."

"I see," said the Senator.

He looked at Johnnie, watching his son without speaking for seconds that seemed minutes. At last he said, "John, I won't claim to have been a good father . . . but you are my son, and you're important to me. Is this something *you* want to do—not to spite me, not to please your uncle?"

Johnnie licked his lips. "Yes, father," he said.

"I want to be very clear about this, John," the Senator continued. "You aren't simply being asked to join a fleet. You're being requested to take part in an enterprise which—whatever the details—is far more dangerous than ordinary mercenary service."

He glanced at Uncle Dan. "That is correct, is it not, Commander?"

Dan nodded, still-faced. "That is correct. And the danger is increased by the fact that Johnnie won't have time to go through the ordinary training procedures."

"Father, I want to go," Johnnie said.

The Senator rose. "Then may God be with you, John," he said. "And may God be with us all."

4

Yes, the Large Birds o' Prey
They will carry us away,
And you'll never see your soldiers any more!
                                    —Rudyard Kipling

The squall dumped gray water in sheets and ropes across the clear dome of Wenceslas Dome's surface platform. Where the rain met the sea, there was a chaos of foam.

Below that margin, shifting with the swells that buoyed the platform, was the water of the ocean itself. It was green with nutriments and microscopic life.

Very occasionally, a streamlined vision of fins and fangs brushed along the edge of the platform and vanished again into the farther reaches of the ocean. One of the visitors took almost a minute to cruise past as Johnnie watched in amazement.

The hydrofoil that would take them to Blackhorse Base was occasionally visible also—through the homogeneous waters of the ocean, not the streaming wall of rain. The hundred-ton vessel rocked on her main hull with her outriggers raised. Her helmsman kept her headed into the wind with the auxiliary thruster. It was running just above idle, creating a haze of bubbles in the sea beneath the hydrofoil's stern.

The squall's fury could not have prevented the hydrofoil from operating at full speed had the situation required it; but the few minutes the passengers for Blackhorse Base would gain by loading now were outweighed by the needless discomfort of going out in the brief storm.

Besides, some of the passengers still hadn't finished their goodbyes.

Dan wore baggy khaki utilities instead of his dress creams, but he looked as crisp as if he'd been sleeping innocently for the past twelve hours. He grinned at Johnnie and said, "How's your head?"

Johnnie managed to smile back. "My head's fine," he said, more or less truthfully. "My stomach, though. . . . Is this what shipboard's going to feel like?"

After Commander Cooke enrolled his nephew at the Blackhorse recruiting office, he had gone off "on personal business"—leaving Johnnie in the charge of his servant, Sergeant Britten, with orders to have a good time. Britten's notion of what *that* meant involved at least a dozen of the dives in Wenceslas Dome's warehouse district.

His uncle shrugged. "This dock's got an unpleasant period," he said. "The dampers are set to smooth tidal lift and fall, but they've got too much stiction to be comfortable in a storm."

The landing platform was as large as the Common thousands of feet beneath it on the sea floor. It was a closed, buoyant structure—of necessity, since the elevator tube joining the platform to the Wenceslas Dome had to adjust to variations in sea level.

The platform could hold a thousand people. Fewer than twenty were present now, scattered in clots and morose handfuls across the clear metal like litter on the floor of an empty amphitheater.

All the uniformed passengers were men. The fleets and their surface bases were male enclaves, though the mercenary companies employed some women as technicians and administrative personnel in the domes.

Sergeant Britten was a stocky man whose shaved head made him look older than his years. He played privy solitaire with his back discreetly turned to his master. His seat was the powered pallet holding the slight kit Dan, Johnnie, and the sergeant himself were taking to base.

Over the past five years of association, Wenceslas Dome had become a second home for the men of the Blackhorse. Most of them kept a fully-stocked apartment in the dome for the time they spent on leave and administrative duty. There was no need to carry luggage between here and the base.

When men died, their effects were sold to the survivors and replacements. No need for transport in that event, either.

"A destroyer's a lot worse, of course," Dan went on. He was letting his eyes slide across the landing platform; concentrating on nothing, missing nothing. "But as my aide, you'll be stationed on one of the dreadnoughts, and your stomach won't mind that."

He grinned again. "Even when you're hung over."

"I'm fine," Johnnie said.

A couple sat on a bench a hundred yards from the stage at which the hydrofoil was berthed. The man wore khaki; he was middle aged, balding and powerful. If Dan's hard features suggested an axe blade, then this man was a sledge hammer.

The woman was only a few years younger, but at least from a distance she looked beautiful rather than pretty. They sat side by side. Each had an arm around the other's shoulders, and their free hands were intertwined on their laps.

"Captain Haynes," Dan said, though his eyes seemed to be on the gray, bobbing hull of the hydrofoil. The rain was slacking off. Patches of white sky appeared briefly through the roof before further spasms of rain obscured them. "And his wife Beryl."

"Companion," Johnnie said. "None of the domes recognize legal marriage to a mercenary."

Dan raised an eyebrow at the venom in his nephew's voice. "Companion," he agreed.

Johnnie licked his lips. "Like my mother. Now."

"Yeah, like Peggy," the older man said. "It's been— too long, six months, I think. Since I saw her. But she's doing pretty well."

Dan checked/pretended to check the clock on his wrist. "She's with Commander LaFarge of Flotilla Blanche," he added. "A good man for executing orders, though maybe not the best choice to deal with the unexpected."

Johnnie looked at his uncle. "He's the one she ran off with?"

"That was a long time ago, Johnnie . . . ," Dan said. He shrugged. "No, that one didn't work out. He was killed later, but Peggy'd already left him. She's been with LaFarge for a couple years, now."

The sky was definitely clearing, but the western quadrant—the direction of Blackhorse Base—was still gray.

"If a destroyer's bad," Johnnie said, "then that little thing's going to turn me inside out, huh?" He nodded toward the hydrofoil.

"Don't you believe it," Dan replied. "When one of those is up on its outriggers, she's the best gun-platform you could ask for. Stable as a rock. I remember once . . ."

His voice trailed off when he realized that his nephew was staring fixedly at the Haynes couple again.

"He looks like he loves her," Johnnie said in a low, grating voice.

"Haynes?" Dan said. "I'm sure he does. Beryl's . . . well, I won't insult her by calling her his lucky charm. She's an estimable woman. But she's also the thing Haynes *trusts* when it's all coming apart and it doesn't look like there's a prayer of surviving."

He chuckled. "Something we all need, Johnnie. That or another line of work."

"But she's just a prostitute!" Johnnie snarled. "A *whore!*"

Sergeant Britten looked toward them. The sergeant's face was expressionless, but his big scarred hand was already sliding the cards away in a breast pocket where they'd be safe if he had to move suddenly.

Dan put his arm around Johnnie and turned him away. When the younger man resisted the motion, the mercenary's fingers pinched a nerve in his elbow. Johnnie gasped and let himself be manhandled to face the hydrofoil again.

"That was a long time ago," Dan repeated quietly. "If you get wrapped up in some minor problem of your father's from twenty years ago, then the real stuff's going to steamroller you right into the ground. And the world won't even know you existed."

"I'm sorry, Uncle Dan," Johnnie whispered.

"Don't be sorry," the mercenary said. "Be controlled."

He gave his nephew an affectionate squeeze. "That's the best advice you'll ever get, lad. Follow it and you'll rise just like me and the Senator."

A klaxon blatted above the docking valve. "El-seven-five-two-one, ready to ship passengers for Blackhorse Base," warned a voice distorted by the echoing vastness of the platform.

Men sauntered toward the valve. Some women waited; some turned and walked toward the elevator even before the mercenaries had boarded the craft which would take some of them away for the last time.

As Johnnie walked beside his uncle, his mind repeated, "... *me and the Senator*...." It was like pairing fire and ice.

5

West and away the wheels of darkness roll,
Day's beamy banner up the east is borne,
Spectres and fears, the nightmare and her foal,
Drown in the golden deluge of the morn.
                                    —A. E. Housman

The door behind the dozen passengers closed, sealing the surface platform from the spray or worse that would enter when the outer lock opened. The air was hot, not warm; the humidity was saturated.

Captain Haynes turned in the passageway and stared first at Johnnie, then at his uncle. "Who's the civilian, Cooke?" Haynes demanded.

"John Gordon, Captain Haynes," Dan answered in a polite rather than merely correct tone. "He's a recruit."

The passageway rose and fell with a teeter-totter motion that didn't disconcert Johnnie as much as the slower rocking of the platform itself. The wet floor was treacherous, despite its patterned surface and the suction-grip soles on Johnnie's new sea boots.

"I believe Personnel still falls within the duties of the XO, doesn't it, Cooke?" Haynes said with heavy sarcasm. "Have I signed off on him? Because if I haven't, he shouldn't be in uniform."

The outer door opened with a slurping sound and

a gush of algae-laden water. A rating from the hydrofoil looked in and shouted, "Will you get your butts—" before he realized that the hold-up in the passageway was caused by the Blackhorse executive officer. He ducked back out of sight.

"Captain," said Dan quietly, "this isn't something I want to discuss without Admiral Bergstrom, and it isn't something I want to discuss *here*."

He nodded back over his shoulder where the remainder of the passengers, enlisted men and junior officers, waited blank-faced. A few of them pretended not to listen.

Johnnie was rigid. He'd spent his life thus far training to be an officer in a mercenary fleet. His studies and simulations ranged from small arms to fleet fire control, from calisthenics to the logistical problems of feeding thousands of men with the usual assortment of dietary quirks, taboos, and allergies.

But he'd always been the son of Senator A. Rolfe Gordon. He'd never been treated like an object: like a side of meat of doubtful quality.

The passageway rose and fell; and rose. More seawater sloshed in. The sky was a hazy white like glowing iron, and the atmosphere weighed on Johnnie's shoulders like bags of wet sand.

"His name's Gordon?" Haynes said.

"That's right."

Haynes grimaced, then turned. "We'll discuss it with the Admiral," he muttered over his shoulder as he stomped aboard the waiting vessel.

L7521 was a torpedoboat. There were three long grooves on either side of her main hull, like the fullers of a knifeblade. For the hydrofoil's present duty as a high-speed ferry, those weapon stations were empty, but torpedoes could be fitted in a matter of minutes by trained crews in a carrier's arming bay.

A tub forward held a pair of .60-caliber rotary-breech machine-guns, while at the stern was a cage of six high-velocity ramjet penetrators which could punch a hole in anything lighter than the main-belt armor of a battleship. Several additional automatic weapons were clamped to L7521's railings, perhaps unofficially by crewmen who wanted to be able to shoot back with *something*, even if the rational part of their mind knew it was something useless.

It was an impressive display, though Johnnie knew the vessel's gun armament was minor compared to that of the hydrofoil gunboats whose duty was to keep hostile torpedoboats from pressing home their attacks on the main fleet. And compared to a dreadnought of sixty, eighty, or a hundred-thousand deadweight tons. . . .

The hydrofoil's real defenses weren't her guns, of course, or even her speed—though her ability to maintain seventy knots as long as there was fuel for the thrusters was certainly a help. The thing that had kept L7521 alive through previous battles and which might save her again was the fact she was so hard to see.

Powered aircraft played no part in the wars which puffed in brief fury across the seas of Venus like so many afternoon squalls. No combination of altitude and absorbent materials could conceal from modern sensors an aircraft's engine and the necessary turbulence of powered flight. And after the quarry was seen—

Battleships and cruisers carried railguns as secondary armament. The slugs they accelerated through the atmosphere hit at a significant fraction of light speed; significant, at least, to anything with less than a foot of armor plate to protect it.

No powered aircraft could survive more than three seconds after coming within line of sight of a hostile fleet. Gliders, travelling with the air currents instead of through them and communicating with their carrier through miles of gossamer fiber-optics cable, were a risky but useful means of reconnaissance; but under no circumstances could a glider become a useful weapons platform.

Light surface craft could be designed to carry out most of the tasks of an attack aircraft and survive.

Survive long enough to carry out the attack, at any rate. War is a business of risks and probabilities.

The advantage a boat had over an aircraft was the medium in which it operated. Unlike the air, sea water is neither stable nor fully homogeneous. Swells, froth, and wave-blown droplets all have radically different appearances to active and passive sensors.

If the vessel was small—in radar cross-section—over-the-horizon systems could not distinguish it from the waves on which it skittered. Look-down Doppler aircraft radars were a technically possible answer, but an aircraft with a powerful emitter operating was even more of a suicide pact for its crew than an aircraft that *wasn't* calling attention to itself for a hundred miles in every direction.

Torpedoboats like L7521 were skeletonized blobs built of plastics which were transparent through much of the electro-optical band. Their only metal parts were in their gun mechanisms and powerplants, both of which were shielded by layers of radar-absorbent materials. If a hostile emitter did manage to lock on at short range, the little vessels mounted an electronic suite that could be expected to spoof the enemy for up to ten seconds—

Long enough to drop all six torpedoes before counter-fire ripped the launch platform to shards of plastic and bloody froth.

The best countermeasures were teams of similarly-designed hydrofoil gunboats to extend the fleet's sensor range. Vicious battles were fought on the rolling wastes of No-Man's-Sea between opposing fleets. The gunboats' heavy armament meant that these blazing encounters almost always spelled death to the torpedoboat—but a regularly-spaced line of patches across L7521's main hull proved that she'd survived once; and therefore might survive again.

"Sir," said the young officer in the central cockpit, nodding to Captain Haynes. "Sir . . . ," and a nod for Commander Cooke.

The hydrofoil's cockpit had seats for four and room for several more standees. It looked like the best place to stay reasonably dry and still see what was going on, though the countermeasures/torpedo control station within the main hull forward was probably more comfortable.

Seamen among the passengers were already snapping lifelines to the vessel's railing. The small-boat men seemed cheerful, but the battleship sailors were grumbling seriously.

"Morning, Samuels," said Uncle Dan. "Get me a couple helmets and you can stand down the forward watch for this run. I'll take the gun tub with Recruit Gordon here."

The young officer's face blanked to wipe his incipient frown. "Ah, sir . . ." he said. "One of the scout gliders thought he saw some activity along our route back. I think I'd like to keep a qualified crew at the weapon stations."

"Ensign Samuels," said Dan sharply, "I was qualified on hydrofoil twin-mounts before you were out of diapers. Commo helmets, if you please."

Captain Haynes had appropriated one of the cockpit seats. He looked up from the control console with an unreadable expression. Johnnie expected him to speak, but apparently the XO wasn't willing to argue against the privileges of rank—even when it was Commander Cooke's rank.

The hydrofoil's commander gave Dan a flustered salute. "Aye-aye, sir," he said.

He turned and called forward, "Alexander and Jones, you're relieved. Give, ah, give your commo helmets to the Director of Planning and his assistant."

Two ratings had climbed out of the forward position before Johnnie and his uncle reached it along the narrow catwalk.

One them grinned as he handed Johnnie a helmet made of the same gray-green plastic as the torpedoboat itself. "Enjoy yer ride, kid," the seaman said. "It's just like the battlewagons—showers in every stateroom."

Johnnie donned the helmet and started to sit in the low-mounted assistant gunner's seat. The AG's job was to pass fresh magazines and take over if his Number One—necessarily more exposed—bought it. Dan smiled and waved his nephew to the main seat instead.

"Go on," Dan said. "You've got simulator hours on the twins, don't you?"

"Yeah, but I'm not qualified—"

The older man waved a hand in dismissal. "*I'm* qualified to judge," he said. "Maybe you'll—"

He touched the keypad on the side of the helmet he wore. "Set your helmet on 3," he continued, his voice now coming through the earphones in Johnnie's helmet. "That'll give us some privacy."

As Johnnie obeyed—hesitating, but managing to find the correct button without taking the helmet off to look at it—Dan continued, "As I say, maybe we'll find you something more interesting that a simulator target."

L7521 got under way, rumbling away from the dock on the single thruster at the stern of its main hull. The outriggers, one at the bow and two at the stern—the latter with thrusters of their own—began to crank down into the sea. When waves clipped the foils' broad vees, rainbows of mist sprayed about the vessel.

Johnnie thumbed the gunsight live. The holographic sight picture was exactly like that of his simulator back in Wenceslas Dome: a rolling seascape onto which the data banks would soon inject a target.

Reality might do the same.

The vessel worked up to about ten knots on the auxiliary thruster alone. The bow started to lift in a sun-drenched globe of spray. The stern-foil powerplants cut in and L7521 surged ahead.

"You think we're going to have to fight on the way to the base, then?" Johnnie asked, wondering if his uncle could hear him over the wind and drive noise.

The helmets did their job. Dan's chuckle was as clear as it had been in the Senator's office. "I think there's usually something on the surface of Venus that'll do for target practice," he said. "Why? Are you worried?"

Johnnie checked the traverse and elevation controls in both handgrips. The action felt normal, natural. The simulator had prepared him very well, though the amount of vibration through the seat and the baseplate was a surprise.

"I'm . . . ," Johnnie said. The wind pushed his head and shoulders fiercely, but the boat continued to accelerate. They must already be at fifty knots, though the absence of fixed objects disoriented him.

"Uncle Dan," Johnnie said, "I'm afraid I won't be good enough. I'm afraid I'm going to embarrass you. . . . But I'm not afraid of fighting."

"That's good, lad," Dan said in a matter-of-fact voice. "Because you're going to be fighting. If not on this run, then real soon. *That* I can promise."

The vibration of L7521's drives and hull reached a harmonic. For a moment, it seemed as though the vessel herself was screaming with mad laughter as she rushed toward the western horizon.

6

Rolled to starboard, rolled to larboard,
when the surge was seething free,
Where the wallowing monster spouted his
foam-mountains on the sea.
                                        —Alfred, Lord Tennyson

Johnnie reflexively set the gunsight controls to search mode—then realized he wasn't alone in a simulator where he'd be graded by electronics. He looked at his uncle in embarrassment, poising his hand to switch back to direct targeting.

Dan raised an eyebrow.

"Ah, was that right?" Johnnie asked. "The sights?"

In search mode, the holographic sight picture relayed the image from the masthead sensors above the cockpit, the highest point on the little vessel. At the moment their image was a three-dimensional radar panorama: 320° of empty sea, with a sprinkling of low islands on the northern and northwestern horizon.

"Sure," said his uncle. "Isn't it what your simulator told you to do?"

"Yeah, but . . ."

L7521 was running at speed, slicing over the swells

43

like an amusement-ride car on rails. Froth and flotsam snapped by to either side of the hydrofoil at startling speed, contrasting queasily with the large-scale hologram which scarcely changed at all.

"John, I designed your training programs myself," Dan said. "They couldn't cover everything, but what they taught you is Blackhorse standard."

He grinned, devil-may-care Uncle Dan again. "Life can't cover everything either, lad. Though it took me a while to figure that out myself."

Johnnie traversed the guns ten degrees, using the left-grip control, to swing them to the marked bearing of one of the distant islands. He then touched the right grip, bringing the sight picture back to direct.

For a moment, the hologram was an electronic image of the sea itself. Then the hydrofoil crested a swell and the sights centered on a blur of a gray slightly darker than that of the water. Johnnie dialed up the magnification to its full forty powers and thumbed in stabilization. The gun barrels rose automatically as L7521's bow slid into another kilometer-wide trough.

Just before the gunsight's direct viewpoint was covered by waves, the men in the gun tub saw something with jaws of yellow fangs lift above the vegetation and stare toward them. Nictitating membranes wiped sideways, dulling the eyes.

An image of sea water rose to fill the gunsight. Johnnie switched back to search mode.

He looked at his uncle, hunched below the tub's armor in the assistant's seat. The halo of spray from the steerable front foil soaked Dan as thoroughly as it did the younger man, but there was no sign of discomfort on his smiling face.

"You've been planning for . . . for years to do this, haven't you?" Johnnie said. "Bring me into the

Blackhorse as soon as you could—twist the Senator's arm."

Dan shrugged. "The training programs? I wouldn't have forced you, lad. You wanted to learn, so you might as well learn the right way. Even the Senator agreed with that. Otherwise you might have run off and joined some jackleg outfit that'd get you killed—if you were lucky."

The implications of what he'd just heard spread across Johnnie's mind like the base of a slime mold, then burst into feculent words: "You don't think I'm good enough for a real company, Uncle Dan? You don't think I could get into the Blackhorse without you pulling strings?"

The older man shook his head. "Wrong wording," he said calmly, as though he were unaware of the shock and horror behind his nephew's flat statement.

"*You* don't think that any real company's going to enlist the son of A. Rolfe Gordon against the Senator's will, do you?" Dan explained. "War's a business, Johnnie. Admirals put their lives on the line, sure; but they're gambling on a lot more than the chance of getting killed. Nobody competent—nobody competent enough to command a successful company—would offend the most powerful politician on Venus."

"He may not be for long," Johnnie said in mingled regret and anger. "Heidigger and Carolina won't let him stay if they win."

"Even then no fleet is going to offend the Senator for nothing," Dan continued. "Nobody in the history of Venus has been able to do what your father's already managed—a free association of three domes, forced by the populace and against the will of the oligarchs who'd been running the show until then."

"But if he fails—" Johnnie said.

"If he fails *this time*," his uncle said, riding over the

interjection, "there's still the chance he'll be back in power later. Politicians have long memories—and so do Admirals."

Dan focused on the sight picture, then frowned and rose from his seat to look over the armor. "Cover that," he ordered, pointing off the right bow. "Samuels is going to pass too close."

The sights went direct when Johnnie swung the guns with his right-hand control. The panoramic blur of land against sea became a huge mass to the left— probably the sub-continental Omphalos Sathanou, though that meant the hydrofoil's speed had been above the seventy knots Johnnie was guessing. To the right was an unnamed islet from which trailed a fur of water-brushing tree branches.

"All weapon stations, track right," Johnnie's earphones ordered in a voice that wasn't his uncle's.

The strait separating Omphalos from its minor satellite was a quarter mile broad, but only within a hundred feet of the islet was there a band of water which had enough current to clear it of mud and tannin. To the islet's right—south—clumps of reeds warned that the water there was dangerously shallow also.

Dan charged and aimed the automatic rifle which had been placed between his seat and the armored tub. "Bloody cowboy," he muttered.

"What is it?" Johnnie asked, trying to scan both the holographic image and the expanse of green/brown/ corpse-finger white beyond it. "What am I looking for?"

"Any damn thing that moves."

"Watch it," the ensign in the cockpit ordered.

Dan glanced sideways toward his nephew. "Remember," he said, "this is who you get crewing hydrofoils. Don't ever pretend people are going to be other than you *know* they're going to be."

L7521 slammed past the islet, her drive noise echoing as a *thrum/thrum/thrum* from the vegetation. The vessel's outriggers threw up triple roostertails. The wakes hunched waist-high across the shallows, churning mud from the bottom.

A ripple of fans waved nervously, the raking gills of giant barnacles or tube-worms.

A tentacle—a tendril?—shot out of the forest toward the L7521. It was gray and featureless, suggesting neither the plant kingdom nor the animal. Everything behind the rounded tip was a twisting cylinder a yard in circumference. The creature's lunge carried it a hundred feet over the water churned by the disappearing hydrofoil.

A sailor on the stern rail fired his machine-gun. The pintle-mounted weapon wobbled, throwing its helix of golden tracers above the creature. Johnnie, glancing over his shoulder at the target his own weapons wouldn't bear on, thought a few of the bullets might possibly have hit.

Possibly.

"What was it?" Johnnie asked.

"Cover your sector," his uncle ordered, gesturing the twin mount forward as his right hand returned the rifle to the slot beside his seat. "Don't worry about the stuff that's over."

"Yessir," Johnnie muttered, his face cold. The hydrofoil banked slightly, hiding the creature which was already withdrawing into the vegetation from which it had sprung.

Uncle Dan grinned. "Good job, John," he said. "A lot of veterans would've shot off ammo they might need later."

"I won't get out of position again . . . sir," Johnnie said.

"Wish I was sure that *I* wouldn't," Dan said.

The older man looked back past the stern, where even the islet was rapidly disappearing. "What was it?" he added. "Something big and nasty and fast. But not fast enough. May all our problems be like that."

"Uncle Dan," Johnnie said, keeping his eyes rigidly on his sight hologram. "Is the Senator a coward?"

"Arthur?" the mercenary officer said. "Hell no! Where did you get that idea?"

"He joined the Blackhorse when you did—"

"Right. He met your mother when she was seeing me off for training."

"—but he resigned after his first battle. He was afraid."

"He wasn't any more scared than I was," Dan said. "The *Elizabeth* got hammered out of line. Damned lucky we weren't sunk. . . ."

He put his arm on Johnnie's shoulder and kept it there until the younger man met his eyes. "Listen to me, Johnnie," Dan went on. "Arthur's first battle convinced him that Venus had to be united, so that some day there wouldn't *be* any battles. That doesn't make him a coward."

Johnnie nodded. "But he was wrong, wasn't he? I mean, you can't change human nature, can you?"

Dan grinned without humor. "I hope Arthur wasn't wrong," he said. "Because it convinced me of the same thing."

7

The Devil is driving both this tide,
and the killing-grounds are close,
And we'll go up to the Wrath of God. . . .
                    —Rudyard Kipling

Fifteen miles from the Braids, Johnnie cranked up the gunsight magnification and added computer enhancement to eliminate the haze. He panned the guns slowly for an early view of the band of swampy islands and shallow channels through which L7521 would pass. Beside him, Dan dictated into a pocket workstation.

A command overlay pulsed slowly in the upper right quadrant of the gunsight hologram, then disappeared.

Johnnie blinked. He reached for the keyboard—and remembered he was in a gun tub, not at a control console. He slapped down his visor, manually keyed his helmet's access channel, and said to the artificial intelligence, "Review past minute's visuals."

The helmet went *eep* and projected what Johnnie had seen a minute before into his visor. The visor image formed a ghost over the nearly identical view currently in the gunsight, but this time Johnnie was ready for the warning pulse.

Dan put the pocket unit away and watched intently as his nephew worked.

"Sir," Johnnie said, "we've been painted by radar."

As he spoke, the pulsed overlay reappeared in the gunsight, echoing the data sent to the main unit in the cockpit.

Dan touched his helmet keypad and said, "Twin mount to bridge. We're under radar observation. Over."

"Bridge to twin mount," replied Ensign Samuels in a wary voice. "We're approaching the Braids. You're—"

Samuels remembered who was on the other end of the link. "You may be seeing reflections scattered from islets. Over."

"Negative!" Johnnie hissed, bending close to his uncle to avoid using the intercom. "That's—"

"Bridge, that's a negative," Dan said sharply. "That's track—"

"—track-while-scan!" Johnnie concluded, identifying the pattern of high-power and low-power pulses which swept the torpedoboat.

"—while-scan," Dan continued. "Who the hell do you have on your EW board? Over."

Details sharpened in the view of the islands toward which L7521 sped. Computer enhancement at long range smoothed objects into a calculated sameness. As the need for enhancement lessened, the foliage appeared in its spiky, curling multiplicity.

There were mangroves and a breeze riffling reed tops into amber motion; but there was no sign of man.

"Shit!" said Ensign Samuels.

Then, in a controlled voice, the torpedoboat's commander continued, "Bridge to twin mount. Sir, the electronic warfare console was disconnected. The console is operating again now. You—"

Operating now that it's too late, Johnnie thought.

"—were right, of course. Over."

"Samuels," Dan said, "ask Captain Haynes to lock into Intercom 3, please. *Soonest!*"

The click of another station joining Johnnie and his uncle cut off the first syllable of Captain Haynes' voice saying, "—mander, is this some joke of yours?"

Dan rose to his feet and looked toward the cockpit. Haynes was standing also; their eyes met. Johnnie glanced from one man to the other—and turned back to the holographic display.

"No joke, Captain," Dan said. "If you haven't decided to lay on an escort for us—"

" . . . f course not!" Haynes' protest was stepped on by the ongoing transmission.

"Then we have to assume that somebody's stationed here to make sure that you and I don't get to Blackhorse Base," Dan said. "Tell Bradley to turn ten degrees to port so we're headed toward Channel 17 instead of 19. That should get us more sensor data."

Johnnie ran a chart of the Braids on his visor. If he flexed his helmet to the tit on the gun mount, he could convert the sight into an omni-function display—

But right at the moment, it looked as though having the gunsight working was more important.

"I can't believe either the Warcocks or Flotilla Blanche would act so dishonorably!" Haynes said.

L7521's front foil nosed into the turn. The port stern outrigger telescoped enough to keep the deck more or less perpendicular to the "down" of centrifugal force; the torpedoboat heeled like a motorcycle.

The Braids were a thousand square miles of weathered pillow lava over which the sea had risen at the end of the terraforming process. The result was thousands of islands, ranging in size from specks to narrow blotches that straggled along for several miles at low water.

None of the land rose more than ten feet above the
level of high tide; none of the channels wandering
through the mass was more than twenty feet deep
when the solar tide was at its lowest; and the sum of
land and water together was very nearly mean sea level.
The through-channels were numbered, but no one had
bothered to name any of the swampy islands.

"Do you think the people running Carolina Dome
are that honorable, Captain?" Dan said sharply. "You
know as well as I do that some of the smaller mercenary companies are no better than pirates, picking
up salvage on the fringes when the big fleets engage.
A few politicians could hire one of them under the
table. . . ."

Johnnie touched his helmet keypad and whispered
orders to the artificial intelligence. His gunsight, at full
magnification, was centered on the point at which the
target should first appear. The sight picture was still
an empty channel choked from either side by black
mangroves, but the electronic warfare suite was beginning to draw a picture of the ambusher.

Radar signals from the other craft located the emitter but could not identify the hull on which the radar
was mounted. When the waiting vessel started its engines in reaction to the torpedoboat's course change,
L7521's passive sensors fed back the faint sound signatures for comparison to known templates.

When the vessel moved—out of Channel 17 and
away from the hydrofoil rather than on a direct interception course—the torpedoboat's data bank achieved
a 98 percent probable identification. The lurking vessel
was a surface skimmer whose flexible skirts balanced
it above the water on a cushion of air.

The air cushion worked as well on land as water.
In shifting away from L7521, the skimmer slid over
a neck of land which the chart showed as being above

water level at the present tidal state. The ambusher settled again in a slough connected to Channel 19.

"Sir," Dan said, "I have small-craft experience that you don't. Ensign Samuels will of course command his vessel . . . but with your permission, I'll take overall control of the operation."

Johnnie risked a glance around to see the captain's face, raised above the cockpit coaming. The rivalry between Cooke and Haynes was as bitter as many religious conflicts; but the men were, literally, in the same boat.

Haynes licked his lips. "We can't turn and run, then?" he said.

"From their acceleration," Dan said, proving that he'd kept an eye on his visor display while talking to his superior, "they're running light—no torpedoes. They'll have at least thirty knots on us, flat out. Our best hope is that they don't know we've noticed them."

"All right, Cooke," said Captain Haynes. He swallowed. "You're in operational command. I'll make room here in the cockpit."

"No time, Captain," Dan said as he tried to unscrew the cap which protected the hard-wire connector on the gun mount. It stuck. "I'll run it from here, if—"

Johnnie rapped the cap twice, sharply, with the butt of his service knife.

His uncle twisted again. The cap spun loose from the grip of microlife which had managed to root into the threads of supposedly impervious plastic.

"I'll run it from here," Dan concluded as he pulled glass-fiber line from the tit and connected it to his helmet.

L7521 rushed toward the Braids at seventy knots. Channel 17 wasn't an ideal route since it narrowed halfway through the mass to little more than the width of the torpedoboat. That was something to worry about *if* they got so far.

Dan converted the gunsight display to a holographic chart of a square mile of the Braids. A blue line and a red bead plotted the torpedoboat's planned course and the ambusher's location, respectively.

Johnnie swallowed and flipped up the twin mount's mechanical backsight. Blurred vegetation hopped and quivered through the sighting ring. The mechanical sights were for emergencies only—

And the lord knew, this was an emergency.

"Three to bridge," Dan said. "Is the Automatic Defense System—"

As the commander spoke, the miniature four-barreled Gatling roused on the centerpost of the cockpit coaming.

"—right, we need it live," Dan said approvingly. "Now, take us up Channel 18 instead. Over."

"Sir," Samuels blurted, "that's blocked—" Then, "Aye-aye, sir. Sorry."

The ADS fired high-velocity 50-grain flechettes. The unit had its own scanner and, when live, operated independently to engage any target that came within a hundred yards of the torpedoboat on an intercepting course. The weapon was switched off at most times—it would riddle an approaching admiral's car in harbor as cheerfully as it would bat a hostile missile—but it gave the torpedoboat a modicum of protection against guided weapons in combat.

"Sir?" Samuels added. "We'll have to throttle back to make the chicane at the mouth of Eighteen. Over."

"That's fine, Ensign," Dan replied absently as the AI ran possible scenarios, one after another, on the sight display. "So long as we don't try to run, it'll just look as though we're having problems with our charts. Over."

He looked at Johnnie, keyed intercom, and muttered, "Which thank god we're not. These charts—"

Dan nodded toward the holographic web of waterways. The glowing blue line—L7521—maneuvered against the red line of the surface skimmer, until a line of red dots joined the two.

The blue line ended.

"—are all that's going to save us. If anything does."

He grinned at his nephew. "That and you spotting the radar signal when whoever was at the EW console slept."

"Is Haynes sitting at that console?" Johnnie asked.

Dan shook his head. On the display's next scenario, the blue line cut across a reed bed that Johnnie didn't think was a channel.

It *wasn't* a channel. The line carried forward on inertia, then stopped—hopelessly aground. Red dots indicating gunfire from the ambusher touched the point which marked the torpedoboat.

A new scenario began.

"I don't like Haynes," Dan said. "But he's a fanatic about getting whatever job's in front of him done. By the book—but done."

The low-lying islands formed a mottled backdrop to the display now. Through the cut-out in the hologram for the iron sights, Johnnie scanned the foliage for any sign of the surface skimmer.

Nothing. Of course nothing. You could hide a battleship, much less an air cushion vehicle, among the dense vegetation of the Braids.

The ambush might very well have gone unnoticed—until it was sprung. Personnel on a boat ferrying people back from leave couldn't be expected to be very alert.

And as Dan had noted, the surface skimmer could run the hydrofoil down if necessary.

L7521 heeled hard to starboard, slowing and

juddering as her wake overran the decelerating foils. Sailors swung and cursed. They were trying to hold on with one hand while their real concern was for the weapons they might have to use at any instant.

The mouth of Channel 18 was lost to sight among scores of mangrove-dripping notches in neighboring islands.

While his uncle attempted to bend the future into an acceptable pattern on the big hologram, Johnnie kept a real-time course display in one quadrant of his visor. The youth grimaced at the situation.

The other vessel had stopped using radar when L7521 came within ten miles; passive sensors were sufficient for it to accurately track the oncoming torpedoboat. Though the ambusher quivered as its prey changed direction, the commander of the surface skimmer did not bother shifting from his hiding place in the relatively-broad Channel 19 as the torpedoboat twisted into the neighboring waterway.

Johnnie kept the twin barrels of his guns aligned with the pointing line in his visor—a vector drawn by his AI toward where the surface skimmer lurked a mile up the parallel channel. He could see only foliage, though from fifty feet or even closer there was an obvious bright diversity of other life growing in the mangroves.

"They'll sweep across a low spot with all guns blazing, then, sir?" Johnnie asked over the intercom. He spoke quietly so that his uncle could pretend not to have heard if the chart demanded his full attention.

The torpedoboat sliced through a stretch of open water so narrow that reed tops slapped the bow like gunshots. Branches wove together above them, throwing the vessel into shadow.

A thirty-pound frog leaped from a mangrove trunk and sailed a hundred feet through the air on its broad feet. Its open-mouthed course took it, like a whale swallowing plankton, into a mass of insects startled aloft by the hydrofoil.

The frog slid neatly into the water. The jaws of something far larger clopped over the amphibian in a shower of spray.

L7521 banked to port, then starboard again, as it followed the meandering waterway. The directional changes were so great that Ensign Samuels cut the hydrofoil's speed to scarcely more than that required to keep it up on the outriggers.

"No, they won't take that risk unless they have to," Dan replied. "They'll stay out of sight and pop at us with indirect fire until a shell or two gets through."

Instead of course plots, a view of the long island separating Channels 18 and 19 now filled the display. Dan's artificial intelligence overlaid bright lines across the swampy land. The individual lines ranged in color from orange through yellow to chartreuse.

"I . . . ," Johnnie said. He swallowed and squeezed tighter on the grips of the twin mount.

The channel broadened into a mirror of black water. The mangroves no longer closed the canopy above. The hydrofoil's bow wave faceted the surface into dazzling jewels.

"I wouldn't think pirates, looters, would have that kind of equipment," Johnnie said as he visualized death dropping unanswerably from the sky.

"Jack de Lessups of Flotilla Blanche is a friend of mine," Dan said calmly. "But *I* don't think he's too honorable to put me out the way before a battle—if it could be done without anybody knowing."

The torpedoboat accelerated again as the channel straightened. Halfway through the Braids, Channel 18 ended in a marsh too shallow, even at high tide, for a hydrofoil to navigate. Until that point, it provided a deceptively open course.

Dan grinned at his nephew. "You might say that Jack respects me," he added.

Johnnie wouldn't have heard the *choonk* of the mortar firing if he hadn't been expecting it. Even then it might have been his imagination—

Until the miniature Gatling gun on the cockpit lifted like a dog raising its muzzle to sniff the air.

There was a black speck in the sky, a shell just above the zenith of its arc. The Automatic Defense System twitched, locked, and ripped the air with a burst at the frequency of a dental drill. Yellow flame stabbed out of the spinning barrels; though the rounds were caseless, propellant gas puffed from the breech mechanism and blew grit over the men in the open cockpit.

The mortar bomb exploded, a flash of orange in a splotch of filthy smoke. Fragments of hot casing shredded leaves and created a circular froth in the channel. The bits which pattered onto the torpedoboat's deck weren't heavy enough to do damage at this range.

Light winked in the sky. A camera in the nose of the shell sent television pictures down a fiber-optics line to an operator aboard the surface skimmer. The operator had planned to steer the shell's tailfins by commands sent up the same line. Now the gossamer trail of glass drifted harmlessly from the sky, writhing in the turbulence from the explosion.

The operator would be shifting his console to control one of the two further rounds which burped from the clip-fed mortar as soon as the ADS detonated the first bomb.

L7521 had been accelerating. Samuels continued pouring the coal to his thrusters, closing the range to the hidden ambusher. The Blackhorse vessel was in trouble if it came off the outriggers here, because the depth of the channel might not be enough to float the hydrofoil's main hull.

They were in trouble no matter what.

Johnnie checked for at least the tenth time to be sure that his twin mount was set to fire explosive bullets. If he got a shot at the enemy, his burst had to count. He figured his best bet was to blow gaping holes in the hovercraft's plenum chamber, disabling the craft for hours and possibly—just possibly—giving the hydrofoil a chance to run clear.

The ADS snarled like a bumblebee larger even than the jungles of Venus had spawned. One of the pair of guided shells exploded at its apex. The speck of the other continued to drop while the Gatling spun to track it, then fired again.

The blast rocked Johnnie down in his seat. Something whined angrily off the neck flare of his helmet. Water just off the torpedoboat's bow spouted six feet high where a large chunk, perhaps the nose cone, hit.

The surface skimmer was paralleling them unseen on the other side of the island to starboard. Johnnie aimed where the AI told him to, praying for a target.

Nothing but mangroves, tens to hundreds of yards of rippling black trunks. Too dense for sight, too dense for bullets to penetrate.

The chart in the holographic display unrolled as L7521 sped down the channel. Because of the chart's reduced scale, its movement appeared leisurely compared to that of the trees and the squawking, startled animals ducking to concealment among them.

Over the scream of wind and the thrusters, the hostile mortar went *choonk, choonk, choonk*. The enemy had fired a full clip. There wasn't a prayer that a single ADS would detonate all three of the guided rounds.

Two crewmen with set, powder-blackened faces poised on the edge of the cockpit. One held a fresh drum of ammunition for the little Gatling; the other sailor would jerk the spent drum out of the way when the gun stuttered to silence. The Automatic Defense System blazed out a hundred flechettes per second— and the feed drum held only five hundred rounds.

A blue line unrolled across the chart display, marking a neck of land so marshy that the water stood on it. At top speed, L7521 *might* be able to cut over that part of the island before her outriggers ripped off and—

"Uncle Dan!" Johnnie screamed. "A mile ahead there's—"

"Too far!" Dan shouted.

The ADS fired, blasting the first of the shells. The Gatling turned, cracked out a single flechette, and froze with its ammunition supply exhausted as the two remaining bombs bored down under the guidance of their operators.

Ensign Samuels emptied his handgun skyward as his men struggled to reload the Automatic Defense System. Even if the bullets chanced to hit, they didn't have enough energy to explode the shells.

The shore to starboard sucked away from the torpedoboat. Molluscs riffled the air above a sandbar; the water in the slough beyond was too deep for mangroves, but great carnivorous lilies spread across its protected surface. The land beyond the slight embayment was marked by a yellow-green line on the chart.

Johnnie's hand curved back to his own pistol.

Dan, controlling all L7521's systems through his helmet, fired the cage of armor-piercing missiles on the torpedoboat's stern.

The crash of the first-stage rocket motors was echoed an instant later by a sharper *crack* as each 5-inch missile went supersonic and the ramjet sustainers ignited. The six rounds rippled off in pairs. Their backblasts enveloped the vegetation to port in steam and yellow scorch marks. Chips of mangrove wood exploded from the dense growth hiding the surface skimmer from its prey.

The missiles had sharp noses and enough velocity to damage the armor of a battleship, an ideal combination for penetrating brush with minimal deflection. Dan had waited to fire the salvo until the forest between him and the ambusher was thin as it was going to be—

At any time before shells blew L7521 to scraps and foam.

The guided bombs staggered in the air as their operators lost control. The shells dropped into the channel ten yards to either side of the torpedoboat, raising harmless columns of mud and water. Various forms of scavengers arrowed toward the circles of dead fish.

A smoke ring, then a huge waterspout rose from Channel 19. The concussion rocked the torpedoboat to port before its outriggers could compensate. It must have been a secondary explosion, shells and fuel aboard the surface skimmer, because the armor-piercing missiles didn't have warheads.

"Sometimes you get lucky," Dan said softly. He unplugged his helmet, then collapsed into the assistant gunner's seat as the flex wound back within its cradle. The display became a normal holographic gunsight again.

"First you have to be good," Johnnie said. "Sir."

"Blackhorse Three to bridge," Dan said with his eyes closed. "Your ship again, Ensign Samuels. I suggest you take us through Channel Seventeen when you get her turned around. Nineteen's got better clearance, but there may be somebody there still able to shoot. Three out."

"I doubt it," Johnnie said. "I doubt there's anything left the size of a matchbox. You did. . . . Uncle Dan, you were perfect."

His uncle smiled. He didn't open his eyes.

They had reached the point that the chart had marked with a blue line. The channel was deeper here. Samuels slowed L7521 and dropped her onto her main hull to turn around.

Johnnie stared at what he'd thought from the display might be a connection by which they could enter Channel 19 and get a direct shot at their attacker. Though there *was* standing water, there was also a solid belt of mangroves. The youth couldn't see the far channel through them.

"We couldn't have gotten through here after all," Johnnie admitted over the intercom.

Dan surveyed the terrain with a practiced eye, then shrugged. "We'd sure have tried if I hadn't gotten lucky with a missile," he said.

And if neither of those mortar shells had blasted us to atoms, Johnnie's mind added.

Aloud he said, "It's solid trees, Uncle Dan. They would have torn us apart if we'd hit them."

L7521 accelerated, kicking up a triple roostertail as she rose onto her foils.

Commander Cooke smiled humorlessly at his nephew. "I didn't say it was a good choice, lad," he said. "But losing is the worst choice of all."

A great, anvil-topped cloud of black smoke marked where the surface skimmer had exploded. As the hydrofoil passed that point in the parallel channel, Johnnie heard the crackle of a fuel fire across the narrow island.

8

They bit, they glared, gave blows like beams,
*   a wind went with their paws;*
With wallowing might and stifled roar
*   they rolled on one another. . . .*

*   —Leigh Hunt*

Blackhorse Base was an atoll rather than an embayment of one of the larger land masses. Dozens of separate islands, most of them waving green plumage, formed a pattern like the individual blotches of a jaguar's rosette. Even where the connecting reef rose only occasionally above the sea, life forms clawed at one another for light and food and the sheer joy of slaughter.

By focusing his gunsight past one of those low spots in the reef, Johnnie glimpsed the great gray shapes of Blackhorse dreadnoughts in the central deep-water anchorage.

With a motion more like that of an elevator than a vehicle, L7521 slowed and settled toward the surface of the sea. The main hull slurped down and wallowed as the auxiliary thruster took over the load; the outriggers came out of the water.

Johnnie blinked. Something with suckers and bright,

furious eyes stared back at him from the blade of the bow foil. It dropped away with regret as direct sunlight baked the plastic surface to which it clung.

How the creature had ever managed to get and hold a grip at seventy-plus knots. . . .

"Why did we stop out here?" Johnnie asked. They were half a mile from the nearest island, and he could see that the entrance to the central anchorage was some distance farther around the circuit of the atoll.

"Twelve knots only feels like being stopped," Dan chuckled. "And—it isn't good form to come racing up to a fleet's base. Even when it's your own and you're expected."

He pointed to the nearest of the islands which had been cleared for occupation. Railguns, dug into coral revetments, were tracking the hydrofoil.

Johnnie started to focus his gunsight for a closer look at the installations, but his uncle caught his hand. "*Real* bad idea," Dan said. "Aim your guns straight up."

L7521, now operating as a conventionally-hulled craft, puttered past an island at a safe three hundred yards from its luxuriant vegetation. Something looked out of a mangrove thicket and snarled. A machine-gunner along the starboard railing snarled back with a short burst.

The next island in the loose chain had an oddly leprous appearance. Johnnie thought he saw the shapes of heavy equipment, but there were also patches of vegetation whose green was brighter than that of the other islands.

He squinted. His uncle took a pair of flat electronic binoculars out of the breast pocket and scanned the island.

"We've only cleared three of the islands," Dan explained. "Now that the Blackhorse is expanding— thanks to the Senator—we decided we needed more room for facilities. This latest flap caught us after we'd made an initial pass on Island 4, but long before we'd gotten the soil sterilized. All available personnel are busy bringing ships up to combat standard, so the clearing operation's had to wait."

He handed the binoculars to Johnnie.

Construction equipment including bulldozers, rock plows, and support structures which looked like stranded barges, stood as though choked by the vegetation that crawled over the machines and the ground alike. A sheep's-foot roller had eight-foot trees growing from the soil which clung to its great studded wheels, and another huge device was anonymous within a wrapper of green tentacles.

"How long has the work been abandoned?" Johnnie asked.

"Twenty-seven days," the older man said with grim amusement. "Lets you know why our ancestors decided to colonize the sea floor instead of the land, doesn't it?"

Dan touched the keypad of his helmet and said in a different voice, "L7521 to Base Control. Request permission to engage life forms on Island 4 with the twins. Over."

"Wow!" said Johnnie.

Something had just lifted its head from the prey it was devouring beside a bulldozer. As the actinic radiation bathing Venus mutated the creature's ancestral germ plasm, its legs became shorter and thicker; its body slimmed; and its wing-cases shrank to vestigial nubs to be displayed during courtship rituals.

"Base to L7521," said a bored voice. "Permission denied. We've still got equipment on 4 and it's not for target practice. Over."

The creature's head and great shearing mandibles were still those of a tiger beetle.

"Base, let me rephrase that request," Dan said in a tone that suggested he had a rasp for a tongue. "Director of Planning Cooke aboard L7521 requests permission to engage life forms on Island 4 with the twins. Over."

"Base to L7521," said the voice, no longer bored. "Permission granted. Out."

Johnnie swung the powered mounts and lowered the gun barrels as part of the same movement.

"Wait one," his uncle said as he turned and waved to the hydrofoil's commanding officer in the cockpit.

"Roger, go ahead, sir," Ensign Samuels responded over the com set.

The tiger beetle's head dipped, then rose again. Its jaws were working furiously on the strip of white flesh gripped in its mandibles. The creature's eyes did not shift to follow the vessel, but the sun glinting on different sets of the faceted lenses gave the impression of movement.

Johnnie thumbed his sights to x2, then x5 when he'd acquired the target. He projected a translucent orange ghost ring. At the higher magnification, the broad ring hopped and wobbled with L7521's motion, almost unnoticed until then. Johnnie dialed in mils of elevation until the bottom of the ring no longer skipped down into the bulldozer, then locked the mount's stabilizer—

And pressed the firing tit.

Though the twin-sixties were heavy armament in Johnnie's terms, their use on a torpedoboat was more to disconcert enemies a thousand times larger than in the realistic hope of destroying an opponent. The feed drums were loaded with every other round a tracer. The guns spat a lash of glowing fireballs—a sight to make a hostile gunner flinch, even if he was behind 20-inch armor and watching through a remote pick-up.

The guns belched two solid, pulsing lines of gold which converged at the laser-calculated range to the target. The lining of Johnnie's helmet clamped firmly over his ears like a punch to both sides of his head. The muzzle blasts slapped his face as the guns recoiled alternately.

Blinking with the double shock to his vision and skin, Johnnie lifted his thumb from the trigger.

The tiger beetle charged. It climbed over the bulldozer with a swift fluidity which suggested it had scores of legs instead of six.

The charge was blind reflex. The creature's head had vanished. The short burst of high-explosive .60-caliber bullets had blown eyes and brain to jelly in a dozen red flashes.

All the guns mounted on the starboard rail began firing. Passengers joined in with automatic rifles and even pistols. The beetle's armor sparkled with the dusting of tiny bullets exploding harmlessly across it.

While the others banged ineffectively at the headless creature, Johnnie switched his feed selector from X to S—solids instead of high explosive. He squeezed the trigger again and held it down. His long burst halted the charging beetle, then knocked it backward.

Though the mechanism still fed from the same loading drums as when the guns were set to the S position, the bursting charges in the bullets did not get the jolt of electricity necessary to prime them. Instead of exploding against the first object they struck, the bullets smashed their way through to the creature's vitals, ripping the heart and the ganglia controlling the shimmering legs.

Johnnie stopped firing. He raised the barrels of his gun and rotated them in line with the vessel's axis again.

Lubricant and powder smoke oozed out of the mechanism, filling the gun tub with their sickening mixture.

The tiger beetle lay on the island's margin. The right side of its thorax was staved in and leaking white fluid. Its legs twitched feebly, but smaller predators were already appearing both from land and water to feast on the unexpected bounty. .

Uncle Dan smiled at Johnnie. "Told you I'd find you some target practice," he said.

L7521 burbled past Island 3, a mass of shops and barracks formed of concrete and stabilized earth. There were variations of style and color, but no semblance of formal art. Despite—or perhaps because of—that, the buildings made a pleasing whole and seemed in keeping with the harsh ambiance of sea and sky around them.

The net-protected entrance to the central lagoon was between Islands 3 and 2. Railgun emplacements flanked it. On the tip of either island was an openly displayed depth-charge mortar.

"Shouldn't they be in pits?" Johnnie said, nodding toward the mortars as winches drew open the outer pair of nets.

"They aren't for submarines," the Blackhorse officer explained. "Subs wouldn't get this close through the outer ring of sea-bottom sensors. But some of the local life forms are about as dangerous as a hostile sub."

The torpedoboat slid through the narrow opening, then waited at idle as men on shore made certain that nothing had entered *with* L7521. Only when security was satisfied did the inner nets part to allow the little vessel into the lagoon.

Long quays reached out from the three inhabited islands. Vessels up through the size of cruisers were moored to them, three and four deep. There were scores of submarines, their smooth black backs awash almost to the conning towers. Johnnie suspected that there were more than the ninety subs which Wenceslas' data bank credited to the Blackhorse.

The heavy ships, the dreadnoughts and the two carriers, were anchored out in the lagoon. Swarms of lighters, some of them of five hundred tons but looking like water beetles by comparison, surged between the big ships and the quays.

A railgun crashed angrily. Johnnie jumped and touched his grip controls. The shooting was just the weapon on the west end of Island 1 discouraging a visitor—perhaps another beetle—from the uncleared portion of the atoll.

Four heavy vessels were visible only as portions of superstructure poking out above the drydocks on Island 1. "New construction?" Johnnie asked, nodding.

"Two of them are," Dan agreed. "Work's stopped for now while we concentrate on the ships we'll be able to use within the next week . . . which itself may be a little optimistic on time. The other two are battle damage."

He brushed his lips with the back of his hand, a trivial gesture unless you happened to be watching his bleak eyes as he did it. His voice had gone slightly harsh as he added, "The *Catherine* may be ready in time. The *Isabella* won't be."

"The *Isabella* was your squadron flagship three months ago, wasn't she?" Johnnie said.

"Yep," said Dan. He laughed—or cackled. "But you should see the other guy."

Then he shook himself like a dog coming in from the rain; and when he met his nephew's eyes again, he was wearing his familiar, insouciant grin.

L7521 slid up to a landing stage built out from a quay on Island 2. Seamen at bow and stern belayed lines tossed from the stage, but they didn't tie them off.

Ensign Samuels cursed as his vessel slipped back from the worn rubber fender and grunched solidly against the stage. "All passengers ashore," he ordered over the cockpit loudspeaker. "And step on it. If you please. Sirs."

Uncle Dan took off the borrowed commo helmet and set it on his seat.

"Let's go, Provisional Recruit Gordon," he said with a smile. "And see if we can get Admiral Bergstrom to confirm you."

The passengers from the stern and cockpit were already hopping onto the landing stage. Captain Haynes jumped with surprising grace; looked back over his shoulder at Dan and Johnnie; and began striding down the catwalk—toward the Base Operations Center.

9

The refrigerated air of the Base Operations Center made Johnnie stumble as he stepped through the door. Dan looked at him in amusement and said, "You've acclimated quickly. That's good. I hadn't counted on it."

"How cold do they keep it?" the younger man asked as he looked around the entrance hall. It was dim and a little dingy as well as being cold. Not cool, *cold*.

"Eighty degrees," Dan said. "Which is wrong—it ought to be pegged to no more than ten degrees below the ambient, but people like to be comfortable when they can . . . and they don't worry about what's going to happen in action, even on a dreadnought, when the cooling plant takes a direct hit."

The door marked "Commander in Chief" was open, but that was just the outer office. The secretary/receptionist at the central desk and electronics console wore the bars of a senior lieutenant.

"Good morning, Commander," the lieutenant said. "Admiral Bergstrom asked if he might have a few

minutes alone with Captain Haynes before you joined
them."

*Captain Haynes demanded a few minutes alone with
Admiral Bergstrom*, Johnnie translated. His face grew
taut. He remembered what his uncle had said about
control, but he wasn't able to relax.

Despite all the sophisticated hardware associated
with the desk, there was an acetate-covered sign-out
chart on one wall of the room. It was printed with
boxes in which the names and destinations of officers
were written in grease pencil. On the opposite wall was
a holographic seascape: pelicans banking over dunes
sprinkled with sea oats, while a gentle surf foamed up
the strand.

The seascape showed a memory of Earth. Nowhere
on Venus was there a scene so idyllic.

"Sure, that's fine, Barton," Dan said easily. "We'll
wait in the hall and keep out of your hair."

There were bulletin boards in the hall. One of them
listed a handful of apartments in Wenceslas Dome. Dan
nodded to it and said, "Leases that got opened up three
months ago. They've been pretty well picked over by
now."

"Is it going to be all right?" the younger man asked
tightly. "With Haynes already there?"

"We'll make it all right, won't we?" Dan said. "Just
follow my lead, is all."

He grinned in what seemed good humor and
added, "You can think of it as your baptism of
fire, John. Only, no matter how bad you screw up,
nobody's going to die."

The expression changed minusculy. "For a while,
that is."

"You know," Johnnie said, "in all the years I've
known you, Uncle Dan, there's only once I've seen you
really angry."

Dan chuckled. "You've seen me angry, lad? When was that?"

"Yesterday. In the Senator's office, when you told him he was a—that he didn't have any balls."

"Oh, that," the older man said. He chuckled again. "And that's why you decided your father was a coward, is it? Well, you mustn't mistake tones for emotions. The Senator reacts very emotionally to anything involving you—that's just biology, after all. So I—"

He spread his right hand and looked critically at the nails. "—had to get his attention on the level at which he was operating."

Johnnie blinked and turned away. "Then it wasn't true?" he said, trying to keep the tremor out of his voice.

"Look at me," his uncle said. "*Look* at me."

"Yessir."

"What's true is that Mankind has a chance to survive and spread to the stars," the mercenary officer said without raising his voice. "What's true is that I'll do whatever I need to do in order to protect that chance."

Johnnie was standing rigid. Dan relaxed with a visible shudder and attempted a grin.

"One more thing and we'll drop this, John," he said. "I want you to remember. I've killed people because it was my job. I've killed people because I was scared. But I've never killed anybody because I was angry."

Johnnie nodded. "Sure," he said. He would have made the same reply if his uncle had told him it was noon, and the information would have made as much difference to him.

"Commander?" called Lieutenant Barton from the office doorway. "The Admiral will see you now."

Dan put his arm around Johnnie's shoulders. "Buck up," he said as they strode forward. "'Forward into ba-at-tle, see our banners go!'"

"I'll be fine, Uncle Dan." He really believed it now.

"Sure you will, John," Dan replied. He settled himself and his sweat-marked uniform into the semblance of the third-ranking officer in the premier mercenary fleet on Venus. "You wouldn't be here if I weren't sure of that."

Dan motioned Johnnie through the inner doorway first. Captain Haynes, seated in one of the two chairs in front of the Admiral's desk, snapped, "Not him."

Johnnie paused. Dan's touch moved him into the office.

"Yes, him, Captain," Dan said as he closed the door and stepped past his nephew. "Recruit Gordon's presence is necessary for this discussion."

He nodded toward Admiral Bergstrom. "But the explanation won't take very long."

Admiral Bergstrom's office was large without being spacious. It was filled with enough scrap and rusted metal to suggest a salvage yard.

One wall held a stenciled swatch of a gunboat's bow panelling. The last digit of the number, Z841–, had vanished into the hole blown by an explosive shell.

Above the panel was a hand-held rocket launcher of a pattern at least thirty years old. Beside them both was the sun-bleached, shrapnel-torn pennant of a flotilla commander; and, to the right of that in the corner beside the door, was the empty circular frame which had once held the condensing lens of a high-resolution display.

All four walls were similarly adorned, and larger pieces of junk took up floor-space besides.

Souvenirs of a life spent in the service of war.

Admiral Bergstrom looked like a clerk with tired, nervous eyes. His left hand was withered, though he used it to play with a miniature mobile of shrapnel chunks as he looked from one to another of his visitors.

The rumor Johnnie had overheard in conversations in his father's house was that Bergstrom had a maintenance-level drug habit. The Admiral's dilated pupils suggested the rumor might be true.

Dan sat. "Sir, it's necessary that Recruit John Gordon be given officer's rank and made my aide without the usual formalities. His background is such that he'll be a credit to the company, but—"

"That's absurd!" said Haynes, his face darkening.

Don't be sorry. Be controlled.

"But it isn't because of *that* that I make the request," Dan continued. "I presume you've realized that Recruit Gordon is my nephew . . . and Senator Gordon's son. Unfor—"

"If there was ever a good time to provide, uh, untrained civilians with commissions," Haynes said, "it's not now when we're facing the most severe test in the Blackhorse's history."

The catch in the captain's voice suggested that he'd intended a less flattering phrase than "untrained civilians." Discretion, and memory of just how powerful a politician's brat Johnnie was, had bridled his tongue.

"Untrained . . . ," Dan repeated, as if savoring the word on his tongue. Then, sharply but not hostilely, "Johnnie, keep your eyes on me!"

"Yessir!"

"There's a lens frame on the wall behind you. Shoot withi—"

The double *cra-crack*! of the pistol shots surprised everyone in the office except Commander Cooke; even Johnnie, especially Johnnie, because if he'd thought of what he was doing he'd never've been able to do it. Two rounds, and he didn't turn until the second was away, shockingly loud in a room without a sound-absorbent lining.

Johnnie thumbed the catch and replaced the

partial magazine with a fresh one from his belt pouch. His fingers worked by rote. His first round had starred the concrete wall just beneath the eight-inch ring; his second had struck in the center of the target. Both of the light, high-velocity bullets had disintegrated in sprays of metal against the hard surface.

The door burst open. "*What the—*" shouted Lieutenant Barton. His eyes widened and his hand dropped toward the butt of the pistol he carried in a flapped service holster.

Johnnie slipped his own weapon into his cutaway holster and turned his back on Barton. His ears rang, and the air was cloying with the familiar odor of powder smoke.

"That won't be necessary, Lieutenant," Dan said, lifting one leg lazily to hang it over the arm of his chair. "Everything's under control here."

The door closed. Johnnie focused his eyes on a signed group photograph on the wall above Admiral Bergstrom's head.

"Under control . . . ," Haynes said. "Cooke, you're insane."

"Now that we've covered the matter of Recruit Gordon's training," Dan said, "there's the serious matter of why—"

"There's more to training than skill with small arms, Daniel," said the Admiral quietly. "As you know."

"As I know, sir," Dan agreed. "In everything but hands-on experience, Recruit Gordon compares favorably to the best of our junior lieutenants. But the reason it's necessary that we commission him isn't that we need another officer—useful though that may be . . . but rather, because Senator Gordon doesn't trust us."

"What?" blurted Captain Haynes.

What? Johnnie's mind echoed in equal surprise.

"The Senator has been following our attempts to associate a supporting company with increasing irritation," Dan continued smoothly. "He called me to him to demand an explanation—"

"That's not yours to give, Daniel," Admiral Bergstrom said with an edge to the words that Johnnie hadn't thought within the capacity of the commander in chief.

"I know that, sir," Dan continued, nodding. "But I know my ex-brother-in-law also, and there was nothing to be gained by claiming those negotiations were none of my affair, so he'd have to talk to one of you."

He dipped his head first to Bergstrom, then to Captain Haynes.

"But that's ridiculous," Haynes protested. "There've been some delays, certainly, but they weren't through any fault of ours."

"I told the Senator that, yes," Dan said, bobbing agreement.

"And in any case, now that I'm back it's just a matter of working out the last details of our agreement with Admiral Braun of the Angels," Haynes continued.

"That I *couldn't* tell the Senator," Dan said, "because as you know, I don't believe it myself."

"Right!" blazed Haynes. "You don't believe it because Admiral Braun's a friend of mine. What do you propose, Commander? Working a deal with your great good friend de Lessups in Flotilla Blanche?"

Johnnie couldn't see his uncle's face as he met Haynes' glare, but his voice seemed as calm as if he were ordering lunch as he replied, "Admiral de Lessups offered me his number two slot last year, Captain. But neither he nor I would expect the other to act dishonorably when our companies were already engaged by rival domes.

"Any more," Dan continued in a sudden, jagged snarl like that with which he had hectored the Senator, "than

I'd expect your Admiral Braun to act honorably at any distance greater than pistol range!"

"Listen, you—"

"Gentlemen!"

"If Braun meant to sign, he'd already have signed!" Dan shouted.

"I needed to take care of business back at Wenceslas," Haynes retorted with a hint of defensiveness. "I'll meet him face to—"

"You had to see your wife, you mean!"

Admiral Bergstrom's right fist rang deliberately on a section of dimpled armor plate on his desktop. "*Gentlemen!*" he shouted.

Captain Haynes had jumped into a crouch. He blinked like a sow bear at her first sight of Spring sunshine, then sat—or flopped—into a chair again. His right hand clenched and relaxed; and clenched again. Johnnie couldn't be certain, but he thought the visicube on the desk before Haynes contained an image of his wife.

"Now that I'm back," Haynes resumed in a voice that was almost falsetto, "I'll go to Paradise Base and knock down the final details." He raised his eyes to meet those of the Admiral. "With your agreement, sir?"

Bergstrom grimaced. "Yes, yes," he said without enthusiasm. "I would have thought that perhaps Hackney's Wizards were a better bet, but—"

"The Angels have the big-bore throw weight that'll be crucial, sir," Haynes said earnestly.

"Yes, well," the Admiral said. "It's really too late to begin negotiations with another fleet, now. And anyway, the Angels will certainly be satisfactory. Almost any company would be, given our own strength."

Almost under his breath, Bergstrom added, "I don't understand why they seem to be treating the Blackhorse as a pariah. We've always kept up the highest standards. . . ."

"Yes *sir*," Haynes said. He rose. "I'll take a hydrofoil to Paradise immediately."

"And you'll take Ensign Gordon with you," Dan said from his seat.

"I'll do no—"

"Because by taking Senator Gordon's trusted observer," Dan continued with icy, battle-order precision. "The Senator's spy, if you will . . . we'll be proving to him that we have nothing to hide."

Dan stood, a smooth uncoiling of his body from the seat as graceful as the motion with which his nephew drew and fired behind his back. "Isn't that so, Admiral Bergstrom? We have nothing to hide."

Bergstrom grimaced again. He closed his eyes briefly, looking more than ever like an overworked bookkeeper at the end of the day.

"Yes, of course," he said at last. "You'll be taking some staff with you to Paradise Base, Captain. I don't see any reason why Ensign Gordon shouldn't be among them."

Johnnie was looking at his uncle. Commander Cooke grinned.

10

*From many a wondrous grot and secret cell
Unnumber'd and enormous polypi
Winnow with giant arms the slumbering green.*
                    —Alfred, Lord Tennyson

The forward gun tub was decorated with the hydrofoil's stencilled number, M4434, and a freehand rendition of her unofficial name: *Bellycutter*. There was also a cartoon of an oriental figure to explicate the name for anybody who hadn't seen the casualty rates for torpedoboats.

The lone sailor on duty behind the twin guns was dozing, but there wasn't much reason for him to be alert. They had sped from Blackhorse across open sea and through the Kanjar Straits. The run was without incident until a pair of skimmers came out of Paradise Base, inspected M4434 as she dropped off her outriggers, and howled back within the harbor at high speed.

Johnnie stood in the bow, bracing himself against the roll with a hand on the tub's armored rim. The continent of North Hell was a mass of greens and earth tones ahead of M4434, punctuated by concrete and plastic constructions on both jaws of land enveloping the Angels' fine natural harbor.

The Angels, like Flotilla Blanche and the Warcocks, were based on the periphery of the Ishtar Basin. That would make link-up between the Angels and the Blackhorse—whose atoll was in the Western Ocean—tricky, though not impossible. Even if the direct route via the Kanjar Straits was blocked, there were scores of other passages through the archipelago sweeping around the south and east of the basin.

The Angels' main installations were on the southern arm of the harbor. They were protected by a wall; beyond the wall a fence which sparkled as high currents fried life forms attempting it; and beyond the fence, strings of flashes and explosions. Guns were firing from the wall, blowing swathes in the nearest vegetation in an attempt to knock it down before roots and branches became a threat to the inner defenses.

There were signs that the Angels had recently started to clear an area further out so that the present barrier could be given over to expanded facilities. The attempt had been abandoned, probably for the reason Blackhorse had done the same: all available men were working to put the fleet on a war footing.

If the Angels were preparing for war, then Captain Haynes must be right. What would that do to Uncle Dan's maneuvering?

The northern landspit was defended but almost unoccupied. At its tip were heavy batteries: railguns and, for engaging enemies over the horizon, conventional artillery in massive casements. The only other installations were those facing the threat of the jungle, which on this side of the harbor was muted.

While the southern jaw had been in existence for millennia, its northern counterpart was the creation of a volcano within living memory.

The lava poured out at 4,000°. Though the pullulating life of Venus had robbed the surface of its virginal sterility even before it cooled to air temperature, the fresh rock nonetheless formed a sufficient barrier against the largest and most dangerous of the predatory vegetation.

A low electrified fence, supported by chemical sprayers and flame guns, protected the gun emplacements from surface roots and the occasional large carnivore which burst from the jungle beyond the two hundred yards of russet lava. In a century—or even a few decades—rain water and the jungle would break the raw rock into permeable soil, with disastrous results for the gun crews on duty when it happened.

But that would be another day, and the concerns of a mercenary were for the far shorter term. . . .

Except maybe for Uncle Dan.

Dan had said to observe *everything* about Paradise Base, the way he'd reflexively observed Admiral Bergstrom's office as he entered it. Bergstrom and Haynes probably thought Johnnie had been briefed on what to expect during the interview; the exhibition of shooting had impressed them, even Haynes, despite that.

But the test had been much more extreme than that. Commander Cooke had wanted to see how well his nephew's training responded to genuine field conditions. " . . . *your baptism of fire, John.* . . ."

Walcheron, the sailor manning the gun tub, suddenly snapped to alertness.

Johnnie's left hand made an instinctive grab for the rifle butt-upward beside the unoccupied assistant gunner's seat. His head rotated quickly, scanning to find the cause of alarm.

There didn't seem to be anything amiss.

A pair of gliders wheeled high in the white sky, no

threat even to a torpedoboat wallowing along on its main hull. The only other vessel in sight was the Angels' net-tending boat. The distance between the jaws of land was too great for the protective nets to be operated from shore, as at Blackhorse Base. Instead, a double-ended fifty-ton vessel equipped with winches accomplished the task from the center of the channel.

The net-tender was lightly armed, even by torpedoboat standards. Besides, some of the crewmen aboard her were waving cheerfully at the visitor which would break the utter boredom of their duty.

The man in the gun tub turned to Johnnie. "Your name Gordon?" he asked.

"Yes—ah, yes," Johnnie replied, catching himself barely before he, an officer, called a seaman "sir."

The gunner tapped his commo helmet. Johnnie hadn't been offered one—and hadn't wanted to ask—on this trip. "Cap'n Haynes wants t' see you in the stern," the seaman explained, gesturing with his thumb.

Johnnie opened his mouth to ask what he realized before speaking was a silly question.

"He wants t' tell you something private, I guess," said the sailor, giving the obvious answer anyway.

Captain Haynes had made this run (as the previous one, from Wenceslas Dome to Blackhorse Base) in the cockpit. Now he got up from his seat at the control console and made his way sternward. His stocky body rode gracefully through each chop-induced quiver of the deck.

Haynes didn't bother to look over his shoulder to see that Johnnie was obeying the command.

"Right," Johnnie said, picking his way carefully along the railing. He wasn't at all steady, though he was sure he'd learn the trick of walking along a pitching deck if he managed to avoid drowning in the near future.

"Careful, kid," warned a pipe-smoking petty officer

amidships. He reached out to steady Johnnie as the youth passed by.

The sailor was amusing himself by blowing smoke rings onto the sea. Water boiled as predators attacked the insubstantial prey.

Johnnie wondered if Haynes would permit the torpedoboat to stop and rescue him if he fell overboard. Judging from the way teeth instantly tore the smoke rings, it probably wouldn't matter. . . .

The deck widened astern of the cockpit. Breathing hard from the earlier portion of the forty-foot journey, Johnnie reached the captain's side.

Haynes had drawn his heavy pistol. He was looking back over the wake. He didn't turn around.

Johnnie curled the fingers of his left hand firmly around the cage of ramjet penetrators. "Yes sir?" he said, uncertain whether or not the captain knew he'd arrived.

"I've been ordered to bring you along, Ensign Gordon," Haynes said.

He spat. The gobbet sailed to a point six inches from the surface of the water. A fish that was all teeth and shimmering scales curved out of the wake and snatched the spittle from the air.

Haynes fired, blasting a waterspout just short of the target. The explosive bullet sprayed bits of miniature shrapnel into the fish so that it left a slick of blood as it resubmerged.

Seconds later, the wake surged in a feeding frenzy more violent than a grenade going off.

Johnnie relaxed. *If that was meant to impress me . . .* he thought.

He'd almost put two rounds of his own through the head of the fish before it went under; but he had a task to carry out for Uncle Dan. This wasn't the time or place to show off.

Haynes holstered his weapon without reloading and gave Johnnie a satisfied smirk. "I'm under orders to bring you along," he repeated, "but that doesn't mean you'll be present during the negotiations. I'm *not* taking a chance of some untrained kid blurting the wrong thing and putting the whole deal at risk. Do you understand?"

"Yes sir," Johnnie said. He even agreed. After all, a deal with the Angels would be the best proof possible that the Blackhorse wasn't attempting some phony game to fool Senator Gordon.

"And don't try to scare me with what your father's going to say," Haynes continued in a rising voice. "The deal I cut with Admiral Braun will *prove* that the Blackhorse has been negotiating in good faith."

"Yessir," Johnnie said. He wondered if Haynes was stupid—unlikely, given his position—or whether the captain just thought that everybody he disliked was stupid.

"There'll be bars open at Paradise Base," Haynes continued. "Or you can stay with the boat if you like. Just keep out of trouble or I *swear* it won't matter who your relatives are."

"Yessir."

Haynes strode past him, back to the cockpit.

Johnnie rubbed his right palm on his thigh. His uniform had been soaked with spray on the high-speed run, but the hammering sun dried the cloth in minutes after the M4434 dropped off her foils.

He really wished he'd showed up Haynes' clumsy marksmanship; but there'd be another time. . . .

He wiped his gunhand again and returned to the bow while the torpedoboat rocked and waited for the outer net to open. He could just as easily have waited where he was, but then somebody might have thought he was afraid to chance the narrow catwalk amidships.

Johnnie reached the bow in time to steady himself against the gun tub when the auxiliary thruster accelerated M4434 through the minimal opening which the net-tender drew for them.

Reverse thrust slowed the hydrofoil again. A derrick on the net-tender's bow slid the folds of net forward again to mate with the line of buoys holding up the fixed portion of the meshes. The water was a deep blue-green, slimed with wastes discharged from the base installations.

Something else had entered with M4434. A paddle-tipped tentacle as big around as a pony keg curled out of the water and wrapped itself around the net-tender.

For an instant, all the chaos and violence was of the squid's doing. A second long tentacle encircled the little vessel. There was a flurry of foam and a mass of shorter tentacles, writhing like Medusa's hair, drew six feet of the squid's mauve body up the net-tender's starboard side.

The vessel bobbed. Waves lapped its starboard rail.

Three, then a dozen guns opened up from the hydrofoil and the net-tender itself. Explosive bullets dimpled the sea, the net-tender's hull, and the squid. Johnnie snatched out the automatic rifle as the gunner spun his twin-sixties to bear.

"Not those!" Johnnie shouted. "You'll sink them!"

When the big guns continued to rotate, the side of Johnnie's fist slammed the sailor's helmet hard enough to knock the man out of his seat. There was no time for delicacy.

"Use solids!" he warned, but he didn't have a commo helmet so nobody could hear him over the gunfire . . . and anyway, nobody would've listened to a young ensign-in-name-only.

But he was right.

A young officer leaned over the net-tender's rail with a sub-machine gun and fired most of the forty-round magazine straight down into the squid. Sparkling explosions blew the eyes to jelly and raised a cloud of lime dust from the huge parrot beak.

Sepia flooded the water around the squid; pigment darkened its flesh from mauve to greenish black.

A pair of tentacles unhooked from the rail and seized the Angels' officer. A third twisted the gun from the youth's hand as skillfully as if the squid still had eyes.

Johnnie switched his rifle to solids and fired a three-shot burst between the monster's eyes. He began walking down the squid's torso with further short bursts, probing for the ganglia. Bullets that exploded on the skin couldn't possibly kill the huge invertebrate.

The creature suddenly spasmed and blushed a pinkish white color. Its tentacles went slack, though the long pair still crisscrossed the net-tender amidships.

The young officer dropped onto the squid's sagging body. Its beak closed reflexively over his waist, but his bullets had powdered the hooked tip which would otherwise have punctured his intestines and crushed his spine.

One of the net-tender's crewmen with more courage than sense jumped into the roiling water and grabbed the stunned officer. In three frog-like kicks he made it back to the vessel's side. Four pairs of hands reached over desperately to pull him and his burden back aboard.

There was a quiver of movement from deep within the water.

"Look out!" Johnnie screamed as he pointed his rifle at where the newcomer would break surface—directly under the struggling men. It was no use trying to shoot *through* the water, but the target would appear jaws-first. . . .

A net-tender crewman, bleeding from a pressure cut on his cheek and forehead, tossed something that looked like a six-pack of beer over the side.

It must have been a bundle of rocket warheads with a short time-fuze, because it went off with a blast that was still bright orange after being filtered through the water.

The gout of water slammed the two vessels apart and lifted their facing sides. Johnnie fell down, but the net-tender's crew used the surge to help them snatch their fellows safe aboard.

A fragment of the squid's tentacle floated near M4434.

The other creature must have been a fish with a swim bladder to rupture in the explosion. It sank to the bottom, unseen save for a flash of terror through the bullet-spattered water.

"Cease fire!" roared Captain Haynes over the cockpit public-address system. "Cease fire! We're not here to waste ammunition!"

Johnnie's left hand was patting the magazine well of his borrowed rifle. He had ejected the empty magazine by rote, but he didn't have a full one with which to replace it.

11

Oh stay with company and mirth
And daylight and the air;
Too full already is the grave
Of fellows that were good and brave
And died because they were.

—A. E. Housman

"Sure you don't wanna come, sir?" said Walcheron. Instead of being angry, the sailor seemed pleased that Johnnie had knocked him down in order to save the Angels from the tender mercies of his twin-sixties. "There's an officers' club if you don't wanna . . . ?"

Johnnie forced a smile and waved. "No, I'll just wander. I—I've been in bars, but haven't had a chance to look at a fleet's base before."

"Hang on," warned the Angel driver as he engaged the torque converter of his prime mover. The flat-bed trailer, loaded with sailors from the hydrofoil in place of its more normal cargo, jerked at the end of its loose hitch toward the base cantina.

Captain Haynes and the two staff lieutenants who made up the negotiating team had already been carried two hundred yards to the Administration

Building in a slightly-flossier conveyance, an air-cushion runabout. That left Johnnie and a single disconsolate sailor—the watch—alone with the M4434.

Johnnie nodded to the sailor and walked down the dock, coming as close to a saunter as the hot, humid air permitted him.

Paradise Base was a smaller, less polished version of Blackhorse Base. The Blackhorse torpedoboat was docked at the destroyer slip; the Angels had no hydrofoils of their own. The next facility around the circumference of the harbor was a drydock holding a dreadnought. The combination of concrete walls and a battleship completely hid everything else in that direction.

Johnnie walked past, looking interested but nonchalant. Dan had told him to observe everything, but not to make any notes or sketches until M4434 was at sea again. Johnnie didn't know what his uncle wanted—and he couldn't imagine that it made any difference, since the Angels' precise strength would become a matter of record as soon as the deal was done.

But Johnnie had his orders, and he was going to carry them out.

He reached the land end of the quay, facing the Admin Building and a series of barracks. He turned left to pass the drydock.

There were twelve destroyers in the slip. All of them seemed to be combat-ready—but that was the full extent of the Angels' strength in the class. Though destroyers weren't capable of surviving the fire of heavier vessels for more than a few seconds, they provided the inner screen against hostile torpedoboats—a particularly important mission for the Angels, who didn't have hydrofoil gunboats of their own.

Johnnie walked on. The drydock had been cast from

red-dyed concrete, but under the blasting sun it seemed to glow a hazy white. Sweat soaked the sleeves of Johnnie's cream tunic, and he could feel the skin on the back of his hands crinkle.

One side of the quay beyond the drydock was given over to cargo lighters hauling supplies to the dreadnoughts anchored in mid-harbor. Traffic was heavy, and there were several railcars backed up on the line leading to the quay from warehouses within the base area.

Two cruisers were drawn up in the slip to the other side. They were middle-sized vessels, armed with rapid-firing 5.25-inch guns rather than the heavier weapons that might have been able to damage a battleship. In effect, they were flagships for the destroyer flotillas; and the pair of them were the only vessels of their class in the company.

Mercenaries have been called the whores of war. Like many prostitutes, the Angels found specialization the best route to success.

The Angels specialized in dreadnoughts.

There were four of the mighty vessels anchored in deep water. They quivered in the sunlight like gray flaws in the jeweled liquid splendor. The ships looked as though they had just crawled from the jungle which ruled the shore encircling most of the harbor.

The most distant of the battleships, the *Holy Trinity*, was huge even by the standards of her sisters. Her armor could take a battering as long as that of any vessel on the seas of Venus, and shells from her 18-inch main guns would penetrate any target they struck.

By themselves, the Angels were suicidally out of balance. The company had no scouting capacity of its own; its light forces were insufficient to screen its battleships; and the handful of submarines Johnnie saw moored to a rusting mothership might be useful to test the Angels' own antisubmarine defenses during maneuvers, but they certainly weren't a serious threat to another fleet.

None of that mattered *now*: Admiral Braun could have the deal he wanted, because the Angels' five dreadnoughts would be the margin of victory in the coming fleet action.

A man on a two-wheeled scooter—nobody at Paradise seemed to walk when they were out of doors—had left the cantina and raced up the quay from which Johnnie had come. Now the vehicle was back, revving high and leaned over at sixty degrees to make the corner onto the harbor road.

Johnnie stepped to the side. There was plenty of room for a truck, much less the scooter, to get around him, but he didn't trust the driver to have his mount under control.

He was probably over-sensitive. There were no personal vehicles in the domes: the slidewalks took care of individual transportation. He'd have to get used to—

The scooter broadsided to a curving halt in front of Johnnie.

The driver jumped off, leaving his machine rocking on its automatic side-stand. He was young, Johnnie's age, but his skin was already burned a deep mahogany color by the fierce light penetrating the clouds of Venus. He wore ensign's pips on his collar and the legend *"Holy Trinity"* in Fraktur script on the talley around his red cap.

"Is your name Gordon?" the Angel ensign demanded.

"Ensign John Arthur Gordon," Johnnie said. His mind was as blank and white as the sky overhead.

We regret to inform you that your son, John Arthur Gordon, was executed as a spy. May God have mercy on . . .

The other youth smiled as broadly as a shrapnel gash

and thrust out his right hand. "Right!" he said. "I'm Sal Grumio, and you just saved my brother's life!"

"Huh?"

"Tony, you know?" Sal explained as he pumped Johnnie's hand furiously. "He was in command of the *Dragger*, you know, the guard boat?"

"Oh," said Johnnie as the light dawned. "Oh, sure . . . but look, it wasn't me. One of his own people jumped in after him. That took real guts, believe—"

"Guts, fine," Sal interrupted. He waved his hands with a gesture of dismissal. "We're all brave, you bet. But *you're* the one had brains enough to use solids and kill the squid. That was you, wasn't it?"

"I, ah . . . ," Johnnie said. "Yeah, that was me."

Sal jerked a thumb in the direction of the cantina. He gestured constantly and expressively. "Yeah, that's what your gunner said in there. Said you're screamin' '*Use solids, use solids!*' and shootin' the crap outa the squid with a rifle. Tony'd 've been gone without that, and hell knows how many others besides."

"Well, I . . . ," Johnnie said. "Well, I'm glad I was in the right place."

"Hey, look," Sal said with a sudden frown. "You don't want to wander around out here in the sun. Come on, I'll buy you a drink or ten."

"Well, to tell the truth . . . ," Johnnie said. "Look, I'm so new I haven't been in the Blackhorse a full day. I've never really *seen* a base or any ship but a torpedoboat. I'd just—"

"Hey, you never been aboard a dreadnought?" the Angel ensign said, grinning beatifically. "Really?"

"Never even a destroyer," Johnnie said/admitted.

"You got a treat coming, then," said Sal, "because I've got one of the *Holy Trinity*'s skimmer squadrons. Hop on and I'll give you a tour of the biggest and best battleship on Venus!"

Sal swung his leg over the saddle of his scooter and patted the pillion seat.

"Ah," said Johnnie, halting in mid-motion because he was sure Sal would take off without further discussion as soon as his passenger was aboard. "Look, Sal, is this going to be OK?

. . . your son, John Arthur Gordon, has been . . .

"Hell, yes!" the other youth insisted. "Look, nothing's to good for the guy who saved Tony's life, right? And anyway—"

Johnnie sat, still doubtful. The scooter accelerated as hard as it could against the double load.

"—you guys and us 're allies, now, right? *Sure* it's OK!"

12

There is never a storm whose might can reach
Where the vast leviathan sleeps
Like a mighty thought in a mighty mind. . . .
                         —John Boyle O'Reilly

"Fasten your belt," Sal ordered, stuffing his cap in a side pocket as he dropped into the pilot's seat of the skimmer bobbing like a pumpkinseed at the end of the ferry dock.

He latched his own cross-belted seat restraints and added nonchalantly, "It won't matter if we flip—there won't be a piece of the frame left as big as your belt buckle—but at least it'll keep you from getting tossed into the harbor when we come off plane."

"Right," said Johnnie, realizing that the scooter ride was going to be the calm part of the trip.

The skimmer had a shallow hull with a powerful thruster, two side-by-side seats, and a belt-loaded 1-inch rocket gun mounted on a central pintle. The weapon could either be locked along the boat's axis or fired flexibly by the gunner . . . though the latter technique meant the gunner stood while the skimmer was under way.

Other recruits had learned to do that, so Johnnie figured he could if he had to. For now, it looked tricky enough just to stay aboard.

Sal touched two buttons on his panel. First the thruster began to rumble; then the bow and stern lines unclamped from the bollards on the quay and slid back aboard the skimmer as their take-up reels whined.

"Hang on!" Sal warned unnecessarily. He cramped the control wheel hard, then slammed it forward to the stop in order to bring the drive up to full power.

The skimmer lifted; its bow came around in little more than the vessel's own length. Within the first ten feet of forward motion, almost nothing but the thruster nozzle of the tiny craft was in the water. A huge roostertail of spray drenched the dock behind them.

"Yee-*ha*!" Sal shrieked over the sound of the wind and the snarling drive.

The seat back and bottom hammered Johnnie as the skimmer—the ass-slapper—clipped over ripples in the harbor surface that would have been invisible to the eye. He braced his palms against the armrests, letting his wrists absorb much of the punishment and—incidentally—permitting Johnnie to look forward past the vessel's rounded bow. The *Holy Trinity* was expanding swiftly.

Johnnie knew Sal was giving him a ride as well as a lift—but he was pretty sure that the pilot would have been running in a similar fashion if he'd been alone in his ass-slapper. What Dan had said about hydrofoil crewmen was true in spades about the skimmers.

But it was true at higher levels also. The battle centers of the great dreadnoughts were buried deep below the waterline and protected by the main armor belts. All the sensor data—from the vessel itself and from all the other vessels in the fleet—was funneled there.

The battle center was as good a place from which to conduct a battle as could be found in action. The muzzle blasts from the ship's main guns jolted the battle-center crews like so many nearby train-wrecks, but even that was better than the hells of flash and stunning overpressure to which the big guns subjected everyone on the upper decks. Enemy shell-hits were a threat only if they were severe enough to endanger the entire vessel.

In the battle center, hostile warships were a pattern of phosphor dots, not a sinuous dragon of yellow flashes and shells arching down as tons of glowing steel. Friendly losses were carats in a holographic display rather than water-spouts shot with red flames and blackness in which tortured armor screamed for the voiceless hundreds of dying crewmen.

The battle center was the best place from which to direct a battle . . . but the men down in the battle centers were clerks. The commanding officers were on the bridges of their vessels, emotionally as well as physically part of the actions they were directing.

It made no sense—except in human terms.

But then, neither did war.

The *Holy Trinity*'s mottled hull swelled from large to immense behind the rainbow jeweling of sunlit spray. Part of the blurred coloration was deliberate camouflage, shades of gray—gray-green, gray-brown and gray-blue applied to hide the great dreadnought in an environment of smoke and steam . . . but the environment had similar notions of color. The natural stains of rust, salt, and lichen spread over even a relatively new vessel like *Holy Trinity* and provided the finishing touch that outdid human art.

They were getting *very* close. Sal heeled his pumpkinseed over in a curve that would intersect the dreadnought's armored side at a flat angle instead of a straight-on, bug-against-the-windshield impact, then throttled back the thruster.

For a moment, the skimmer continued to slap forward over the ripples; the major difference to be felt was the absence of drive-line vibration. Then they dropped off plane and Johnnie slammed forward into his cross-belts, hard enough to raise bruises.

Sal let the reflected bow wave rock the skimmer to near stasis, then added a little throttle to edge them forward at a crawl. He was chuckling.

"How d'ye like that?" he asked Johnnie. "Are you going to specialize in ass-slappers yourself?"

"Ah, no," Johnnie said, answering the second question because he was going to have to think about the first one for a while before he was sure. "I'm supposed to be serving as aide to my uncle, so I guess that means battleships. Ah, my uncle's Commander Cooke."

Sal raised an eyebrow. "Commander *Dan* Cooke?" he asked. "I've heard of him. No wonder you're good."

Johnnie beamed with pride and pleasure.

Sal had brought the skimmer to a tall, six-foot-wide slot at the waterline, some hundred and fifty feet astern of the cutwater. For a moment, Johnnie thought the hole was either battle damage or some general maintenance project, as yet uncompleted.

"Starboard skimmer launch tube," Sal explained with satisfaction. "Come to think, you don't have ass-slappers in the Blackhorse, do you?"

"Ah," said Johnnie. "I don't think we use them, no."

"Gunboats look all right," his guide said scornfully, "but what they really are is bigger targets. *This* baby—" he patted the breech of the rocket gun "—can chew up torpedoboats and spit out the pieces. And besides, they can't hit *us*."

Try me on a hydrofoil's stabilized twin-mount, Johnnie thought, but it would've been rude to speak aloud. Rocket guns coupled a serious warhead with the low recoil impulse which was all a skimmer could accept, but neither their accuracy nor their rate of fire were in any way comparable to the armament of a hydrofoil gunboat. The ass-slappers made a bad second to hydrofoils for fleet protection—

But they were better than nothing, and nothing was the alternative which economy would force on the Angels.

Sal rotated the skimmer on her axis again.

Johnnie was looking up at the side of the *Holy Trinity*, expecting to see a derrick swing into view to winch them aboard. "What are we—" he started to say.

Sal accelerated the boat into the tight, unlighted confines of the tube meant for launching ass-slappers in the opposite direction.

The skimmer bumped violently to a halt on inclined rollers. Its wake sloshed and gurgled in the tube, spanking the light hull another inch or so inward.

Sal cut the thruster. "Anybody home?" he called. He switched on the four-inch searchlight attached to the gun mount and aimed it upward.

They were in a cave of girders and gray plating. A dozen other skimmers—eleven other skimmers—hung from a curving overhead track, like cartridges in a belt of ammunition.

"Anybody?" Sal repeated, flicking the searchlight around the large cavity in a pattern of shadows. His echoing voice was the only answer.

The skimmer magazine was in a bulge outside the battleship's armor plating. A sliding plate, now open, could be dogged across the launch tube's opening when the vessel was at speed, though neither protection nor the watertight integrity of the main hull were affected if it stayed open.

Forty feet overhead was a large, grated hatch in the

forecastle deck, the opening through which the ass-slappers were meant to be recovered by derrick. There was also a man-sized hatch into the main hull. The latter looked like a vault door and was probably much sturdier.

The little boat was sliding slowly back down the launch rollers. Sal added a bit of throttle and ordered, "Grab that—"

The searchlight indicated an empty yoke on the overhead track. The skimmers already in place were hanging from similar units.

"—and bring it down to the attachment lugs. There oughta be somebody on duty down here, but they've drafted everybody and his brother from the watches to get the *St. Michael* refitted in time."

Sal grinned. "We'll get a better price from Admiral Bergstrom if we bring five dreadnoughts 'n four, right?"

"I think . . . ," said Johnnie. He stood on his seat, then jumped to grab the yoke. Its telescoping midsection deployed under his weight, allowing him to ride it down.

"I think we'll kick the Warcocks 'n' Blanche's ass just fine with four," he went on, because he *did* think that. "But sure, more's better."

Together they locked the skimmer into its yoke; then Johnnie watched as his guide operated the winch controls to hoist the little vessel up with its sisters.

"Now," Sal said, "let's look at the best damned ship in the world!"

There was a large handwheel in the center of the personnel hatch, but a switch—covered with a waterproof cage which Sal opened—undogged and opened the massive portal electrically.

The hatch was tapered, like the breechblock of a heavy gun. It swung into the skimmer dock, so that a shell impact would drive it closed rather than open. The hatch, and the forward armor belt of which it was a part, were twelve inches thick.

"In battle," Sal explained, "all the watertight doors are controlled from the bridge. If the bridge goes out, control passes to the battle center. I guess that's a bitch if you're trying to get from one end of the ship to the other in an emergency—but it beats losing watertight integrity because somebody didn't know the next compartment was flooded."

"Everything's a trade-off," Johnnie said; agreeing, but balancing in his mind an expanding pattern of decisions. Dreadnoughts and skimmers, against fewer dreadnoughts, a carrier, and hydrofoils.

Above that, the Blackhorse on retainer to Wenceslas Dome: using the permanent arrangement to expand in power and prestige faster than rival companies . . . but facing *now* utter defeat and humiliation, because of the jealousy and fear of rivals who were no longer peers.

Above *that*, Commander Cooke and the Senator juggling war in the service of what they said was peace, would *be* peace, if. . . .

All in a pattern that took Johnnie's breath away in a gasp, though he knew that he saw only the base of it and that the superstructure rose beyond the imaginings of even his father and uncle.

"Yeah, well," Sal said as the hatch closed behind them. He grinned because he misunderstood Johnnie's sudden shock. "It's not as though it matters to *me* whether they got the door back here dogged shut."

There were lights on in the passageway behind the armor belt. Sal led the way briskly, commenting that, "There's nothing much at main-deck level, just bunks, chain-lockers and the galleys. I'll take you down t' the battle center 'n' magazines, then give you a look at the bridge."

They had turned into a much wider passage, one which could hold hundreds of men rushing for their action stations in a crisis. On one side was a barracks-style bunk room whose three double doors were open onto the passageway. On the other side of the passage was what Johnnie presumed was an identical facility, but it was closed up.

"We've got just a skeleton watch with the drafts working on *St. Michael*," Sal explained, "and they're trying to keep the power use down so that we'll have max fuel available if the balloon goes up real sudden."

Johnnie tried to match the other ensign's knowing grin. Sal had *been* in action before. All the training in the world couldn't make Johnnie a veteran. . . .

"Anyhow, they're just running the air-conditioning to the one sleeping area—and where there's people on duty, of course, the engine room, the bridge and the battle center."

The accommodations were spartan. Cruises of more than a week or two were exceptional for vessels of the mercenary fleets. There was no need to provide luxury aboard warships when the crews would be back at base (or on leave in a dome) within a few days.

On the other hand, *space* wasn't at a premium on a battleship. Automation permitted 350 men to accomplish tasks that would have required a crew of thousands in the days of the early dreadnoughts on Earth, but the hull still had to have enough volume to balance the enormous thickness of armor covering the ship's vitals.

Here on the *Holy Trinity*, sleeping crewmen had only a simple bed and a locker for a modicum of their personal effects—but the bunks were individual, and they were clamped to the deck at comfortable distances apart. Sleeping quarters in the domes themselves were far more cramped for any but the richest and most powerful.

Sal began clattering down a companionway. "No elevators?" Johnnie asked as his own boots doubled the racket on the slatted metal treads.

"We'll go up by the bridge lift," Sal said. "Most of 'em are shut down, like I said . . ."

He looked back over his shoulder with his wicked smile. "Besides, I can't think anyplace I'd less like t' be than trapped in an elevator cage because the power went off when the ship was getting the daylights pounded outa her."

They'd reached the lower-deck level, but Sal kept going down. He waved at the huge, dim shapes beyond the companionway. "Generator rooms for the forward starboard railguns," he said.

The companionway ended on the platform deck. The air was dank and seemed not to have stirred for ages. Instead of a single long passageway, the corridor was broken by watertight doors every twenty feet. For the moment, they were open, but a single switch on the bridge or battle center could close them all.

"Next stop, A Turret magazine," Sal said cheerfully. "How do you like her so far?"

So far she seems dingy and brutal and no more romantic than a slidewalk installation, Johnnie thought.

"She's really impressive," he said aloud.

The armored wall of the barbette enclosing the magazine was sixteen inches thick. The mechanism opened smoothly, but it seemed an ungodly long time before the drive unit withdrew the hatch far enough that the hinges could swing the plug out of the way.

"How long does it take to open it by hand if the power's off?" Johnnie asked.

"Hey, this is a battleship, not a ass-slapper," Sal laughed. "Things take time, right?"

The powder room was circular, with spokes of sealed, side-facing pentagonal bins in double racks built inward from the walls. The two ensigns had entered one of the wedge-shaped aisles between racks. Above them was a track-mounted handling apparatus, empty at the moment.

The air had a faint, not unpleasant odor. The room could have been a linen store.

"There's a four-man crew in each powder room during action," Sal explained as he unlatched one of the bins. "If everything's going right, they just sit on their hands . . . but with the shock of the main guns firing, stuff jumps around like you wouldn't believe."

Johnnie grinned tightly. "And that's if the other guys' shells aren't landing on you, I suppose?" he said.

Within the bin—filling it to the degree a cylinder could fill a pentagonal case—was a powder charge sheathed in transparent plastic.

"The inner casing's combustible," Sal noted. "But then, if something penetrates to the magazine, you got pretty big problems already."

"It's *huge*," Johnnie said, looking at the garbage can of propellant.

"And that's a half charge," Sal said complacently. "A full charge takes two bins—over twelve hundredweight. And if you think that's something, the shells—"

He pointed at the steel floor, indicating the bilge-level shell room beneath them.

"—weigh thirty-six hundredweight apiece. How'd you like to be where *they* land?"

The center of the powder room was a ten-foot diameter armored shaft. Waist-high hatches, big enough for men but intended for the powder charges, were positioned at the center of each aisle where they could be fed by the automatic handling apparatus—or, in an emergency, by the sweating human crew struggling with charges on a gurney.

A ladder led up from the powder magazine in a tube

beside the hoist shaft. Sal strode to it and began to climb. "Come on," he directed. "This leads to the gun house."

"Isn't this hole dangerous in case the powder explodes?" Johnnie asked.

Sal laughed. "It's the blow-off vent," he explained. "The idea is, maybe it'll channel the blast up instead of blowing the sides out."

Johnnie blinked. "Will it work?" he asked. "The vent?"

"I'm just as glad I'll be a mile or so away if it comes to a test," Sal said. He laughed again, but his words were serious enough.

The vent plating was relatively light—two-inch, thick enough to redirect the powder flash which even the heaviest armor couldn't contain. Sal opened the hatch into the turret's gun house while the vent continued up its own angled path to the deck through the barbette wall.

"This," said Sal, rapping his knuckles on the barbette armor, "is a thirty-two-inch section, just like the turret face. Because it's above the main belt, you see, so it may have to take a direct hit by itself."

"Right . . . ," murmured Johnnie as he stared at the huge machines around him. He wasn't really hearing the words.

A computer program could perfectly duplicate scenes of war as plotted in a dreadnought's battle center. A man who never left the keeps could become as expert in strategy and fleet tactics as the most experienced admirals of the mercenary companies. But that led to an impression of the instruments of war as being items of electronic delicacy—

And they weren't. Or they weren't entirely, at any rate. Here, in a gloom relieved only by the glowstrips that provided emergency lighting, were the triple loading cages—each of which lifted a shell weighing over two tons from the central hoist and carried it up a track into the turret above.

The loading cages rotated with the turret so that the guns could be fed in any position. A rack-and-pinion drive, powered by a massive hydraulic motor, encircled the top of the barbette. This was the apparatus that trained the guns by swinging the whole turret with the precision of a computer-controlled lathe.

Friction wasn't a factor: the turret bearings were superconducting magnets. But the sheer weight of the rotating mass must be over a thousand tons. It was inconceivable until you saw it—

And even *then* it was inconceivable.

"Pretty impressive, right?" Sal noted as he began clambering up the ladder into the turret.

"That's not the word," Johnnie said as he followed.

He wasn't sure quite what the word *was*, though. A dreadnought in action would be a foretaste of Hell.

The door at the back of the turret was open. Johnnie blinked and sneezed at the light flooding in. Powder fouling and burned lubricants gave the air a sickly tinge; all the surfaces were slimed with similar residues.

The breeches of the 18-inch guns were closed. Their size made them look like geological occurrences, not the works of man. Johnnie tried to imagine the guns recoiling on their carriages; the breeches opening in a blast of smoke and the liquid nitrogen injected to cool and quench sparks in the powder chambers; hydraulic rammers sliding fresh thirty-six-hundred-weight shells from the loading cages and into the guns as the twelve-hundredweight powder charges rose on the track behind the shells. . . .

A vision of Hell.

"Really something!" Sal noted cheerfully. "The guns can be fought from here—" he pointed to the four seats, each with a control console of its own "—if something goes wrong with the links from the bridge and battle center."

Or something goes wrong with the bridge and battle center. . . .

Johnnie walked to the door. The armor, even on the back of the turret, was so thick that it gave him the impression of going through a tunnel. "I'm about ready for some sunlight," he said.

It struck Johnnie that he'd never *seen* direct sunlight until the day before . . . but the carefully balanced illumination of the domes had nothing in common with the crude functionality of this huge weapon's artificial lighting. The heat and glare on deck were welcome.

The deck had a non-skid surface, but at the moment it was under a glass-slick coating of blue and green algae. Sal spat over the side and muttered, "They need to hose this off with herbicide, but everybody's so damn busy with the *St. Michael* and loading stores that it'll maybe have t' wait till we're under way."

At the land perimeter of the base, a sort of battle had broken out between the guard force's flame-throwers and what were probably roots, though they moved as swiftly as serpents. Human weaponry created enormous evolutionary pressures on the continental life forms, ensuring that whatever lived or grew in the immediate vicinity of fleet bases was tougher and more vicious than similar forms elsewhere in the planetary hellbroth.

A tall barbette raised B Turret so that its guns could fire dead ahead, over A Turret. Just abaft and starboard of the barbette was one of the ship's four railgun batteries. Johnnie looked with interest as they walked past it.

From the outside, the installation was a fully-rotating dome whose only feature was a pair of armored slots

which could open from +90° to -5°. That spread was
wide enough to permit the railguns to engage anything
from a missile dropping out of orbit to a hydrofoil a
pistolshot out.

The tubes themselves were too fragile to survive on
the deck of a ship under fire, so the weapons were
designed to accelerate their glass pellets up a helical
track. That way, their overall length could be kept
within an armored dome of manageable size.

Given enough time—and not a long time at that—
railguns could blast through anything on the surface
of Venus, whether a dreadnought or a mountain. But,
though they could destroy a target in orbit, they were
unable to engage anything over the horizon from them.
Furthermore, the power requirements of a railgun in
operation meant that only dreadnoughts had the generator capacity to mount such weapons.

They were lethal and efficient within their limitations; but those limitations made railguns primarily
defensive tools, the shield of the battleships slashing
at one another with the sword of their big guns.

There was another enclosed companionway leading
up the exterior of the shelter deck superstructure to
the bridge whose wings flared out beyond the line of
its supports. Sal opened the hatch, then paused.

"Those," he said pointing to the railguns, "would
have to be ungodly lucky to hit us in the ass-slappers."

They can hit a plunging shell, Johnnie thought, *so
they could damn well hit a skimmer if they wanted to
waste the ammunition.*

"And *those,*" Sal went on, indicating a turret holding twin guns of the dreadnought's secondary armament, "the five-point-two-fives, *they* couldn't hit us if
they had angels riding on every shell. Sure you don't
want to transfer to us and ride ass-slappers, Johnnie?
Safest job in the fleet, I tell you!"

"Aw, my uncle's a big-ship man," Johnnie lied with a grin as the two of them began echoing up the slotted treads of the companionway.

The skimmers weren't safe even when nobody was shooting at them. The bow wave of a friendly vessel—or the back of a surfacing fish—could either of them flip one of the little pumpkinseeds in the air like a thumbed coin. If that happened and the ass-slapper's own speed didn't kill the crew, the life teeming in the sea would finish the job in minutes if not seconds.

No, skimmers were romantic—and now that Johnnie had seen a dreadnought close up, he realized that the big ships surely were not. But battles were decided by the smashing authority of the dreadnoughts' main guns. Everything else, necessary though it might be to a successful outcome, was secondary to big-gun salvoes.

Everything but perhaps strategy was secondary to the big guns. Uncle Dan hadn't risen to his present position simply because he knew how to press a firing switch.

Johnnie had thought he was in good shape . . . and he was, for the purposes for which he'd trained. He hadn't been running up and down staircases on the planet's surface, though. His legs were so rubbery that he used his grip on the handrail to boost him up the last few steps to the hatch marked: "Bridge/Access Controlled."

"It's closed," Sal explained as he touched the switch, "because they've got the air-conditioning on inside. Scratch a big-ship man," he added, smiling to take the sting out of the words, "and you find a pussy."

A puff of cool air spilled down the companionway as the immensely thick hatch cycled open. It revived Johnnie like a bucket of cold water. He wasn't sure that the constant change from Venus-ambient to artificially-comfortable wasn't a lot less healthy than acclimating to the natural temperature—

But for now it sure felt good.

There were six men already present on the bridge. One of them was the senior lieutenant acting as Officer of the Day. The armored shutters were raised so that Johnnie could look out at the harbor area through glazed slits; but it seemed to him that the banks of displays, both flat-screen and holographic, gave a better view.

The OOD was talking to a control console. He looked up and frowned as the ensigns entered the bridge. "Roger," he said as his right hand threw switches. "Roger. Out."

"Just showing a visitor the *Holy Trinity*, sir," Sal said cheerfully, before the lieutenant could ask.

"Well, keep out of the way, will you?" the senior officer said sourly. "Base wants us to help with the yard work."

"Turret Eye-Eye live, sir," said a technician at another console.

"Bring it to seventeen degrees until they give us final corrections," the OOD instructed. "They'll pipe them in, they say. And load with incendiaries."

"That's the forward starboard five-point-two-five turret," Sal explained, though Johnnie had already figured out the reference. "There's four secondary turrets on either side amidships."

"Want me to ready Beta Battery, sir?" called a junior lieutenant from the far wing of the bridge.

"No, I do *not* want you to light the main drives, Janos," the OOD snapped. "Besides, for what they want, the secondaries'll do a better job than the railguns would."

There was a horrible squeal of dragging metal, through the fabric of the ship as well as the air. The turret's superconducting gimbals had not come up to full power before the mechanism started to turn.

"That ought to be repaired!" the OOD said.

"It has been, sir," replied the man at the gunnery board. "That mount, it always does that. I think it's the power connections to—"

"Mark!" said the OOD.

A pattern of lines overlay a map display on the active gunnery screen. They shifted suddenly without any action by the tech at the console. The ship vibrated as gears drove Turret II a few seconds of fine adjustment.

Johnnie stepped to the window. The glazed slit was eight inches high, but the thirty-two-inch bridge armor it peered through made the opening seem as narrow as the slots in a jalousie.

The *Holy Trinity* was deep within the bay and closer to the northern side than the main occupied area on the south. That was desirable for the present purpose, since the mile or more the shells had to travel would give them a chance to stabilize, thus limiting the chances of a wild round. The 5.25-inch guns were only secondary armament for a dreadnought, but their shells were big enough to cause real problems if they landed among the base defenses they were firing to support.

The bridge was forward of the secondary battery amidships, but holographic displays inset every two yards beneath the viewslit showed the entire vessel— a quick reference for purposes of damage assessment. Seven of the eight secondary turrets were aligned with their twin guns perpendicular to the ship's axis. The front turret on the right side pointed just off the bow.

"Fire one," said the OOD.

The right-hand of the pair of guns in hologram flashed and recoiled. The *Holy Trinity* rang like a railroad collision, and a ball of orange powder gases hid the viewslit for an instant.

If these are the secondaries, what happens when the big guns fire?

The spark of the shell landing was almost lost in the jungle beyond the gash of bare No-Man's-Land, but it bloomed into a cloud of devouring white smoke. The consoles twittered inaudibly with exchanges between base control and the guard units engaged with the non-human threat.

Johnnie turned to Sal, standing beside him, and asked, "Are the turrets manned, then?"

"All automatic," Sal said with a shake of his head. "You only need people if there's a problem—or if director control goes out."

If the superstructure is a flaming ruin, with sensors and communications disrupted and scores of dead . . . then the turrets could fight on alone.

"Fire for effect," said the OOD.

For a while.

The guns began to belch flame at a rate of a shot every five seconds, WHANG WHANG WHANG WHANG WHANG—

A pause.

WHANG—

"Cease fire!"

The target area was a roiling mass of smoke. A huge root burst out of the soil halfway between the jungle and the human defenses; it writhed and died before flamethrowers were able to bathe it.

"Sir, the left tube has a stoppage," announced the man at the gunnery console.

"I know it's got a bloody stoppage!" snarled the OOD. "I can bloody hear, can't I? Get a crew to clear it."

There were patterns of compression and rarefaction rippling across the algae which slimed the dreadnought's forecastle. The marks were vestiges of the muzzle blasts.

"Ah, shall I wake the off-duty watch?" the technician asked.

Something huge leaped from the jungle where the shells had landed. It was a mass of flames. A track of yellowing leaves followed it for hundreds of yards through the forest.

"No, dammit, go yourself," said the OOD. "I'll have Rassmussen send somebody from the engine room. Two of you ought to be able to handle it."

He turned to another technician. "Graves, bring up Turret Eye-Vee in case they need—"

The OOD broke off as his commo helmet spoke to him. He looked at Johnnie. "You," he said. "Are you Ensign Gordon?"

Johnnie drew himself up stiffly. "Yessir."

"Then you're about to go home," the OOD said. "They're bringing your hydrofoil alongside in a few minutes."

The man beamed. For the first time, Johnnie saw him looking cheerful.

"I think," the Angel lieutenant added, "that we've got a deal!"

13

Venus looked on Helen's face,
  (O Troy Town!)
Knew far off an hour and place,
And fire lit with the heart's desire;
Laughed and said, "Thy gift hath grace!"
  —Dante Gabriel Rossetti

Sal pushed the hatch control. "Come on, Johnnie," he said. "You up to a fast ride down?"

"Elevators at last?" Johnnie asked. "Sure, I'm up to anything."

"Bring 'em around to the starboard quarter, Lieutenant Hammond," the Angel ensign called back to the OOD as the hatch closed behind them. "Anything it is, my friend. You're going by the skimmer winch."

They clanged down the companionway from the conning tower more easily than they'd come up it, and perhaps a little faster; but a part of Johnnie's mind kept imagining his uncle sneering, "*Arthur, your idiot son broke his neck running down stairs. . . .*"

The air was thick with powder fumes. The breeze riffling across the harbor brought with it faint hints of burned vegetation and phosphorous—though that might have been Johnnie's imagination.

Voices cursed from the forward 5.25-inch turret. The men sent to clear the stoppage began to hammer, an uncontrolled sound that struck Johnnie as a doubtful way to deal with high explosive.

Sal opened a coverplate on the starboard foredeck and lifted up a folded, telescoping derrick. The cover was cross-dogged, but even so Johnnie doubted that it would survive the muzzle blasts of the 18-inch guns firing above it. After a battle there would be considerable damage to all the dreadnoughts, whether or not they'd been struck by enemy shells.

Sal spread the extensions that were meant to clamp the lifting points of a skimmer. "Hop in," he said. "Your limousine awaits."

His face turned serious. "Ah—but if you think you might slip, we'll go by the regular landing stage."

M4434 had pulled away from the dock and was curving toward the *Holy Trinity*. Flotsam and the opalescent stains of oil wobbled in the hydrofoil's wake; the motion brought bright flashing teeth to life in the harbor as well.

"I'm fine," said Johnnie, setting one boot on either clamp and gripping the hinge where the arms joined. He was sure he'd be all right; and he'd rather drop into the watery killing ground below than admit to Sal he was afraid. "Lower away!"

With a loud squealing—from the winch brakes rather than the monocrystalline cable—Johnnie dropped smoothly toward the harbor. Sal waved from the control box.

As the dreadnought's gray-green hull slid past, Johnnie looked down—and rotated dizzyingly as the motion changed his center of mass. A skimmer would be held by three arms, not two and the hinge. He braced himself erect again, as though he were preparing to be shot.

"I don't want us staving our sides in with this nonsense!" Captain Haynes shouted from close by. "Be ready to fend off forward!"

Strong hands caught Johnnie by both forearms and pulled him in, over the amidships rail. "Step back, sir," said Walcheron.

Johnnie obeyed. Because the sailors were holding him, he didn't fall back into the cockpit when his heel stubbed the coaming.

"I'm okay," he gasped, realizing as he spoke that he really was.

"Bring us around, Watkins," Haynes ordered the torpedoboat's commander. "Let's get *home*, man!"

The cable hummed its way back onto the take-up reel. Johnnie looked up. Sal was peering down past the pronounced flare that directed waves like a plowshare instead of sweeping them into the superstructure when the dreadnought was at speed.

The young Angel officer waved. Johnnie started to return the gesture, but he had to grab the rail as the M4434 accelerated in a tight turn.

"Good hunting, John!" Sal shouted past the rumble of the auxiliary thruster.

Johnnie started forward toward the gun tub.

"Ensign Gordon," Haynes ordered. "Come into the cockpit with me."

The guard boat, more than a half mile away, had already drawn back the net's inner layer. The hydrofoil headed for the gap at all the speed the hull motor alone could provide. The little vessel bucked and pitched as it crossed the vestiges of its own wake.

Johnnie swung his legs over the low bulkhead, trying not to kick any of the five men already in the small enclosure. "Yes sir?" he said. He wondered if he ought to salute.

Haynes, seated at one of the paired control consoles, looked up at him. "Who told you to go buggering off on your own, Gordon?" he demanded. "It would've served you right if I'd just left you to find your own way back, you know."

The hydrofoil's helmsman and the commanding officer—an ensign—kept their eyes studiously on the business of running the boat, but Haynes' two staff lieutenants stared at Johnnie with sycophantic amusement.

"I—" Johnnie began, but this was a test too—life was a test—and he wasn't going to tell *this* man what directions he'd gotten from Uncle Dan.

"Sir," he resumed, "I thought this was a good opportunity to familiarize myself with the Angels' operation, seeing that we may be acting in concert with them in the coming action."

"Did you think that indeed, Ensign?" the captain said with a sort of heavy playfulness. Even his initial attack had lacked the anger Johnnie would have expected to underlie the words. "That we'd be 'acting in concert' with Admiral Braun?"

"Yessir," Johnnie said.

The helmsman throttled back as the torpedoboat entered the netted lock area. Crewmen had rifles and grenade launchers ready in case there was a repetition of the excitement when they locked through from the open sea.

The guard boat's hull bore a line of fresh patches where stray bullets had raked her. All the visible members of her crew were waving.

"Well, Gordon," Haynes said, "you're right. Perhaps I shouldn't judge you by the maternal side of your family."

Johnnie kept his lips pressed together. Uncle Dan didn't need a junior ensign to defend him, and anyway—*don't be sorry. Be controlled.*

The hydrofoil's commander muttered an order. M4434 speeded up again. The bow slapped, then rose, and the outriggers began to extend in iridescent domes of spray. Johnnie gripped the coaming behind him with both hands.

To his amazement, Captain Haynes squeezed deeper into the console and motioned Johnnie down onto the corner of the seat beside him.

"Admiral Braun is calling a company meeting right now, Gordon," the captain said. "He and Admiral Bergstrom will handshake by radio, probably before we've gotten back to Blackhorse Base. Would you like to know how I arranged it?"

"Ah, yessir." He had to put his mouth close to the pick-up over the ear of Haynes' commo helmet to be sure the captain heard him.

"Not more money," Haynes said, gloating over his triumph and his captive audience. "That's what your uncle would have tried, but I know Admiral Braun. I offered him the chance to merge his fleet with the Blackhorse on favorable—though reasonable—terms."

Johnnie waited for more. "Yes sir?" he prompted when he saw Captain Haynes' face darken at what he was reading as dumb insolence.

"Yes . . . ," Haynes said, purring the word like a zoo-fattened lion. "Quite reasonable. All the Angel officers and men in the rank of lieutenant or below transfer with an additional ninety days in grade for the purpose of bonus distribution. That's fair, isn't it, Ensign? For an additional five battleships plus supporting units?"

"Yes sir," Johnnie said. "That seems a very fair deal." It did. Johnnie didn't see where the catch was, unless

Haynes were simply preening over his success . . . and there seemed to be more in his tone than that.

The hydrofoil had risen to full speed. With a load of torpedoes aboard she would have been a few knots slower, but the additional weight might have damped some of the high-frequency vibration Johnnie noticed now that he was out of the wind's buffeting.

"And as for Admiral Braun himself," Haynes continued, "he receives the rank of captain and moves into the number three slot in the Blackhorse. Director of Planning."

"That's Uncle Dan's position." Part of Johnnie's mind was amazed by the cold lack of emotion with which his tongue had formed the words.

"It *was* Commander Cooke's position," Haynes smirked. "He'll move, I think—obviously Admiral Bergstrom and I need to work out the internal details—Commander Cooke will become Commodore of Screening Forces. . . . A position of expanded responsibility since Blackhorse is being reinforced by the Angels in that category too."

"Sir," said Johnnie's ice-cold tongue. He was speaking loudly to be heard, but he wasn't shouting; he was sure he wasn't shouting. "The Angels are heavy in capital ships, not destroyers. Their adjuncts to our screening forces are insignificant."

And the water beneath is wet and full of hungry things, Johnnie's mind gibed at him, *since we're stating the bloody obvious now.*

"Yes, well, Ensign," said Captain Haynes. "Our first duty is to our employers, Wenceslas Dome, you know. I'm sure your father could explain that to you if you don't understand it already. If some individuals have to pay a price in the accomplishment of that duty, well—soldiers have to be willing to pay the price, don't they?"

"Sir," said Johnnie. "I request permission to join Seaman Walcheron in the forward gun tub."

Haynes made a contemptuous shooing motion with the backs of his fingers. "Go on, then, Gordon," he said. "Maybe your uncle will take you with him to Flotilla Blanche—if he really has an offer from Admiral de Lessups the way he claims. *And* if there's anything left of Flotilla Blanche after we engage them!"

Johnnie sat in the assistant gunner's seat with his head cradled in his hands. The sunset was fiery and brilliant, hurling the torpedoboat's distorted shadow hundreds of yards astern of the racing vessel, but the young ensign had no stomach for visions of the new surface world of which he'd become so recently a part.

Walcheron's commo helmet was hooked into the base-to-ship frequency. He heard the message sent to Captain Haynes when M4434 was only three miles from Blackhorse Base, then repeated the gist of it for Johnnie.

Heidigger and Carolina had just declared war. They had hired Flotilla Blanche and the Warcocks, as expected.

The Angels had signed with Heidigger Dome as well.

Admiral Braun had suckered Captain Haynes. There wasn't a chance now of associating another company before the Blackhorse alone faced her triple opponents.

14

*No counsel is more trustworthy than that which
is given upon ships that are in peril.*
—Leonardo da Vinci

Captain Haynes was off M4434 and jogging toward
the Base Operations Center before the hydrofoil had
been secured to bollards. His pair of lieutenants hesitated, then jumped after him. They were big-ship men.
The jig the torpedoboat did as the vessel rebounded
from a fender made one of the aides sprawl full-length
on the floodlit dock.

Johnnie's reaction to the bad news—the disastrous
news that doomed the Blackhorse, Wenceslas Dome,
and perhaps all of Mankind—was relief. Commander
Cooke had been right all along; Captain Haynes looked
a fool and an incompetent.

Johnnie knew his reaction made sense only on the
emotional level, not intellectually . . .

But he was beginning to realize that most people
acted on a primarily emotional level, himself included.

Johnnie jumped to solid ground. Like Haynes and
his team, he was superfluous to the business of docking
and shutting down the hydrofoil's systems.

Unlike Haynes, he hadn't any idea of what he ought to do next.

"Did you have a good trip, then, John?" called a voice from the pool of shadow at the base of one of the light standards.

Johnnie turned and blinked. "Yessir," he said.

He felt his lips rising in a cruel grin. "A better trip than Captain Haynes did, Uncle Dan. *I* carried out my mission."

Insects brought out by darkness buzzed enthusiastically around the men. The living sound almost buried the hum of the high-frequency generators in the epaulets of Blackhorse uniforms which repelled the bugs.

Johnnie slapped his cheek. *Most* of the bugs.

Dan gestured in the direction of the BOC. The two men fell in step with an ease that had nothing of training to it, in at least Johnnie's case; he and his uncle were just in synch.

"Haynes didn't let you into the negotiations, did he?" Dan asked when the dock and the men busy there were ten yards behind them.

"No sir." *Should he have insisted on being present?* "I didn't insist." *No excuses.* "I viewed the base arrangements and went aboard one of their battleships, the *Holy Trinity*."

Dan looked at him sharply. "*That* one," he said. "What's her status?"

"Combat ready. She's dirty because most of her crew's working on the *St. Michael*, but she's ready to go."

He cleared his throat. "Uncle Dan," he said, "they were going to move you to the screening forces. If the deal had gone through."

"Two birds with one stone, hey?" Dan chuckled. "That's better strategic planning than I'd have given Haynes credit for."

Johnnie's mind revolved possibilities as they marched toward the Operations Center. One of the aides opened the door for Haynes, and the trio disappeared inside.

"If we move very fast," Johnnie said carefully, "I don't think the Angels can have the *St. Michael* ready for action."

Dan pursed his lips and made a scornful *pfft*. "The *St. Michael* isn't going to turn the battle," he said. "For that matter, the *Holy Trinity* isn't going to turn the battle if it's just one more ship in the line. . . ."

The BOC's lighted facade loomed in front of them.

Johnnie rephrased the question in his mind and said, "Shall I wait in the lobby for you?"

His uncle pushed the first set of doors open. The air conditioning and anticipation made Johnnie shudder.

"No," said Dan. "I need you. To give honest answers to any questions you're asked—"

Johnnie opened the inner doors.

"—and to cover my back if we have to shoot our way out."

Johnnie blinked. Uncle Dan was smiling.

Probably the last clause was a joke.

Lieutenant Barton and Haynes' two aides waited in Admiral Bergstrom's outer office. The Admiral's secretary smiled tightly and said, "Commander, the Admiral and Captain Haynes are waiting for you."

"Right," said Dan. "For me and Ensign Gordon."

He reached for the door latch.

"Not—" began one of Haynes' men as he rose from his chair.

Uncle Dan's eyes met the lieutenant's and spiked him. Johnnie's right hand flexed instinctively as he turned also. He no longer assumed Dan had been joking.

The lieutenant sat down heavily.

"Right," Uncle Dan repeated. He pushed open the door.

"Captain Haynes," he said even before his foot had followed his hand into the inner office, "you excluded Senator Gordon's son from the negotiations which you—"

"Cooke, what are you—" the captain blustered.

"—botched. *Botched*," Dan continued in a rising voice as his left hand gestured Johnnie through the door beside him and let it close of its own weight. "For that reason alone it would be necessary for Ensign Gordon to be present now."

"Then I want Lieutenant Platt—"

"Walter," snapped Admiral Bergstrom, "for God's sake, *shut up!*"

The room froze.

"Gordon," the Commander in Chief resumed in a tired voice, "sit down. No trick shooting this time. Daniel, you sit down also."

He looked from one of his senior officers to the other. "We don't need to chew each other up, gentlemen," he said. "There are three very competent fleets out there—" he gestured "—ready and willing to accomplish the task."

Johnnie slid cautiously into the seat nearest the door. It was plainer than the units in his father's office, but the data bank/hologram projector linkage was state-of-the-art.

"Sorry, sir," muttered Captain Haynes. "I'm—"

He grimaced. There was a visicube of his wife on the console of his seat. His hands revolved it. "We're all upset."

"Perhaps," Uncle Dan suggested quietly as he too sat, "Koslowski, Molp, and Randleman should be present?"

Bergstrom shook his head. "We'll need the other

squadron commanders when it's time for detailed planning," he said. "But first we have to decide what to do . . . and that's a matter for the three of us, isn't it, gentlemen?"

He nodded ironically toward Johnnie. "And for Senator Gordon's representative, of course."

"There's no certainty in battle," Haynes said, speaking distinctly but toward the image in his hands. "Sure, we're outnumbered, but that doesn't mean we can't engage and win."

"If we met the others one at a time," said the Commander in Chief, "we could possibly defeat them all in detail. But—"

"If we station ourselves *in* the Kanjar Straits," Haynes said eagerly, "if we do it right away—they can't use their full strength against us. Then—"

"Then they put out a screen of subs and light forces on the ocean side of the Straits and let us rot until our hulls are foul and we have to return to base to refuel," Uncle Dan broke in without raising his voice. "When we attempt to do that, their combined fleets sail from base—clean and fully prepared—run us down while we skirmish with their screen, and send us to the bottom."

"Are you saying we should surrender now?" Haynes demanded. "Are *you* saying that?"

Dan didn't speak. Admiral Bergstrom played with a piece of rusty shell casing on his desk, then looked directly at Haynes. "Frankly, Walter," he said, "I don't see much point in fighting a battle we're certain to lose, either. Lose badly."

"Sir," said Haynes, "honor demands we fulfil our contract to the best of our abilities."

"Honor won't win a battle against overwhelming strength," Uncle Dan said.

He ignored Johnnie completely. The other senior

officers kept flicking their eyes toward the man they thought was the political envoy from Wenceslas Dome.

"Honor won't even bury us," Dan continued calmly. "Though of course that won't matter so long as the fish are on the job. I could not in good conscience recommend we engage if I didn't think we could win."

Captain Haynes opened his mouth—and closed it without speaking.

"Daniel," Admiral Bergstrom said. "This isn't a time for games."

"Sorry," Dan said; sounding for the first time in Johnnie's hearing as though he felt he'd made an error.

Dan's fingertips worked the projector controls of his chair. He cleared his throat and resumed, "My aide, Ensign Gordon, reconnoitered Paradise Base for us during the negotiations. John, will you sketch in the location of the Angel units for us now?"

A holographic representation of Paradise Base, plucked from the BOC's data banks, glowed in the air of the office. Johnnie snapped open the cover of his own controls, slid the magenta cursor along the docks with his joystick, and began tapping a function key. The software was the same as that he'd trained on. . . .

"Twelve destroyers *here*," Johnnie said crisply. His pulse slowed and the nervous flush left his face now that he had a task to perform. "Two cruisers, bow inward, on the west side of this dock—"

He hit a different function key twice, then used his joystick to adjust the attitude of the holographic images. "They appeared to be combat ready, but I have no hard evidence on the subject. Here—"

Tap—

"—was a mothership with five submarines. Six, actually, but one had floats attached for buoyancy and I can't imagine that she's serviceable."

"It's not their bloody subs that we're worried about,"

muttered Captain Haynes as he stared at his wife's picture. "I only wish it was."

"The dreadnought *St. Michael* here in drydock," Johnnie said, ignoring the comment. "Local personnel believed that she'd be combat ready shortly, perhaps as soon as twenty-four hours. The *Holy Trinity*—"

He toyed with the joystick to align the huge ship's image correctly near the harbor's jungle margin to the north.

"And three more dreadnoughts, which I believe to be the *Azrael*—"

Tap—

"—the *Spiritus Sancti*—"

Tap—

"—and the *Elijah*, though with these three I'm going by silhouette matching, not local information."

"That doesn't matter," said Uncle Dan.

"Perhaps you'd like to tell us exactly what *does* matter, Commander Cooke?" Haynes said sharply. "Where the vessels are when they form a battle line against us may be important, but—"

Uncle Dan faced his rival and said, "The *Holy Trinity* matters. I propose taking fifty men on two of our submarines and cutting her out tomorrow night. Stealing the most powerful unit in the three fleets we face."

"There's a way through the minefields and nets?" the Commander in Chief said in amazement. "You've found a path?"

"No sir," Dan said. "We'll go overland *here*—"

He slid the cursor to jungle-clad neck of land to the north of the harbor, beyond the plug of igneous rock which protected the outpost on the tip.

"—carrying boats with us, then board our target at night. She has only a skeleton crew."

"No," said Admiral Bergstrom. "Through the jungle— that's suicide."

"I don't believe so, sir," Dan rejoined. "With proper planning—and I *have* been planning this for some time, as a contingency in the event—"

"As a plan for throwing away fifty men, there are easier ways," Haynes snapped.

"—in the event Admiral Braun behaved as *I* expected him to," Dan went on forcefully. "With proper planning, and the special skills which Ensign Gordon here brings to the endeavor, I believe we have a high likelihood of success."

He looked at Johnnie; looked at the Commander in Chief; and said, straight toward Captain Haynes with their eyes locked, "I will of course expect to lead the cutting-out expedition myself."

Johnnie's face turned toward the display, but his mind fleshed out the holographic blur with memories of the green-black Hell he'd seen from the deck of hydrofoils and the dreadnought herself.

Haynes glared at his rival, then glanced down at the visicube in his lap. "Commander," he said to his wife's image, "I don't question your personal courage. But if you choose to commit suicide, there's no reason to take forty-nine other men with you. We'll need them for the battle."

"The *battle*, as you propose it, would be suicide on a much larger scale, Captain," Dan said coldly.

"You'd scuttle the *Holy Trinity* with explosives, then?" said Admiral Bergstrom. "Interesting, but surely it wouldn't require so large a force . . . would it?"

"We'll need a considerable force to fight our way through the neck of jungle," Dan explained. "I'm not pretending that this will be an easy job—only that it's possible, practical."

He cleared his throat. "And no, we won't be sinking the ship, we'll be stealing her. As I said. It's actually safer to leave the harbor with a dreadnought under us than it would be in any other fashion—"

"You can't sail a dreadnought with fifty men!" Haynes said.

"We can't *fight* a dreadnought with fifty men," Dan replied. "We won't try. We *can* sail her out of the harbor and join the rest of the Blackhorse."

Haynes stared but did not speak.

"One ship isn't going to tip the balance," Admiral Bergstrom said musingly. For the first time during the meeting, his voice had animation. "Though the *Holy Trinity* is a very large ship. . . ."

"That's part of the plan," said Uncle Dan as his fingers sorted files from the data bank and picked one. "The other part involves the probable response by our . . ."

The image of Paradise Base vanished and was replaced by a large-scale map of the entire Ishtar Basin.

" . . . the response by our opponents."

As his uncle began to lay out the details of the plan on which he proposed to venture his life and Mankind's future, Johnnie's mind filled with visions of vegetable dragons and great, fire-wrapped beasts crashing through the jungle toward him.

15

Gather ye rosebuds while ye may,
Old Time is still a flying;
And this same flower that smiles to-day
To-morrow will be dying.

—Robert Herrick

"Welcome to the penthouse, lad," said Uncle Dan as he unlocked the door of his suite and waved Johnnie through.

"Good evening, sir," said Sergeant Britten, "Mister Gordon."

"*Uh!*" said Johnnie.

Commander Cooke's suite was on the top—third—floor of a barracks block. While it was scarcely a penthouse, the furnishings of the living area were striking in the extreme.

"I told Personnel that I'd billet you here for the night," Dan went on. "They can find you permanent quarters after you come back from tomorrow's operation. Assuming that you do, of course."

His familiar grin didn't change the truth of what he'd just said.

The table and chairs of the combined living/dining

area on which the door opened were of good quality but ordinary design. All four of the walls, however, were hidden within changing holographic vistas.

Johnnie glanced back at the door by which he'd entered. It was now a shop entrance in a good district of Wenceslas Dome. Pedestrians hurried past, chatting silently and looking at window displays. He couldn't be sure how long the hologram loop ran, but it didn't repeat during the time his eyes followed it.

The wall in front of which Sergeant Britten stood, smiling imperturbably, was the seascape that had made Johnnie gasp.

Seascape—not a beach scene. It showed the green-gold water ten feet below the surface, probably in a lagoon like that around which Blackhorse Base was constructed. A mass of silvery fish, none of them more than a finger long, flicked into sight like magnesium raining from a star shell.

The school of fish vanished as abruptly as they had appeared, with and perhaps because of the appearance of something with spines, tentacles, and nodes that could be either eyes or the receptors of a vegetable life form. It slid just over the bottom, raising curls of sand. Johnnie thought the newcomer was the ugliest thing he'd ever seen in his life—

Until a section of bottom the size of a bedsheet roused itself and wrapped the spiny creature in a flurry of blood and bubbles.

"I like my surroundings to remind me that there are alternatives," Dan said drily. "It helps prevent me from becoming too rigid . . . or it may be that I'm just a little weird."

As before, the smile didn't affect the truth of the statement.

The wall on Johnnie's right was jungle. At first glance it seemed relatively static. A closer examination showed

that one of the strangler vines crawling up a massive
trunk was in turn being attacked by a swarm of ants.

Worker ants were hacking through the cortex with
their pincers and bringing up globules of sap which
they loaded on their backs. Tendrils curled from the
flanks of the vine, but a cordon of warrior ants, twice
the one-inch length of the workers, was burning back
the vegetable defenses with squirts of acid from their
tails.

A gray-white shadow like a mass of ash swept across
the scene, then vanished upward into the canopy again
with a snap of its ghostly wings. The ants, workers
and warriors alike, were gone. There was a deep semicircular gouge missing from the vine where they had
been.

Swarms of flying insects arrowed to the vast well
of sap now that the ants were no longer present to fend
them off.

Across from the wall of jungle was an image that
Johnnie couldn't place. Mountains in the middle distance thrust up into a sky that was an unfamiliar streaky
mixture of white and blue, like partly-mixed paint.
Closer by were rutted white fields across which
meandered black streaks like the tracks of giant slugs.
The foreground—the portion of the scene that Johnnie
could have touched were it not a hologram—appeared
to be water, but there were chunks of white rock floating in it.

"Recognize it?" Uncle Dan said, waving toward the
image on which the younger man's eyes were focused.
He was smiling, but he almost always smiled; and this
was not an expression of real humor.

"No, I don't," Johnnie said. "Where is it?"

"It's one of the outlet glaciers of Vatnajökull," his
uncle explained. "On Earth. Before."

Johnnie looked hard at the scene. Ice, then; sliding

across the land and carrying streaks of dirt and crushed rock with it to the sea. Hard to imagine such a volume of water cold enough to freeze—and under an open sky, as here. . . .

But that had been Earth.

"I like," Dan repeated softly, "to be reminded that there are alternatives. This particular view reminds me that some alternatives are closed off forever, because of what men like me did or failed to do a very long time ago."

"Ah," said Johnnie. "It's disconcerting, I guess. To me, at least."

He forced a smile. "But maybe that's good."

"Come into the office with me," Dan said, stepping toward the wall of jungle. "I want to go over the table of equipment for the operation—unless you're too tired? I was going to have Britten make up a bunk for you in the office after we'd finished, but you can have my bed if you'd like."

His hand swung back a door which seemed to be part of the trunk of a fallen giant. A pack of mutated slime molds now slithered their way through the foliage, leaving gray, burned patches behind them. The section of office visible through the opening was even more dissonant than the lines along the corners where the holographic images joined.

"I'm fine," Johnnie said. "I—look, I'm doing fine, but I couldn't sleep now anyway, Uncle Dan."

"Nothing wrong with living on your nerves, John," the older man said with a chuckle as he led Johnnie into the office. "Myself, I've been doing it for years. Britten, why don't you get us all something to eat?"

The sergeant's face split in a grin. "Hearty meals for the condemned, you mean, sir?" he said.

"Don't laugh, boyo," Dan called back through the closing door. "You're going too, you know."

"Indeed I am, sir," Britten said in a muffled voice. "You didn't think you could keep me away from an operation this bughouse crazy, did you?"

Britten sounded cheerful; Johnnie was scared.

Not scared of the jungle, exactly, though his view of their likelihood of success in reaching the harbor by the back way was nowhere near as sanguine as the one Uncle Dan had polished in Admiral Bergstrom's office. . . . And not scared about the risks involved in first capturing a dreadnought, then sailing away in it while pursued by at least three other battleships. Johnnie hadn't been able to think that far ahead.

He wasn't afraid the operation would fail: he was afraid it would fail because of *him*.

"Are you sure you're all right, John?" his uncle said.

"I don't want to mess up, Uncle Dan."

"Join the club," the older man replied; and again, there was very little humor in his smile.

The office was smaller than the Senator's—Commander Cooke had no need to impress anyone here. The walls were cream-colored, enlivened neither with real windows nor by holographic views like those of the living room.

The desk was double-sided. A light-pen lay in front of the identical consoles which faced one another; a similar pen was in its holder at the other station. Three visicubes aligned with the long axis of the slate-colored expanse were the only other ornamentation.

"Well, sit down," Dan said as he slid into one of the consoles. "I didn't really figure the Admiral would agree to fifty men—the second submarine doubles that aspect of the risk, after all—but I think thirty will be sufficient for what we need to do."

The senior officer's right hand played over the keypad while his left removed the pen from its holder. Columns of names and figures, the

Blackhorse personnel roster, glowed in the air between them. The holograms shifted as they began to sort themselves according to skills and efficiency ratings.

Johnnie was staring at the visicubes.

"You won't know the men, of course," Dan said, "but—"

He looked at his nephew and paused.

"I'm sorry," Johnnie blurted in embarrassment, raising his eyes.

"Oh, they're worth looking at, lad," his uncle said with an honest laugh.

Each cube held the image of a different woman: a blonde, a redhead, and a brunette with white skin and almond eyes. The blonde was a statuesque beauty; the redhead was heavier than some men's taste, though Titian would have painted her as Venus; and the brunette was bone-thin.

Their expressions were equally alluring, even frozen in the visicubes.

"Go ahead, touch them," Dan said.

"Are they all your . . ."

"Friends?"

"Wives, I meant," Johnnie said.

His index finger tapped the touch-sensitive patch at the bottom of the first cube. The blonde's face suddenly brightened in a smile. Her voice, lilting despite the limits of the reproduction medium, said, "Hello, Dan. I'm really looking forward to seeing you again, so don't do anything foolish. All right?"

The image blew a kiss.

"Companions, yes," his uncle agreed without expression.

Johnnie touched the second cube, as much as anything so that he had something to look at instead of the older man. "Do they . . . know about each other?"

"Dan," said the plump redhead, "You don't want to

hear how much I love you . . . but when you come home, I'll make you as happy as a woman can make a man."

"They'd almost have to, wouldn't they, lad?" Dan said coolly. "I don't volunteer any information, and they don't ask me. But sure, I assume they know, all three of them."

The dark-haired woman lifted an eyebrow, then adjusted the scooped neckline of her violet blouse. She grinned, but the image did not speak.

"Don't they care?" Johnnie said. He looked up. "Don't they *care*?"

"Johnnie," said his uncle, "life isn't simple. I don't put any restrictions on them that I wouldn't keep myself. They find that acceptable, I suppose, or they'd find someone else."

He licked his dry lips. "But that's me, and them. We're individuals. And my sister—your mother—is an individual too, living her own sort of life. With men and women, there aren't certainties for everybody. Not the way your father thought there ought to be; and not the way I live my life, either."

Dan reached out and squeezed the younger man's hand against the desktop.

"Sorry," Johnnie said. He twisted his hand palm-up and returned the grip.

Uncle Dan grinned impishly. "These cubes can be programmed to take a double message, you know?" he said. "And keyed to a particular fingerprint as to which they play."

He touched the third visicube with the little finger of his right hand. The brunette pulled the puff sleeves of her blouse down to display her breasts. They were well-defined though small, and the areolae were almost black.

"Dan, darling, dearest Dan," the image said in a

husky voice, "I wish you were here with me now so that you could kiss my nipples, so that you could *bite* my nipples the way you do, because that's ecstasy for me. . . ."

Johnnie stared at the wall. His face felt hot and he was sure that he was blushing.

"Everybody's different, lad," Dan said with a chuckle as the visicube returned to its innocent static state. "Figure out how you want to live your own life and don't worry about other people. Especially about relatives."

The door opened. Sergeant Britten, carrying a platter with two place settings, a dish of chicken and dumplings, and a visicube, stood silhouetted against the glacial scene on the opposite wall.

"Ready now, sir?" he asked.

"Ready for raw Pomeranian," Dan said, patting his flat stomach. "Set it right down here."

"When I unpacked," Britten said as he doled out the plates and flatware with the skill of a croupier, "I found this, sir. I didn't know where you wanted it placed."

"This" was a visicube containing the image of a plumpish, attractive woman of middle age—Beryl Haynes.

"Umm, yes," said Dan. "I had one of our techs make it up for me back at the dome. It's by way of being a gift for Captain Haynes . . . but I'd rather he didn't know about it. Since you know Greider, his batman . . . can you get it into his quarters to replace the cube he usually keeps in his combat uniform?"

Sergeant Britten grinned. "With what Greider owes me from poker last month? You know I can! I can get you Haynes' desk and Greider'll help me carry it."

Dan began spooning out the savoury dish onto his plate and Johnnie's both. "You're a jewel, Britten," he said. "Try to come back from this operation, will you?"

"No fear," snorted the sergeant as he left the office with the cube and the empty platter. "If *you* buy it, try to get swallowed whole, will you? I don't want to have to carry a—"

The door closed. Vaguely through it: "—bloody corpse back."

16

If the red slayer think he slays,
Or if the slain think he is slain. . . .
                    —Ralph Waldo Emerson

Viewed through the image intensifier in Johnnie's visor, the water at the creek-mouth boiled with life.

And death.

The jungle glimpsed from a fleet's base or in the holographic environs of a simulator seemed to be the army of Nature arrayed against Man. Here the battle was just as intense and Man was not even an incident. The varied factions of Nature were too busy fighting one another to notice the beached submarine.

"For God's sake, hurry with that chute!" said the submarine's commander, Lieutenant van Diemann.

As though the words had flown straight to heaven from his lips, there was a hiss from the bulky apparatus four of the party were deploying from a cylinder welded to the sub's deck. A tube two meters in diameter, stiffened by a glass plate floor, began to extend slowly in the direction of the shore. Sergeant Britten, carrying a flamethrower, rode the tip of the protective chute.

"You may have to edge a little closer," said Commander Cooke. "I'm not sure the hundred feet will be enough."

"I can't!" van Diemann snapped. "We're already aground!"

Dan turned with the easy motion of a marksman and said, "I know you're aground, Lieutenant. I said you might have to edge a little closer to shore through the bottom muck. If you're incapable of carrying out the maneuver, I'm sure it's within the capacity of Ensign Gordon here."

Uncle Dan is scared, and he's taking it out on other people . . . who are scared too.

Something huge had died or been washed up at the creek-mouth; Johnnie couldn't be sure whether the creature had come from the jungle or the sea to begin with. Now the corpse was a Debatable Land for scavengers and things which preyed on scavengers . . . and those who devoured them in turn.

Crabs a foot across the carapace backed together to form iron rings which rotated slowly across the carrion. One large pincer tore the flesh into strips of a size that the mandibles could worry loose, but the other pincer was always raised to threaten any creature that moved nearby.

Occasionally something with a long beak or armored paws would pluck at the defensive circles, but for the most part the crabs were safe—

Unless two groups collided. When that happened, the rings flattened against one another and all thought of food or defense was lost in a ravening urge to slay their closest kin—and therefore closest rivals. Other predators coldly picked their victims from behind or simply waited for crushed and fractioned debris to be flung away by other crabs.

"Sorry, sir," said van Diemann. "But we—I mean,

a stranded sub would be a dead giveaway to an Angel reconnaissance flight, wouldn't it?"

"If you weren't the best submarine commander in the Blackhorse, Ted," Uncle Dan said, "I'd've picked somebody else for the mission. You're good enough to work her loose before daylight and the thermals."

"Shall I . . . ?" The lieutenant offered.

Dan shook his head. "The chute's going to reach. I was nervous, and you say things when you're nervous."

Something slithered from the sea, dripping with soft phosphorescence. Johnnie thought it was a root or a tentacle, but it bore jaws that slashed a chunk from the carcass. The whole creature vanished back the way it had come with a bulge of meat working its way down the throat. Moments later the fish was back for another piece, but this time an insect as large as the lid of a garbage can slid across the water's surface and stabbed.

There was a flurry like the explosion of a depth charge. As much as ten yards of the fish writhed to the surface at one time, but the insect kept its grip with suicidal intensity until both combatants were lost in the roiling water.

Life on Venus was a constant round of struggle and slaughter, meaningless except perhaps in some greater framework hidden from the participants. The humans on the surface of the planet—the mercenary companies—conformed to the same paradigm.

"Ready the lead element," snapped Sergeant Britten as the inflating tube neared the shore at the speed of a staggering walk.

"Lead element report," Johnnie ordered, letting the artificial intelligence in his helmet route the request to the men of his team. A block in the upper right corner of his visor glowed yellow, then went green in nine quick increments as the lead element reported ready.

The lead element. The forlorn hope.

"Lead element ready," Johnnie said crisply.

Long, trailing branches swayed toward the carrion from the canopy as if carried by a breeze, but the air was still. One of the tendrils curled vaguely in the direction of the beached submarine.

"Watch tha—" Johnnie said, butting his rifle to his shoulder.

As he spoke, a spark that the troops' visors blanked to save their vision slapped between the bare tips of two of the hanging branches. A squadron of crabs and hundreds of the lesser creatures crawling around them froze in varied attitudes of death. The tendrils began to twine around the quantity of freshly-electrocuted meat, ignoring the carrion.

Johnnie fired with the flash. His explosive bullet whacked the base of the branch questing toward the men. It dangled from a strip of bark for an instant, then fell into the water where a boil of teeth met it.

Others of the men on the cramped deck jerked around in surprise to look at the young ensign.

"You'd think," said Commander Cooke, removing all question about the propriety of the shot, "that the jungle would let us come to it . . . but I suppose it's a case of the early bird and the worm."

"The worm's got teeth," said Lieutenant van Diemann, who was about twenty-five years old. "Nice shot, kid."

"Send the lead element forward," said Sergeant Britten's voice in the helmet earphones. Johnnie, as head of the lead element, was part of the command net.

"Lead element forward," Uncle Dan—Commander Cooke—ordered.

"Lead element, follow me," said Johnnie as he slipped the magazine with one round fired into the pouch from which he'd just taken a fresh reload. He stepped into the tube; and, as soon as the protective walls were around him, began to jog from eagerness and a desire to release tension.

The chute was a standard design which most of the free companies used for fire-fighting and expanding their bases into the jungle. The walls were woven of fine-spun quartz monofilament, refractory in themselves and interlaid with bands of beryllium which could be electrified if necessary. Mounting one on the deck of a submarine was awkward, but nowhere near as difficult as most of this operation.

The chute would take the expedition to the edge of the jungle in safety. For the rest of the way they were on their own.

For a moment, Johnnie's boots echoed alone on the walkway; then the chute rocked in a multiplying rhythm as the members of his lead element clambered out the submarine's hatch and joined him.

Three of the men carried flamethrowers—Red Section; three of them carried reload tanks for the flamethrowers—Blue Section; and the remaining three men of Green Section had quad-packs of armor-piercing rockets. Many of the men were half again Johnnie's age; all of them had vastly more experience than Johnnie did—

And the raw ensign was leading the force because nobody knew as much about the jungle as the simulator had taught him. The Blackhorse fought nature only as an incident to fighting men.

The block of light in Johnnie's visor was still solid green. He could have asked his helmet for a remote view from any or all the men in the lead element, but they weren't going to get lost—and the jungle ahead needed his full attention.

Johnnie paused at the edge of the chute beside

Sergeant Britten; aiming his weapon—outward, not at a specific target, for there was none. He projected a compass bearing in his visor, then moved back a half step to make room for the section leader who was supposed to be immediately behind him.

"Red One," he said. Johnnie didn't know the names of the members of his section, but their military job descriptions were all that mattered now.

He indicated an arc by moving his left hand beneath the barrel of his rifle/grenade launcher combination. "Sweep twenty degrees with a three-second shot."

Red One braced himself behind the nozzle of his flamethrower, but he didn't fire. "What am I aiming at?" he asked.

"Red One, you're relieved!" Johnnie shouted. "Report to the center element for assignment. Sergeant Britten, take over Red Section."

Britten's flamethrower snarled like a dragon waking. A pencil-thin rod spat from the nozzle in a flat arc. The fuel was magnesium-enriched; its flame was almost as bright as the electrical discharge from the tree a moment before. Foliage curled and crackled as the sergeant walked his lethal torch waist-high across *precisely* twenty degrees in *precisely* three seconds.

Johnnie's helmet visor automatically blanked the high-intensity core of the flame, but the reflections— from water, leaves, and even the smooth bark of some trees—made a dazzling pattern all around him. Something screamed horribly over the roar of the flame; he wasn't sure whether it was an animal or steam escaping from the trunk of a dying tree.

The white flame and its soul-searing noise cut off. Orange sparks puffed and showered; occasionally one of them flew against the breeze in a vain attempt to escape the destruction it carried. A wide section approximately fifty yards into the jungle was either clear or too stunned to pose an immediate threat to the expedition.

"Good work, Britten," Johnnie said. "Lead element, follow me."

He hadn't been sure of exactly what was in the section the flamethrower swept, but he knew that where the jungle met a beach or stream bank, the flux meant that the nearest life forms were particularly savage and determined. Once the team had penetrated the immediate wall, they had a chance with the jungle's ordinary denizens.

"What?" blurted Red One, who hadn't understood— and hadn't understood that orders must be carried out *instantly* if they were any of them to survive. "Wha . . . ?"

"Force Prime to all personnel," said Uncle Dan's voice over the earphones, "Lead Prime, your orders transferring Red One and Force Two are approved. Red One, trade weapons with Force Two so that he's got a full bottle. And *move out!*"

John Gordon, ensign in the Blackhorse for a matter of days, stepped forward as point man in an operation that was at least as dangerous as anything the veterans behind him had ever attempted in their years of service.

It felt good.

17

One had a cat's face,
One whisked a tail,
One tramped at a rat's pace,
One crawled like a snail. . . .

—Christina Rossetti

Light enhancement gave Johnnie a good view of outlines, but he switched his visor to thermal imaging as he stepped out of the chute's protection. Sensors in his helmet mapped the temperature gradients around him down to variations of a half degree. His AI fitted the blotches of heat into patterns which it highlighted on the visor when required.

Vines were at air temperature. The stick insect, poised vertically along a tree bole near the course Johnnie planned, was several degrees warmer. Though "cold-blooded," the insect had warmed itself by muscle contractions so it could strike with maximum speed and suppleness when the line of men passed beside it.

Johnnie switched back to light-enhanced vision and aimed, using the lower set of sights.

"Sir, what're you—" Sergeant Britten said in a low voice.

The grenade launcher beneath the rifle barrel went *bloonk!* The heavy recoil jarred Johnnie's shoulder, even though he let it rock him back instead of trying to fight it.

The grenade detonated with a bright green flash, blowing the insect's head to pulp and throwing the fifty feet of body into furious motion as dangerous as that of a runaway bulldozer. Medium-sized trees crashed as the not-yet-corpse careened through the jungle in a series of jointed motions.

"God almighty!" said Sergeant Britten.

"Right, let's move," Johnnie said as he stepped into the reality of a forty-pound pack that he hadn't worn in the simulator. Some food, some medical stores. . . .

Mostly ammunition. For his rifle, grenade launcher, and the little pistol on his hip. The raiders couldn't shut off the jungle just because they'd emptied their magazines, and Nature's scoring program had very tough sanctions for losers. . . .

Twenty yards away, a patch of ground quivered in the midst of the ash and embers. Leaves lay on it, but the sheen of mud was bright around their edges.

"Watch it," Johnnie whispered, facing his first real test. "That looks like a swamp-chopper burrow. I'll move close and when it rises I'll—"

"Excuse me, sir," said Sergeant Britten blandly. He held the nozzle of his flamethrower in his left hand so that his right was free to unhook a heavy grenade from his belt. "Let's try it my way first."

The veteran lobbed the grenade like a shot put, putting his upper body behind the throw with a grunt. The missile arched down and entered the soft ground with a sullen *plop*. The explosion that followed was a mere burp of sound, more a quiver through Johnnie's boot soles than a blast.

A column of mud and water shot ten feet into the

air, then subsided. Bubbles with a sheen of blood rose and burst for thirty seconds more.

"I thought that might be simpler, sir," Britten said. "No . . . extra credit for neatness here, you see."

"Right," Johnnie said, tight-lipped. "Thanks." He set off past the lair, now harmless.

There was a trail near the end of the burned wedge, worn by God-knew-what and headed in something close to the planned bearing. Johnnie decided to follow it, since the ground was likely firmer than that of most of this low-lying area. They'd still have creeks to cross, and there *wasn't* a safe way to do that.

But then, there wasn't a safe way to fight any war— unless you were a politician.

The lead element proceeded several hundred yards without incident. Johnnie was on point, and his men were spaced at six-foot intervals behind him—tighter than would be safe against human enemies. He moved slowly, looking in all directions and switching his visor repeatedly between modes of vision.

"Don't forget the canopy," he warned on the general net. "Keep looking up. That's where the real bad ones'll be."

Some of the real bad ones.

The hot, saturated air felt like a bucket of molasses as he slogged through it, and the broad straps of his pack were knives. He *couldn't* let discomfort affect his alertness, but he didn't see how he could avoid that happening.

Too little light penetrated the forest canopy for there to be a heavy growth of green plants at ground level, but masses of fungus in a variety of forms made up for the lack.

Johnnie paused. Thermal mapping told him that the figure crouching beside the trail wasn't the lizard it seemed to be. It was a toadstool, a Trojan Horse fungus, which had grown into a distorted shape that would attract rather than repel larger, hungry predators. Therefore—

"Red Section," he ordered, pointing. "Together on my count of three, hit that. One, t—"

A member of blue Section fired off the magazine rifle he carried in addition to a flamethrower reload. The surface of the lizard-form puffed out yellow spores launched by chambers of compressed gas within.

"Flame!" Johnnie shouted, knowing it was too late even through Sergeant Britten had anticipated the order by triggering his flamethrower. Helmet filters clamped over Johnnie's nostrils; he squeezed his lips shut against the urge to suck in air through his mouth when his nostrils were constricted.

The white dazzle of Britten's flame-rod touched the fungus and turned it into a soft gush of light as its methane chambers exploded. A second flamethrower intersected with the sergeant's.

The third member of Red Section didn't fire. He lay on his back, arching in convulsions. Either the man had sucked spores in through his mouth, or he'd gone into anaphylactic shock from mere skin contact.

His tongue was black, and there was no life behind his bulging eyes.

The bare backs of Johnnie's hands prickled.

"Right," said Johnnie. He felt cold, as though he'd just stepped into ice water, but that was merely his sweat. "Force Prime, lead element has one fatal. Force Two, take the fresh flamethrower. Blue Two—" the man who'd fired his rifle "—carry the sergeant's flamethrower besides your own equipment."

"Hey, I can't carry—"

Johnnie slapped the side of the man's helmet with his rifle butt.

"You dickhead!" he screamed. "You just killed him,

don't you see? That toadstool was waiting to be attacked so its spores would have first crack at fresh meat to grow on! And that's just what you gave them! Your buddy!"

The dead man's face was entirely black now, but the color was more than chemical reaction. Tiny fingers of fungus were already reaching up from the skin, speeded by the warmth of the flesh and the violent struggle for place through which life here had evolved.

"Oh," said the rifleman. He took the heavy flame-thrower Sergeant Britten held out to him. "Oh."

Johnnie turned and vomited off the side of the trail.

"Lead element, are you able to proceed?" Uncle Dan demanded from his position back with the rear guard.

Johnnie spat, then wiped his mouth and swallowed. "Roger, lead element proceeding," he said in a voice he didn't recognize as his own.

That was the first time he'd seen a man die.

It wouldn't be the last.

Dawn was a blaze of heat and enough additional light that the enhancement circuitry in the helmet visors was no longer necessary. Colors became real— and therefore more boringly uniform, black/green/gray, than the computer had made them for the sake of contrast.

The expedition was making very slow progress; but they *had* time, since there was nothing they could do when they reached the harbor shore except wait until midnight.

The trail met a creek, black with tannin and decay products. Track and watercourse together twisted off to the southeast, away from the harbor. The shallow banks were less than ten feet apart, an easy jump for the men if they hadn't been carrying their loads of weapons and equipment.

"Force Prime," Johnnie said as he eyed the water. It didn't look very deep, but they were going to have to check that before they entered it. "We've reached a stream. We'll need fencing."

The heavy equipment—the three boats, the mats for soft ground, and the fences to block a safe pathway through running water—were in the relatively-safe center element. Those burdened troops were almost defenseless, but their two unladen guards needed to watch only the flanks.

"Roger, I'll send some forward," Uncle Dan replied calmly . . . as calmly as Lead Prime, Johnnie himself. "What width do you—"

There was a roar and screams, audible through the air as well as over the helmet radios. Rifles ripped out their magazines in single, barrel-melting bursts. A pair of back-pack rockets added their *whack-SLAP!* sounds to the jungle-muffled din.

Johnnie's men spun around, staring vainly through the undergrowth. A few of them started to move toward the sound of the guns.

"Lead element, circle around Lead Prime!" Johnnie ordered sharply. "The sound will bring—"

And it did, sweeping like a flying carpet ten feet high above the water of the creek: head grotesquely small against the forty-foot expanse of flattened ribs on which it glided, but still wide enough to swallow a man whole.

It was genetically a snake, but the skill with which evolution had molded its body into an airfoil permitted it to fly for more than a mile if it found a tall enough tree from which to launch its attack.

Johnnie fired a grenade, but the creature banked and presented its body edge-on as he did so. The projectile sailed harmlessly above it and detonated in a mass of vegetation which hid even the flash.

The snake wasn't heading for the lead element but

rather for the commotion which had caught its attention. Sergeant Britten raised and swung his flamethrower, but the weapon was too heavy to track at the speed of the flying target.

Johnnie sighted on the saffron scales of the snake's underside and slid an embroidery of three-shot bursts along them, working from mid-section to head as the target flashed past. The creature suddenly buckled in the air, braking its flight just long enough for Britten to whack the flat body in half with his rod of ravening flame.

The pieces fell separately, on to either side of the stream. As they did so, Green One punched a rocket through the front half.

"God almighty . . . ," Sergeant Britten muttered again. He took his right hand from the flamethrower's grip and waggled it in the air. The fine hairs were singed off the back of his fingers. The weapon's nozzle glowed orange from the long stream he'd fed through it.

"Keep watching the front and sides," Johnnie ordered in a pale, distant voice. "Somebody else will take care of what's behind us."

He fumbled with the fresh magazine. He'd gripped the rifle so hard that his fingers were almost numb.

The roars from the following elements had died away. It took repeated orders from Force Prime before the shooting there stopped, however.

"Lead Prime," Uncle Dan reported, "the fence is coming forward now. We won't be able to recover all of it, so try not to cross any more creeks, okay?"

Johnnie could hear men panting up the trail toward him. "Ah . . . Force Prime, what's the problem with the fencing?" he asked.

"No problem with the fence," his uncle said bluntly. "We just don't have the men to carry it any more."

Sergeant Britten had fitted his flamethrower nozzle

to a full container of fuel. The container he'd used, completely empty, lay on the ground beside him. Rootlets were beginning to explore it for the possibility of food.

Two men of center element, uninjured but with harrowed looks on their faces, struggled forward with their loads of electronic fencing.

"What happened back there?" a rocketeer demanded.

Johnnie opened his mouth to tell the questioner to do his job and leave center section to its personnel—

But the rocketeer had already taken one end of the bundled fence; and anyway, Johnnie wanted to hear the answer as badly as his men did.

"It was a spider," the other bearer muttered. "I didn't see anything, it just . . . somebody shot, and it knocked me down like, like, I don' know. . . ."

"The rest a you, keep watching," Sergeant Britten ordered gruffly. "We're maybe going to get more company."

There was a post in the center of each roll of fencing. The troops set them in the soft ground of the creek bank, about six feet apart. The bearers—engineering techs—unfastened the small control pods atop the posts.

"It grabbed Bodo and Taylor, both of them," the first tech amplified. "I tried to . . . I tried to hit it with the boat—"

"You were carrying the fence, weren't you?" Blue Three objected.

"Watch the trees!" snapped Britten.

"Bodo here had fence, Taylor 'n' me, we had the boat," the bearer corrected in a voice without emotion. He depressed a button. The post rotated. The free end of the fencing began to extend itself through the water like a sliding door of fine mesh. His partner at the other post did the same.

"They hit it with rockets, but it didn't stop," the second tech said, resuming the story. "Only it turned and grabbed the rocketeer instead."

"Saved my life," said the first bearer. "Saved *my* life."

The three rocketeers of Green Section shied. They darted their eyes across the waste of fungus and trees with new alertness.

The fences were hung from jointed drive rods. They reached the far bank and crept up it a few feet in two roughly-parallel lines. Their metallic fabric was flexible enough to follow the contours of the muddy ground. There was a bright spark from within the stream; a bubble of steam burst to the surface.

"They hit it with a flamethrower," the first tech said. "The hair, it was burning all over it, burning and stinking . . . but it kept sucking on Taylor and he just sagged like a balloon going flat. . . ."

"Let's go," said Johnnie.

"Just a moment, sir," Britten said as he unhooked another grenade, this time an incendiary, from his belt. He armed it, and tossed it into the fenced portion of the stream. "You guys better get back."

"Yeah, we gotta get the boat," one of the techs said. They stumbled off together, oblivious of the grenade fuze sizzling in the creek behind them.

The main charge went off with a roar of colored steam. Globules of fire darted from the haze and vanished. Dark water, drawn from both up- and down-stream, surged through the net and set off further sparks as creatures were electrocuted.

The fence combined a battery of sensors with a sophisticated control system—and a high-voltage power pack in its anchor. Water did not short the current paths—as it would have done without the computer control. When the sensors detected contact with an object which had an electrical field of its own—a

living object, whether plant or animal, large or small—
a surge fried the interloper.

The grenade burned out. Water continued to splutter
and roil for several seconds longer.

"Mighta been safe before, sir," Britten said. "But
again, that mighta been just the wrong stretch of
bottom between the fences. I figure it's clear now,
though."

"Lead element, follow me," Johnnie said as he
stepped into the bubbling water. His trousers were
moisture-sealed, but the fabric felt hot and clammy as
it pressed against him.

He knew more about the jungle and its threats than
the others did; but the veteran sergeant knew the
importance of using all the firepower you had available.
In war—with men or nature—no force was excessive if
you were the one still standing at the end. . . .

The two men in front of the column with powered
brush saws waited while Johnnie compared the relief
map projected on his visor against his hand-carried
inertial locator. Machines—even (especially) the most
sophisticated machines—fail. When something as
important as the expedition's precise position in a lethal
jungle was involved, an ounce of redundancy was more
than justified.

"We're almost there," he said. He'd settled his pack
on the ground while he took the bearings. The release
of weight felt like a long rest. "Well, almost to where
we'll wait for, for . . . to go off tonight. Another three
hundred yards."

Thunder boomed a regular drumbeat in the middle
distance, its direction diffused by the surrounding leaves
and branches.

"Whazzat?" demanded a rocketeer, spinning in an
attempt to face all directions during the time something

could reach him. Green Section had been windy ever since they'd heard what happened in center element.

"That's the Angels shelling some tree," Sergeant Britten replied with cool scorn as he continued to examine the arc of jungle he'd assigned himself to cover. "Normal base maintenance. Don't get your bowels in 'n uproar, huh?"

Johnnie bent and thrust his arms through the packstraps again. He held his rifle upright between his knees. "There's more Trojan Horse fungus ahead to the right," he said. "Give it a wide—"

A thirty-foot-long iguana—its ancestors had been iguanas—poked its head through a mass of reeds. It clamped shut the flaps over its nostrils, then came on at a rush. Green Prime was staring straight at the creature when it began its charge.

Some plant-eating forms had evolved into carnivores on Venus, but the iguanas remained vegetarians. Fronds of brush dangled away from the corners of the creature's mouth, then fell away as it bleated a challenge.

The bulls and rhinoceroses of Earth had been vegetarians also. That meant they attacked out of ill-temper and territoriality rather than from need for food; a distinction without a difference for the corpses they left behind them.

Green Prime knelt and aimed his weapons pod. Johnnie, struggling to free himself from his pack, saw the four rocket nozzles staring back at him. He flung himself to the side, abandoning his rifle.

"Watch it, you damned—" shouted Sergeant Britten.

Green Prime's first rocket ignited. The man who'd been beside Johnnie hadn't moved. The backblast caught him, and his flamethrower reload exploded.

The scream and white-hot glare of fuel threw the rocketeer off. The remainder of his ripple-fired pod raked the foliage to the side of the intended target.

The first missile had struck the bony scutes protecting the iguana's skull. If the range had been slightly longer—if the rocket had reached terminal velocity—it could have drilled straight through a comparable thickness of armor plate. The difference of a second's burn-time (the disadvantage of a rocket compared to a gun) was the difference between life and death for Green Prime.

His missile glanced from the lizard. The impact staggered the beast. That was not enough to keep it from clamping its jaws over the rocketeer's torso, then spewing out the remains in a froth of blood as the creature twisted for another victim.

Sergeant Britten's flamethrower licked across the blunt head at point-blank range. A ruff of red, orange, and blue flame enveloped the iguana as horny skin burned and colored its white destroyer. The creature lashed out in blind pain, flinging Britten in one direction and his flamethrower in another.

Johnnie rolled as though driven by the ball of fire incinerating his pack and the man beside it. The brush-cutting team had dropped their saw and were firing rifles. Explosive bullets glittered across the iguana's flank; even solids would have been useless against a creature of such bulk and armor.

Johnnie's pistol was useless also. He fired anyway, aiming at the back of the creature's knees as it strode forward. The splayed legs of the lizard's ancestors had been modified into a graviportal stance suitable for the giant's elephantine bulk.

The iguana—eyeless, lipless, and terrible—turned. Something clasped Johnnie's nose. He screamed and tried to lash free of the grip while the lizard lumbered toward him.

Nothing was holding him. His filters had just closed for protection. Sergeant Britten, moving feebly, had collapsed the clump of Trojan Horse fungus when he landed. The lethal spores were drifting out in their broad-spreading trajectory.

One of the brush cutters threw down his rifle and ran. The other tried to reload but dropped one, then another, full magazine.

The iguana doubled itself in a sideways arc, then sprang straight again and flopped over on its spiny back. Its right legs kicked violently, but the left pair were frozen.

A rocketeer walked his load up the iguana's rib cage. The third and fourth missiles were close enough to terminal velocity that they exited the far side of the animal, sucking with them a puree of the creature's heart and lungs.

"Cease fire," Johnnie ordered. He forced his numb lips to blow out the words while he breathed only through his filters. "Cease fire, it's dead. Cease fire."

Under normal circumstances the iguana would have been invulnerable to the spores of the Trojan Horse, but Sergeant Britten's flame had burned off the lizard's nostril flaps. Black, questing streaks of fungus were already taking possession of the giant corpse.

"Lead Prime, report!" Uncle Dan's voice demanded in Johnnie's ears. "Any lead-element personnel, report!"

Sergeant Britten had risen to his knees. He crawled some distance away from the crumpled fruiting body before he got fully to his feet.

"Force Prime," Johnnie wheezed, "this is Lead Prime. Hold in place for a few minutes. We're ahead of schedule. Just keep off our backs for a while, okay?"

His filters opened so that he could breathe freely again. He didn't stand up until he'd finished reloading his pistol.

✧   ✧   ✧

The expedition's twenty-two survivors set up a tight perimeter, just within the strand of Paradise Harbor. By extending a fiber-optics periscope through the jungle, Commander Cooke and Ensign Gordon could view their target and the remainder of the Angel installations without risk of being observed themselves.

Shortly after dusk, the boom of gunfire from the *Azrael* and *Holy Trinity* ceased. Either the jungle had gone to sleep when the high-energy actinics no longer drove its motion, or the perimeter guards had drawn back for their own safety until daybreak.

The expedition members were physically and mentally exhausted. Half of them at any one time were detailed to watch, but the off-duty men were permitted to sleep if they could manage it.

Johnnie wondered if any of them really slept. For his own part, he found he was afraid to close his eyes.

18

Then honor, my Jeany, must plead my excuse;
Since honor commands me, how can I refuse?
                                    —Allan Ramsay

"Hold it," said Johnnie, poised in the lead with a power saw in his hands. The clear patch of beach was the obvious point from which to launch the boats—

But there was a reason for the mud to be clear.

The image intensifier in his visor caught the ripple an instant before the anemone broke surface. Johnnie lunged, his finger on the saw's trigger, trusting that no one on the ships could hear the high-pitched whine over the night-sounds of the jungle and the vessels' own mechanical systems.

The cutting-bar sparked on the anemone's sting-clad arms before squelching through the support tube. Bits splashed Johnnie and an arc twenty feet out in the harbor.

The tube, now harmless, sucked back under the water. The head and fragments of severed arms writhed on the mud—still dangerous to a bare hand but unable to crawl high enough to strike above boot level.

"Is it safe now?" demanded a tech, understandably nervous with both hands gripping the boat.

"It's safe," snapped Uncle Dan, "unless you wait long enough for something to move into the area that the worm—"

It was an anemone, not a worm, Johnnie thought—

"—kept clear for you!"

The techs set the first collapsible boat into the harbor strand and hooked up its pump and generator. Sergeant Britten marshalled the squad of men who waded gingerly to the edge of the shore and knelt, knives out and peering through visors to spot any serious threat moving toward them through the water.

Johnnie, holding his saw, stepped onto the end of the line opposite Britten. The water was too good a heat conductor for thermal imaging to be of much use, but color-highlighted ripple patterns would/might be enough warning.

The boat made a slurping sound, then clicked as the segments locked into place. The inner material became a colloid and expanded 300-fold when it contacted water. The colloid provided the core and stiffening for the boat, while microns-thick panels of vitril hardened the surfaces to create a practical vessel.

One of the nervous men on guard gasped and stamped his feet. What he'd thought was an attacker was only the sucking mud. "Wish we were bloody aboard!" he grunted.

"*I* wish we were back in Wenceslas Dome for the victory celebration," said Britten. The sergeant had a concussion grenade in either hand for an emergency. No one else was permitted to use explosives at this stage of the operation. "But we ain't."

"Boat's ready," murmured the tech.

There was a general sloshing movement as most of the men in the water and a few of those watching the jungle behind started to slide the boat deeper into the harbor. The man beside Johnnie tried to clamber over the gunwales. Johnnie grabbed him by the shoulder and held him till the moment of panic had passed.

Men from the rear guard boarded, according to the plan. Uncle Dan was the last aboard.

"Sorry, sir," muttered the sailor.

The first boat moved a few feet out from the shore with a muted burble from its underwater thruster. More techs dropped the second boat into the place of the first and got quickly to work. The last of the little vessels had been abandoned when it became obvious that there wouldn't be enough survivors to require all three.

"We're not exactly headed for a tea party, you know," Johnnie said to the man beside him as they both looked for trouble. Years of human occupation and entrance nets must have thinned out—maybe eliminated—really large forms from the harbor.

"Sir, I *know* ships," the sailor replied. "But I been shit-scared ever since I stepped outa the submarine."

Eliminated. Dream on.

The saw whirred like a nervous cat. Johnnie's finger had tightened more than he'd intended.

"Boat's ready," said a tech as he twisted over the side. He lifted his feet high against the chance of something making a late grab at him.

Half the waiting men lurched into the boat while the others slid the hull toward deeper water. The technique worked well enough, but it was completely spontaneous.

This time the man who'd jumped early waited, shivering with fear or anticipation, until Johnnie clapped him on the back and said, "Go! Go on!"

Light winked on the deck of the *Holy Trinity*. Someone had opened a hatch and spilled some of the interior illumination.

Coming or going? Someone headed in to his bunk, or out onto the rail from which he'd be able to raise the alarm . . . ?

"Sir?" grunted Sergeant Britten. "*Sir.* C'mon!"

Johnnie had been walking outward at the bow of the boat. He was waist-deep in the water. He tried to lift himself over the gunwale. Britten caught him beneath the armpit and pulled hard. "Throw that damned—"

Johnnie dropped the saw, no longer necessary.

"—saw away!" the sergeant growled.

Johnnie flopped into the boat. It was already full beyond its designed capacity.

There was a flurry from the water as something struck the tool and rose with it, thrashing violently. Johnnie looked back over his hips, but the creature and its frustrating prey had sunk again.

"Quiet back there!" snapped the earphones in the voice of Uncle Dan, who must have thought the fish was part of the second boat's boarding process.

The collapsible boats started across the harbor. Johnnie was in the bow of the second. He could barely see the other vessel, twenty feet ahead of him. When Sergeant Britten completed raising the heat/light/radar-absorbent camouflage net, the second boat became equally hard to spot, even to someone expecting it.

The camouflage nets blinded the boats' crews as completely as they did outside observers. The coxswains steered by the images projected in their visors—constructs from the helmets' data banks and inertial navigation equipment.

The boats slid across the water at less than a walking pace. The wake of the leader rocked the following vessel less than the slight harbor chop. The dreadnought that was their target grew slowly in Johnnie's visor, but knowing that he saw an image rather than the actual guns and hull somehow robbed the vision of its reality.

Although: the *Holy Trinity* was real, and the hologram projected into the helmet visor was as much the object as sky glow reflected from the gray armor onto Johnnie's retinas would have been.

The dreadnought lay at an angle to the boats; they were approaching its port side. "Force Prime," Johnnie warned, "the skimmer port on the starboard bow—the right side of the bow—" *How did you say 'port port' without being confusing?* "—is open. I'm not sure the one on this side is."

The first boat slowed. The careful computer simulation in Johnnie's helmet showed the wake travelling on ahead as the boat dropped to a crawl. Johnnie rocked as his coxswain cut power to keep station.

"Lead Prime, this is Force Prime," said Uncle Dan's voice. "Take over the lead. Bring us in, John."

"Coxswain," Johnnie said, "take us around the bow. The port we're looking for's about a hundred fifty feet back."

The thruster wound up, a hum through the hull instead of a sound. Men swung to and fro again, their heavy packs emphasizing the gentle acceleration.

"Coxwain," Johnnie snapped, "we're not in a hurry."

But they were, all of them were; in a hurry to make something happen themselves. All they could do now was wait for a burst of automatic gunfire to gut their boats and a few men, leaving the remainder to splash for a while as they provided food and entertainment for the harbor life.

The simulated bows of the *Holy Trinity* loomed above them. The boat was beneath the bow flare, invisible to anyone on the dreadnought's deck. Sergeant Britten ripped back the netting—not before time, because they were headed for the chain of the bow anchor.

The coxswain saw the obstacle without need for the warning and curses from the men in the bow, but it had been a near thing. The software controlling the simulation needed a little tinkering. . . .

The skimmer port was a black rectangle against slate gray. Water gurgled doubtfully through it. The coxswain throttled back still further.

"Easy . . . ," breathed Sergeant Britten, as much to himself as to the coxswain.

Johnnie stood up in the bow. He wasn't afraid. He didn't have leisure to be afraid.

"Here, sir," Britten murmured.

The grip of a sub-machine gun touched Johnnie's right hand from behind.

He'd been about to attack a superdreadnought with nothing but a .30-caliber pistol.

"Right," said Johnnie. He quickly snapped the weapon's sling into his epaulet, then paused. The collapsible boat was slightly broader than the opening. Johnnie braced his arms onto the armor while his feet thrust back, preventing the little vessel from crunching into the huge one. Then he jumped aboard the *Holy Trinity*.

There was no guard in the skimmer magazine. All twelve of the water-stained pumpkinseeds hung from their davits, swaying gently. Johnnie caught the line Britten threw him and made it fast to the rail so that the boat would hold its station. The remainder of the assault force followed him, splashing awkwardly on the water-covered rollers and cursing. Sergeant Britten was the last man—

As expected.

The boat gurgled as the sergeant stepped out of it; he'd pulled the scuttling strip, opening a six-by-thirty-inch hole in the bottom. They didn't want the boats floating in the harbor and perhaps arousing suspicion, but it was still disquieting to see the transport which had brought them this far slipping beneath the black water.

Britten reached for the line. Johnnie had already cut it with the diamond saw which formed the back edge of his fighting knife. A metal edge wouldn't have worked its way through the monocrystalline cord until dawn broke. . . .

The second boat slid to the mouth of the opening. Commander Cooke tossed Johnnie another line and clanged aboard himself. His men followed him.

"Have you opened the hatch yet?" Uncle Dan demanded.

"Ah, no, I—" Johnnie said.

"Out of the way," his uncle ordered brusquely.

Dan pushed past Johnnie and clambered over the railing to where the first boatload already waited. He pulled a suction cup on a line of thin flex from his helmet and stuck it onto the wall. "Team leaders report," his mushy voice ordered.

"One."

"Two!"

"*Three present!*" There was a bang as the leader of section three slipped on the rollers as he hastened to board.

"Four."

Ordinary helmet communications were only useful at line of sight for this operation, since the massive armor walls of the *Holy Trinity* blocked spread-frequency radio as effectively as they did incoming shells. The leaders of the various sections—bridge, bow, stern, and engine room—reported via radio since they were all in the same room, but in action they would use the same system Uncle Dan had just tested.

The transmitter in the suction cup fed the signal through the fabric of the ship itself. It could be received directly through the helmets, but replies would have to be made with the men's similar units.

A squish and a gurgle marked the scuttling of the second boat. Johnnie cut the line. Sergeant Britten reached over the railing and helped the young ensign up to the front of the assault force.

Johnnie charged his sub-machine gun. There were similar *clacks* throughout the compartment as all the men readied their weapons to fire.

"Remember," said Uncle Dan calmly, "if we don't have to fire a shot, then we've done a perfect job. But if there's trouble, finish it *fast*. We don't have any margin for error."

He touched a button. The hatch whined and slowly cranked its way outward.

19

Up the close and down the stair,
Out and in with Burke and Hare.

—Anonymous

The teams separated immediately. The eight men picked to capture the engine room, and the pair who would cut the stern cable, went directly aft on the platform deck. The remainder, the bridge assault team and the two men for the bow and bow anchor, took the companionway up two levels to the main deck before dividing again.

The dreadnought's off-duty crewmen should be sleeping peacefully in the air-conditioned comfort of their lower-deck quarters, but none of the assault force would be on that level to chance a meeting.

The bridge team, with Dan, Johnnie, and Sergeant Britten attached as supernumeraries, was officially led by Turret Captain Reiss, a senior warrant officer. As a practical matter, when Commander Cooke was present, Commander Cooke was in charge—

And when Ensign Gordon was present, he was jogging forward on point, his eyes wide open to catch movement at their peripheries and the borrowed

sub-machine gun ready to end that movement before
the victim knew what had hit him.

There was no cover in the dreadnought's empty,
drab-painted corridors. Somebody could step out of a
compartment at any time and see the Blackhorse
assault force, armed to the teeth. There was no
reason a member of the *Holy Trinity*'s crew *should* be
here . . . but there was no law of nature forbidding
them, either.

Training had made Johnnie good at this sort of
business. Now he realized that success required that
he—that they—also be lucky, or at least not unlucky.

Of course, the most immediate bad luck if the
raiders were discovered would be that of the Angel
crewman, smashed into a bulkhead by Johnnie's burst
of explosive bullets.

The armored curve of A Turret barbette bulged
into the corridor. Visible beyond it was the barbette
supporting B Turret. Johnnie broke stride, trying to
remember the layout of a dreadnought from schematics
studied at leisure and the brief glimpse he'd had of
the *Holy Trinity*'s armored reality as he followed Sal
Grumio.

"Sir, should we—"

—*enter the barbette and go up to the shelter deck
through the turret?* he would have concluded if Uncle
Dan, a rifleman faceless behind his reflective visor,
had not broken in with, "No, the next compartment
forward should be the lower conning room. We'll take
the access ladder straight from there to the bridge."

"And take it *easy* when we're in the ladderway,"
Sergeant Britten added in a low-voiced snarl. "Remember, even if they're all half asleep, they're going to
wonder if it sounds like there's a soccer crowd stampeding toward the bridge."

The lower conn was well within the main armor belt,

so the compartment's bulkheads were thin, barely splinter-proof. Even so, the hatch cycled slowly and unwillingly, a minor mechanical fault that Maintenance hadn't gotten around to correcting.

Johnnie took a deep breath in the enforced pause. His body shivered with reaction.

"Let's go," Dan said, leading through the hatchway.

Lights went on as soon as the presence of humans tripped a circuit. Johnnie crouched to spray the first movement, but the lower conn was empty save for the Blackhorse raiders. The hatch to the ladderway was open, for ventilation or from the sheer lazy disinterest of the last man through.

"Sorry, sir," Johnnie muttered to his uncle.

"Nothing to be sorry about," Dan said as he entered the armored staircase behind the muzzle of his rifle.

The helical treads of the ladderway were barely wide enough for men to pass in opposite directions, and there was no way that ten booted humans could climb them without sending a mass of vibrant echoes through the narrow confines. Johnnie reminded himself that the constant flexing of the dreadnought's whole tens of thousands of tons was loud enough to conceal the ringing footsteps from the bridge watch, but there was no emotional comfort in what he knew intellectually was true.

Dan paused briefly on the landing outside the conning tower, directly below the bridge. Again the hatch was open and the compartment empty. Vision slits, presently unshuttered, gave a shadowy view forward over B Turret.

"Force Prime," muttered the command channel in Sergeant Britten's voice, "*I* ought to be leading."

"No sir," Johnnie gasped. Because of the weight of his pack and the monotony of the steps, he'd had to make a conscious effort to keep his eyes lifted above the next tread. "*I should.*"

"Both of you, shut—" Commander Cooke snarled.

The *tak-tak-tak* of gunfire, not loud but penetrating because it was the sound they all feared, cut him off.

A fuzzy voice over the intra-ship channel crackled, "*. . . at the accommodation la . . .*" and blurred off as the sound of another burst rattled the night. It was impossible to pinpoint the direction of the echoing sound; from the words, the stern team had run into guards at the accommodation ladder raised along the dreadnought's aft rail.

Johnnie plucked the transmitter cup from his helmet. "*Forget that!*" bellowed Uncle Dan. "Come on!"

The massive bridge hatch was opening. An enlisted man, slinging a sub-machine gun and looking back over his shoulder to hear a shouted order, was halfway through the opening when Dan's rifle blew him back in a sparkle of explosive bullets. Muzzle blasts in the confined space stung Johnnie's bare hands and chin.

Dan jumped through the hatchway, firing. The hatch staggered, then began to close. Johnnie brushed both the hatch and its jamb as he followed his uncle into the bright-lit interior.

A junior lieutenant lay against a bulkhead painted with his blood. He'd been reaching for his pistol, but his outstretched left hand had already thrown the master switch that closed and dogged all the bridge hatches.

Dan fired. His shots blasted a console and the bulkhead beyond the ducking officer of the day.

Johnnie killed three techs still at their consoles, two of them scrabbling for pistols and the third—the dangerous one—shouting into his communicator.

Training held. A pair of explosive bullets hit each man in the head. One of the techs leaped to his feet and sprang across the bridge, caroming between consoles and bulkheads and spraying blood in a fountain. The officer of the day jumped up, screaming in horror at the sight.

This time Dan's bullets stitched him across the chest.

Somebody fired a pistol from the far wing of the bridge. The bullet was a solid which ricocheted off the armored roof, as dangerous to surviving Angels as it was to the attacking force.

"Get the hatch control!" Johnnie shouted to his uncle as he charged the gunman.

The muzzle of the pistol poked cautiously up from behind a console. Johnnie jumped to the top of the unit, surrounded by a flare of holographic movement triggered by his boot soles.

A pair of Angel technicians huddled on the other side. One had his hands folded over his head and his face against the decking; the other held his pistol as though it were a crucifix and Johnnie was Satan himself.

Not Satan but Death. The explosive bullets splashed bits of the man's terrified face in a three-foot circle.

"Get up!" Johnnie shouted to the remaining technician, the only survivor of the bridge watch.

The man moaned. Johnnie jumped down and kicked the fellow. "Get up!" he repeated. He continued prodding the prisoner with his boot until the man obeyed, still hiding his face with his hands.

The air-conditioning made Johnnie shiver. His pack was suddenly an unbearable weight. He'd meant to take it off just before the attack, but there hadn't been time. . . .

He shrugged off the load of equipment and ammunition—a dead man's load replacing the one he'd lost in the jungle—and let it thump to the bloody deck. He turned.

Uncle Dan was bent over an undamaged console. He snapped switches with his hands while he spoke through the intra-ship transmitter flexed to his helmet. Muted queries rasped through the *Holy Trinity*'s own intercom.

The bridge hatch hadn't closed completely because of the corpse slumped in it, but it had only cycled a body's width open by the time Johnnie looked around. Sergeant Britten rushed through with his rifle poised— locked onto the two figures standing at the far wing of the bridge—

"Don't!" Johnnie screamed as he flattened.

Britten's rifle slammed the prisoner into the armored bulkhead and held him there in an explosive dazzle until the magazine was empty. When the Angel technician finally fell, there was almost nothing left of his body from the beltline to collar.

"Don't shoot!" Johnnie called. He lifted the butt of his sub-machine gun a hand's breadth above the console. *"Don't shoot!"*

"Omigodsir!"

Johnnie raised his head. Sergeant Britten had frozen with the empty rifle still at his shoulder. Now he flung it down as though it had bitten him. Its barrel glowed white from the long burst. The rest of the assault team had stopped behind the sergeant.

"Omigodsir!"

"Fayette," ordered Uncle Dan without looking up from what he was doing. "Take over here while I try to raise Team Two. Benns and Forrest, reinforce Team Three. They've captured the engine room, but they're a couple of men short because of things breaking early."

Nobody moved.

Uncle Dan raised his head. "For God's sake!" he shouted. "Did you think this was going to be a picnic? Get *moving*, you men!"

The Blackhorse raiders shuddered back into action. Two men disappeared back down the ladderway to replace casualties from the attack on the engine room. A tech slid into the seat the commander vacated to finish locking a selection of the dreadnought's watertight doors. The console's holographic display showed that the crucial hatches, to the battle center and to the crew's quarters forward, were already sealed beyond the capacity of those within to countermand.

A pair of men, unordered, began shifting the corpses of the bridge watch to a corner where they would be out of the way and not particularly visible.

Uncle Dan looked around somberly. "Believe me," he said, "you're going to see worse before this is over."

20

Johnnie took a deep breath. He was one of several members of the raiding party who were gawking like spectators, and there wasn't time for that now.

"U—ah, sir?" he said. "I'll bring up the weapon systems. I can do that."

Dan gestured brusquely toward a console. He touched the mute on the helmet through which he'd been talking to the survivor of Team Two. That sailor was now waiting to blow the cable of the bow anchor. "Get to it, then, Gordon," he said.

He looked up almost at once. "Ignore the eighteens— and whatever you do, don't switch the railguns live until you're ordered to. The overload will shut down the power boards and then we're screwed for good 'n' all."

Having delivered the necessary information with the same crisp skill he would have spent on a computer keypad, Uncle Dan went back to his business.

Johnnie lowered himself halfway into the seat, then grimaced and shifted to the console next to that one. There was a pool of congealing blood and brains on the first.

The layout of the *Holy Trinity*'s bridge consoles differed from those in the training program Johnnie had used—but as a practical matter, every ship differed from the next, even those laid down as sisters in the same stocks. Bridge consoles did the same job, and an ensign who couldn't figure out the idiosyncrasies of a new layout had no business in the Blackhorse.

The system was already live. An Angel tech had spent the last moments of his life checking the vessel's fresh-water supply. Johnnie switched screens blindly twice, then got hold of himself and found a menu. He cut quickly to the armament-status panel.

"Engine room secured," said a voice over the *Holy Trinity*'s own communications system. "We've unlocked all the boards." The man speaking wasn't Freisner, the warrant officer who'd led Team Three before the shooting started.

"Acknowledged," Dan responded as his fingers whisked across the control panel. "Send two men forward and check the status of the battle center, will you? I want to make sure that they stay sealed up until all this is over."

"Ah, Force Prime . . . ," said the man in the engine room.

"Team Three?" Dan said sharply. "Are you too shorthanded? Shall I—?"

"Negative, negative. We'll take care of it, you just get us the hell outa here."

Johnnie began opening circuits to the *Holy Trinity*'s profusion of weapon systems. Uncle Dan lit the three engines, cold while the dreadnought was at anchor, and brought up the fourth to full drive capacity. Fayette closed watertight doors, both as protection against Angels who might be loose in the ship and because the *Holy Trinity* was likely to need all the buoyancy she could get. Another technician busied himself with the cameras of the ship's damage assessment/internal security system.

There was a distant ringing sound from forward as the crewmen sealed into their sleeping quarters hammered on bulkheads. The internal divisions of the ship weren't comparable to the thirty-two-inch main belt—but even so, the two-inch bulkheads would hold despite anything unarmed personnel could bring against them in the next century.

The huge vessel sighed as she came to life. Multiple levels of vibration quivered through her fabric; but the change, so evident to those aboard her, was lost in the sounds of human pleasure and the jungle, so far as the residents of Paradise Base were concerned.

The top overlay on the armament board was the 18-inch turrets, but Johnnie knew to ignore them even if Uncle Dan hadn't made that a direct order. The minuscule Blackhorse crew was barely able to operate one of the big turrets, quite apart from the more important tasks involved in getting the *Holy Trinity* out of Paradise Base. He touched a key and shifted to the secondary turrets.

There were manual interlocks on the 5.25-inch guns, but the legend for Turrets II and IV—those nearest the bow on the starboard side—said READY on Johnnie's display. Those were the guns which had been firing in support of the base perimeter. Though they should have been locked down again when firing was complete, nobody had bothered to do so.

Johnnie powered up the turrets one by one, so as not to overload the boards with a surge before the main drives were operating at full capacity. That was a once-in-a-million event to occur from just the power requirements of the secondary batteries—but it only had to happen once to scuttle the mission.

As the 5.25s came up in sequence, Johnnie checked the railguns. The four domed batteries, one on each corner of the superstructure, were on yellow, STANDBY, status. That meant that although they were shut down, the permanent self-testing procedure indicated that they would operate normally as soon as the correct switches were thrown.

Which would not be until Commander Cooke personally was sure that generator output was sufficient to the load.

"Fayette," said Uncle Dan, "take the helm. Can we turn without backing?"

"Going to be close, sir," muttered the technician. He split his screen, a holographic chart of the harbor on the right and a display of figures and arcs, the *Holy Trinity's* turning circles under various conditions, on the left. "Gonna be damn close."

Besides the secondaries and railguns, the *Holy Trinity's* decks carried scores of multi-barrelled automatic weapons to suppress skimmers and torpedo craft at short range. The guns could be aimed and fired either from the weapon installations, like L7521's gun tub, or from consoles on the bridge and in the battle center.

"We can make it," Dan muttered, though it sounded as if he were stating a hope rather than a conclusion. "Rudder full starboard, and port screws alone."

Then, almost under his breath, "We've had it if we back and fill. Why in *hell* couldn't they line her up with the harbor mouth before they anchored?"

Johnnie aimed his light-pen at the icon which would switch on all the automatic weapons—then paused. Not yet.

The multiple installations' sleet of explosive bullets could be useful in a few minutes; but with guns of that sort, there was always the possibility that the charging command would fire a round.

Small arms firing within the dreadnought's armored sanctuary hadn't alerted the shore defenses, but a 1-inch slug screaming over the barracks sure as hell would. There would be time enough to ready the light weapons after the alarm was given.

"I dunno," Fayette said. "Sir. Maybe if you back one of the starboard screws, that might do it. Might."

"Ah. Secondary batteries ready, sir," Johnnie said. "Turrets Eye-Eye and Eye-Vee are unlocked and prepared for loading."

"Which are those, Gordon?" Dan demanded. "I don't know the layout of this ship."

"Forward starboard, sir," Johnnie said, swallowing. Being treated as just another member of the team had advantages. It gave him the feeling of being a cog, rather than the person on whom the whole operation would stand or fail.

Dan nodded. "Reiss and Mertoh," he said to the man who, bloody-handed, had finished moving the corpses behind a shattered console. "Go unlock the secondary guns on the port side. When you're done, stay in the forward turret and crew it if needs be."

The sailors trotted off the bridge, obviously pleased to have a job within their competence. As they disappeared, the voice of one of the men drifted back, saying, "But we can't keep 'em firing, just the two of us, can we?"

"Team Two," Uncle Dan said, using the intra-ship communicator from his helmet to reach the man waiting at the bow. "Report."

"Ready. Ready, ready," buzzed the answer in Johnnie's earphones.

Fayette touched a control. A combination of hum and high-pitched whine from the dreadnought's stern made her quiver.

"Team Three, report."

"Engine room ready, sir," replied the unfamiliar voice over the ship's intercom. "All four powerplants are at eighty percent or better."

"Team Four, report."

Johnnie wondered if his own face was as set and strained as those of everyone he could see on the bridge. His light-pen poised, ready to click the automatic weapons live.

"Ready t' go, sir. I see movement on the shore."

Of course there was movement on the shore: this was a busy naval base. But it was lonely enough on the bridge with a group of other men; what must it be like to crouch on the stern of a hostile warship, unsure whether the next sound would be an order from your distant leader—or the challenge of a party of heavily-armed Angels?

"Full starboard rudder, sir," said Fayette before he was asked.

"All right, gentlemen," Dan said. "Then let's do it." He slid a control forward. "Teams Two and Four, fire your charges."

Johnnie looked forward, out the unshuttered viewslit. There was a bright white flash as the ribbon charge which was coiled around the anchor cable went off. The noise was sharp but, for the men on the bridge, almost hidden by vibration from the drive shafts Dan had just engaged.

The *Holy Trinity* gave a double lurch as both the bow and stern lines parted.

The raiders could have hoisted the anchors easily, but that process was both time-consuming and extremely noisy. The quick and dirty method was the only way this operation was going to work.

Johnnie thought of the Angels' bridge watch, bit his tongue; and thought about the crisp holographic display in front of him instead.

"Base to *Holy Trinity*," said the ship-to-shore link in a voice which combined boredom and petulance. "Report your status. Did you have an explosion aboard? Over."

"*Holy Trinity* to Base," Dan answered calmly. "Everything here is nominal. Over."

Lights on the shore were moving noticeably through the viewslit. The two engaged drive shafts were turning at only a handful of rpm, but the torque of the huge screws was enough to swing the dreadnought even at that slow speed.

"Base to *Holy Trinity*," the voice said, no longer quite so bored. "Are you drifting? Over."

"Negative, Paradise Base," Dan said in a voice too sullenly emotionless to trip any warning bells in a listener's mind. "Our position hasn't changed in a month and a half. Suggest you check your database. Over."

Not only did the dreadnought move in relation to the fixed lights of the land, the bow was curving closer to the harbor's southern shore. On the holographic plot, the stern of the docked *St. Michael* stuck out dangerously far. Johnnie remembered the helmsman's doubts about whether they would be able to clear the shore installations.

"*Holy Trinity*," ordered the duty officer on shore, no longer in the least bored, "put the officer of the day on at once. At once!"

"Base," said Dan, "the Oh-Oh-Dee's in the head and—"

A raucous klaxon sounded from the center of Paradise Base. Jungle beasts echoed what they took for a challenge.

"Fuck your mother with a spade," said Dan very distinctly.

Johnnie clicked his light-pen, waiting all this time.

"Starboard screws astern," said Fayette. "She wallows like a pig! *Astern starboard!*"

Uncle Dan slammed back one of the slide switches he'd configured as a throttle. Johnnie moved his pen, poised, and clicked it again. The *Holy Trinity* exploded in glare, smoke, and racket as all her automatic weapons fired at once.

Johnnie didn't bother to aim individual tubs; that wasn't the point. He was trying to create confusion with guns that were too small to do serious damage.

And at the moment, confusion was the most serious damage the Blackhorse raiders *could* do.

Some of the bullets arched into the wilderness, shredding foliage in a minor sideshow to the destruction the jungle regularly wreaked upon itself. A few rounds hit the other dreadnoughts anchored in mid-harbor, scarring paint or even starting minor fires.

A plurality of the streaming tracers, randomly aimed but as heavy as the first rush of a rainstorm, raked the Angel shore installations. Lamp standards went down, windows blew out; concrete walls cracked and cratered under the wild shooting.

Smoke from the multiple machine guns wreathed the *Holy Trinity*, fogging the muzzle blasts and turning the tracers into fingers of lightning which reached from a stormcloud. Minutes of constant operation caused one weapon after another to jam and drop out of the fusillade. The barrels of those still firing glowed an orange which verged on yellow.

Johnnie looked from the forward viewslit toward the plot in front of the helmsman; then back again. The reality of the great drydock growing before their bow was more vivid than the hologram, but they both indicated the same thing: *Holy Trinity* would collide with a mass of concrete and steel through which not even her own size and power could carry her.

There was a long, shuddering tremor as the outer starboard propellor began to bite the water in reverse while the port screws continued to drive forward. The bow swung sideways, like the head of a horse fighting a hand jerking its reins.

They were clear.

There was a puff of powdered concrete as the dreadnought's swelling port side ticked the end of the drydock—tens of thousands of tons slipping past one another on either side, touching in a lovetap that could be repaired with a bucket of paint, if anybody cared.

The *Holy Trinity* headed for the harbor mouth, answering to her rudder alone. Uncle Dan shifted all four drive-shaft controls into their full-forward position, but it would be many minutes before the inertia of the huge screws and the mass of water they churned permitted a response.

Most of the automatic weapons were silent, choked by feeding jams or chambers so hot that rounds had exploded within before the breeches were closed. Johnnie shut down the few remaining guns. A pall of powder smoke drifted like an amoeba above the harbor.

Audible across the bridge in the relative silence, Dan spoke into a handset coupled to the dreadnought's radio, "Six, this is Three. The situation is Able, I say again, Able."

Sergeant Britten hovered behind the commander. He winced as he heard the words and warned, "Sir, sir—we don't have compatible code sets aboard this bitch. You're broadcasting in clear."

Beyond the *Holy Trinity*'s cutwater, the running lights of the *Dragger*, guarding the harbor mouth,

spread from a single blob to individual points. There
was a series of red flashes from the tender's deck, then
a stream of machine-gun tracers. If the bullets struck
the dreadnought at all, their impacts were indistinguishable in the noise of the ship working.

"Six," Dan continued, "we will rendezvous at
Reference Point K, I say—"

"Sir!" Sergeant Britten blurted.

"—again, Reference Point K. Three out."

He laid down the handset and met Britten's eyes.

The sergeant was wringing his hand. "Sir," he
mumbled, "oh, sir, we're screwed. Two years ago we
were operating with the Warcocks and they *know*
Reference Point K is the Kanjar Straits. They'll cut off
to the west, and Flotilla Blanche'll come tearing
through to block the Straits for our main fleet."

The *Holy Trinity*'s vibration lessened somewhat. The
starboard screws had slowly accelerated, so that Fayette
was able to lessen the amount of rudder needed to
keep the vessel on a straight course.

"They'll try, at least," Uncle Dan said calmly.

A bullet from the *Dragger* struck the viewslit and
blotched the armor glass with gray metal.

"Sir, they'll *do* it!" Britten cried. "Even if our ships're
already in the Straits—"

"They're not in the Straits," Dan interrupted crisply.
He swept his cold eyes around the faces of the other
men on the bridge, all of them staring at him. "There's
just a submarine surfaced fifty miles back in the ocean,
broadcasting as if it was Blackhorse Command."

He took a deep breath. "That'll work until morning,
when they can get up a full complement of gliders on
the thermals. The real fleet has entered Ishtar Basin
from the southeast, in the direction the Warcocks are
going to force us to turn. And then—"

The *Holy Trinity* staggered as she cut the heavy

cable supporting the inner net across Paradise Harbor. The guardship vanished beneath the dreadnought's bow. Moments later there was a barely perceptible crunch. The white froth of the bow wave was speckled with debris, fragments of the *Dragger* and her crew as they slid back inexorably toward the churning propellers.

"—we'll have another surprise for them." Dan continued.

For a moment, his mask of clam slipped into something equally quiet but much more bleak. "Assuming that the Angels don't take care of us themselves before then," he said.

The *Holy Trinity*, accelerating with the ponderous grace of an elephant, crashed through the outer cable as well. There was a metallic scream astern as something—net, cable, or a portion of the shattered guardship—fouled one of the dreadnought's screws.

But they were out of the harbor—and out of the series of events they could control. Whatever happened next was a matter for others—and for God.

21

*An' now the hugly bullets come peckin' through
the dust,
An' no one wants to face 'em, but every beggar
must. . . .*

—Rudyard Kipling

The port outer drive shaft was shut down. The length of cable, caught in the free-spinning screw and streaming back in the wake, still twisted the *Holy Trinity* with a rhythmic vibration.

An hour and a half of the jolting, with no real work to take Johnnie's mind off it, was putting him to sleep.

His head jerked up an instant before it touched the console. His skin was flushed and his head buzzed. He looked around quickly to see who might have noticed his lapse, but all the faces he saw were drawn and focused on their own internal fears.

Even Uncle Dan.

". . . glider activity," one of the technicians was reporting earnestly to the commander, "and the masts of destroyers are already on the horizon."

"The battleships must be under way by now,"

Fayette chipped in gloomily. "I can't get this pig above twenty-three knots with a fouled screw. No way. Sir."

"We're here to draw them, aren't we?" Dan said. The words were nonchalant, but there was nothing light in either his tone or his expression. "We're just doing a better job than we'd counted on."

"We ain't going to run as far southeast as planned, neither," somebody muttered.

Dan had connected the main radio to the ship's internal communications system, so that the scattered Blackhorse parties would know as much about the situation as he did himself. As a result, the message from Blackhorse Command, broken oddly by static because of the nature of frequency-hopping transmission, came through the public-address speaker in the center of the bridge.

"Three," said the emotionless voice. "this is Six. There is heavy enemy activity to your north and west. The plan is inoperative. I say again, the plan is inoperative. Six over."

Everyone looked at Dan. He licked his lips and said, "Six, this is Three. What are your orders? Three over."

During the perceptible pause before the response came, Sergeant Britten removed the magazine from his rifle, checked it, and reloaded his weapon. There were beads of sweat on his face.

"Three, this is Six," said the distant voice. "Use your own initiative. I have no orders for you. Six out."

"Six, what do you *mean*?" Uncle Dan shouted into the pick-up wand. "We don't have any initiative! One of the props is fouled. Six, what are your orders? Three over!"

"Three, this is Six," Headquarters repeated. "I say again, we have no orders for you. Save what you can. Six *out*."

Dan put down the wand. "Fayette," he said calmly,

"bring us onto a course of one-twenty-three degrees. Flank speed."

He grinned. His face looked like a skull stained dark by oxides. "Or as close as we can get to flank speed, with three screws and a sea anchor," he added.

The helmsman made a series of quick control changes. The *Holy Trinity* was too big to react suddenly to anything, but Johnnie felt the ship slowly heel as she started to come around in the severe course change.

"Hey, cheer up, guys," Dan said brightly. "That was all an act for the other side. *You* know that."

Johnnie tried to smile. He *did* know that the exchange of messages had been scripted.

The words still felt real when he heard them delivered; and for that matter, the *Holy Trinity*'s situation was just as bad as if the whole thing were exactly as their allied enemies were intended to think.

"The destroyer bearing three-four-zero degrees absolute," said a worried technician, "is pinging us with his laser rangefinder."

"John, that was good work," Uncle Dan said. "With the machine guns."

"Thank you, sir."

"Not a cloud in the sky," Fayette muttered as he stared at the unsympathetic prop-revolution read-outs. "We need a bloody storm, and we get the best weather I've seen in seven years on the surface."

Dan touched a control on his console. "I'll take over gunnery now, Gordon," he said as his display duplicated the holograms before Johnnie.

The commander's finger tapped a key in a short, repetitive motion. At each downstroke, the *Holy Trinity* staggered as her generators accepted the demands of the railguns' warming coils. READY/READY/READY/READY replaced the STANDBY legends on Johnnie's display.

Johnnie was redundant now.

"The destroyers aren't closing, but they're moving up on either quarter," said the tech who was running the surveillance boards. "I think they're trying to get us in a scissors for a torpedo attack."

"Right," said Uncle Dan, throwing another switch. "Britten, take Lajoie from the bow and man the forward starboard five-two turret. If there's a jam—"

"I'll go with him," Johnnie interrupted. "Sir."

Dan looked at his nephew. There was nothing in his eyes but calculation. "Right," he said again. "If you can't clear a problem fast, just shift back to the next turret."

"Yessir!" Sergeant Britten said, starting for the hatch before the commander finished speaking.

Johnnie was only a step behind him.

"Good luck!" Uncle Dan called to their backs; and he certainly meant the words, but Johnnie knew the wish wasn't the most important thing on Commander Cooke's mind just now.

The ladderway amplified vibration from the fouled drive shaft into a high-frequency buzz. Sergeant Britten had both hands free. He hopped three steps at a time, guiding himself by the handrail. Johnnie's sub-machine gun was slung over his right shoulder, where it clanged against the curving bulkhead as he followed.

If they ran into Angel crewmen still loose, Britten might regret abandoning his rifle on the bridge . . . but that was probably the wrong thing to worry about.

The hatch from the ladderway out onto the shelter deck was open. Reiss and Mertoh must have left it that way when they passed through on their way to unlock the port 5.25-inch turrets. Johnnie wasn't sure that was a good idea with the ship going into action—but it speeded him and Britten now, and he didn't take the time to close it himself.

There was a lengthy whine and series of clanks from

above them. Johnnie skidded, unslinging his sub-machine gun as he looked upward to find the cause. There was nothing to see on the superstructure looming against the gray sky.

"Forget it, kid!" Sergeant Britten shouted as he disappeared into Turret II. Interior lights went on, turning the hatchway into a rectangle with rounded corners. The sergeant's voice resumed, blurry and dull with echoes, "They're just shuttering the bridge viewslits."

Johnnie took a final look at the horizon astern. He could see nothing, but he had no doubt that destroyers maneuvered there like hunting dogs preparing to cut out a wildebeest.

Turret II made a keening noise as its magnetic gimbals raised it from the barbette. Johnnie jumped through the hatch just as the turret began to rotate its guns sternward.

The turret was being operated from the bridge. Sergeant Britten bent over a control panel, but that was set to the holographic remotes from the magazine and lift tube.

The personnel hatch in the turret floor was closed and dogged. Johnnie doubted that it would be worth-while trying to clear a malfunction below, but standard operating procedure required that the turret crews keep in touch with all portions of the operation.

There wasn't much standard about this operation.

"Secondaries report," ordered a crackly voice from the speaker in the roof.

The breeches rotated an eighth of a turn to unlock the interrupted-screw locking mechanism, then drew back. The 5.25-inch bores looked incredibly small against the thick tubes of metal encircling them.

"Forward port ready," said Reiss' voice from the speaker.

Cased rounds—not separate shells and powder charges as with the 18-inch main guns—moved up for the lift tube and into the paired loading cages. The cages paused for a moment, then ratcheted forward to ram the shells home ahead of the closing breeches.

Britten threw a switch. A panoramic display quivered to life on the turret face above the guns. It showed the horizon with a speck that swelled into the blurred image of a warship's superstructure as the sergeant turned a control.

"Turret Eye-Eye ready," he reported with satisfaction.

"Stand by," warned the bridge.

"For swattin' destroyers," Britten said to Johnnie, "these—"

He pointed to the 5.25s just as the breeches lowered to elevate the muzzles from their rest position. The guns were poised like hounds, waiting for the gunnery controller to slip their electronic leashes. "These're better'n the big mothers, the eighteens. Now, with only two turrets live, we might have a problem if the Angels had a decent destroyer force, which they—"

The guns slammed, one and the other. The breeches spewed out the empty cases as the rammers fed fresh rounds into the smoking bores and the lift tube raised the next sequence for the loading cages to grip. Ten seconds after the first shots, the next salvo was on the way and the third was loading.

Johnnie's helmet protected his ears, but the floor jumped and the blasts echoing through the open hatch behind them were punishing blows. The air was a hazy gray from smoke. When his nose filters clamped down, Johnnie opened his mouth. Though he only breathed through his nostrils, caustic gases seared the membranes at the back of his throat.

Hammers struck the *Holy Trinity*, in time with the recoiling guns of Turret II but syncopating them. Turret

I on the other side of the superstructure was firing at another of the shadowing destroyers.

There were rhythmic red flashes from the ship on the display. For a moment Johnnie thought he was watching their own shells hit, but it was too soon for impacts on a distant target.

The flashes came in threes—bow, bow, and stern—while Turret II salvoed shells in pairs. He was watching the muzzle flashes of the destroyer's own guns.

Aimed at him.

Sergeant Britten pointed and grinned. "Don't sweat that, kid," he shouted over the deafening pulse of the 5.25s. "Torpedoes can hurt us, but—"

The center of the destroyer's image disappeared behind a waterspout—a near miss, short. By the dreadnought's standards, the 5.25s were small guns, but the explosion of one of their shells lifted *tons* of water.

There was another spout on the far side of the target. The fire director had straddled the destroyer with the first salvo.

The second, third, and fourth pairs of shells landed before the destroyer's captain could even start to maneuver out of the killing zone. The bursting charges were a deeper red than the muzzle flashes with which they mingled, and their sullen light was dirtied further by tendrils of the black smoke from which they erupted.

A shell casing stuck in the breech of the left-hand gun, just as the deck rippled with a *clang!* that knocked Johnnie off balance. He grabbed a stanchion while two more Angel shells rang against the dreadnought's hull.

"Come on, kid!" Sergeant Britten shouted. There was a toolrack welded to the side of the turret. Britten snatched a pry-bar from it and leaped to the jammed gun.

The right-hand tube continued to cycle at ten-second intervals, but the left was frozen in the full-recoil position. The breech stood open, but the empty case was jammed into the threads deep in the cavity.

Johnnie reached for another pry-bar but seized a maul instead when the ship quivered to another shock. He didn't know what he was supposed to do anyway, so one tool was as good as another.

He staggered across to join the sergeant. He was suddenly terrified that he'd stumble into the path of the recoiling gun and be crushed like a bug on a windshield.

The destroyer they had been engaging sheared away. Her superstructure glowed orange, and flames licked above her mast peaks. Pairs of shells still in the lethal circuit continued to strike and smash, fanning the blaze.

Turret I had ceased firing, but the *clang!* of a hostile shell hitting astern echoed through the *Holy Trinity*.

The sergeant thrust the point of his bar into the breech opening and levered fiercely to free the stuck case. His bare arms were black with powder fouling except where drops of sweat jewelled the skin.

The image of the burning destroyer dropped over the horizon. A pillar of spark-shot smoke trailed back along the crippled vessel's course.

A huge orange bubble swelled into the display, then shrank back. The destroyer's bow and stern lifted momentarily as if they were vertical brackets enclosing the space of the explosion.

The right-hand gun ceased firing, though shells already on the way continued to lift columns of spray and debris on the far horizon.

In the silence of the gun turret, Johnnie thought he heard the screams of men burning, men cartwheeling toward the jaws rising from the waves to meet them. But the cries were only in his mind.

22

When he turn'd at bay in the leafy gloom,
In the emerald gloom where the brook ran deep
He heard in the distance the rollers boom,
And he saw in a vision of peaceful sleep,
  In a wonderful vision of sleep. . . .
                                    —John Davidson

"Kid!" Britten shouted as he turned his head. When the sergeant saw that Johnnie was already at his shoulder, holding a maul, anger cleared from his expression.

"Right!" he said. "Hit it! Right here!"

Britten tapped a thick finger on the curved hook of his pry-bar. The point was deep in one of the eight slots across the breech threads, but the strength of the sergeant's arm alone was not enough to break the deformed casing free and extract it.

Johnnie hammered the end of the bar.

"Harder! The sergeant shouted. "Put 'cher back—"

Johnnie slammed his maul into the bar, making the shaft spring back with a belling sound. The tool vibrated out of Britten's grasp, but the shell case slid loose also and rattled onto the turret floor. Foul gases curled from the case mouth. They smeared like grease when they touched solid objects.

"Bloody hell!" the sergeant muttered as he stepped backward and flopped into a pull-down seat beside the hatch. "Bloody hell."

They could feel the gear-driven vibration of one or more of the port 5.25-inch turrets rotating, but all the *Holy Trinity*'s guns were silent. No hostile shells were falling aboard the dreadnought, either, though by this time the remaining Angel battleships should have had time to catch up with their fleeing consort.

"Now our course is right across the Ishtar Basin," the sergeant said as if idly. "That's deep water, twenty thousand feet some of it."

He glanced sidelong at Johnnie, then looked away quickly when he realized the young officer was watching him.

"You can drown in two inches," Johnnie said, answering what he thought was his companion's concern. *Or be eaten by what lives in the wrong two inches.*

"Naw, not that," Britten said scornfully. "I mean it's deep enough water t' hide our subs. They could come up to combat depth when the Angel screen was past and give the dreadnoughts something to think about besides us."

He looked at Johnnie. "If they was there?" he prodded.

"Sergeant . . . ," Johnnie said, trying to match the two images of the man beside him: the burly, competent veteran; and the enlisted man of moderate intelligence, who had to trust his officer superiors to balance the risks that *he* wouldn't understand even if they were laid out before him in meticulous detail.

"Sergeant," Johnnie continued, "we need to draw them on. Not just the Angels. The Warcocks and Flotilla Blanche besides, because if just *those* two have time to choose where and how they'll fight us, we lose. The Blackhorse loses. Ambushing the Angels wouldn't help."

"Except," said Britten, "it'd save *our* butts." The expression on the sergeant's scarred, blackened face did not appear to be anger, but neither had it any sign of compromise offered to superior rank.

"I don't think that's at the top of anybody's priority list, Sergeant," Johnnie said as cooly as he could manage.

Britten shrugged and looked at the open breeches, almost clear of smoke by now. "Naw," he said, "I don't guess it oughta be, even. But it gripes my soul to think how Cap'n Haynes'll laugh if Cookie bites the big one on this."

The squawk box in the turret roof suddenly cleared its electronic throat, then piped in an unfamiliar voice saying, "*Holy Trinity*, this is Angel Command. Come in, *Holy Trinity*, over."

"Why are *they* calling us?" Johnnie muttered.

He didn't realize he'd spoken aloud until he glanced to his side. Sergeant Britten's eyes had widened at proof that the officers didn't know what was going on, either.

"Blackhorse Dreadnought *Holy Trinity* to Angel Command," rasped Uncle Dan's reply. "I hope you're calling to offer your surrender, Admiral Braun, because we don't have anything else to discuss. Over."

"Hoo, Cookie's in great form t'night!" Britten crowed. He sounded as though he had forgotten that "Cookie's" nephew sat beside him, and that the most likely result of Commander Cooke's baiting would be a sheaf of large-caliber shells.

Of course, the shells would come soon enough anyway.

"*Holy Trinity*," said Admiral Braun. The words were

slurred as if Braun had a speech impediment, but that might be because the Angel leader was choking with anger. "You've made your point. Now it's time to talk. You're cut off from, from your fleet by overwhelming forces. We know they've abandoned you—"

"We haven't been abandoned, Braun!" Dan said, ignoring transmission lag in the knowledge that his words would step on those of the enemy commander.

"Listen to me!" Admiral Braun snarled. "The Blackhorse fleet is blocked at the Kanjar Straits! They've *told* you you're on your own, you fool! The only thing you can do now is die in vain if you refuse to listen to reason."

Braun didn't sign a transmission break, but he paused as if to give his opponent a chance to respond.

"S' long as they talk," murmured Sergeant Britten, "they're not shootin' our asses off. Which suits me."

He frowned. "Course," he added, "they maybe ain't in range yet. Quite."

"*Holy Trinity*," the Angel admiral resumed in attempted calm, "come about now. We'll take your vessel out of service for the duration of the war. All—"

"Bingo," said Johnnie. "They're talking because they don't want to—"

"—of your party will be returned to Blackhorse—"

"—lose the *Holy Trinity*. They're willing to do just about—" said Johnnie.

"—Base immediately, free to fight. We're not—"

"—anything to keep from pulling the plug—" said Johnnie.

"—asking for your paroles. And you—"

"—on their own best ship!" said Johnnie.

"—must have injured personnel. We'll provide full medical treatment for them. Angel Command over."

Silence from Uncle Dan.

"This is better than a fair offer, Blackhorse," Admiral

Braun concluded in desperation. "This is a complete victory for your party! Over."

"Gun crews," muttered a different voice, one of the technicians on the dreadnought's bridge. "Stand by."

"No rest for the wicked," Britten grumbled, but there was a cruel smile on his face as he stood. He was holding the pry-bar. Johnnie noticed with surprise that his own hands still gripped the hammer.

"Braun," said Dan with the harsh anger Johnnie had heard his uncle use on Senator Gordon, "this is Commander Dan Cooke. This is my offer. You surrender all your forces immediately. That means when the war is over, you'll get them back as is, including the *Holy Trinity*. You'll still be in business . . . which you won't, if you push things to conclusions. What d'ye say, Braun? Blackhorse Three over."

The turret's panoramic display showed the masts of a ship on the horizon again. Hydraulic rammers whined, sliding the waiting 5.25-inch rounds into the tubes and withdrawing as the breeches screwed closed. The sudden activity made both men jump, but the guns did not yet fire.

"Commander Cooke," Braun said in a voice that stuck to his throat. "Dan. Dan, you know we can't do that. We've got a contract with Heidigger Dome that—"

"Listen to *me*, Braun," Dan broke in. His words buzzed like a rattlesnake's tail. "It isn't some sucker like Haynes you're dealing with this time. You know me, and you know I'll do what I say. You can take my offer, or you can rest assured I'll ram it up your ass. *Capisce?* Blackhorse Three over."

Turret II turned slightly. The motion was barely noticeable against the thumping background of the dreadnought's fouled drive. The guns elevated a few degrees, then stabilized.

"Have it your way, you bastard!" snarled Admiral Braun.

The interior of the turret brightened, lighted by the panoramic display. The image of the horizon had gone orange-red with the muzzle flashes of the pursuing dreadnoughts.

"For what we are about to receive," Sergeant Britten murmured blasphemously, "the Lord—"

The paired 5.25s fired in close sequence, aiming not at the invisible battleships but at one of the destroyers which plotted the fall of the batleships' heavy shells. Johnnie flinched instinctively, but the concussion of the secondary armament was almost lost in the hideous sound of the railguns, firing to raise a defensive envelope above the *Holy Trinity*.

As the big shells lifted toward their target, the four domed railgun batteries sought them with bursts of hyper-velocity slugs which turned metal gaseous on impact. Not even the armor-piercing noses of rounds from a dreadnought's main guns were proof against hosing streams of projectiles which had been accelerated to astronomical velocities.

Shells with bursting charges detonated, blowing themselves apart harmlessly. One of the pursuing battleships was firing solid 16-inch shot. Even those dense projectiles melted under the impacts. They tumbled off trajectory, streaming glowing clouds behind them.

The buzz of the railguns' coils energizing was marrow deep, more penetrating than a mere noise could ever be. When the guns discharged in rapid succession, the ballistic crack of a slug accelerated to thirty thousand feet per second in a few yards shattered the air like nearby lightning.

The *Holy Trinity* mounted four railgun installations. The pursuing dreadnoughts carried a total of thirty-three

16-inch guns, each of which was capable of a higher rate of fire than the *Holy Trinity's* big 18-inch tubes. The mathematics were as simple and inexorable as statistics on aging and death.

Johnnie could *see* shells approaching in the panoramic display: three smears of red, glowing from their passage through the air. They hung almost motionless, swelling, because they were dropping directly toward the pick-up feeding the display.

"—make us thankful," Sergeant Britten concluded as the shrieking railguns detonated one of the shells so close that the flash reflected through the hatch of Turret II.

A waterspout, colored fluorescent yellow by marker dye, rose over the *Holy Trinity* and sucked the huge dreadnought sideways. The other shell hit with a rending crash. The sound went on and on while Johnnie screamed.

The turret lights dimmed, and for a terrifying instant the railguns stopped firing. In the relative silence between shots from the 5.25s, Johnnie heard a distant, overwhelming rumble. It was not thunder, any more than the red glow on the horizon was lightning. He was hearing the sound of guns which reached for his life from twenty miles away.

The railguns took up their defensive snarl again, but the timbre had changed. The port-side stern installation, Gamma Battery, was no longer part of the mix of ravening noise.

"Watch it!" Britten mouthed as he leaped for the lift tube. The round that had just presented itself to a loading cage was skewed in its cradle. The *Holy Trinity* had flexed when the big shell hit, and the motion had jounced the rounds in the loading sequence.

Britten tried to force down the nose of the shell. The left tube's loading cage pivoted and grabbed the round, still at an angle; the sergeant jerked his hands away just in time to save them.

Johnnie ducked under the swing of the right loading cage, reaching for its next shell, and seized the rim of the skewed round's casing. He lifted desperately.

The shell dropped into alignment just as the rammer shoved it into the 5.25's breech.

Three 16-inch shells hit the *Holy Trinity*, two and then one. The turret floor bucked and threw Johnnie into a backward somersault. His head rang on steel. The shock dazed him despite his helmet.

The left-hand loading cage offered itself empty to the gun tube. The rammer and breech mechanism cycled as though the intended load had been thrown out of the cage by the dreadnought's pitching. A fully-loaded 5.25-inch round was bouncing around the turret with Johnnie, the sergeant, and all the tools thrown from the rack.

The shell wasn't likely to explode. The primer was electrical, not impact, and the shell's own base fuze was activated by the violent spin it got in the rifling of the gun barrel.

But it weighed almost a hundred pounds. When it caromed into Johnnie's hips as he started to rise, it knocked him back down with a sharp pain he prayed didn't mean a broken pelvis.

Only one railgun installation was firing. The high-voltage, high-frequency pulses turned the driving cones of its slugs into glowing plasma that hung along the *Holy Trinity*'s course like the track of a snail. The sea beneath boiled with the dreadnought's wake and gurgling fluorescent calderas blown by shells the railguns had not stopped.

Shells roared overhead, deafening even compared with everything else going on. Fayette had made a minuscule adjustment to the *Holy Trinity*'s course, and the three-ship salvo missed—short and over, ahead and astern.

Waterspouts drenched the *Holy Trinity*, sloshing Johnnie through the turret hatch. Only the yellow emergency lighting was on. No railguns were firing.

The right-hand loading cage picked up the next round. It was aligned correctly, but the tortured lift tube had presented it back to front.

Johnnie lurched to his feet. His hip supported him.

"*Run!*" Sergeant Britten screamed, pushing the younger man aside.

Three shells hit the *Holy Trinity* simultaneously. The ship writhed, throwing Britten into the empty toolrack and tumbling Johnnie out the open hatch.

Johnnie braced himself against an exterior bulkhead. Small fish, flung onto the deck by near misses, snapped and writhed beside him in the algal slime.

The sky above was a map of Hell.

For an instant, Sergeant Britten was silhouetted against the turret lighting. He groped for the hatch opening. He'd lost his helmet, and his face was a mask of blood from a cut scalp.

Johnnie started to rise to help him just as the rammer thrust a 5.25-inch round backward into the breech. The casing crumpled, heating and compressing the powder charge. It ignited in something between a fire and an explosion while the breech mechanism was still open.

The first blast set off the remaining rounds in the loading sequence. Orange flame enveloped Sergeant Britten, incinerating the back half of his powerful body and driving the remainder against Johnnie as a mist of blood and tissue.

Johnnie lay against the bulkhead. His eyes were open. He was, so far as he could tell, unharmed.

Above him, the sky roared and blazed. The fish on

deck were making furious efforts to swallow one another down, even as air dried their gills and inexorably slew them all.

After an uncertain length of time, Johnnie got up and headed for the ladderway to the bridge.

23

None of the *Holy Trinity*'s guns were firing. B Turret had taken a direct hit which wrecked the roof-mounted fire director and must have penetrated the gun house, because one of the 18-inch tubes pointed skyward at a crazy angle.

Because the guns were not being worked, the turret and barbette were nothing but armored boxes, as safe a target for incoming shells as any on the dreadnought. If the turret *had* been in operation, one or more of the twelve-hundredweight powder charges in the loading cycle would have burned, sending flames a thousand feet high through the punctured roof.

If the charges had flashed back into the magazine through the loading tube, the whole forward portion of the *Holy Trinity* would have vanished in a cataclysmic explosion.

Johnnie wondered what it felt like to be dead. Did Sergeant Britten care?

He tried to wipe his face, but his hands weren't clean either.

There was a fire on the shelter deck, just aft of the second funnel. Sparks rose in swirling clouds, sometimes lifting sections of lifeboats and wardroom furnishings with them.

There must have been explosions among the flames, but their sound was lost in the greater chaos around them.

Johnnie reached the ladderway to the bridge. The hatch was missing. While it stood open, the shock of an explosion had caught it and wrenched it from its hinges.

Three shells hit the *Holy Trinity*, throwing Johnnie to the deck again. One landed among the flames amidships. A huge fireball lifted into the air, separating from the ship to hang above them like the sun on the day of judgment.

As suddenly as it had formed, the globe of fire sucked inward and vanished. The *Holy Trinity* was alone again with the Hell-lit night.

The dreadnought twisted under hammering shells as the iguana had done when Sergeant Britten's flamethrower bathed it. A shell had pierced the starboard main-belt armor, close beneath where Johnnie pulled himself to his feet. He could not have seen the hole, even if he leaned over the rail, but the fire at its heart threw a bright orange fan across the waves.

The light swept over a mass of writhing tentacles. Squid were battling for the bodies of fish killed by concussion.

Johnnie reached the ladderway again. He clung to the railing, gasping breaths of fiery air in through his mouth because the filters restricted his nostrils.

More shells hit. Johnnie bounced like the clapper in a bell, but he retained his grip on the rail.

If the shell that pierced the main belt had landed ten feet forward and ten feet higher, it would have struck B Turret Magazine instead. Perhaps the barbette would have withstood the impact, but its armor was no thicker than that of the belt which failed.

It would have been quick. Oblivion would be better than this, and even Hell could be no worse.

"You on the bridge ladder!" growled a demon's buzzing voice. "Identify yourself!"

Johnnie shook his head. It seemed a lifetime since he last heard human speech. Words didn't belong in a universe of shock waves that flung men to and fro like the disks of a castanet. The helmet protected his ears, but it couldn't save his soul from the pummeling.

"Awright, sucker—" buzzed the voice.

He was being challenged over the intra-ship communicator. A Blackhorse seaman waited on a dark landing above him, preparing to fire at the figure silhouetted against the firelit hatch.

"—you had your—"

"No!" Johnnie shouted, flinging himself to the side. The shadows might conceal him, though they wouldn't stop a sheaf of ricocheting bullets. "I'm Johnnie Gordon! Ensign Gordon!"

He didn't have time to unclip his ship-structure transmitter, but for this purpose ordinary helmet radio was better anyway. Johnnie and the guard were within a few feet of one another, and the armored ladderway surrounding them acted as a wave guide.

He'd lost his sub-machine gun somewhere. Left it in Turret II, he supposed, though he couldn't remember unslinging the weapon with all that had gone on since he left the bridge.

Johnnie's pistol was in his hand, pointed toward the swatch of darkness which most probably concealed the guard. He'd drawn the gun in an instinctive response to his training, but he didn't think he would shoot even if a blast of shots lit the ladderway's interior.

The Angels' 16-inch shells were killing them fast enough. The Blackhorse team didn't need to join in the job of its own destruction.

"Ensign?" buzzed the guard. "Sir? Geez, you shoulda said something!"

Johnnie got up and holstered his pistol. The stair treads would have been some protection, at least if the guard was firing explosive bullets.

Enough glow leaked into the armored shaft for the light-amplifying visor to work at short distance. The guard—Johnnie recognized him, though he didn't know the sailor's name—squatted in the conning tower. He'd smashed the light fixtures to keep them from going on automatically at a human's presence. He was waiting with his rifle aimed through the part-open hatch.

"What the hell's going on?" Johnnie demanded of the man who'd been about to kill him. "What're you—"

The *Holy Trinity* staggered as another shell hit her and the remainder of a large salvo landed close aboard. Metal screamed.

The ship's whipping motion was magnified because Johnnie was a deck higher than he had been before. He wondered how long the dreadnought could endure the unanswerable pounding her enemies were inflicting.

"It's the Angels, sir," the guard explained sheepishly. When the man stood up to greet Johnnie, he disengaged his flexed transmitter, so his words were relatively clear over ordinary intercom. "Bulkheads sprung when the shells hit forward, so the off-duty crew's loose now."

He frowned as his mind sought accuracy. "What survived the shells're loose. Cookie, he figures they may try to take over the bridge."

Even though the two men were face to face, neither could have heard the other's unaided voice over the bedlam of a battleship dying.

"Right," said Johnnie. If the Angels recaptured the bridge, they would radio their fellows and stop the rain of shells. Somebody aboard the *Holy Trinity* might survive then.

"Well, carry on," Johnnie muttered as he started climbing the last flight of steps to the bridge. He had to pause midway as the treads rang and jounced beneath him in response to a fresh salvo.

Johnnie stepped through the bridge hatch and staggered because the deck was momentarily stable. Dan, Fayette, and another technician were the only living humans present. They did not notice his arrival.

Several of the consoles showed holographic displays of the *Holy Trinity*'s interior. Fires filled compartments, lending their hellish radiance to the as-yet undamaged bridge.

"Uncle Dan!" Johnnie blurted. "Sergeant Britten's dead!"

The three men at the consoles reacted. Fayette ducked, the other technician snatched clumsily for his shouldered pistol—

And Commander Cooke had the rifle from across his lap pointed at Johnnie's chest before his eyes told his brain not to take up the last pressure on the trigger.

Dan lowered the rifle. Johnnie let out his breath.

Sergeant Britten was dead. The entire Angels' bridge watch was dead. Many of the Blackhorse raiders whose packs and equipment littered the deck between the consoles were dead, trying to accomplish whatever final tasks Commander Cooke had set them.

Very shortly, everyone aboard the *Holy Trinity* would be dead. A few minutes one way or the other wouldn't really have mattered to Johnnie.

"Right," said Uncle Dan. He shifted his grip to the balance point of the rifle and tossed the weapon to his nephew. "Watch the hatch here, Gordon. We've got Caleif below in the conn room, but we don't need another surprise like you just gave us."

He turned back to his console. It was set to a damage-control schematic with symbols rather than grim analogue realities to show the hammering the battleship had received. Fayette resumed speaking to someone in the engine room. The other technician continued a program of controlled portside flooding to balance the amount of sea they'd taken in through shell holes at the starboard waterline.

The *Holy Trinity* bucked and shuddered at the heart of a fluorescent maelstrom. Salvoes from all three of the pursuing dreadnoughts arrived simultaneously. Waterspouts dyed red, blue, and yellow sprang up around the stricken vessel, and at least six more of the shells smashed home.

A 16-inch shell landed on the roof of the bridge.

Johnnie felt himself suspended in black air. Every working piece of electronics in the big room shorted as the concussion pulverized insulation and fractured matrixes. The regular lighting went out. The emergency glowstrips which replaced it had to struggle through a suspension of thick dust.

He didn't remember being thrown to the deck, but that was where he found himself lying when the world ceased to vibrate and the dust settled enough for him to see again.

The overhead armor had held. The shutters had been blown away from the viewslit, so another hit on the bridge would surely kill them all. One of the consoles muttered to itself as it melted around the blue flame at its core.

Fayette bawled something unintelligible and bolted

through the hatch. A burst of explosive bullets up the ladderway hurled his corpse back onto the bridge.

"Angels!" Johnnie shouted as he fired an explosive placeholder over the body. He knew bullets fired from this angle couldn't hit anyone when they burst in the ladderway, but he hoped the sleet of zinging, stinging fragments would make the desperate Angels hesitate while Johnnie's thumb switched his feed to solid projectiles that would ricochet.

"Get out of—" screamed someone behind as Johnnie thrust his rifle into the hatch opening, tilted the muzzle down, and triggered a one-handed burst which left as much of his body as possible behind the steel bulkhead.

"—the way!" Dan finished as his body slammed against the same hope of cover Johnnie was using.

Dan fired a flamethrower through the hatch.

Johnnie's helmet visor blacked out the direct line of the magnesium-enriched fuel, but its white streak flooded the bridge like the reflection of an arc lamp. The flamethrower's nozzle tried to lift in the commander's hands, but he kept it aimed down in a perfect three-cushion shot along the shaft's inner surface.

There were only a few seconds' worth of fuel remaining in the bottle. The flame died abruptly. The yellow flash of a secondary explosion in the ladderway, grenades or ammunition, was dull by comparison.

There were still screams.

Johnnie strode through the hatch. Glowing metal walls provided light for his visor to amplify.

Caleif and three Angels sprawled below. Another Angel whose uniform was on fire clawed blindly at the conning room bulkhead.

The living figure turned. Both eyes were gone, and the flesh had melted away from the left half of his face.

Johnnie fired instinctively, sending the screaming

remains of Ensign Sal Grumio to join his brother and the rest of the *Dragger*'s crew.

Nothing else moved. Johnnie stepped back onto the bridge.

Uncle Dan and the surviving technician stared at him. None of the three men spoke.

The deck was tilted at a noticeable angle. Fires were visible across most of the 270° panorama of the unshuttered viewslit. The slime forward had baked dry in the heat of the deck beneath it. The algae now burned with its own smoky flame.

The *Holy Trinity*'s bow dipped toward the sea, but the dreadnought no longer had enough way on to sweep waves across the sullen fire.

No shells had fallen since the horrendous triple salvo.

"Look!" croaked the technician as he pointed to the southwestern sky. "*Look!*"

The horizon brightened as though the red gates of Hell had been thrown open.

Dan was kneading the singed back of his left hand with the fingers of his right. His face was terrible. "Bloody well about time," he snarled.

Patterns of red specks roared high overhead. They were full salvoes from the seventeen battle-ready dreadnoughts of Blackhorse Fleet, slamming Commander Cooke's trap closed on the Angels.

24

Rather the scorned—the rejected—
    the men hemmed in with the spears;
The men of the tattered battalion which fights
    till it dies,
Dazed with the dust of the battle, the din and
    the cries,
The men with the broken heads and the blood
    running into their eyes.

                    —John Masefield

There were ten of them still alive.

Two of the Blackhorse raiders, men from the engine room, were so badly burned that they had to shuffle along with their arms supported by their comrades' shoulders. Johnnie arranged the makeshift harness of packstraps around them with as much care as possible, but the wounded men still moaned and shuddered through their fog of drugs and toxins.

The gunboat D1528—*Murderer* according to the legend painted across the turret of the 2-inch Gatling gun on its foredeck—bobbed in swells reflected from the side of the *Holy Trinity*. Three of the crew used rifle butts as fenders to prevent the gunboat from being smashed into the side of the sinking dreadnought; others received each member of the raiding party as he came down the skimmer winch and passed the shaken men to such comfort and medical treatment as a hydrofoil could provide.

The sea was lighted for miles by torrents of sparks spewing from the *Holy Trinity*'s stern. Flames reflected from waves, from debris, and from the eyes of things which had learned the chaos of war meant a source of abundant food.

The hydrofoil's crew was clearly nervous. The little craft depended on speed and concealment to survive. Here, stopped dead alongside the brightest beacon in the Ishtar Basin, they had neither, but they were carrying out their orders without complaint.

As the men of the raiding party themselves had done; and had, for the most part, died doing.

Men on the gunboat's deck released the second of the wounded raiders and passed him gently to their fellows in the cockpit. Dan winched up the whining cable at the highest speed of which the drum was capable.

It didn't have far to come. The skimmer port was long under water, and the gunboat's railing was now only ten feet below that of the sinking battleship. At any time in the past five years, that would have been an easy jump for Johnnie, even onto the bobbing deck of a hydrofoil.

At any time but now.

"Go ahead," Johnnie said. "I'll winch you down."

His uncle shook his head. "I'm the captain," he said. "I leave last. Hop in."

He pointed to the harness.

Johnnie wasn't sure whether or not the words were a joke, but he knew that he didn't want to argue—with anyone, about anything. He gripped the cable, intending to ride the clamps down without bothering about the harness.

He swayed and almost blacked out. He'd been all right so long as he had the other crewmen to worry about, to fasten into the jury-rigged harness. . . .

Dan caught him. "That's all right, John," the older man murmured. His right arm was as firm as an iron strap. "Here, we'll ride it together."

The slung rifle slid off Johnnie's shoulder. Dan tossed it to the deck and said, "We won't need that now."

The youth opened his eyes. He saw everything around him with a new clarity. "Right," he said in a voice he could not have recognized as his own. "Leave it for some poor bastard to blow his brains out before he drowns or the fish eat him."

The winch began to unreel at a low setting. Dan supported him, but Johnnie's limbs had their strength back again. Hands reached up from the gunboat's deck to receive them.

The Blackhorse line of battle was in sight, approaching from the southwest. The dreadnoughts' main guns spewed bottle-shaped flames which reflected from the cloud cover. Johnnie had never seen anything like it, even when he was hallucinating from a high fever.

The seventeen battleships were proceeding in a modified line-abreast formation. Admiral Bergstrom kept his fleet's heading at forty-five degrees to their targets beyond the horizon, so that the Blackhorse vessels could fire full broadsides instead of engaging with their forward turrets alone.

"For God's sake!" Dan muttered scornfully. "The Angels only *have* three battleships. What's he afraid of?"

No incoming shells disturbed the perfect Blackhorse formation. The dreadnoughts' railgun domes were live, trailing faint streamers of ionized air, but they fired only occasional skyward volleys. The Angels had been battered to the point they had scarcely any guns capable of replying to the ships destroying them.

"Got 'em!" shouted one of the crewmen who grabbed Dan and Johnnie. "All clear!"

The hydrofoil's drive was churning a roostertail even before the winch cable had swung back against the *Holy Trinity*'s side.

The Blackhorse fleet was almost upon the burning dreadnought. The nearest of the battleships would pass within two hundred yards. The wake of the massive vessel, proceeding at flank speed, would have crushed D1528 against the *Holy Trinity* as so much flotsam had the gunboat not gotten under way in time.

Johnnie wondered who had set the fleet's course . . . though subtlety of that sort didn't seem in character for Captain Haynes.

Flames from the *Holy Trinity* picked out details on the hull and superstructure of the oncoming dreadnought, washing the three shades of gray camouflage into one. Johnnie thought the vessel was the *Catherine of Aragon*, but his mind was too dull for certainty and it didn't matter anyway.

The dreadnought's twelve 16-inch guns were now silent, but there were squeals as the secondary batteries clustered along her mid-section rotated to track the hydrofoil as the little vessel turned desperately to bring her bow into the oncoming wake. The paired 5-inch guns glared at D1528 like the eyes of attack dogs, straining at their leashes.

"Bastards!" snarled the ensign commanding the gunboat as he lifted Johnnie over the cockpit coaming. "*They* probably think it's a joke!"

D1528 rode over the wake with a snarl and a lurch. The ensign used the drop on the far side to deploy the gunboat's outriggers thirty seconds before her forward motion alone would have permitted it.

Dan swung himself into the cockpit. The motion was smooth and athletic. He seemed as fit as he had been two days before in Admiral Bergstrom's office.

Unless you looked carefully at his eyes.

"Nice job, Stocker," Dan said to the ensign.

Johnnie blinked. The name stencilled on the gunboat officer's helmet was worn and illegible in this light. Did Uncle Dan know all the Blackhorse officers by sight?

Stocker looked up from the horizontal plotting screen. "Thank you, sir!" he said.

D1528 was beating up to speed. Lifted on her foils, the gunboat was amazingly stable even though crosscutting wakes corrugated the sea.

"Where are you supposed to take us?" Dan asked, as if idly.

He was using helmet intercom. A red bead in Johnnie's visor indicated that Dan had chosen a command channel that the gunboat's enlisted crew couldn't overhear.

The hydrofoil was headed in the opposite direction from the battleships. The big ships were almost hull-down, their locations on the northeastern horizon marked primarily by the glowing discharges from railguns on alert status.

All the guns had ceased firing. The Angels must have surrendered—whatever was left of them—and the Warcocks were not yet in range.

Ensign Stocker looked up from the plot again. This time a guarded expression had replaced the earlier pleasure. "Ah, well, I'm to carry you to the cruiser *Clinton*," he said. "She's the command ship for the rear screen. Plenty of room aboard her and, you know, first-rate medical facilities."

Stocker nodded toward the hydrofoil's electronics bay. One of the wounded raiders sat in the open hatchway, babbling to himself while a gunboat crew-man tried to comfort him.

"Admiral Bergstrom is aboard the *Semiramis*?" Dan asked.

Stocker nodded cautiously. "Yes . . . ," he said. "Sir."

"Take us to the *Semiramis*, Ensign," Dan said.

The cockpit was cramped. Commander Cooke and the two ensigns were within arms' length of one another, but for an instant there was a cold crystal wall between Stocker and the others.

"Sir, Captain Haynes specifically ordered . . . ," the gunboat officer began.

Dan grinned at him.

Stocker braced to attention. "Aye aye *sir!*" he said crisply. He turned to the plotting table, then began snapping orders to his helmsman over an intra-ship push.

There was a pair of jumpseats against the back wall of the cockpit. Dan pulled one down for Johnnie, then sat in the other himself.

D1528 came about in a wide arc, banking on her outriggers. The only certain marker in the sea, the flaming pyre that had been the *Holy Trinity*, began to slide back across the western horizon as gunboat reversed course to pursue the battle line.

"Unc—ah . . . ," Johnnie said. "I mean, sir?"

Uncle Dan put an arm around the younger man's shoulders and squeezed him.

"Uncle Dan, was it worth it? Was it worth—"

Johnnie closed his eyes, but he couldn't close out the crowding memories.

"Ask me when it's over, John," his uncle said. He leaned his head close to Johnnie's so that they could speak without using their helmet radios.

The dreadnoughts were coming in sight again. Rather, the combing bow-waves kicked up by huge vessels moving at speed reflected the sky glow on the horizon.

"You mean, after we've beat the Warcocks and Flotilla Blanche?" Johnnie said. "If we beat them."

"Oh, we'll beat *them*," Dan said. "This war's as good as won; or will be as soon as I'm on the bridge of the *Semiramis* to make sure Haynes and the Admiral don't throw it away from too much caution.

"But what I meant," he continued, "is we won't know if it's worthwhile until there's a united government on Venus and Mankind is at peace."

Johnnie turned from the horizon beyond the cockpit windscreen and stared at his uncle. "*We* won't live to see that," he said. "Will we?"

Dan shook his head. He smiled. His face was as gentle as Johnnie had ever seen it, but the expression was without humor.

"They won't—Man won't—win in our lifetime," he said. "But we might live long enough to see us all lose. Long enough to see Venus turned into a fireball, and the last tomb of Mankind in the universe."

Johnnie nodded, but his mind was too tired to visualize Mankind as an entity.

Besides, his last glimpses of Sergeant Britten and Sal Grumio kept getting in the way.

25

From a find to a check, from a check to a view,
From a view to a death in the morning.
          —John Woodcock Graves

The hydrofoil strained forward like a horse whirling a sulky down the home stretch.

The jumpseats weren't fitted with terminals, but there were data feeds in the flimsy bulkhead behind them. Johnnie uncoiled one against the tension of its take-up spring and plugged it into the input jack of his helmet. After his AI sorted through the options, he settled on viewing the forward gunsight image on the left side of his visor.

The dreadnought filling that magnified picture had her port secondary batteries and at least forty small-caliber Gatling guns trained on D1528. Any one of the Gatlings—much less a single shell from the 6-inch secondaries—could reduce the gunboat to pieces small enough to fit in a matchbox.

"We're being queried by *Semiramis*," said Ensign Stocker.

"I'll take it," said Uncle Dan. He rose, then slid into the command console as Stocker vacated it.

"Kinda hoped you might, sir," the ensign said with a grin.

Johnnie shook his head in wonder at the other young officer. Stocker had decided he was going to have fun with the situation—even though he knew he was being used as a pawn in a high-stakes game between his superiors.

Courage wasn't limited to the willingness to ride a flimsy hydrofoil into battle.

Dan entered his personal code, then authenticated it with his brainwave patterns transmitted by his helmet. "Blackhorse Six," he said, "this is Blackhorse Three aboard the D1528. I need to come aboard the flagship."

Unlike the raiders' transmissions from the *Holy Trinity*, there were compatible code sets on both vessels. It wasn't impossible that the Warcocks' signals intelligence personnel would intercept the exchange—even though it was low-power, tight-beam, and sent in tiny snippets over a broad spread of frequencies. The conversation could never be decrypted in time to have tactical effect, however.

Johnnie couldn't hear the response. He knew the message had been received on the flagship's bridge because the *Semiramis'* Gatling guns all lifted like the arms of troops saluting on the parade ground.

The officer in charge of the anti-hydrofoil batteries had overheard the request. He'd made the instant decision that *he* didn't want to answer questions about why he'd threatened to blow away Commander Cooke.

The 6-inch turrets moved only to track D1528 as the little vessel closed. An officer at another console had made a different decision. Probably a decision involving Captain Haynes' likely reaction.

"Negative, Pedr," Uncle Dan said. He was speaking forcefully, though he called Admiral Bergstrom by his first name. "The *Semiramis* needn't stop or even slow. Order the port accommodation ladder lowered, and my aide and I'll come aboard."

Johnnie felt too decoupled to be afraid. He looked at his uncle.

The *Semiramis* alone could manage about thirty-two knots, but the speed of the battle line as a whole would be slightly slower. The ships would still be travelling fast enough that if someone slipped while hopping from the hydrofoil's deck to the spray-slick surface of the dreadnought's accommodation ladder, impact with the water would be stunning if not fatal.

The creatures in the water would be certainly fatal.

But it really didn't matter.

Ensign Stocker called an order to his helmsman and throttled back. He looked worried. The unspoken basis of Commander Cooke's offer was that Stocker could match the gunboat's speed perfectly to that of the battleship, despite the turbulence of the huge ship's passage through the sea.

"No sir," Dan said, "I can't discuss this by radio. We *must* come aboard."

They were now so close to the *Semiramis* that the 6-inch guns couldn't depress enough in their mountings to bear on the hydrofoil. The turrets continued to track, however, as though hoping that the gunboat would somehow leap high enough in the air to be disintegrated by a salvo of hundred-pound shells.

Powder smoke still drifted from the eight eighteen-inch guns to surround the *Semiramis* like a sickly-sweet aura.

"I appreciate that, Pedr," Dan said. "And the sooner we come aboard, the sooner Ensign Stocker here can carry the rest of my team back to the *Clinton* for that medical treatment."

Stocker looked at Commander Cooke, then toward

the shuddering, whimpering man in the electronics bay. His face was without expression.

The helmsman held D1528 thirty feet off the dreadnought's port quarter. Throttled back to the larger vessel's best speed, the hydrofoil felt sluggish. It had a tendency to follow the corrugations of the sea's surface rather than slicing at the even keel maintained by the telescoping outriggers.

The accommodation ladder hanging from the *Semiramis'* port quarter began to lower toward the water. A pair of sailors rode the stage down, ready to catch the transferring officers as they jumped across.

Dan stood up, swaying slightly with the hydrofoil's motion. "Right," he said. "Take over, Ensign Stocker. Do your usual excellent job and I won't forget you."

Stocker slid into his console and looked up at the superior officer. "Same for me, huh, sir? Cream their ass."

The ensign's words could have referred to the fleets allied against the Blackhorse, but Johnnie doubted it. He was Senator Gordon's son. He'd seen enough politics in his life to recognize them, even when they were being conducted in uniform.

Johnnie unplugged the data feed and rose as the thread-thin optical fiber coiled back onto its spool.

His uncle looked at him sharply. "Are you up to this, John?" he asked. "Because if you're not . . . ?"

"Sure, I'm fine," Johnnie said. He wasn't sure if that was true. He saw everything around him with unusual clarity, but he seemed to be hovering over his body.

It didn't matter.

He followed Dan to the starboard rail. He felt steady; which was a matter of vague intellectual interest to him, because he knew that the deck underfoot was vibrating badly. The drive motors were being run at well below their optimum rate.

Stocker and his helmsman brought the D1528 in smoothly. The accommodation ladder now hung about eight feet above the average level of the sea, but occasional swells surged dangerously near the platform's underside. At thirty knots, the stage would tear loose if it touched the water.

"Go," said Dan, and Johnnie stepped across the six-inch gap.

A dreadnought sailor was ready to grab him, but Johnnie waved the man away. The gunboat was so precisely controlled that there was less relative motion between the disparate vessels than there would have been in getting off a slidewalk.

Dan followed and continued striding toward the steps leading up to the deck. "Come on, lad," he snapped. "Time's a-wasting."

"They'll winch us up, sir!" called one of the sailors.

Dan gestured brusquely, dismissively, without turning around.

"What is it that we've got to tell Admiral, ah, sir?" Johnnie asked as he pounded up the perforated alloy treads behind his uncle.

The gunboat, freed of its shackling need to keep station, curved away from the accommodation ladder in a roar of thrusters coming up to speed.

"I want to make sure they don't throw the battle away," Dan said. "I told you that."

There were splotches of algae on the *Semiramis'* side, but not a solid coating as had been the case with the *Holy Trinity*. This was just the growth since the battleship slipped out of port the day before.

"*I* don't have anything to add," Johnnie said emotionlessly.

Dan had reached the battleship's deck. A section of rail pivoted to form a gate. He turned and looked back at his nephew.

"Oh, you have something to add, John," he said. His lips were firm as the jaws of a vise. "I didn't lie to the Senator about that."

He strode toward a hatch in the dreadnought's superstructure. X and Y Turrets' huge 18-inch guns had blackened the deck and lifted up a sheet of the plastic covering, then plastered it against the railing.

"But *what*?" Johnnie demanded.

A staircase—a ladderway—lay behind the hatch. "In good time, lad," said Dan's echo-thickened voice as his boots clanged upward. "If not tonight, then later. . . . But I think tonight."

As Johnnie closed the hatch behind him, he heard the squeal of the 6-inch turrets. The secondary batteries were returning to the ready position now that they had tracked D1528 out of sight.

26

*The sea is Death's garden, and he sows
dead men in the loam. . . .*
                    —Francis Marion Crawford

A helmeted gunner raised his head from one of the
Quad-Gatling tubs on the shelter deck as Commander
Cooke and his aide strode forward to the bridge.

Johnnie started. The equivalent installations on the
Holy Trinity had been empty. He'd never been aboard
a dreadnought with a full crew.

There were crewmen where Johnnie's subconscious
expected only the heat-warped barrels he'd burned out
as the raiders escaped from Paradise Harbor. He
thought of corpses rising in their coffins.

Corpses didn't do that. But neither did the corpses
in Johnnie's mind sleep.

The bridge hatch was open but guarded by a heavily-
armed senior petty officer.

"Come along, sir!" the man urged. "We don't none
of us want to be out here when the big bastards cut
loose again, do we?"

There was the sound of distant gunfire and an

occasional flicker of light on the horizon, but for the moment action was limited to the screening forces.

Action. Thick armor cracking, perforating. Hell erupting to spew out over the sea, winking from waves and the eyes within the waves.

The hatch ratcheted shut, closing them within the climate-controlled fastness of the bridge. Johnnie trembled because of what was in his heart, not the drop in air temperature.

The bridge of the *Semiramis* was very like Wenceslas Dome's governmental accounting office. The differences were that the warship's bridge crew was uniformed, and that its personnel seemed far more alert.

Of course, accountants would be on their toes if they knew that an 18-inch shell might land in their midst at any moment.

The center of the enclosed bridge was a huge plotting table. In the air above it hung a vertical holographic projection of the same data. The hologram was monochrome, but the air projection aligned itself to appear perpendicular to someone viewing it from any point on the bridge.

The console built into the plotting table was vacant. Uncle Dan slid into it and began keying up data.

"Ah, sir?" said a lieutenant Johnnie had never seen. "That's Captain Haynes' station. He's on his way up from the battle center now."

Dan snorted. "When he heard I was coming aboard, you mean? Don't worry, Bailey. When the captain arrives, I'll vacate."

He unbuckled his equipment belt and hung it, the holstered pistol on one side balanced by loaded magazines on the other, from the seat's armrest. Then he resumed his work.

Admiral Bergstrom was at a console with no visual display up but six separate data feeds plugged into his helmet. He turned, looking like a man whose brain was being devoured by wire-thin worms, and peered at Dan in the seat behind him.

"Commander?" Bergstrom said. "Commander. You had crucial information for us, you said?"

"Right," said Dan, one eye on his console display and the other on the plotting table itself. His fingers danced on the keys. "Have you released the subs yet, sir?"

Johnnie looked over his uncle's shoulder. Strung raggedly along the western edge, barely within the confines of the plotting table at its current scale, were two hollow yellow circles and a yellow X: the electronic remains of the Angel dreadnoughts, sinking and sunk respectively, which had pursued the *Holy Trinity*.

One of the technicians had the last moments of the X marker up on his display. There were more important things for Blackhorse personnel to be considering at the moment, but Johnnie could understand the tech's fascination with the looped image.

Almost anything was more important than that particular ship now.

The vessel had been the *Azrael*, easily identified because it carried its main battery in three quadruple turrets forward. The unusual layout meant that the thick belt protecting the main magazines and shell rooms was relatively short, saving weight without giving up protection.

It also meant that most of the explosives aboard the battleship were concentrated in a small area.

The holographic image was a sixty-degree oblique, transmitted to the *Semiramis* by a glider which had risked the night winds to spot the fall of shot. The *Azrael* was making a course correction, perhaps to bring her heavy guns to bear on the unexpected threat from the main Blackhorse fleet. Her railgun installations blazed blue-white, and her curving wake shivered with phosphorescent life.

The glider's imaging system picked up the dull red streaks of shells plunging down—not by pairs and triplets as Johnnie remembered from the *Holy Trinity*, but thirty or forty at a time. The *Azrael* was the simultaneous target for half a dozen Blackhorse dreadnoughts; there was nothing the victim's railgun batteries could do to affect the result.

"Flotilla Blanche isn't in the killing zone, yet, Commander," Admiral Bergstrom said. "Ah—Commander, what is it that had to be explained face to face?"

Great mushrooms of water bloomed on all sides of the *Azrael*, distorting the wake and twisting the bow as they hollowed the surface into which the cutwater then slid.

A few of the shells which landed aboard the *Azrael* burst with bright orange flashes because their fuzes were over-sensitive. The dangerous hits merely sparked on the surface of the armor and detonated far within the dreadnought's guts.

The stricken vessel's bow lifted as though she were a flying fish making a desperate attempt to escape. The explosion that engulfed her forequarters was black, streaked with a red as deep as the devil's eye sockets. C Turret sprang fifty feet into the air, shedding hundred-ton fragments like so many bits of confetti.

"We don't *need* the submarines to finish Flotilla Blanche," Dan said as he shuffled quickly through data on his console. "Or the Warcocks, for that matter. We can do that with gunfire easily enough—if we slow down the Warcocks with our subs so that we catch them before the two fleets join."

He tapped the Execute key with a chopping stroke of his finger. The display quivered, then blanked. "With your permission, sir," Dan said, "I'll send the wolfpacks in now."

A thousand feet above the fiery cauldron, the column of smoke topped out in a ragged anvil. The stern half of the *Azrael* was sucked into the crater of white water. It bobbed as the sea closed over itself, then vanished with scarcely an additional ripple.

The recorded images ended with a blur of incandescent light.

The loop began again. Johnnie forced his eyes away with difficulty; the technician continued to watch the repeated horror.

There but for the grace of God. . . .

"I *don't* think . . . ," Admiral Bergstrom began, but his glare turned to a grimace.

The ultra-low-frequency pod beneath the *Semiramis'* keel began to transmit orders to the Blackhorse submarine fleet at a frequency of between ten and a hundred hertz. Johnnie's bowels quivered.

Due to the sluggish transmission frequency, there was time to abort the command before it reached the submarines lurking on the bottom three miles down. Instead, Bergstrom said, "Oh . . . yes, I suppose you're right."

The submarines were beneath the thermocline, a differential of temperature and salinity in the deep sea which blocked both active and passive sonar. That helped conceal them from the Warcocks, but the subs' best protection was a matter of psychology rather than physics.

The Angel fleet had run the same course without interference. The Warcocks and Flotilla Blanche, now desperately trying to join forces in the northwest quadrant of the Ishtar Basin, assumed the only dangers they need fear were the Blackhorse surface ships which had reduced the Angels to blazing wreckage in a matter of minutes.

The petty officer, alerted by a message through his helmet, activated the control of the hatch he guarded.

"Right," said Dan. He started to get up.

Johnnie's face was still. His mind visualized a pair of raiders wearing Angel khaki as they burst through the hatchway with a cataclysm of rifle and sub-machine gun fire.

Consoles sparking around stray bullets; the chests of neat cream uniforms exploding in blood and smoldering cloth; fingers which were accustomed to stroke keys flailing wildly for pistols almost forgotten beneath polished holster-flaps.

The stink of gunsmoke, and the greater stink of feces when fear and death voided men's bowels.

Captain Haynes squeezed through the hatch before it was really open enough to pass a man of his solid bulk.

Haynes was panting. He must have walked—run— all the way from the deep-buried battle center rather than chance an elevator when any instant could bring a shell and a power failure.

His face was livid, but that was more from anger than from exercise. His left hand gripped so hard on a visicube of his wife that his knuckles were mottled.

"Commander Cooke," Haynes said in a voice like millstones, "you're at my station—"

Though by the time the words came out, Uncle Dan had moved to an ordinary console nearby. A quick gesture—a twist of his index finger as though it were a boning knife—sent the technician there scrambling out of his seat.

Johnnie followed as if he were his uncle's shadow. He was drifting through this ambiance like a thistle seed in a zephyr. He felt nothing, but his senses were sharper than he ever remembered them being.

Captain Haynes seated himself with the swaggering certainty of a dog staking out its territory. He set the

visicube on the plotting table before him. "Sir," he said
to Admiral Bergstrom, "I felt the ULF communicator
activate while I was on the way here. What—"

"Pedr thought," Dan broke in, "that unless we slow
the Warcocks' withdrawal, they'll be able to join Flotilla Blanche before we bring them to battle. If they
have to zigzag because of submarine attack—"

"Let them join!" Haynes snapped. "Then our subs
take care of both of them!"

The Warcocks' ten battleships were in a straggling
line-ahead on the plotting table. The new emergency
had further disturbed a formation that had been rough
to begin with.

The Warcocks left their base in a rush to block the
Holy Trinity from the presumed destination of the
Blackhorse fleet at the Kanjar Straits to the northwest.
When the stolen dreadnought turned southwest,
Admiral Helwig had thrown his Warcocks into the pur-
suit—as though the Angels' own three battleships would
not be sufficient.

Now they were racing back to the northwest again,
hoping to join Flotilla Blanche as it streamed from the
position it had taken at the mouth of the straits.

The light forces of Flotilla Blanche speckled the
upper edge of the plotting table. The Warcock screen
of cruisers and destroyers formed a broad arc between
their dreadnoughts and the oncoming Blackhorse fleet.
They were well positioned to block torpedo attack by
Blackhorse hydrofoils, but they could do nothing to stop
the one- and two-ton shells from the dreadnoughts
which would rumble overhead as soon as the range
closed to thirty miles or so.

They weren't in a good position to defend against
the submarine ambush the Warcocks had blundered
into the center of, either.

"Subs can't *destroy* them," Dan said, speaking loudly

enough to be heard by everyone on the bridge. "These
are good outfits, both of them. We can just cause
confusion, as we decided in the planning—"

"The Admiral and I—" Haynes shouted.

Admiral Bergstrom's face was suffused with the frus-
trated pain of a child listening to his parents quarrel.
He must have been a decisive man at one time, but
age and his rumored drug habit had rotted away the
hard core of his personality.

"—changed that plan, Commander, while you were
off having your fun playing soldiers!"

"Oh, God!" muttered a lieutenant commander, who
then buried his face in his display. Everyone, even
Captain Haynes, looked embarrassed.

Everyone but Dan and Johnnie. Their burned,
bloodied, torn fatigues left them immune to embarrassment by any of the clean-uniformed personnel on
Semiramis' bridge.

Besides, there was no room in Johnnie's eyes for
embarrassment or any other emotion.

The starboard secondaries opened fire. The enclosed
bridge damped the shock of the muzzle blasts, but the
hull belled as the guns' thick steel breeches expanded
from the pressures they contained.

"Torpedoboat attack in sector A-12," explained a
lieutenant loudly.

Any of the bridge personnel could have learned that
data from their own consoles, but the statement served
its real purpose of breaking the vicious argument
between two of the fleet's most senior officers. Admiral
Bergstrom gave the lieutenant a look of gratitude. The
emotional temperature of the big room dropped to
normal human levels.

"All right," muttered Captain Haynes as he twisted
his face toward the plotting table. "We've got a battle
to fight, let's not forget."

Dan's fingers worked his keypad though he continued to watch the side of Haynes' determinedly-
averted face for some moments longer. A distant—
blurry despite being computer-enhanced—view of the
Warcock line appeared on his console.

The display above the plotting table showed sudden
chaos within the hostile battlefleet. None of the ship
symbols indicated damage, but the dreadnoughts had
started to curvet like theater-goers after someone
noticed smoke.

"Revised estimate of time to engagement," said
public-address speaker in the mechanical voice of the
battle center computer. "Three minutes thirty seconds
for leading El Paso elements; sixteen to seventeen
minutes for all El Paso elements."

Captain Haynes opened his mouth and reached for
the transmit key of his console.

"I'll take care of this, Captain," Admiral Bergstrom
said coolly. He pressed his own transmitter and said,
"Blackhorse Six to all El Paso elements. You may fire
as you bear, gentlemen. Blackhorse Six out."

For this operation, "El Paso" was the code name for
the dreadnoughts.

An ensign at the far end of the bridge shouted,
"Yippee!"

27

Then suddenly the tune went false,
The dancers wearied of the waltz,
The shadows ceased to wheel and whirl. . . .
                                    —Oscar Wilde

On Uncle Dan's display, the second ship from the rear of the Warcock line suddenly wreathed itself in flame and powder smoke. She had opened fire with her main guns. A moment later, all the other battleships visible from the glider joined in.

The Warcocks certainly knew that they were still out of range.

They also knew that they were shit outa luck.

"Ah, sir . . . ?" said Captain Haynes as his left hand stroked the image of his wife. "Do you think it might be better to delay firing until we can overwhelm them with a full fleet salvo?"

"No," said Admiral Bergstrom without turning to face his executive officer. "I do not."

"We'll be eating them up piecemeal, Captain," Dan said. He glancing from his display and then back. "Their formation's strung out for nearly five miles."

Johnnie nodded, professionally impressed by the way

his uncle managed to keep his tone along the thin neutral path between insulting and conciliatory.

"We'll have plenty of concentration on the rear of their line," Dan continued blandly as he examined the desperate Warcock dreadnoughts, "even if only the eighteens can fire for the first ten minutes."

Haynes' face was a thundercloud, ready to burst in a storm of invective unmerited by anything that had happened in the past few minutes. As his mouth opened to snarl, the portside Gatlings blazed in a sudden fury whose rate of fire made the enveloping armor sing.

Johnnie's training held, though his intellect was dissociated from control of his actions. He reached reflexively for the keypad of the console behind which he stood. The only reason his fingers did not shift the display to the gunnery board and echo the Gatlings' target information—

Was that Uncle Dan's fingers were already doing so.

The ship-shivering burst ended three seconds after it began. There was nothing on the targeting display except a froth where over a thousand 1-inch projectiles had ripped a piece of flotsam.

"Omigod, sorry, sorry," muttered the junior lieutenant whose console was the primary director for the Gatlings. "I thought, I mean. . . ."

He caught himself. His face hardened. "No target," he said crisply. "All clear. No target."

The *Semiramis'* main fire director rippled off a salvo from A and B Turrets, four 18-inch guns. The dreadnought shook herself like a dog coming in from the wet. The air of the bridge was suddenly hazy because finely-divided dust had vibrated out of every crack and fabric.

The thirty-inch armor covering the bridge flexed noticeably with the waves of compression and rarefaction. Johnnie could not imagine how the sailors manning the open gun tubs survived the muzzle blasts.

Dan switched back his display. The dreadnoughts had ceased cavorting in wild attempts to avoid torpedoes from Blackhorse submarines. The Warcock line reformed and resumed shaping to the northwest. Anti-submarine missiles from the dreadnoughts and their screen were forcing the subs to concentrate on evasion rather than attack—or to press on and die pointlessly.

Yellow symbols on the plotting table hologram indicated that two of the Warcock battleships had been hit, but they were still keeping station. Half a dozen red symbols marked the destruction of attacking submarines.

Johnnie's face did not change. Ships and shells and men; all were expendable.

The rearmost of the Warcock battleships had been the leaders in the pursuit. They were the fastest and generally the most modern members of the fleet, and two of them mounted 18-inch guns.

Semiramis' six railgun batteries began to tear the universe apart, dwarfing the racket of the Gatlings a minute before. Railgun discharges brightened the images of the Warcock vessels as well, but a splotch of white water beside the last ship marked a shell that had gotten through the defensive barrage.

The rising banshee moan of a dropping shell became a background to the crackling of hyper-velocity slugs. Johnnie's face did not change, but his body began to shudder uncontrollably. The youth's deep-buried lizard brain remembered that sound. Conscious courage—conscious fatalism—could do nothing to quell the tremors.

The shell burst with a dull *crump*, thousands of feet short of its intended target.

" . . .oboats in. . . ." the ceiling speaker said during the brief interval the railguns were silent.

If Johnnie cared to hear the details of the report, he could have flexed his helmet to the console, but the information didn't matter except to the men at the gunnery boards. The 6-inch batteries were firing, both port and starboard; a moment later, the Gatlings added their sharp-tongued chant.

Three shells burst directly above the second ship from the rear of the Warcock line, so close that the red-orange flashes and the blots of filthy smoke they left behind were visible in the image transmitted to Dan's console.

Most of the salvo screaming in a few seconds later struck on or around the dreadnought.

The forward superstructure, including the bridge, warped and shredded. There was a glowing pockmark where armor of particular thickness had been heated white-hot by a sixteen-inch shell.

A shell penetrated X Turret magazine. Instead of an explosion, a yellow flash hundreds of feet high blazed from every interstice of the turret and rear hull. As the initial glare sucked itself back within the blackened armor, the Y Turret magazine flashed over and burned with identical fury.

Johnnie keyed intercom mode on his helmet, the channel reserved for members of the raiding party. Him and his uncle; no one else within range . . . and scarcely anyone else alive.

"They're screwing up," he said flatly. "Their railguns are on automatic mode, but then they only react to direct threats. The poor bastards at the end of the line are on their own."

Like we were in the Holy Trinity.

Dan made a quick series of keystrokes without bothering to check whether or not the input was necessary. "Blackhorse Three to El Paso elements," he said to his console. "Your railguns are now firing on Sector Defense Mode. You will not switch them to Local Defense without orders from the flagship or an acting flagship. Out."

He turned to look up at his nephew. The 18-inch guns boomed out another salvo just then, but Johnnie could see his lips forming, " . . . *safe than sorry.*"

The third and fourth ships from the rear of the Warcock formation winked amidst waterspouts. The second had fallen out of line, her whole stern a mass of flames ignited by the powder flash.

The final vessel seemed to bear a charmed life with no shells falling near it, but her course had begun to diverge from that of the remaining dreadnoughts. Carats on the plotting-table display indicated that several torpedoes had gotten home and had jammed the ship's rudder.

"Sir," said Uncle Dan, "with your permission, I'll signal General Chase." His voice echoed in Johnnie's helmet: he was using an open frequency that everyone on the bridge could overhear, rather than the command channel.

Because he was Commander Daniel Cooke, that wasn't an accident or oversight. He wanted the statement public, because he knew that every one of the pumped-up officers who heard it would regard arguments against General Chase as cowardice rather than caution.

The screens along the bulkheads, taking the place of the now-shuttered viewslits, showed a dozen pyres on the sea. The Warcock light forces were making desperate attempts to slow the hostile battle-line, but the Blackhorse screen and the dreadnoughts' massed secondaries immolated the attackers as victims.

The Blackhorse battleships formed an arc with the ends slightly advanced. The Warcocks were in line-ahead, roughly centered within the pursuing arc. There were between two and six railgun installations on each Blackhorse dreadnought, and every one of them could sweep the sky above all seventeen ships in the formation.

If the Blackhorse formation broke up and each dreadnought proceeded at her own best speed, the defenses became porous.

But it was the only way the Blackhorse could be certain of running down the ships at the head of the Warcock line.

"Sir, I—" Captain Haynes began. Though he spoke to Admiral Bergstrom, he looked across the short intervening distance to his rival.

Dan grinned at him.

Haynes' face suffused with blood and rage. He closed his mouth like a door slamming.

The Admiral turned in his seat. His expression was unreadable. He looked up at the plotting display, then lowered his eyes to his executive officer.

"Yes," he said as the eighteens fired. His lips seemed to be slightly out of synch because his voice came over the radio a microsecond sooner than air would have transmitted the words. "Let's end this, shall we?"

Dan waited an instant to be sure that he, rather than Admiral Bergstrom, was to give the order. Then, with a wink to Captain Haynes, he keyed his console and said, "Blackhorse Six to El Paso element. General Chase. I say again, General Chase. Let's have 'em for breakfast, boys! Out!"

As a period to the command, the secondary magazines of a ship near the center of the Warcock line blew up. For a moment, inertia held the dreadnought on course. Her superstructure was missing and there was a scallop from the middle of her hull as though she were a minnow bitten by a piranha.

The stricken vessel slewed to the side. Her bow listed to starboard, her stern to port.

"Sir!" said a communications tech. "The Warcocks are calling for you on Frequency 7 to discuss surrender. Shall I transfer the call?"

Another heavy shell burst, close enough to be felt but still harmlessly far in the air.

"Yes, yes, of course!" Bergstrom snapped, prodding at his console with what seemed to Johnnie to be drunken precision.

"Blackhorse to all Blackhorse elements," Uncle Dan said. "Cease firing offensive—"

The booming main guns from the battleship immediately to starboard rocked the *Semiramis*.

"—weapons. They're giving up! Cease—"

Captain Haynes rose from his seat. "You have no right to give that order, Cooke!" he shouted.

"—fire, they're surrendering. Out."

The hammering snarl of the railguns was a reminder that at this range, shells would continue to fall for almost a minute—on the Blackhorse and on their opponents.

Flashes covered the stern of another Warcock dreadnought on the display. When the blasts ended, the guns of Y Turret were cocked sideways and the deck aft was a smoking shambles.

Uncle Dan stood up. He moved gracefully and at seeming leisure, like a cat awakening. "Do you have something to say to me, Captain Haynes?" he said.

The railguns cut off. Instead of silence, the bridge filled with the sound of a voice rasping from the roof speaker, "—der unconditionally to you, Admiral Bergstrom. We, I . . ."

The voice broke. Whether it was Admiral Helwig or subordinate promoted into his place by Blackhorse shells, there was no doubt of the sincere desperation of the Warcocks' commander.

Johnnie understood how the man must feel. All the few survivors of the *Holy Trinity* would understand that run-through-a-hammermill feeling.

Captain Haynes swallowed. "Remember we've still got Flotilla Blanche to deal with," he said. His tone was almost an apology.

He started to sit down.

"If you can spare us medical help—" the Warcock officer said.

"Admiral de Lessups can do basic math, Captain," Dan said harshly. "He can match twelve dreadnoughts against seventeen in his head—and he's not so stupid that he'll try the result for real."

"—we'd be very thankful."

Haynes' face worked. Johnnie could see that the stocky captain was still trying to disengage from an argument he had lost as soon as he opened his mouth. "We're low on main-gun ammu—"

"Not so low we can't hammer Flotilla Blanche to the bottom, Captain!" Dan shouted. His face was red, and his voice was full of the ragged fury Johnnie had heard him counterfeit in Senator Gordon's office. "They know that and we know that! *You* know it!"

"That won't be possible until we've dealt with Flotilla Blanche," said Bergstrom over the roof speaker. "As soon—"

"Commander," Haynes said, looking at his clenched fingers, "I think we're both overwrought. I think we—"

"You know what the real problem is?" Dan said rhetorically. His eyes swept the other personnel on the bridge. He waved his arm. "The *real* problem is that Haynes has learned about me and Beryl, and he's willing to give up a victory just so it won't be a victory I planned!"

Admiral Bergstrom turned around and snapped,

"Hold it down, for God's sake!" He straightened to resume his conversation with the Warcock officer.

Several of the listening officers gasped or turned away. Johnnie would have felt shock himself if he were able to feel any emotion at the moment.

Captain Haynes blinked. He was no longer angry; amazement had driven out every other reaction.

"Cooke," he said in wonderment, "were you wounded in the head? That's ridiculous."

Uncle Dan took a step forward and reached out. His index finger pressed the touch-plate of the visicube on the plotting table. He backed away.

"You may proceed to your home port—" Admiral Bergstrom was saying.

"Dan, darling, dearest Dan," squeaked the voice from the image of Beryl Haynes. *"I wish you were here with me now so that you could kiss—"*

"—leaving only enough undamaged vessels at sea to aid those—"

Haynes went red, then white. Johnnie could barely see the seated captain past his uncle's torso.

"—my nipples, so that you could—"

"—which are in danger of sinking," said the Admiral's voice.

Haynes lurched to his feet. His hand groped at his pistol holster.

"—bite my nipples the way—"

"I'm unarmed!" Dan shouted. He raised his hands from elbow level. His holster hung from the chair behind Haynes.

Captain Haynes swung up his pistol.

Johnnie's face was calm, his mind empty of everything but trained reflex. He drew and fired twice over his uncle's shoulder.

Haynes' head swelled as both bullets exploded within his brain.

"—*that's ecstasy for me . . .*" concluded the visicube.

Haynes' arms, flailing as he fell, brushed the image of his wife to the floor.

Johnnie's fingers began to load a fresh magazine into his pistol.

EPILOGUE

When navies are forgotten
And fleets are useless things,
When the dove shall warm her bosom
Beneath the eagle's wings.
        —Frederic Lawrence Knowles

Torpedoboat D992's auxiliary thruster was turning at idle, enough to make the water bubble beneath her stern and to take the slack out of the lines. Despite that, if any of the vessel's crew were anxious for their passenger to come aboard, they took pains to conceal the fact.

Johnnie, wearing civilian clothes, and Captain Daniel Cooke in a clean uniform with the tabs of his new rank on its collar paused beneath a tarpaulin for a moment. The sun was a white hammer in the sky, but the storm sweeping west from the Ishtar Basin would lash Black-horse Base before the afternoon was out.

Heavy traffic sped up and down the quays, carrying materials to repair battle damage and supplies to replace the enormous quantities used up in the action of the previous night. None of the men or vehicles came near the end of Dock 7 where the D992 waited.

Dan said, "I don't want you to misunderstand, John.

You can't stay with the Blackhorse, but I can get you a lieutenant's billet with any other fleet on Venus. Flotilla Blanche, for—"

"No," Johnnie said sharply.

He looked at his uncle, then focused on the lowering western horizon. "I wanted to learn what it was like to be a mercenary," he said. "Now I know."

His lips twisted and he added to the black sky, "I thought the Senator was a coward because he left after one battle."

"I told you that wasn't so," said Uncle Dan.

Johnnie met the older man's eyes. "You told me a lot of things!" he snarled.

"Yes," Dan replied calmly. "And none of them were lies."

A railcar carrying a section of armor clanked along the lagoon front, toward the drydock where the *Hatshepsut* was refitting from her torpedo damage. The dreadnought's gunnery control board had gone down at a critical time. Before the secondary armament could be switched to another console, a pair of Warcock torpedoboats unloaded their deadly cargo.

"Not lies?" the youth said. "Maybe not—by your standards, Uncle Dan."

Then, as his eyes blurred with memories, he said, "You *used* me. From the time you talked to the Senator, you were planning—what I did!"

"For eight years," Dan said coolly, "I've been raising you to be the man I'd need at my side when there was no one else I could trust. I never forced you to do anything—but I wanted you to have the chance to be the man I needed, *if* you had the balls for it."

"Oh, I've got the balls, Uncle Dan," Johnnie retorted. "What I *don't* have is the stomach. I see why you had to get rid of Captain Haynes—he was a normal human being. But I don't—"

The youth been speaking in a controlled if not a calm tone. Now his voice broke.

"—see why you had to pick me to murder him. Wouldn't Sergeant Britten have dropped him in the lagoon some night for you?"

"Captain Haynes killed himself," Dan said. "He'd be alive today if he'd been a man in whose hands the fate of Venus could rest safely."

"He was a decent man!"

"Venus isn't a decent planet, boyo!" the older man snapped. "It's a hellhole—and it's all Mankind has left. I'll pay whatever it costs to be sure that Venus is unified before somebody uses the atomic weapons they figure they need to win a war."

Lightning backlit one, then several of the oncoming cloud masses. Their gray-and-silver forms looked like fresh lead castings. Thunder was a reminder of distant guns firing.

Johnnie stared toward the clouds but at the past. "I don't care if Venus is ever unified," he said flatly. "I just don't want to see more men die."

"Well, you ought to care, boy," said his uncle in a voice like a cobra's hiss, "because if we don't have unity, we won't have peace; and if we don't have peace on this planet, then there's going to be two temporary stars orbiting the sun instead of just one."

Johnnie turned to Dan and blazed, "You don't make peace by killing people, *Captain!*"

Dan nodded. "Fine, boy," he said in the same cold tone. "Then you go down to the domes and help the Senator unify the planet his way—or some way of your own. It doesn't matter how you do it. But don't forget, boy: it has to be done, whatever it takes."

Johnnie closed his eyes, then pressed his fingers over them. It didn't help him blot out the visions that haunted his mind.

He spun around, though Dan had surely seen the tears dripping from beneath the youth's hands.

"Johnnie," said his uncle in a choking voice, "I told you there were costs. I didn't lie to you!"

I thought you meant I might be killed, Johnnie's mind formed, but he couldn't force the words through his lips.

He stumbled toward the hydrofoil waiting to carry him back to Wenceslas Dome.

"Whatever it takes!" his uncle shouted.

And the thunder chuckled its way across the sky.

THE JUNGLE

1

There was an instant of silence as the salvo of 8-inch shells drowned their freight-train roar in the shallow water off the port side of Air Cushion Torpedoboat K67. When the shells exploded, their three blasts erupted together from the sea in a spout of sand and water. Toothed life forms snapped and tore at one another even as they seared to death in the sunlight which burned through the clouds of Venus.

"—to Orange Leader," Ensign Brainard shouted into his commo helmet. "For God's sake, Holman, we can't hold this heading! Over."

They had to veer to seaward or reverse course. They had to do *something*, and do it quick or it wouldn't matter.

When shells began to fall unexpectedly on their two-ship scouting element, Lieutenant Holman had ordered K67 and his own K70 to skim the shallow embayment of one of the nameless islands of Gehenna Archipelago. At first, the order had seemed a good idea to Brainard also. The island's central peak, wrapped in festering vegetation, should confuse the radar of the cruiser targeting the two hovercraft.

But radar was never trustworthy on Venus. Solar radiation and magnetic fields twisted radio beams into corkscrews which might or might not bounce back to the receiving antenna. This time the cruiser's luck was good, and Brainard's luck—

The shockwave hammered them.

Brainard commanded one of the smallest vessels in Wysocki's Herd—Hafner's Herd originally, but a 16-inch shell had retired Cinc Hafner. Brainard gripped the cockpit coaming and glared at the waterspout, as though his eyes could force a response from Lieutenant Holman when a laser communicator could not.

K70, their sister-ship and the patrol leader, rocked out from behind the shellbursts, holding course. Instead of taking station ahead or astern of K67, Holman held his vessel 200 yards to seaward. That might be why the cruiser was still getting a Doppler echo separated from the shore—and an aiming point.

The sky screamed with another salvo. Ahead, the further cape of the embayment approached through the haze at K67's flat-out speed of 90 knots.

"Orange Two to Orange Leader!" Brainard shouted, knowing the volume of his voice wouldn't help carry the words to K70 if the laser communicator didn't function . . . and if Lieutenant Holman didn't want to hear. "Sheer off, for God's sake! Over!"

Newton, the coxswain, steadied K67 against the airborne shockwave followed by the surge of water humping over the shallows to pound the hovercraft's skirts. A ten-foot ribbonfish, all teeth and iridescence, swept up on the narrow deck, then slid into the roiling sea again. The fish had locked its jaws onto something round and spiny. In its determination to kill, it seemed oblivious to the notch some other creature had bitten from its belly.

Despite the oncoming shells and the onrushing land, Newton seemed as stolid as the ribbonfish. Perhaps he was. Newton made an excellent coxswain, but Brainard sometimes suspected that the seaman was too stupid to realize there was anything to be afraid of. He would hold course as ordered, even though he knew running up on the island's jagged shore at 90 knots would rip K67's skirts off and strand her crew in the middle of Hell.

The 8-inch salvo burst squarely between the two torpedoboats, hiding K70 momentarily in another deafening uprush of water. The cruiser was firing armor-piercing shells. Its radar must be treating the paired echoes as a return from a single large vessel. When K67 adjusted course to port as they must do in a moment—*must* do!—they would be squarely in the footprint of the next trio of shells.

There was a salvo on the way. Brainard could hear the howl over the intake roar of the fans pressurizing the bubble of air which filled K67's plenum, driving her across the surface by thrust vectored through the skirts.

The starboard forward fan was running hot. Technician 2nd Class Leaf, the motorman, was half inside its nacelle ahead of the gun tub.

He glanced back toward Brainard. The opaque helmet visor hid Leaf's face, but Brainard could imagine the panic in the motorman's eyes. The same terror stared back at Brainard whenever he looked into his soul—so he didn't do that, he concentrated on his instruments and his duty and to *hell* with Lieutenant Holman.

"Coxswain," Brainard ordered on his helmet's interphone channel, "drop twenty knots and adjust course ten degrees to seaward."

That would clear the jaws of land, barely, and avoid their consort—if she held her course. If Holman chopped K70's throttles also, the high-speed collision of the two flimsy craft would do as thorough a job as the 8-inch shells could have desired.

Officer-Trainee Wilding looked up from his navigation/electronic countermeasures console on the other side of the coxswain. "Sir," Wilding's voice crackled over the interphone, "I've tracked the shells back, and it isn't the Battlestars firing—"

Wilding had a reporting capsule ready to go, a laser communicator which would transmit its message program when it rose high enough to achieve line of sight with the Herd's main fleet. There was no point in releasing the capsule now. The 90-knot windspeed would shred the ascender balloon before the capsule released from its cradle.

Newton adjusted his throttles and helm. K67 took his input, but her slow response was almost lost in the thunderous vibration of the incoming shells. The cloud cover, lighted a translucent white by the sun only 67 million miles away, quivered with the sound.

These weren't shells fired by a cruiser. This was a main-gun salvo from a dreadnought. The cruiser's fire had not taken effect, so she had passed her radar target to a battleship.

"Hang on!" said Ensign Brainard, but he was only clinging to the cockpit rim with his left hand himself. He threw himself back into his seat; the shock harness gripped him.

Brainard's right hand checked the key on his commo helmet. He had to make sure that it was clicked forward to interphone so the crew could hear him. If he filled his mind with duty to his crew there was no room left for fear.

Shells lifted the sea off K67's port bow. Sand,

corals, and innumerable forms of life bulged up and outward in a man-made volcano. The bursting charges released fluorescent green marker dye so that a spotter could differentiate the fall of shot among multiple ships in a fleet engagement.

K67 bucked as the tidal wave swept across her track, but the hovercraft lifted instead of being overwhelmed by the circular chaos. All the world was the white pressure of the shockwave, the simultaneous detonation of several 18-inch shells.

Brainard was weightless. Only the touch of his left hand on the coaming connected him to his vessel. For an instant, he thought that they were safe, that K67 had ridden out even *this* cataclysmic fury—

Then he realized that the hovercraft was dropping off the back side of the wave. When the skirts lifted, they braked K67 like a parachute—but not enough, and their direction was now a vector of their initial course and the 90° side-thrust from the shockwave. K67 was about to slam down on a jagged shoreline at a speed that would rip through the armored belly of a dreadnought, much less a hovercraft's flexible skirts.

Brainard realized one other thing as well. The Battlestars didn't bother with marker dye in their shells. One of the Herd's screening cruisers had seen a big-ship echo where the Herd had no major fleet units. The cruiser had taken the target under fire, then passed the target to a battleship.

From the color of the dye, K67 had just been destroyed by the *Elephant*, the flagship of Brainard's own fleet.

May 10, 382 AS. 2334 hours.

As Brainard and his momentary consort sauntered up the circular ramp, he glanced down through a haze of alcohol at the ballroom's panorama of metal and jewels and the fabrics which shimmered brightest of all.

He'd seen parties like this one before, but he'd never been present in person. Every Keep's holonews focused on the glittering celebrations that the founding families and their retainers held, on festival days or whenever a special event arose.

This time the event was the imminent war between Wyoming Keep and Asturias Keep. The Callahans, whom Officer-Trainee Wilding said were the most powerful of the Twelve Families directing the affairs of Wyoming, had risen to the occasion. A gathering this splendid would occupy the holoscreens until battle news arrived to entertain the mass of the population.

The common people had their own celebrations in every bar and club throughout Wyoming Keep—and Asturias as well, no doubt. Those parties Brainard *had* seen, as officer-trainee and as civilian, for as far back as he could remember.

Because mercenaries—the surface fleets of the Free Companies—did the actual fighting, war was only an economic risk to the populace of the domed keeps beneath the seas of Venus. If the Battlestars, the Free Company employed by Asturias, managed to defeat Wysocki's Herd, the leading families of Wyoming Keep—the folk here in this ballroom—would manage to insulate themselves from the worst effects of reparations payments. The common people had little enough to begin with that less would not significantly degrade their manner of life.

Civilians celebrated because battles were exciting. Mercenaries—and there were ten or a dozen at this gathering besides Brainard, mostly high officers—caroused because they might be about to die.

The woman on Brainard's arm drew herself

possessively closer to him. What *was* her name? He couldn't remember.

The ramp to the chambers on the high second level was designed to permit those on it to see and be seen by the crowd in the ballroom itself. The ramp was broad and sloped gently, making a full circuit of the big room in its ascent.

Two couples were coming down together as Brainard and his companion went up. The women were strikingly beautiful in jumpsuits of pastel chiffon. The fabric was almost transparent.

The men wore lieutenant-commander's braid on the blue-and-silver dress uniforms of Wysocki's Herd.

"Oh, Lieutenant Brainard!" bubbled the woman in chartreuse as she fumbled to take the ensign's free hand. The other three strangers carried drinks, but this woman's expression was brighter than alcohol alone would paint it. "I'm so glad to see you! Prince Hal— Hal Wilding, *you* know—promised to introduce me to you!"

The woman in pink let her half-empty glass fall and said, "Prince Hal is a *very* dear friend of mine!" She tried to insert herself between Brainard and the other woman, but Chartreuse had a surprising amount of muscle in her plump arms. "Would you like me to show you over the house?"

Brainard stared at the two men. Their uniforms were real. Their complexions probably resulted from make-up, but the men looked as if they had the deep mahogany tans which high-energy rays penetrating the cloud layers burned into the exposed skin of Free Companions on the surface.

But the eyes were wrong. The men were phonies, rich civilians in costume, and they turned away from the expression they saw on Brainard's face.

The woman on Brainard's arm gave Pink and

Chartreuse a look as cold as the ensign's own. "Dearests . . . ," she said, drawing out the sibilants into a hiss. "I'm going to show Ensign Brainard the house myself. After all, dearests . . . it *is* my family's house, isn't it?"

Drink buzzed in Brainard's mind. He supposed his consort was a Callahan.

She must have done something with her dress when she saw rivals approaching. Now it was formed of two slitted layers instead of a single piece of fabric. The woman smiled at Brainard and shifted her stance, so that her erect pink nipples peeked out at him.

The two couples passed on down the ramp, snarling among themselves in low voices. From across the ballroom, Officer-Trainee Wilding, surrounded by his own harem and the cameras of a holonews team, glanced up and met Brainard's eyes.

The ensign saluted sardonically. Prince Hal, was it? He'd known that K67's new second-in-command was a member of the Twelve Families; that was how he'd gotten Brainard an invitation to this party, after all. But Brainard hadn't been born in Wyoming Keep, so he'd had no idea that Wilding was prominent even within his class.

A footman in magenta livery with buff facings knelt to pick up the dropped glass. The tail of the servant's coat brushed Brainard's leg. His consort noticed the contact. She squealed and lashed out with her foot, displaying a slender leg and a line of blond fuzz from her pubic wedge to her navel.

Brainard caught her so that the kick missed its target. The footman scuttled away without looking back.

"We had to lay on extra help for the party," the woman said pettishly. "Some of them are worse than useless."

She hugged herself close to the ensign again. "Come along," she said. She giggled. "But not *too* fast."

Brainard's face did not change. They resumed their stately progress up the ramp. His consort wanted everyone to see that she had snagged a certified combat hero for the evening. Well, that was all right with him. . . .

The ballroom's high ceiling was a holographic projection of the terraforming and settlement of Venus. In the opening scenes of the loop, huge cylinders arrived, filled with bacteria gene-tailored to live and grow in the Venerian atmosphere. The waste products of bacterial growth included oxygen and water vapor. Rain fell in torrents that finally, as the atmosphere cleared, reached and pooled in oceans over most of the planetary surface.

The terraformers' centuries-long plan continued. Later cylinders spewed the seeds and eggs of multi-celled lifeforms onto the newly receptive planet. Trees of myriad species; vines, grasses and epiphytes; *all* the diversity of Earth, plus multiple mutations for every original species. Through the burgeoning jungles stalked beasts—insects, arachnids, crustaceans; even the forms of backboned life which were simple enough that the young did not require parental care. All were genetically tailored to the new environment.

The terraformers' success was beyond plan—almost beyond comprehension. Human-engineered changes to gene plasm had coupled eagerly with the virgin environment and the high level of ionizing radiation penetrating the clouds of water vapor. The result was a hell of aggressive mutations like nothing ever seen on Earth. Perhaps the artificial ecosystem was unique in the universe.

The new conditions changed but did not force the abandonment of plans for the human colonization of

Venus. Now the holographic views showed how the planners set up their first colonies in undersea domes at the edges of continental shelves, as nearly barren—and therefore safe—as any region of the planet. Colonization of the surface, turgid with ragingly lethal lifeforms, would come later—when the domed keeps could themselves support the effort.

But before that day came, Earth had destroyed itself in a nuclear holocaust which turned the atmosphere's welcoming blue into a hideous white companion star for the sun.

Human life continued in the Keeps of Venus, but the Venerian surface was reserved for the Free Companies and their proxy wars. Holographic dreadnoughts flashed at one another in the final scene of the ceiling decoration—and the looped image reverted to the lifeless chaos which preceded terraforming.

In the ballroom below, couples danced and drank and laughed in brilliant, tinkling voices.

The ramp ended at the balcony which gave access to fifty upper-level rooms. Most of the rooms near the ramp were already marked by the discreet In Use notations which appeared when the inner lock was turned. A few doors were open. Within, servants in livery changed washable couch-covers, disposed of used glasses and drug paraphernalia, and occasionally removed the torn or forgotten undergarments of previous temporary occupants.

"There's an empty bed further along," Brainard's consort said.

The ensign's brain was foggy with alcohol. The woman's pleasant, contralto voice came from a blur of warm flesh, not a form.

She chuckled. "But the night's still young. They'll be lining up before daybreak."

Though there were toilet facilities just off the dance

floor, there was another set at 90° and 270° from where
the ramp joined this level. Brainard and his consort
were nearing the men's room. Male guests stood near
the door, lounging against the balcony or wall; chatting and looking idly about.

There were empty stalls inside. These folk were held
by ennui or inertia, not need. All were civilians. Their
expressions quivered with various shades of envy as they
eyed Brainard and the woman.

A mercenary officer stepped out of the men's
room—Lieutenant Cabot Holman, Brainard's immediate superior. He was a forceful, blocky man, not as
tall as the ensign but heavier in a muscular way. At
the moment, he was flushed with drink.

Brainard nodded with minimal politeness. He
stepped closer to the rail so that Holman could pretend to ignore him if he so desired. The two officers
would never have been friends, even if it hadn't been
for Holman's younger brother. . . .

Holman looked up, saw Brainard, and let his gaze
glance aside like an arrow sparking away from rock.

Holman froze. His red face went livid, then white.
Brainard blinked at him, wondering if the lieutenant
was about to have a seizure from something he had
consumed in the name of entertainment.

"Stephanie, you slut!" Holman shouted. He looked
queasy.

It took Brainard's dazed mind a moment to remember
that his consort had introduced herself as, *"Stephanie—
Stephanie Callahan, dear one."*

"And with the bastard who killed Ted, too!" bellowed
Holman.

People stared. Doors opened around the second
level; folk in the ballroom below craned their necks
for a better view.

"I didn't kill your brother!" Brainard said. He'd

drunk too much. His tone was more of a snarl than his conscious mind had intended.

Holman punched him in the mouth. It felt like being too close to the breech of a recoiling cannon.

Brainard staggered, numb all over. The balcony rail was against the small of his back. The wide arc to his front was a blur of screams and faces filled with wolfish glee.

Another door slammed open. Captain Glenn, Officer in Charge of the Herd's screening forces, stepped onto the balcony. Glenn was stark naked except for his flat uniform hat, covered with gold braid.

"What in the hell is going on out here?" the captain bellowed. Two girls peeked out of the doorway behind him. Neither of them seemed more than pubescent.

Holman knelt on the balcony and put his hands to his face. The knuckles of his right hand were bloody.

"He killed my brother Ted," Holman sobbed; then he vomited onto the floor.

On the ballroom ceiling, the holographic display again formed itself into a ravening jungle.

2

Leaf's mind split into a part that understood what was happening and another part that still believed he could survive. He'd unlatched the access plate to #2 fan and was sprawled within the nacelle when he felt the torpedoboat lift onto her last crest. Air boomed with the braking effect of the skirts.

Leaf's left hand gripped the fan mount while leg muscles locked his boots against K67's starboard rail and the lip of the nacelle opening. His right hand held the multitool with which he had just loosened journals of the fan's back bearing and squirted in microsphere lubricant. The bitch'd shake herself to shrapnel in forty minutes, but that was half an hour longer than she'd last before burning if the motorman did nothing.

Leaf had had to disconnect the hose feeding cool, dry air to his environmental suit before he crawled into the nacelle. The suit's impermeable membrane trapped his sweat and body heat, steaming him like a shrimp dinner.

The climate wouldn't have time to be fatal, though, because Leaf had also unsnapped his safety line.

Leaf dropped his multitool to grip another handful

of rim. The spring lanyard spooled the tool up snugly beneath his right arm. *It* would come through the next few seconds just fine.

The hovercraft dropped, touched a solid surface, and spun with the momentum of more than 40 knots times her mass.

Leaf's existence was a montage in which serial time no longer ruled:

The barrels of the twin machine-guns in the gun tub cut an arc to port, then to starboard, against the white sky. Yee, strapped into the gunner's seat, swung between the weapons like a participant on a carnival ride.

Ensign Brainard sat like a statue, his head visible through the cockpit windscreen. He was shouting something into the interphone, but Leaf could only hear the timbre of the CO's voice in a universal roar too great for even the circuitry of his commo helmet to sort out.

A palm fought with a blackberry at the edge of the jungle. Thorns probed deep into the palm's hard tissues, but its wounds wept a binary sap which smoldered as its chemicals oozed onto the bramble.

K67's starboard quarter struck hard enough to compress #4 fan against a coral head. The blades exploded upward, through the guards and housing. If that fan had been running hot instead of #2, Leaf would be lunchmeat.

The sea was a huge spout of vivid green against the sky. The dismembered head of something reptilian slammed its jaws on another fragment of its body.

Tools, cups, and the holographic image of a naked woman flew from the torpedohouse aft the cockpit. Tech 2 Caffey, the torpedoman, and his striker were harnessed safely into their seats.

Unlike Leaf.

Instinct anticipated the shocks where intellect would have been overwhelmed.

Right boot shifted, right side tight against the edge of the access port—God! it hurt, but if he'd been flung sideways the three inches of a moment before, the lip would have broken his pelvis.

Down, chest flat against the mesh guards and the fan still howling at full revs. Inertia slams down a thousand times harder, bulging the mesh and crushing the breath from the motorman's lungs.

Forward—his arms took the strain and he screams but they *take* the strain. Right side, *again*, and *worse*, but alive. He's still all right. Not great; the inside of his visor is speckled with what looked like mud but was blood from when he banged his nose. Broken bones or just pulled muscles? But . . . alive.

K67 slammed down squarely, compressed what was left of her skirts, and sprang three feet into the air before coming to rest. Leaf had nothing to brace him against the last shock. He flew out of the nacelle like a bomb from the tube of a mortar.

He tumbled in the air. He'd lost his helmet, though he didn't know how: the chin strap was supposed to be strong enough to tow a destroyer. Slime and water splashed to envelope him. It was a moment before Leaf realized that he was no longer moving.

And that he was alive.

Leaf gasped a lungful of air. He screamed it back out because of the pain in his ribs. He lay on his back in a pool, floating easily because of the air trapped in his environmental suit.

There was ten feet of open water in every direction he could see. Jointed reeds grew from the margins of the pond. They bent their spiky tips toward him slowly.

Leaf tried to turn his body. He screamed again and his head bobbed under water. When he came up, eyes bulging with fear, he saw the quick flick-flicker of a tongue through the reeds to his right.

The snake eased the remainder of its head into view.

Leaf heard nervous human voices nearby. The wrecked hovercraft must be close, though he couldn't see it the way he lay in the water. "Guys?" he called softly.

The snake's head was wedge-shaped and the size of a barrel; there must be at least a hundred feet of gray-brown body behind it. A nictitating membrane swept sideways across the one glittering eye that fixed on the motorman.

"Help!" Leaf shouted.

"Good God, man!" Brainard shouted back. "Don't move!"

That was when Leaf saw the spider peering with its eight tiny eyes from the reeds to his left.

The spider extended its long forelegs cautiously, spanning two yards. Their tips were brushes of fine hair which dimpled the surface of the black water but did not sink through it.

Leaf tried to hug himself in fear, but his head started to sink again as soon as his arms moved. He froze, unwilling to close his eyes but terrified by what he saw through them.

He wasn't carrying a sidearm. The multitool could be pressed into service as a weapon, but he'd be underwater sure if he tried to draw it down from its take-up spool.

The snake cocked its head further to the side, interested in the spider's stealthy movement. The forked tongue lapped the air for a taste of its potential rival. The arachnid poised, more still than the gently-lapping water, while the reed tops bent above it.

Men talked behind him, but Leaf couldn't make out the words. They spoke softly, as if to avoid drawing the attention of the two monsters away from Leaf. He heard a squeal as the gun tub was cranked around by hand. The hovercraft's motors must have shut down during the crash.

Neither of the beasts would die easily. If one was shot, both would go berserk. They'd finish Leaf in their death throes, even if a stray bullet didn't get him first.

The motorman's body stuttered in a sequence of trembles, then tensed with pain. Both spasmodic movements were beyond his conscious control.

"Leaf," Ensign Brainard repeated, "whatever you do, don't move. Do you understand?"

"Yessir." His voice was a cracked whisper, but perhaps they saw his lips move.

The rifle shot startled him. The high-velocity bullet missed *everything*. It lifted a column of spray from the far edge of the pool.

God, he's missed!

The snake struck at the water spout. The spider leaped from the other side of the pool to sink its fangs into the reptile's neck, and the gun tub's twin .75-caliber machine-guns laced both creatures with high explosive.

Something wriggled through the air to the motorman. He shouted in fear before he realized what it was—a safety line—and grabbed with both hands. A firm pull dragged him toward land.

Explosive bullets had blown the spider's abdomen away from its cephalothorax, but its mandibles continued to worry the snake's neck. A long burst from Yee's revolver-breech machine-guns walked down the snake's body.

Something clung to Leaf's legs, then slipped away from the smooth fabric of his environmental suit. The water around the blasted, still battling, monsters blurred, then turned pale.

A hand gripped Leaf's hands. He lunged convulsively to the shore, where Officer-Trainee Wilding knelt to spread his weight better over the liquescent bog.

Leaf glanced over his shoulder. A membrane as pink as the inside of a stomach had risen through the water. It enfolded the snake and spider. The torn bodies, still thrashing, dissolved into pink slime which the membrane sucked in.

May 11, 382 AS. 0109 hours.

Leaf sat on a crate of empty bottles, ignoring the whore who tried to entice him by brushing his face with her pink tits. His back leaned against the brothel's piccolo as it blared out—for the twentieth time in a row—a song that had been popular when Leaf was a kid. He could barely hear the words, but he mouthed them by memory: " . . . *Tennessee*. . . . *Tee for Thelma, She made a fool outa me*. . . ."

Leaf closed his eyes. His glass was empty, but he was too drunk to get up and buy another drink. The bottle rims stabbed his buttocks like a bed of blunt needles, but they were a better seat than the slimy floor, and he wasn't sure he was able to stand just now.

The Año Nuevo's ground-floor reception area was stiff with sound. The orders sailors bawled to the tapster behind the semicircular bar were more often than not misheard, but at this time of night it didn't make any difference. Men drank whatever was put before them.

The separate staircases down to the basement and sub-basement were on either side of a low stage. The sub-basement was a credit cheaper, but it was damp and stank like a sewer; if you cared, which most of the Año Nuevo's customers didn't. The evening's floor show was over. The huge holonews display on the wall behind the stage was tuned to a party thrown by the local upper crust.

"Gonna buy me a shotgun wif a great big shiny bar'l...."

The brothel's star turn was a black-haired, black-eyed minx named Susie. She was a tall woman compressed into five feet of height: large breasts and broad hips, but with a distinct waist separating them. She was a looker by local standards, though that wasn't the main reason for her popularity.

Every evening, the girls collected a half- or quarter-credit from each of the customers to pay for Susie's time, and some lucky guy got a freebie on the stage. Tonight, Susie's choice—a sailor from the dreadnought *Elephant*—had already been too drunk to perform effectively. That made the entertainment even better for the half of the brothel's clientele who weren't battleship sailors.

"Gonna shoot that Thelma...," Leaf sang.

Two couples on the stage now were giving a pretty good informal show of their own. If the sailors thought they were going to save a room charge, they were wrong. Above them, glittering party-goers smirked through interviews on the holographic display, their words lost in the general racket.

"...just to see her jump an' fall."

The music, a vibration through the motorman's spine, ended as the piccolo shut off. Leaf sighed with his eyes closed and fumbled in the pocket of his tunic. He still had a few half-credit coins left. He slipped one out and raised it toward the slot above and behind him, moving by practiced reflex.

"Tee for Texas," he mouthed. *"Tee for Tennessee..."*

A hand closed over Leaf's groping hand.

"Go away, honey," he muttered tiredly. "I'm fucked out, believe me."

"I said, are you gonna shut that noise off or am I gonna bust your head?" a voice shouted in his ear.

Leaf's eyes flashed open. He wasn't drunk any more, but his skin was very cold.

The whore had gone to plow more useful fields. Another sailor bent close to the motorman's face. The tally around his cap read *Elephant*, not a big surprise. He was a young fellow, six inches taller than Leaf and muscular. His flush was drink or anger or both.

Almost certainly both.

"Got a problem with something, sonny?" Leaf said as he rose smoothly to his feet. Leaf wasn't shouting, but the general volume of noise had dropped enough that most of those in the reception room could hear him. He let the coin drop to free his hand. "Can't get your dick stiff, maybe?"

This wasn't the sailor from the floor show, but he'd heard the story. He reacted without hesitation, punching Leaf in the face.

Leaf had ten years in the Herd and a lot of bar fights behind him. He shifted his head so that the fist glanced along his jawbone. It would leave a bruise, but for the moment Leaf scarcely noticed it against the rush of alcohol and adrenaline.

He flung himself backward into the piccolo as though the punch had caught him squarely, then sprawled on the floor. If the other sailor was smart, he'd try to put the boot in—and then it was going to get interesting.

He wasn't smart. "And *leave* it fucking off!" the battleship sailor shouted as he turned toward the bar instead of finishing what he'd started. "Flitterboat pussies!"

Leaf came off the floor. The crate of bottles was in his hands, swinging in a sideways arc.

Shouted warnings started the kid's head rotating to see what was happening behind him, but it was already too late. The crate hit him at the center of mass.

Bottles flew out. The impact smashed ribs and flung the victim over the bar. He caromed off the tapster who had already jerked down the alarm lever.

It was too late for that as well. Even before the crate landed, battleship sailors and crewmen from smaller vessels began to fight one another all over the reception area.

Some of the girls joined in, shrieking with fury. It wasn't any business of theirs . . . but then, all the sailors were from the same Free Company.

Leaf ran for the stairs to the sub-basement. He collided with a redhead in a string top which displayed all the little she had. The whore seemed to have lost her client below. She grabbed Leaf with both hands and began mechanically to proposition him.

"Move it, bit'h!" the motorman snarled, realizing that the right side of his jaw was numb. He pulled himself free.

There was an emergency exit from the sub-basement into a drainage tunnel, and this was an emergency by Leaf's standards. In a matter of minutes the Año Nuevo would be full of stormtroopers with truncheons and stun gas, Wyoming Keep's Patrol or the Herd's own shore police. Leaf didn't intend to be around while the authorities sorted out how the fight had started.

The holographic display was still tuned to the upper-crust party. Leaf dived past it, but the voice of the commentator followed him down the stairwell saying, *"And why is Prince Hal wearing the uniform of a high officer in Wysocki's Herd? Because it's his uniform! Yes, really, darlings, the most eligible bachelor in Wyoming Keep is a Free Companion!"*

3

"Wilding," said Brainard, extending a hand over the rail to help the officer-trainee back aboard, "see if you can get a response on the radio. I can't raise a thing."

Wilding was barely able to move after boosting Leaf on board. Heat, the weight of his environmental suit, and the boggy soil into which he sank knee-deep at every step combined crushingly. "Sure," he gasped. *How did you explain to a man like Brainard that other people had limits?* "In a minute. Are the balloons okay?"

Radio communication was as undependable as radar imaging in the charged Venerian atmosphere. The alternatives were long-wave communication through the sea itself, and modulated laser. Long wave was slow, and the apparatus was too heavy to be mounted on a hovercraft. Laser commo was fast and virtually proof against interception, but it was line-of-sight only.

The answer was to raise the transmitter a thousand feet or more above the surface by balloon, bringing distant receivers above the horizon.

Brainard shook his head. "Sorry," he said. "All that gear's gone."

Wilding was exhausted, but the man he had rescued moved like a zombie in a suit twice the proper size. Bozman, the assistant motorman, supported Leaf's bulging body to his station just aft the torpedo controls.

"I got the auxiliary running, chief," Bozman chattered. "We'll have you plugged into the air conditioning soonest."

Leaf's suit dribbled pools of slime on the deck as the motorman moved. "How's the main motors?" he asked.

Wilding found the motorman's words remarkable both for their huskiness and for the fact that they were directed at his regular duties.

"They're fucked," said Caffey in a grim voice. "The commo's fucked. And we're fucked."

The torpedoman had clipped a light machine-gun—his personal weapon, since they weren't stock issue for hovercraft—to the seaward rail. The gun tub was rotated inland, covering the pool fifty feet away where the giant snake and spider had hunted, but no direction was safe.

Brainard glanced at Caffey without speaking. The torpedoman grimaced, then broke eye contact by calling to his striker, "Wheelwright! Bring another drum of ammo."

Wilding slid into the cockpit and reconnected the hose to his environmental suit. The seepage of cool, dry air through the suit's lining steadied his mind before it could make any practical difference to his body.

Brainard had brought the console displays up as soon as the auxiliary drive provided power for them. The radio transmitted an any-station emergency signal; K67's main computer would key the crewmen's commo helmets if there were a response.

There wasn't a damn thing else to do, except check

the balloon ascender gear. The console had a scarlet Not Ready message under that heading.

A glance astern showed why. K67 had been inverted at some point as she spun ashore. The last five feet of the deck had been scraped, carrying away two decoy launchers and the long-range communications apparatus.

For the first time since a cruiser invisible over the horizon began to shell them, Wilding had leisure to consider their situation. Caffey was right. They didn't have a prayer.

K67 lay in a salt marsh inside this nameless island's outer barrier of coral. The coral had shredded the hovercraft's skirts, but that was probably the reason any of them were still alive. A rigid-hulled vessel would have disintegrated on impact, but the tough, flexible skirts had scrubbed away K67's velocity as they abraded.

Air-cushion torpedoboats hung their pair of primary weapons in the plenum chamber. Both torpedoes had been torn from their mountings as K67 bellied into the bog. Their safety mechanisms kept them inert despite the shock.

The torpedoes lay like a pair of broken sticks in the path the hovercraft tore through the vegetation. The body of one had been crushed like a pinched grass-blade, while the warhead of the other lay askew with half its attachment lugs stripped. Hungry reeds nuzzled the weapons in vain.

The warheads contained a nominal thousand pounds of barakite explosive. Their blast was designed to penetrate the main armor belt of a superdreadnought. If either weapon had detonated during the crash, there would have been nothing left of K67 and her crew.

Inshore, the jungle ascended in terraces of dark green toward the peak that the hovercraft's database indicated was a thousand feet above mean sea level.

Mist and the foliage bulging from the slopes prevented Wilding from checking the accuracy of the charts.

Far to seaward, a storm or the broadsides of massed battlefleets thundered. The jungle responded with a fluting cry that seemed even more terrible because of its supernal beauty. Wilding shivered.

"I could maybe get Number One fan spinning, sir," said Leaf. "The blades are dinged, that's all. But we can't pressurize the plenum chamber with just one fan."

"You've studied this stuff, haven't you?" Brainard said.

"There aren't any skirts left to patch, anyhow," Caffey said morosely. He massaged his chest where the crash harness had held him during the multiple impacts. The gesture reminded Wilding of how much his own ribs hurt.

"Where's Holman?" Newton asked. "When's he comin' back for us?"

The coxswain sounded curious rather than aggrieved. He stared out to sea.

There was no sign of K67's consort, but the surface boiled in a natural frenzy. Living things devoured one other and the flesh of creatures the salvos had killed.

"Wilding!" Brainard snapped. "You studied surface life, didn't you? Your file said you did."

Wilding turned around, blinking in surprise. *The CO had been talking to him. . . .*

Brainard's face was hard. Not angry, but lacking any sign of weakness or mercy. The ensign was three calendar years younger than Wilding himself, but Brainard had been born with a soul as solid as the planetary mantle. He belonged here, and maybe the other crewmen did as well; but Hal Wilding would vanish into this environment as swiftly as the tags of bloody froth where the sharks fed.

"Yessir, that's right," Wilding said aloud. He heard

with horror the crisp insouciance with which he clothed his words. It was the only protection he had, and it was no protection at all. "I have some course work in ecology."

Brainard wasn't one of his Twelve Family acquaintances, before whom Prince Hal needed to conceal serious endeavor. "Ah, I completed a degree program, as a matter of fact."

Wilding looked up at the jungle humping into the white sky behind them. "I don't have a great deal of specific knowledge, though. The rate of mutation here is so high that new data is generally obsolete by the time it's catalogued."

"I'll tell you where that bastard Holman is," Caffey muttered to the coxswain. "He's left us here because he's too chickenshit to risk coming ashore to take a look for us."

Brainard turned and pointed his right index finger at the torpedoman. "Drop that," he said quietly. "Nobody's been abandoned."

"That last salvo may have been right on top of them," Wilding suggested. He tried to remember the moments in which the man-made waterspout swelled to engulf K67. "They were—"

"*Drop that!*" Brainard repeated, the syllables sharp as gunshots. Wilding's tongue and heart froze.

"We aren't K70's problem," Brainard continued softly. "We're *our* problem. We're alive, we've got our equipment. So we're going to make things all right."

"We got fuel for three months, just running the auxiliary," Leaf said. His voice was surprisingly perky considering the shape he'd been in minutes before.

"If the auxiliary don't pack it in, you mean," retorted Caffey.

"We should be all right for food," Wilding said, pretending that he didn't believe the torpedoman's gloom was a realistic assessment of their chances. "We can supplement emergency rations with the flesh of most of the animals. Maybe even a few plants."

"The laser communicator can double as a portable," Brainard said, ignoring everyone else's comments. "Is it still functioning?"

"Look, Fish," Leaf said to the torpedoman, "the auxiliary'll still be running after you 'n me 're fertilizer. Anyway, I could rig Number One motor to power the air system."

Wilding unlatched the laser unit and lifted it so that the prongs feeding power were free of the jack on the bottom of the chassis. The self-contained module had its own sighting and stabilization apparatus. It was supposed to be capable of an hour's continuous operation on its integral batteries.

Wilding switched the unit on. It ran its self-test program without hesitation. "Checks out," he said and lowered it into its cradle again. A weight of fifteen pounds made the module portable but not exactly handy.

"Hey!" shouted Yee from the gun tub. "*Hey!*"

Everyone turned to follow the line the twin guns pointed to starboard. Thirty feet from K67, a bubble of methane rose to the surface of the bog and plopped.

Twenty feet beyond, in line with the wrecked torpedoboat, a six-foot dimple in the marsh marked the spot where a previous bubble had burst.

Yee fired a short burst. The muzzle blasts flattened a broad arc of the nearest vegetation. Explosive bullets cracked into the reed tops with dazzling flashes. The gun tub would not depress low enough to rake the semi-solid ground.

"Cease fire!" Brainard ordered. "Cease fire! Everybody get sidearms. We'll wait by the rail for it to surface!"

Reeds smoldered where the bursting charges had ignited them. The air was bitter with the mingled stench of explosives and burning foliage. A gray haze drifted away from the torpedoboat.

Another bubble broke surface ten feet closer.

Caffey struggled to unclamp his machine-gun from the port rail. Leaf, moving without wasted effort, unclipped an automatic rifle from the motormen's station and tossed it to his striker. The short blade clicked from his multitool. Newton and Wheelwright scrambled for their personal weapons. The CO was already pointing his rifle over the rail at a 60° angle.

Wilding wore a pistol as part of his uniform. He knew from his several attempts at qualification firing that the weapon might as well be back at the Herd's shore installation for all the good he could accomplish with it. He ran to the bow, skirting Caffey in a tense pirouette as the torpedoman freed his machine-gun and turned with it.

Wilding's air line disconnected and reeled itself back into the cockpit. The suit's impermeable outer skin slapped him like a wet sandbag. The two decoy dispensers forward had come through K67's grounding without damage. They were simply spigot mortars from which small propellant charges lobbed the decoys.

"Look," one of the crewmen cried, "he's running!"

Wilding wasn't running. There was no place to run.

The decoy was a bomb-shaped projectile weighing about fifty pounds. At the first dispenser, Wilding broke the safety wire which locked the fuze until the dispenser fired. He spun the miniature propeller on the projectile's nose to complete the arming procedure. The decoy was not supposed to burst until it was at least thirty feet from the vessel launching it. . . .

The arming propeller came off in Wilding's hands and tinkled onto the deck, arming the decoy. He lifted the decoy in a bear hug and staggered to the starboard rail with it. He couldn't see past the bulky cylinder.

"Get b—!" he shouted and slammed into the starboard rail. The impact knocked the breath out of his body and tipped the projectile nose-first into the bog.

Brainard grabbed a handful of Wilding's suit and jerked the officer-trainee back to safety as the decoy fell.

The nose of the decoy sank into the soft ground before the bursting charge went off with a *whump*! and drove a pair of binary chemicals together. The mixture expanded as a bubble of heavy gas which formed a skin with the moisture in the air and ground.

The gas was a brilliant purple-gray and so hot that it blistered the hovercraft's refractory plastic hull. At sea the decoy would skitter over the tops of the waves, drawing enemy fire and attention until it cooled and flattened into an iridescent slick. Here—

K67's crew stumbled to the vessel's port side, driven by heat from the swelling decoy. A claw eighteen inches long drove through the glowing boundary layer of decoy and atmosphere, clacked twice, and then withdrew on its jointed arm. The muscles within the crustacean's translucent exoskeleton had already been boiled a bright pink.

Five guns dimpled the decoy's opaque surface with automatic fire.

"Cease fire!" Ensign Brainard ordered again. "We'll need the ammo soon enough."

Wilding got his breath back. He straightened. Brainard released him. The decoy began to ooze sluggishly away from the torpedoboat. It seared a broad track into the reeds behind it.

"All right," said Brainard without emotion. "This boat's shot. That's too bad, but we're still okay ourselves."

He looked from one crewman to the next, his eyes

hard and certain. Wilding held his breath while Brainard's glance rested on him. "We're going to need more height in order to lase a signal to somebody who can rescue us. Since we don't have the ascender apparatus any more, we're going to climb that mountain."

He nodded in the direction of the island's hidden peak.

"God almighty, sir!" Caffey gasped. "We can't march through that jungle. Nobody could!"

Brainard looked at the torpedoman. The ensign's face was as calm as the sea, now that the feeding frenzy had burned itself out.

"No, Fish," Brainard said. "We're going to do it. Because that's what we have to do to survive."

November 6, 381 AS. 1500 hours.

"I don't think," said the Callahan, a man of fifty whose features were as smooth and handsome as the blade of a dress dagger, "that we need wait for the others."

His finger brushed a control hidden in a tabletop carved from a single mother-of-pearl sheet. The chamber's armored door slid shut, separating the Council of the Twelve Families from the crowd of servants in the anteroom.

The panel staggered as it mated with the slot inlet in the jamb. The machinery made a grunching sound.

Hal Wilding looked around the council chamber, cloaking his disgust beneath his usual sardonic smile. Nine of the twelve chairs around the circular table were occupied, but in three cases the occupant was only physically present.

The McLain was senile.

After a series of brutal tongue-lashings by the

Callahan, the Hinson had learned to keep his mouth shut during council meetings; a success of some degree for a man with an IQ of 70, but a dog could have been trained more easily.

The Platt had mixed recreational drugs in an unfortunate combination. For the past ten years he had little more brain activity than a wax dummy. His family continued to send him to council meetings, because if they acted to remove their titular head, they would be faced with an internal struggle for succession.

The Wilding's seat was filled by the eldest son of the House. . . .

"I called this meeting when I saw the catch projections for the next twelve months," said the Callahan with his usual lack of ceremony. "They can be expected to drop to sixty percent of their current levels in that time—and current levels are already a third down on really satisfactory quantities."

The Galbraith frowned and fluffed his lace shirt out from beneath the sleeves of his frock coat. "Can't we build more netters and bring in more food, then?" he asked.

"That's the problem, you see, Galbraith," Wilding said. "We're already overfishing our grounds. That's the main reason the stocks have crashed."

The Callahan nodded. "Yes, that's correct," he said. "The problem is with empty holds, not lack of netting capacity."

Whenever the Callahan looked at Wilding, it was with cool appraisal for a potential rival. Wilding understood the attitude very well.

Wilding smiled coldly. With the rate of mutation and adaptive radiation on this planet, it was easy to imagine the appearance of life forms able to prey upon even the huge submarine netters which supplied the keeps with fish.

"Well, it's not as though anybody's going to starve, is it?" the Penrose said. "There'll still be plenty of vegetable protein."

"It's not starvation we need to worry about, it's riots," said the Callahan.

"You'd riot too, Penrose, if you had nothing to eat but processed algae," gibed the Galbraith.

The Penrose chuckled and patted the vest over his swollen belly. "No, no," he said. "We certainly can't permit that. What's the alternative?" He was looking at the Callahan.

Wilding interjected crisply, "We could colonize that land. *That* would provide additional resources." Wilding felt cold. He hadn't been consciously aware of what he was going to say until the words were out of his mouth. As soon as he spoke, he realized that the substrata of his mind had planned the statement from the moment he decided to attend the council meeting.

He wasn't sure of what response he expected. What he got was averted faces from everyone in the room except the Callahan.

The Callahan said in an icy voice, "Master Wilding, if you wish to dance through life, that is your right. You do *not* have the right to interfere with those of us who are keeping the system going."

The two men stared at one another. At last, Wilding shot his cuff, withdrew a snuffbox carved from a block of turquoise, and snorted a pinch from the crease of his hand and thumb.

"I believe the best course is to send our netters into the grounds of Asturias Keep," the Callahan resumed. "That will mean war within six months, so I suggest we start negotiations with one of the mercenary companies at once."

"Wysocki's Herd did a good job for us three years ago," the Galbraith said. "Shall we try them again?"

"I'm not sure six months is soon enough," said the Penrose, frowning. "The shortages will be obvious well before then. Perhaps we ought to speed matters up by leaking our plans directly to Asturias, rather than letting them learn when our netters are spotted."

"Oh, I believe the time frame should be adequate," said the Callahan. "We'll just need to inflate all their initial statements before we release them to the public. Say, three months before Asturias realizes what we're doing, and another three months of drawing out negotiations before it comes to war."

The Dahlgren was by far the eldest of the functional council members, but he lacked the drive that made the Callahan a leader. He nodded and said, "Yes, that's the better course. Twice the effect for the cost, very practical."

"I fail to see the practicality," said Wilding in tones of chilled steel, "since Asturias Keep has almost certainly overfished its own grounds as badly as we have ours. We need to expand our sources of sup—"

"I'm afraid you've missed the point, *boy*," said the Callahan. "The war emergency will take the mob's attention off the shortages. Shortages will be expected, in fact. Then, in the six months or so that our grounds go uncropped, the stocks will rebuild—whether or not the netters bring an ounce of protein from Asturias' grounds."

"I thought in past years," said Wilding, enunciating perfectly and locking his glare with that of the Callahan, "that Wyoming Keep's apparent lack of direction was because I heard council decisions filtered through my father's perceptions." He sniffed. "Or lack of perceptions. But I now realize that he was perfectly accurate. If this is an example of the policy of the Twelve Families, then the policy of the Twelve Families is bankrupt. Manipulating the common people to accept wretched conditions is pointless when we could be improving those conditions."

"You know, *boy* . . . ," the Callahan snarled.

All eyes in the council chamber were on Wilding. Some expressions were hot, some cold; all were full of hatred.

" . . . when I was informed that you would be representing your family, I was pleased." The Callahan nodded around the table. "Yes, pleased. Because I foolishly thought that you might be turning over a new leaf. I see now that I was wrong. You're simply a destructive dilettante, looking for something new to smash."

"You should let your father come in the future," said the Penrose. "After all, all the Wilding did was drool—and that was easy enough for the servants to clean up after the meetings."

Wilding stood. His whole body was trembling. He could not have spoken, even if he could think of something to say.

"You know, Prince Hal," said the Galbraith, "if you're so concerned about injustice to the common people, you should give up your perquisites and join them. Once you acclimate, I suspect you'll find the mob's round of drink, drugs, and sex much the same as that of your own circle."

Wilding began walking toward the door. He could not see for the red blur blindfolding him, but he heard the groan of the armored panel start to open.

On the threshold, with his back to the council, Wilding paused to shake imaginary dust from the tails of his frock coat.

4

From the deck Brainard looked at the wall of jungle beyond the tide-swept marsh. Vines, branches, and flowers like bright sucking mouths entwined in twisted agony.

There was movement. A stand of slender, black-trunked trees quivered back instead of leaning toward the humans over the salt-resistant reeds.

"What's happening with them?" said Wheelwright. "The trees."

That was the question that Brainard was afraid to ask. Brainard didn't know anything about the situation—except that he was terrified of having to think beyond the immediate next step.

"Morning stars," said OT Wilding coolly. "Plants can't normally move as fast as animals, even here, but these store energy by drawing back their stems like springs. When we come within fifty feet, they'll snap forward and grab us with the spikes in their branches."

"The edge of the jungle is worse than anything we'll find inside it," Brainard said. "It's like a warship's armor. Once we penetrate the shell, we'll be all right."

To build and maintain their bases, the Herd and

other Free Companies fought a constant war against nature. There had been lectures on surface life forms during training, but Brainard had pretty much dozed through them.

Active duty hadn't given him any practical experience either. Large vessels, dreadnoughts and cruisers, provided the perimeter guards who battled the jungle's attempts to retake Base Hafner.

The line Brainard parroted was the only thing he remembered from the lectures. The words sounded empty.

Leaf frowned in puzzlement. A scar trailed up the little motorman's left cheek and into his hair where it continued as a streak of white. "How can we get through that, sir? We got two cutting bars and our knives."

He wasn't arguing. He just wanted an explanation of a plan that his mind couldn't make practicable.

"We can burn it," said Caffey unexpectedly.

"Go on, Fish," Brainard said. His face was expressionless; his mind was empty of useful ideas.

"It takes a fuze to make barakite explode," the torpedoman said. "If you just light a wad of it, it burns like the fires of Hell. And we've got a ton of the stuff we can take outa them two." He thumbed in the direction of the crumpled torpedoes.

Brainard nodded. "Right," he said. "Caffey and Wheelwright, begin removing the warheads. Newton— no, I'll guard you myself. Wilding—"

"Sir, we can't carry much, just the two of us," Wheelwright blurted.

"Boz and me'll lift a deck panel," Leaf volunteered. His boot tapped the ribbed sheets of radar-absorbant plastic which covered the hovercraft's upper surfaces. "We'll bend the end up and make a skid. You can dump the stuff on that."

"Wait," Brainard said. He thought for a moment. Barakite explosive was a white, doughy substance, as seemingly harmless as so much taffy. He'd seen what happened to a warship when a barakite torpedo exploded in her belly, though. . . .

"Just take the backplate off one of the warheads," he said. "The casing'll direct the flames out, like a flamethrower."

"Jeez, we better make sure we unscrew the fuze first!" Wheelwright gasped.

"Yes, you had better," said OT Wilding with a twist of his lips.

"Wilding," Brainard continued, "take charge of loading useful items into packs. Weapons, ammunition, food if you think we'll need it. You're the environmental expert. Remember that we'll carry loose barakite from the other warhead. We may need it farther along." He swallowed. "I'll take the communicator myself," he said.

The laser communicator was their one hope of rescue. With that solid security in his hands, Brainard thought he might be able to get through the hours until they reached the peak. Might.

Everybody looked at him. "Caffey, what are you waiting for?" he snapped. "Let's move!"

The two torpedomen swung immediately to the hovercraft's rail. Caffey snubbed up at the end of the hose connected to his environmental suit and paused. He looked back at Brainard.

Next problem. One at a time. "Until we're through the, the frontal wall of the jungle," Brainard said, "you can wear your suits or not as you choose. After that, they'll be too heavy and confining. We'll leave them."

They all *stared* at him. The tough suits were armor, real armor against the lethal surface environment, but men wearing them couldn't carry a load as much as a hundred yards with the air hoses disconnected.

"I'm going to take mine off now," said Brainard. His body began to obey his mouth, opening the catches and taking the direct shock of heat and saturated humidity. His mind watched the events as if they were taking place on the holonews.

Caffey unclipped his hose and clambered over the rail, followed by his striker. For the grace period Brainard had offered them, the discomfort of a disconnected suit was more bearable than facing the surface unprotected.

Leaf knelt and began cutting the tack welds with his multitool. The motorman directed Bozman as if his assistant were a barely-sentient tool himself.

Wilding gave orders in a clear, precise voice, separating into manageable loads the objects that would keep the crew alive during its trek. Everything was under control.

Brainard stepped out of his suit. He felt naked and afraid. He jumped quickly from the deck before he could lose his nerve.

Stupid. He sank to mid-calf in the muck. Wheelwright glanced back. Men were looking at him from deck also.

"Get on with—" Brainard called.

A leech the length of Brainard's arm rose from the mud. It twisted toward his face. It was green with white stripes the length of its body, and its mouth was a black pit.

Brainard tried to scream but his tongue stuck to the roof of his mouth. He thrust out with the rifle in his hands. The creature engulfed the weapon's muzzle in a hideous sexual parody.

Brainard pulled the trigger and nothing happened, *nothing happened*! He jerked the rifle upward convulsively. The leech clung for a moment, then slipped off and writhed through an arc over the marsh. A tube worm shot from its armored housing near the shore and snatched the leech while it was still in the air.

Brainard stared at his rifle. The selector was still on Safe. He rotated it to Automatic and began to drag his legs forward. He was almost blind from fear. He knew that unless he moved at once, he would be unable to move ever again.

"Newton," ordered Wilding, "I told you to bring the remaining bandoliers from the arms locker. Get moving!"

It was a good thing they had Wilding along. He'd been born to lead. Most officer-trainees were kids who went blind with fear in a crisis. . . .

July 12, 381 AS. 0933 hours.

"I've brought your new XO, Tonello," Lieutenant Holman called to the officer bent over in the cockpit of the hovercraft docked on a shallowly-submerged platform.

Holman prodded Officer-Trainee Brainard between the shoulderblades. Brainard, his hard-copy files clutched in his hands, hopped convulsively from the quay to the vessel. The gray deck shivered beneath his sudden weight. The hovercraft was 60 feet long and 28 feet across the beam, but her mass was deceptively slight because most of the volume was the empty plenum chamber.

Lieutenant Tonello straightened with an engaging smile and extended his hand out of the cockpit well. He was a lanky man several inches taller than Brainard's own five-foot-eleven. "Welcome aboard K67—" his eyes read the name tape sewn over the left breast pocket of Brainard's utilities "—Brainard. You had three months aboard the *Kudu*, I believe?"

Tonello's grip was firm, but he didn't play finger-crushing games the way Lieutenant Holman had done half an hour earlier. Brainard handed his new CO his file with some embarrassment. "Ah, no sir," he said. "I'm straight out of training school."

"That was Officer-Trainee Suchert," Holman said from the quay. "He, ah, went to K44 instead."

A score of small craft, both air-cushion and hydro-foils, were moored to either side of the quay. No combat aircraft was survivable in an environment of the beam weapons and railguns mounted on capital ships. High-speed torpedocraft could blend closely enough against the sea to remain effective. They carried out the reconnaissance and light-attack duties which would once have been detailed to aircraft.

It was a dangerous job—but war is risk, and no man is immortal.

A head watched Brainard from K67's gun tub, and another popped out of a hatch forward that must give access to the plenum chamber. Enlisted members of the hovercraft's crew were sizing up the new junior officer.

Lieutenant Tonello riffled through Brainard's file, then glanced up at Holman with a thin smile. "Wanted somebody with experience to hold your brother's hand, did you, Holman? Well, that's all right with me. Brainard here's got two years of technical school behind him. Just the sort a flitterboat needs."

Holman's chin lifted. "Ted doesn't need anybody to hold his hand," he snapped.

"I didn't say he did," Tonello remarked, looking down as if he were going through Brainard's file more carefully. "*I* didn't say it."

Holman spun on his heel. He strode down the quay

to where K44 was moored. The scar-faced man looking from the plenum chamber grinned at Brainard,
turned his head, and spit into the oil-rainbowed
water of Herd Harbor.

Tonello dropped Brainard's file on a console and
grinned again. "What do you know about hovercraft,
Brainard?" he asked.

"Not much, sir," Brainard said, wishing there were
some way he could lie and expect to get away with it.
He'd assumed his first assignment would be to a ship
whose scores or hundreds of crewmen could cover for
his own inexperience. "Just that you've got eight-man
crews."

"And two torpedoes, Brainard," the lieutenant said.
He was still smiling, but his lips now had the hard
curve of a fighting axe. "Don't forget those. Because
if we do our jobs right, the other side won't forget
them." Tonello's expression softened again. "No problem. I'll give you the grand tour." He gestured forward.
"That's Yee at the gun tub," he explained. "If a mission goes perfectly, we'll get in unobserved and he
won't fire a shot."

"Fat chance," remarked one of the men who had
risen from the scuttle aft the cockpit.

"If things don't go perfectly," Tonello continued in
an equable voice, "then nobody *likes* a faceful of
tracer fired from twin seventy-fives. If our problem's
with a boat more or less our size, Yee may well settle
matters."

Tonello turned to indicate the man who had
just spoken. "That's Tech Two Caffey," he said, "our
torpedoman. If I do my job, the fish'll track to their
target by themselves. Caffey and his striker are there
in case I'm not perfect. Their station's got imaging and
control along fiber-optics cables, so they can thread the
torpedoes through the eye of a needle if they've got to."

"A big fucking needle," the torpedoman grunted, but he was obviously pleased.

"And that's Tech Two Leaf," the lieutenant said, turning toward the scarred fellow looking out of the plenum chamber. "When he's on duty, he's the best motorman in the Herd—"

Leaf grinned.

"—and when he's off duty, he's my worst discipline problem," Tonello continued—and the motorman continued to grin. "What are you working on, Leaf?"

"Replacing the impeller on Number One fan, sir," Leaf said. "I got Newton and Bozman in the water wearing suits, while I tighten fittings." He waved a multitool. "RHIP."

"You remember that when you go on leave, Leaf," Tonello said. "Because the next time you're caught in a bar fight, you'll have neither rank nor privileges. I promise."

Leaf gave a mocking salute with his multitool, then ducked out of sight.

Quietly, so that none of the enlisted men could hear, Tonello said, "We've got four fans to float us on a bubble of air and drive us. If one goes out, we can still maneuver, but we're sluggish and a target for anybody with so much as a popgun." He nodded forward. "In the eighteen months Leaf has been motorman, K67 has never lost a fan to maintenance problems." Tonello continued in a normal voice, "Your station's here, Brainard." He pointed to the left of the three seats across the cockpit. "In action, your primary responsibilities are navigation and electronic countermeasures, but you may be called on to do *any* job on the vessel, so you have to know every man's duties."

The lieutenant gave his axe-blade smile again. "In particular," he said, "you may have to command the vessel if something happens to your commanding officer. So stay alert, hey?"

He clasped Brainard's wrist and gave it a gentle shake for emphasis.

Brainard would have swallowed, but the lump in his throat was too big.

5

Leaf had known plenty of brave men—

"Keep her moving!" ordered Ensign Brainard, darting quick glances in all directions as he walked ahead of the six-man crew at the draglines. Leaf was the man nearest the skid on the left side. "Don't lose your momentum!"

—but he'd never met somebody as willing to hang his balls on the wall as Brainard. *Don't waste ammo*, he says, so when a leech goes for *him*, he don't even bother to shoot it, just swats it away.

"Sir, should I . . . ?" Yee called from behind them, in K67's gun tub.

Leaf looked up. Sweat blurred his vision, but if those morning stars weren't within the fifty feet Wilding gave as their trigger range, they were sure damned close to it.

Only thing was, Brainard was out in front.

"Not yet!" the CO said.

They were using safety lines as drag ropes for the skid. Reeds flattened into the slippery ooze, creating a perfectly lubricated surface over which to pull the massive warhead—but the same muck gave piss-poor traction to the boots of the men tugging the sucker toward the wall of jungle.

Leaf wheezed and staggered in the discomfort of his heavy suit. It didn't seem to him that he was pulling his weight, but somebody among the six of them must be doing the job. The skid moved, and the twisted trees were goddam close.

At least they hadn't had problems with large animals. Leaf had been raised in Block 81 of Wisconsin Keep, a slum; he understood territories. The snake and spider he'd attracted had kept this stretch of marsh to themselves. There hadn't been enough time since the local bosses got the chop for replacements to take over.

The crew gave the pond itself a wide berth. Whatever lived on its bottom had been given a big enough meal to occupy it for a while, anyhow.

"Mr Brainard?" gasped Wilding, on the far end of Leaf's rope. "I think—"

Brainard had offered to take a rope and let Wilding control the operation. The officer-trainee refused, saying he'd be useless as a guard because he couldn't shoot. Leaf didn't figure a pansy like Wilding'd do much good on the line, either; but at least he was trying.

"Right," ordered Brainard. "Everybody down. Yee!"

Leaf flattened. He clapped his hands over his ears and opened his mouth. The man beside him, Newton, was still upright. He either hadn't heard the order or—more likely with Newton—hadn't understood it.

Leaf grabbed the butt of the coxswain's slung rifle and tugged it hard. Wilding must have been pulling from the other side, because Newton flopped down an instant before Yee's twin seventy-fives cut loose over their heads.

Even fifty feet away, the big guns' muzzle blasts punished bare skin and stabbed agony through the ear

Leaf had uncovered to save Newton. The ballistic crack of the supersonic bullets snapping just overhead was worse for the motorman's nerves.

These rounds were aimed high deliberately. Too often in Leaf's small-boat service, a *snap!snap!snap!* meant the enemy was about to correct his sight picture and put his next burst through your hull.

Ropes of brilliant scarlet tracers raked the edge of the jungle, concentrating as planned on the copse of morning stars. The explosive bullets went off with white flashes against the black bark, hurling bits of wood in all directions.

The explosions released tension within the trunks. Sawed-off boles leaped into the air. Their spiky branches slashed at one another during the moments it took them to fall.

The guns scythed a 10° arc through the living barrier, then stuttered into silence. Yee had shot off the entire contents of his ammo drums. Powder gases, explosive residues, and the thick smoke of green vegetation burning hung in the air. A beetle the size of a cheap apartment stepped into the cut, then rushed away through a path it tore for itself.

"Come on!" Brainard shouted. His voice chimed through the ringing in the motorman's left ear. "Move! Move! Move!"

Leaf got up. For an instant he thought he was having difficulty because he was exhausted; then he noticed that during the time he hugged the ground, reeds had grown about him. Their tips probed at the folds of the environmental suit. He swore and tore himself free.

"Come on!" the CO repeated, reaching back to grip the upturned front of the skid. "Before something else moves in!"

Leaf threw his weight against the rope. The skid had begun to sink into the marsh. They got it moving again, somehow. The warhead's weight had one advantage: it dimpled the plastic decking into a cradle, so there was no risk that the burden would roll off the skid.

Ten feet. Twenty feet. A shrapnel-pithed frog, three feet long with lips of saw-edged bone, flopped in a ragged circle at the edge of the jungle in front of them. A dozen blood-sucking insects gripped it. An ilex tree stabbed a branch down from the canopy, harpooned the frog, and withdrew more slowly with its prey.

If the frog had not been there—

"That's enough!" Brainard ordered. "Go back, get your packs, and prepare to move out. Watch yourselves!"

He looked at the motorman. "Leaf, light the warhead. But *don't* get in the way."

In order to give himself a moment to catch his breath, Leaf deliberately fumbled with the multitool slung beneath his armpit. The hot, humid air his lungs dragged in wasn't much help. The suit suffocated him, but it was his only hope of staying alive. . . .

The warhead was a black steel dome twenty-three inches in diameter. It lay sideways on the skid with its flat base pointing in the direction of the jungle. Caffey and Wheelwright had unbolted the thin baseplate, exposing the cream-colored barakite.

They'd also removed the fuze from its pocket in the nose.

Heat alone wouldn't set off barakite. Heat *would* set off the booster charge in the fuze, and *that* would detonate the unburned portion of the barakite. The blast would kick what was left of the hovercraft back out to sea, let alone what it did to the crew.

The motorman's powered multitool was a compact assortment of grippers, drivers, cutters—and an arc welder. Leaf snapped the arc live and touched it to the upper surface of the exposed barakite.

The white spark went blue. A puff of vapor spurted from the explosive. Leaf stepped aside.

Not far enough. Ensign Brainard grabbed his shoulder and pulled him, just in time.

A billow of flame with a blue heart roared outward in all directions. The barakite burned back so that the casing could direct the blaze. After a moment, it steadied into a forward-rushing jet. Combustion products from the explosive and the plasticizer which made it malleable boiled outward in a vast white cloud.

"Don't breathe that!" the CO shouted from a vast distance. He released Leaf's shoulder and strode back toward the packs waiting on the torpedoboat's deck.

Leaf didn't move. He had sucked in a double lungful of the poisonous vapors. He viewed his world from multiple viewpoints.

The initial gush of fire baked a wide fan of marsh to the consistency of a cracked brick. The reeds had vanished. Now that the flames had steadied, green tendrils were already breaking their way to the surface at the fringes of the cleared area.

The warhead was designed to release all its energy in a microsecond flash, shattering battleship armor and sending a spout of seawater a thousand feet in the air. When the barakite was ignited instead of being detonated, the energy release spread over a minute of furious burning—but there was just as much energy involved.

A twenty-three inch hose of blue-white flame roared into the jungle. It vaporized everything in its direct path and shriveled vegetation ten feet to either side.

Leaf watched:

A man-sized salamander lunged up as the concealing leaf mold burned away. It bit at the gout of flame as though it were a quivering serpent. The salamander's head vanished in the 2,000° heat, but the tail and body writhed away.

Reeds, stunned by the fire's temperature, recovered enough to squirm over Leaf's boots. They were looking for entrance to his flesh as he stood transfixed.

A bright golden reptile sailed from a tree top and performed three consecutive loops. The diameter of the loops increased as the creature's feathery scales burned away. It finally plunged toward the sea, trailing smoke behind it.

Crewmen caught the packs Yee tossed them from the hovercraft's deck. They began to waddle toward the jungle again.

Marshy soil humped a few inches upward in a line that extended toward Leaf at the speed of a slow walk. Reeds bowed aside from the intrusion among their roots.

"Leaf!" Ensign Brainard shouted from the hovercraft. "Are you all right?"

A free-standing walnut tree burned furiously on the side toward the devastation pouring from the warhead. Its branches flailed downward, stabbing the flames with hollow tips through which herbicide squirted. This enemy could not be poisoned. The branches added fuel to the self-devouring blaze.

OT Wilding dropped his pack and began to run toward Leaf. He tugged his pistol awkwardly from its holster.

Most of the barakite had burned. The tongue of flame shrank back and curled, like a tiger clearing away traces of a recent meal.

Leaf's boots had sunk six inches into the muck. The line of raised soil was within a yard of him.

Wilding fired into the ground. He was almost close enough to touch his target. The first bullet splashed mud a hand's breadth from the motorman's ankle; the second round was lost somewhere in the unburned jungle.

The third shot punched through the side of the mound. Six feet of mud slid upward from an iridescent surface. Blunt horns extended from the front end as the creature nuzzled the oozing bullet wound.

Leaf came to in an eyeblink. Suction and the questing reeds gripped his feet firmly. He triggered the welding arc of his multitool and raked it in a long line across the slimy surface of the monster.

Flesh blackened and shriveled, twisting the creature into a writhing knot. A tongue armed with glittering conical teeth extended from the mouth.

Reed-tops touched the body and clung, sucking greedily.

"Mole slug," Wilding wheezed. He grabbed the motorman's shoulder to balance himself. His pistol wavered in a dangerous circle that included the feet of both men. "Ah, are you okay?"

Leaf bent and seared the vegetation away from his boots. "Yeah," he said, "I'm fine. I'm great."

His mouth was dry. He chewed his cheeks and tongue to release the juices. The warhead had burned out. A breeze carried the remaining fumes toward the jungle.

"I'm as good," Leaf said deliberately, "as I've been since I joined this fucking outfit."

April 1, 372 AS. 2214 hours.

The hand-lettered sign outside the door announced that Enrique's Bar was closed for a private party. One of the neighborhood regulars rattled the latch anyway. His eye appeared at the small triangular window in the door panel. When he saw that the "private party" was a Free Company's recruiting drive, the man vanished as if whipped away by demons.

Inside, the woman who writhed on top of the bar wore nothing. Her hair was blond. It was held in a high, drifting fan by a process that must have cost as much as a drug dealer in Block 81 earned in a week.

The woman's face was aristocratically beautiful, but her eyes were a million miles away. She rotated slowly, ignoring the thirty-odd young men crowded into the room.

The handsome lieutenant wore a row of medal ribbons on the right breast. Over the left pocket was a nametag reading CONGREVE, in blue letters on silver to match the color scheme of his uniform. "Well, I must have made a mistake," he said in a sneering drawl. "I thought there were men here, but *men* wouldn't leave a poor girl in that state."

Congreve leaned against the bar in a pose of false relaxation. An electronic data file was open beside him. He watched everything in the room from beneath drooping eyelids.

Tub Caffey stood up suddenly. His brother-in-law tried to pull him back to the table. All the guys on that side of the bar ran with the 3d Level gang.

"I'll give the bitch what she needs!" Caffey muttered. He headed straight for the woman. He could have been on the other side of Venus for all the notice she took of him.

Leaf was the only member of the 5th Level gang in the bar tonight. He knew Caffey pretty well. His index finger absently traced the knife scar up his cheek to his hairline.

Lieutenant Congreve stepped between Caffey and the woman. Jessamyn, the senior sergeant who worked the floor with Congreve, moved his big body between the potential recruit and the friends who might have other ideas for him.

"Here you go, lads," Jessamyn said, holding out three puce applicators on the back of his left hand. The knuckles of the clenched fist on which the drugs balanced were a mass of white scar tissue. "Let's all stay happy, shall we?"

Caffey's brother-in-law and the two men who had jumped up at the same time hesitated, then accepted the applicators and sat down again. Jessamyn smiled. His front teeth had been replaced by metal the cold blue-gray of a gun barrel.

Caffey laboriously signed the screen of the data file. The imager built into the lieutenant's signet ring had already snapped the recruit's retinal prints and encoded them into the electronic contract.

Congreve tapped the woman's instep with a finger. "Back room, Kimberly," he said. He opened the bar's swinging gate so that the new recruit could stumble through.

The woman stepped down and walked through the door into what was normally Enrique's private office and storage area. She didn't look behind her.

Caffey collided with the redhead who came out of the back room as the blonde entered it. The door closed.

Someone moved close to Leaf. He looked to his side and saw the sergeant. "Here you go," the mercenary said. He offered a three-striped mauve applicator in the middle of his left palm.

Leaf squinted at it. He didn't recognize the markings. "What's this?" he demanded.

The redhead mounted the bar and began a slow dance. Her diaphanous garments concealed nothing, but she used the floor-brushing length of her own hair as a curtain to display and reveal alternately.

"Tsk," said Jessamyn. "A good time, lad, that's what it is."

The big noncom touched the applicator to the inside of his left elbow and squeezed, releasing the contents into his bloodstream. He turned his hand palm down, then up again with another applicator on it in a feat of minor legerdemain.

Leaf flushed and took the drug.

The redhead turned her back. Her long-fingered hands now lay on the cheeks of her buttocks, spreading and closing the white flesh. Her fingernails were the color of fresh blood.

"The girls look like they just stepped off a holo-screen," Leaf whispered.

The familiar barroom had a glow over it now. Everything blurred except for the woman at whom he stared. She faced the audience again. Her left hand was behind her back; her right was in front of her. She was manipulating herself with her index fingers.

The woman's pupils were dilated so wide that the color of her irises was indeterminable.

"They've been on the holos, often enough," Jessamyn murmured. "And at the very best parties, they have. Ashley, there, she's a Callahan from Wyoming Keep, she is. That's one of the best families there."

"Who'll be man enough to give little Ashley what she needs?" Lieutenant Congreve asked in a cajoling tone. "You can see how she's looking forward to meeting a real man."

Jessamyn put a big, gentle hand on Leaf's shoulder. "I can see you're a hard one, lad," the mercenary said. "She likes that, I can tell you. All her sort like that."

There was a tinge of bitter sadness in Jessamyn's voice. Leaf heard the tone, but it didn't matter any more.

He got up. His legs propelled him toward the woman in the center of a rosy haze.

6

"Let's go, let's go!" Brainard ordered. "Newton, carry your pack, don't try to sling it. You'll be taking off your suit in a hundred feet and you can put the pack on then."

The coxswain blinked at him. He made one last, half-hearted attempt to thrust his arms, doubled in size by the baggy fabric of his environmental suit, through straps which could not possibly hold them.

The walnut tree blazed in the center of the area its poison had cleared. The ferns and bamboo in the warhead's direct line had vanished; those on the edges now smoldered and struggled to pump life into the shrivelled foliage before undamaged neighbors strangled them.

Bright green shoots speared up from the devastated swath.

Footlockers, like bunks and air-conditioned quarters, were for the crews of major fleet elements. The personal gear of a crewman aboard a hovercraft was limited to the contents of a .8-cubic foot backpack which could be hung, slung, or stuffed into what little space the flitterboats offered.

Now the packs were stuffed with dried food, ammunition, and wads of doughy barakite scooped from the warhead of the second torpedo. Brainard didn't know how much good the explosive was going to be, but he knew they needed *something*.

"These black balls on the soil," Wilding called. He pointed to a sphere the size of a snooker ball. There were dozens of them, obvious against soil from which all the cover had been burned away. "Leave them alone. *Don't* for any reason touch them!"

Wilding ought to be in charge. He was educated, so he knew the environment. To Brainard, it was all a lethal blur. He was afraid to focus on anything except the peak that was his goal . . . and the peak was invisible, merely something taken on faith from the charts.

K67 hadn't been equipped to support her crew on an overland trek. The rifles and Caffrey's slightly heavier machine-gun were the security blankets with which men convinced themselves that they wouldn't be helpless against enemy gunboats if the twin seventy-fives were put out of action.

OT Wilding had only a pistol. Wilding claimed he couldn't hit anything with it, but Brainard had seen the aristocrat nail the slug while he was running to save Leaf.

As for Leaf. . . .

"Leaf, do you want my pistol?" Brainard said aloud. The handgun was part of an officer's insignia of rank, but Brainard also brought a rifle and bandolier of magazines aboard K67.

The motorman carried his pack at arm's length in one hand and his multitool in the other. He looked at the ensign. Leaf's complexion was sallow beneath its tan. "Naw, I got this," he said and waved the multitool.

"All right, but you're welcome to something that'll shoot," Brainard said.

Leaf resumed his trudge forward. "This'll do for me," he muttered.

Brainard brought up the rear while OT Wilding led the crew through the flame-cleared corridor. They hadn't discussed the arrangements, it just happened that way. Wilding knew what he was doing . . . and he was a *born* leader, never mind rank.

Brainard remembered to step around one of the black spheres in the path. A shoot which had broken through the baked surface nearby nuzzled the sphere, preparing to rip through the husk and suck whatever nourishment was within.

The sphere exploded with a puff of steam. Barbed rootlets lashed in all directions. Some of them pierced the earth; others seized the shoot that had triggered the sphere's opening.

"Everything all right?" Wilding called from the front of the line.

"A couple plants trying to eat each other," Brainard shouted back.

He tried to look behind him while he still watched where he put his feet. There were too many things he *had* to see. Even though he'd taken off his environmental suit, his backpack and the laser communicator strapped to his chest restricted his movements.

"Fern spores," Wilding explained. "They get an extra growth spurt from whatever sets them off."

A man's foot would be better a better meal than a bamboo sprout. Sea boots weren't designed to stop steam-driven clusters of needle-sharp roots.

They had to climb to high ground and call for rescue. That was all Brainard knew.

Wilding reached the far end of the flames' hundred-yard path, to where the vegetation was seared but not consumed. Just as the lecturer said, the jungle floor was much more open than that of the unpierced wall, where competition for the abundant light created a solid expanse of foliage.

Brainard looked up. The deadly struggle of branch and vine in the canopy hundreds of feet overhead was the best protection available to men in dim corridors among the trunks beneath. Green shapes moved above him, striving to absorb every needle of sunlight before it could benefit the leaves of rivals below.

"All right," Brainard ordered. "Get your suits off, two at a time. Caffey and Leaf."

The chiefs looked at Brainard, then looked away. Caffey began slowly to unseal his protective garment.

"Now!" Brainard snapped. They would collapse in the first half mile if they tried to climb in the heavy suits. They would die, and he would die with them. . . .

"Sir," begged the motorman. "I'll wear mine, okay? It's all that saved me when, when that pond ate the snake and sp-sp-spider."

"What saved you then, sailor," Wilding said in a tone like a blade of ice, "was obeying your CO's orders to lie still until we could divert your neighbors and pull you clear. You will obey him now—because we can't afford to let you die the way you want to do. *Do* you understand?"

"Fuck," whispered Leaf. "Fuck it all." He released his multitool on its spring lanyard. He began stripping off his suit. His eyes were closed.

Brainard turned, to keep watch and to hide his face. He didn't know what to do, and when he did know they ignored him. They were all going to die because their commanding officer had no business being an officer.

Something moved in the darkness. Brainard aimed his rifle, then relaxed. Ivy rotated toward the crew from the edges of the cleared area. The tendrils moved like corkscrews, growing from the tips rather than being thrust out from the main body of the vine. A collar of barbed thorns sprouted every time a tendril threw out another trio of leaves.

The barakite flame had burned through the boles of several giant trees, opening the canopy and releasing a flood of sunlight to the forest floor. Energized by the light, the ivy grew at the rate of several inches a minute—amazingly fast, but still no risk to the humans. They'd all have changed out of their suits and gone on before the vines reached them.

Caffey saw the motion. "Watch it!" he shouted. He triggered a burst, firing his machine gun from the hip. Bullets plowed the fire-hardened soil. The muzzle blasts made the foliage quiver as if with anticipation.

"Cease fire!" Brainard shouted. *They were never going to make it.* "Cease fire!"

Clear, poisonous sap filled and sealed the nip one bullet had taken from a tendril. The tip resumed its rotary advance.

"We'll need that ammo," Brainard muttered to himself.

He glanced up into the canopy to avoid meeting Caffey's eyes. Strands of cobweb drifted there. He hadn't seen it when he looked a moment—

The cobweb was drifting down on them. It was a circular blanket ten feet in diameter, as insubstantial as smoke.

"Move!" Brainard shouted. "Run! Run!"

Wilding glanced upward. "This way!" he cried, leading the way deeper into the jungle.

The crew stampeded forward. Bozman dropped his pack. The cobweb banked lazily around the bole of a forest giant and followed. The humans were hindered by grasping foliage, but the blanket moved in open air beneath the mid-canopy. It easily followed its prey.

Brainard stood transfixed. He didn't know what to do. He opened his mouth to call his men back, but Wilding knew about the dangers, and anyway it was too late.

Brainard should—

Brainard should—

He raised his rifle and fired at the creature a hundred feet in the air. He was a good shot. The yellow muzzle flashes hid the cobweb for an instant, but there was a spark of light as a bullet hit something.

He fired again, another short burst, and the creature curved toward him with the grace of a shark moving in for the kill. Fifty feet, thirty. It gleamed like a diffraction grating as a beam of direct sunlight caught it.

Brainard didn't realize his finger had clamped down on the trigger until the rifle butt abruptly ceased to recoil against his shoulder. He threw down the empty weapon and ran for the nearest cover, the burned-off stump of a fern that had been three hundred feet tall.

The cobweb swooped. The edges of gossamer fabric extended like the wings of a bat driving food to the waiting jaws. Brainard saw the glitter in the corners of both his eyes. The stump was too far to—

An ivy tendril caught him. He tripped forward on his face. He flung his hands out, just short of the stump he had hoped would shelter him.

The creature swept over him as a shimmering shadow. It wrapped itself around the stump.

Brainard stared. The crystal fabric humped itself, driving spikes a foot long into the smoldering wood. The holes released spurts of steam which hung for a moment in the saturated atmosphere.

Wilding ran over to him. "You saved us, sir!" he cried. "That was brilliant! You saved us all!"

Brainard gaped at Wilding. He moved his foot in a disconnected attempt at removing it from the ivy's hooked grasp.

July 23, 381 AS. 0244 hours.

Officer-Trainee Brainard's console was a holographic triptych.

To the right, between Brainard and Watkins, K67's coxswain, the navigation board displayed the Gehenna Archipelago. Tonello's hovercraft and her consort, K44, probed for the Seatiger squadron which Cinc Wysocki believed was lurking there in ambush. Low islands and shallow straits scrolled down the panel of coherent light.

Brainard bent close to the left-hand panel which displayed schematics of the torpedocraft's signatures:

Thermal—

Fan #3's intake glowed 4° above ambient. Brainard touched keys to reroute the overdeck airflow, scattering the warmth in turbulence. Leaf, hunched over against the wind, ran toward the drive module to work on the underlying problem.

Electro-optical—

All the hovercraft's emitters were shut down. The blotched gray polymer of K67's hull quivered at between an 83% and 95% match for the surrounding sea in color and albedo. That was a closer copy than stretches of seawater a mile apart could achieve.

The vessel's computer fed low-voltage current through connections to the hull and skirts, modifying the camouflage pattern by the plastic's response to its electrical charge. It didn't require operator input.

Audio—

K67's sonic signature required an act of God to do it any good. There was damn-all Brainard could even attempt now that the CO had called for flank speed. Intake baffles flattened to smooth the path of air howling to feed the fans. Wind rush—over the deck, the gun tub, the cockpit and the crew stations—blended its myriad turbulences into the roar. Exhaust flow, ducted at high velocity to drive the vessel forward, hammered the night.

You couldn't have speed and silence. The best you could do was diffuse the cacophony so that it might come from anywhere in a mile radius instead of giving the enemy a sharp aiming point.

Brainard was doing what he could with the low on-deck air dams. He thought he'd shifted the calculated center of noise starboard and 3° astern, though the sonic ghost-vessel would keep a parallel course. Maybe the line of swampy islands a mile to starboard on the navigation screen would produce a confusing echo, but that was a matter for luck—temperature and air currents, nothing that a hovercraft's electronic countermeasures operator could do.

But something had to be done. Cinc Wysocki had been right. Brainard's center screen showed that the Seatigers had at least a pair of heavily-armed hydrofoil gunboats in the archipelago, five miles away and closing on the Herd patrol at 42° off the port bow.

Brainard heard the *boonk*! over the wind roar, but he didn't recognize the sound until the high-altitude *pop* followed three seconds later and the heavens turned lambent white in the glare of a star shell. The gunboats opened fire.

K44's gun tub fired back.

Brainard was lost in the virtual environment of his console. Nothing was real, not even the coxswain and Lieutenant Tonello beside him in the narrow cockpit.

K44's signature brightened by ten orders of magnitude near the center of the situation display.

"Don't shoot!" he screamed. "For God's sake, *don't!*"

Outside the cockpit, the Seatiger gunboats disappeared behind the dazzle of their tracers and muzzle flashes. Each hydrofoil mounted a 3-inch gun in the bow and 1-inch Gatlings in tubs abaft the cockpit to either side. On the gunboats' present closing course, all their weapons could fire.

K44's tracers mounted in a high arc as the gunner attempted to achieve an impossible range. The scarlet marker compound burned out before the bullets started their vain downward tumble.

"Tonello to crew," rasped the CO's voice, distorted by static on the interphone's masking circuit. "Do not fire. Yee, I've locked the gun tub. Do not attempt to fire. Break. Blue Leader to—"

Brainard screamed silently as a pip glowed on the signature display. It was all right, tight-beam laser directed at K44 as Tonello gave orders to their consort, but *nothing* was all right.

"—Blue Two, cease fire and—"

K67 staggered. There was a bang and a puff of hot gas at the port bow on Brainard's thermal schematic. The CO had fired a decoy from the spigot mortar there.

"—conform to my movements. Out."

The sky ripped and roared. White streaks quivered like heat lightning in Brainard's peripheral vision. A sheet of spray lifted just ahead of the hovercraft, better shielding than anything the console provided, but the *whack/whack* from low in the hull added noise drumming through a double hole in the plenum chamber.

The decoy bloomed into a satisfying blob on Brainard's situation display, but centrifugal force shoved him to the left and the ghost image he had created on the audio schematic vanished in the modified airstream. Watkin's elbow blurred the navigation display for a moment as the coxswain fought to hold K67 in a tight starboard turn.

Brainard braced himself and began reworking their sonic signature. The CO was headed for the strait separating a pair of islands like pearls on a necklace. The hovercraft of the Herd patrol had thirty knots on their hydrofoil opponents, but Tonello was determined to hunt the narrow confines of the archipelago rather than return to Cinc Wysocki with word of a pair of screening vessels.

A triple crackling noise vibrated K67. Brainard's left-hand display vanished, then resumed before the curse reached his lips and his finger could stab the back-up control.

The islands would blur the hovercraft's horrifying racket. Maneuvering in tight waters was the CO's concern, not Brainard's.

Brainard had to concentrate on eliminating the torpedocraft's signatures.

Or he would die.

The night to the left exploded in hard white flashes as a gunboat slammed its six-round burst into a skerry as K67 roared past. Fragments of rock, shell-casing, and barnacles three feet in diameter sprang into the air. They rained down on the hovercraft's deck. Shreds of barnacle flesh gave the air a fishy tinge and brought shoals of toothed creatures to the surface.

The firing was behind them. A series of low islands concealed the gunboats from K67's sensors. K44 had managed to join her leader, but hot spots on Brainard's situation display indicated the other hovercraft had battle damage.

"Tonello to crew!" the CO crackled over the interphone. "The Seatigers may think this is a great place to hide, but we'll see how well they dodge torpedoes in narrow waters!"

Something touched Brainard's shoulder. He turned around in shock. Tonello had loosened his harness in order to lean over to the countermeasures console.

The CO raised his visor and shouted over the wind rush, "Brainard, I've never known a man to stay so cool in his first action. I'm proud to have you aboard!"

Tonello swung back into his own seat.

Brainard stared at him. The CO's words had been distinct, but they didn't make any sense.

Wind buffeted Brainard at chest height. He shut down the signature display for a moment. There was a circular one-inch hole in the plastic behind the holographic panel.

Brainard wondered dully how the Gatling bullet had managed to miss him on the continuation of its course.

7

Wilding offered Brainard a hand. Brainard stared as if he were unable to comprehend the gesture.

The enlisted members of the crew ran back to their officers. Leaf picked up Brainard's rifle by the sling and demanded, "What was that? What the *hell* was that?"

"Goddam if I know," the ensign said in an emotionless voice. He levered himself to his knees, then stood upright. His bandolier swayed, making the magazines clatter against one another.

Wilding rubbed his hand on his thigh to give it something to do. "It's an ice mat," he said, looking at the crystalline form. Pale, stunted shoots sprang from nodes over the spikes driven into the tree. "A seed pod of sorts. It's descended from a thistle—the parent plant is, I mean."

Brainard took his rifle from Leaf. He touched the barrel; winced as the hot metal burned him. "All right," he said. "Let's get moving."

Wilding had forgotten the weight of the pack during the moments of panic. Now the straps cut into his shoulders. He was suddenly sure that the forty-pound

315

loads which he had set—conservatively, he thought—were too heavy, at least for him.

"Yes sir," he said as strode back into the jungle.

The edges of the cleared area were already a tangle of thorns and poison. Wilding reopened the path with the powered cutting bar he carried, one of the two in K67's equipment locker before the crash. Caffey fell in behind him with the machine-gun.

"But it was alive," Leaf insisted from mid-way back in the line. "It wasn't just falling, it was *coming* for us."

"It doesn't have a mind," Wilding said. He knew he should concentrate on the terrain in front of him, but a part of his mind insisted that he dwell on Ensign Brainard's cold courage. "It has a very discriminating infra-red sensor, though. It would have avoided an open flame, but the CO lured it into a charred stump that had cooled to just above blood heat."

That was the second part of what Brainard had done. First, while Wilding ran in terror thinking, *Let it take one of the others*, the CO used the hot, expanding propellant gases of his rifle to draw the ice mat toward himself. Brainard's combination of nerve and diamond-hard calculation was almost beyond conception.

The interphone only worked through K67's computer, but the visor-display compasses in the helmets were self-powered. Wilding set his on a vector to the peak. He began to follow it.

Almost immediately, the ground lurched up in an outcrop too steep for the thin soil to cling to its surface. Wilding gripped rock, lifted himself, and kicked for a foothold from which he could push up the rest of the way.

A gigantic fig overhung the outcrop. The lower twenty feet of its folded bark bubbled with bright red spittle. A colony of scale insects hid within the frothy protection.

"Don't touch the red!" Wilding shouted. "Anything that showy is probably poisonous."

"Give me a hand," Caffey said peremptorily. "Sir." He lifted his machine-gun.

Wilding grasped it by the barrel. He almost over-balanced. The gun weighed nearly thirty pounds with its ammunition drum.

The torpedoman clambered up the rock and took the weapon back. He bent to offer Yee, the third man in line, a hand.

A stand of yellow-barked willows was in the direct path. Wilding skirted them. There was a broad corridor through the copse, but bones and the sections of insect exoskeleton there showed its danger.

Trees at the front and back of the corridor wove closed when a large creature stepped within. The boles in the middle of the track squeezed down slowly and crushed their victim into a nitrate supplement for the poor soil.

"Okay," said Caffey, "that's how." The torpedoman panted softly, like a dog, between phrases. "About the ice mat, I mean. But how *come*? Or does it just like to kill things?"

"Like you, you mean?" Leaf gibed from behind them.

"Hell, like us, if you want to be that way," said Caffey. "Like anybody in a Free Company."

"Not me, Fish," Leaf replied. "I just—" the motor-man paused to grunt his way over a steep patch "—keep the fans spinning."

Wilding's whole body hurt. He swung the cutting bar mechanically because it had become too much mental effort to decide when a sweep of the blade was necessary.

"The ice mat needs nutrients to grow," he said. He spoke aloud, but he wasn't sure that his words were distinct enough for the torpedoman to understand. "Animals are the best source of complex nutriments," he continued. "Insects, reptiles, it doesn't matter. Any animal has to be able to modify its body temperature against the ambient to function, so that's what the seed, the ice mat, homes on."

The lecture took Wilding's mind off the pain of moving; but the pain was still there, waiting for him.

The moss hanging from branches a hundred feet in the air was so thick that its shade had cleared the ground beneath to sandy red clay. Wilding altered course slightly from the compass vector to take advantage of the open area.

Through interstices in the trunks of moss-hung trees, Wilding glimpsed a steep terrace covered with bamboo. That was going to be a problem. They would either have to go around the tough, jointed grass or cut through it. Given that the belt might encircle the peak—and might be hundreds of feet deep—neither alternative was a good one. Perhaps—

Caffey and Yee both shouted. Caffey's voice choked off in mid-bleat.

Wilding spun around. The weight of his pack threw him off-balance. A strand of moss had spooled down and wrapped around the torpedoman's neck. Other strands bobbed just beneath the main mass on the branch, preparing to follow.

The tendril trying to strangle Caffey had snagged the barrel of his machine-gun as well. The gun muzzle crushed painfully against the torpedoman's forehead, but the rigid steel saved his larynx.

Yee fired two deafening shots, trying vainly to blast the gray streamer apart. The moss parted like tissue paper when Wilding swiped his cutting bar through it.

Released tension lifted the severed strand fifty feet in the air. The tip continued to contract around its victim. Wilding and Yee tugged against the moss with their free hands. The cutting bar was too clumsy to use near Caffey's throat.

The short blade of Leaf's multitool snicked through the loop of moss. Half came away in Wilding's hand. The remainder uncoiled and dropped to the ground.

"Fish!" Leaf shouted. "Fish! You okay?"

The torpedoman sat down heavily. His eyes were unfocused. There was a line of red spots across his throat.

Wilding looked down at his own hands. Miniature thorns in the moss had pricked him also. He hoped the points weren't poisonous, though the inevitable infection would be bad enough.

Overhead—

"Do you need help?" Brainard demanded from the end of the line.

"Come on!" Wilding snarled, grabbing Caffey by one shoulder. "Help him! Move!"

Yee took Caffey's other arm. They pounded through the deadly clearing together. The torpedoman was barely able to keep his legs moving in time with those of the men supporting him, but for the moment Wilding forgot about weight and pain. Leaf, the machine-gun's sling in one hand and his multitool in the other, was on their heels.

When he reached the bamboo, Wilding looked back over his shoulder. The whole crew followed at a staggering run. There were no further problems. The moss reacted too slowly to be a serious threat to men who were prepared for it.

Wilding gasped for breath. A clearing meant danger. It was his fault. He'd been too tired to realize the obvious, and it cost—

"Caffey, how do you feel?" Ensign Brainard demanded before Wilding could remember to ask.

The torpedoman massaged his throat. "I'm okay," he wheezed. "Just gimme a minute, okay?"

The bamboo shoots were thumb-thick. The stems were yellow, and the lower leaves were yellow-brown.

The undersurface of each leaf was a hooked mat. The foliage began to tremble outward as the plants sensed human warmth.

God alone knew how thick the belt was.

Wilding bent and swung his cutting bar. Contact triggered the 20-inch blade in a petulant whine. Stems toppled, but their leaves clutched at Wilding's arm as they fell.

"Right," Brainard said. His voice was as calm as that of an accounting adding figures. "We need to get moving. Yee, take the Number Two slot and Caffey will fall in just in front of me for a while."

"Ah . . . ?" Yee said. "How about the gun?"

"Fuck you," said Caffey. Instinct, not intellect snarled in his voice. The injured man hugged his heavy weapon to him with both arms.

Wilding resumed cutting. The bamboo rustled as it fell. Sometimes the stems remained upright, gripped by the mass of their neighbors. Wilding forced them aside. His uniform was in shreds, and a sheen of blood coated his arms.

The bamboo went on forever. Wilding cut, and stepped, and cut. He lost track of time and was only conscious of dull pain.

"Hey," a voice said.

Wilding swung. The bar cut on either stroke, but the rotator muscles of his shoulder screamed with pain after ten minutes of alternate backhands.

"Sir?" said the voice. "I hear something."

Wilding swung. He couldn't see for the sweat in his eyes and the burning red haze which overlaid his mind.

Yee grabbed him by the shoulder. The bar dropped

from Wilding's nerveless fingers. "Sir!" the gunner said. "I *hear* something."

So did Wilding, now that his body had stopped moving. His mind re-engaged. A rhythmic crunching sound, amazingly loud. He couldn't tell what direction it came from because of the scattering effect of the dense stems.

Wilding looked over his shoulder. Leaf had paused six feet behind Yee; the next man in line was hidden by the walls of the ragged trail. Nobody wanted to bunch up here. . . .

"Pass the word back to Mr Brainard," Wilding whispered to the nervous gunner. "Tell him that—"

The wall of bamboo crashed forward. Wilding shouted and grabbed for his cutting bar. The net of interlaced stems sprang down and held him as immobile as an insect in amber.

A three-ton grasshopper smashed its way across the trail. Its legs were modified to graviportal stumps. One of its clawed feet came down squarely on the net of bamboo which held Wilding.

The stems took up some of the shock, but Wilding screamed in despair as he felt tendons go in his right ankle.

November 24, 379 AS. 0211 hours.

A dozen of them sauntered down the Palm Walk together, giddy with drink and the odor of the tropical blooms among the trees. The clubs were still open, but establishments in this restricted area had no need for garish advertisement. The entrances were lighted in pastels which set off the broad corridor rather than illuminating it.

Wilding was at the front of the loose group. The woman on his arm was a short-haired blonde from a cadet branch of the McLain family. He thought her name was Glory, but he was too drunkenly cautious to risk a scene if he were wrong.

The blonde said, "I want to go—*ooh!*"

Wilding tried to fold her in his arms. "I want to go ooh with you too, darling," he said. "Let's—"

The blonde twisted away from him. Wilding goggled at her in amazement.

"Oh my god!" grumbled one of the men. "Is Tootles still around? He stayed in the Azure, didn't he?"

"Hal?" called a woman's half-familiar voice.

Wilding turned. The figure shambling toward him was only a blur against the arbor in which she had waited, but her eyes were well adapted to the Palm Walk. "Oh, Hal," she blurted, "thank God it's you! You've got to help me."

"Patrol!" the blonde shrieked. "Patrol! Where are you, you lazy bastards?"

There were discreet cameras and audio pick-ups every hundred yards down the corridor. As soon as the blonde screamed, a bright blue strobe light flashed a quarter mile away at the guarded entrance which separated the Palm Walk from the public areas of Wyoming Keep.

"Now, you haven't any business here, madam," Wilding said, queasy with the shock of the unknown. It *couldn't* be anyone he knew. He still couldn't make out the woman's features, but her body odor and the stench of cheap perfume flared his nostrils. "If you don't cause any trouble, then I'm sure the Patrol will let you—"

"Hal, my God, it's *me*, Francine!" the figure cried. "You've got to help me see Tootles."

Good God, it *was* Francine.

"Tootles picked her up somewhere," a man explained to his companion. "Then she found him in bed with her maid and hit him with a bottle. She tried to *kill* him!"

A Patrol scooter, silent except for the hiss of its tires against the pavement, sped toward the disturbance. Its strobe pulsed across Francine's swollen features. She looked as though she had applied her make-up in the dark.

"Tootles isn't here, Francine," Wilding said. He wondered if she was armed.

Chauncey Callahan, Tootles, had started the evening with their party but he'd dropped away hours ago. Nobody else in the group knew Francine as well as Wilding himself did.

Francine snatched his wrist. Her trembling grip had no strength, but her false nails felt like the touch of broken glass. "Hal, you're my friend," she wheezed. "You've got to explain to Tootles that it was just a mistake, that I *love* him."

"Sent her back where she belonged, of course," said an ice-voiced woman in answer to a question Wilding hadn't heard. "Which was nowhere."

The Patrol scooter pulled up so hard that it squealed. Three men jumped out. One of them swept the group with a hand-held spotlight. The white glare steadied on Francine's raddled, desperate face. Her dilated eyes glowed red in the beam.

"Hal, *please*," she begged as the other two Patrolmen seized her elbows. Her nails left scratches as she lost her grip on Wilding. "Hal, you remember me! You *remember* me!"

Francine's blouse was of a natural material from the planetary surface, a soft clinging fabric that fluoresced in white and blue-white light. The cloth blazed now in spotlit radiance, but that only emphasized the stains and tears which had made the garment too worthless to barter for drugs.

Francine pulled the blouse open. Her breasts sagged. "You remember!" she screeched.

"Get her out of here!" Wilding shouted as he turned his face.

One of the Patrolmen injected Francine with something. She sprawled limp and let the pair of them load her into the scooter.

The third Patrolman switched off the spotlight. The strobe pulsed twice more, then cut off also.

"I'm very sorry for this problem, ladies and gentlemen," the senior Patrolman said. His tone was unctuous over an edge of real concern. This could mean his rank, his job, or—or he could fall back into the bleak emptiness reserved for those who had basked in the favor of the powerful, and then lost that favor. Empty days filled with algal protein and holonews images of the glittering folks with whom he had once been in daily contact. A life like that of Francine, drooling in the back of a Patrol vehicle.

"Unfortunately, the man at the entrance recognized the woman and didn't check her name against the updated admissions list," the Patrolman continued. The filament of his spotlight was a fading orange blur. "I trust that none of you were injured, or . . . ?"

"You useless bastards!" the blonde shrilled. "We could have been—"

Wilding grabbed the woman's shoulder. "Shut *up*," he said very distinctly.

Glory, if her name was Glory, gasped and nestled against him.

Wilding waved at the scooter and its contents. "Get her out of here," he demanded. His voice rose. "Get her out of my life!"

"At once, Mr Wilding," said the Patrolman in

relief. He leaped aboard the vehicle. The driver had already started it rolling.

The scooter sped back toward the entrance to the Palm Walk and oblivion. Its tires keened like a woman sobbing.

8

We been rammed by a fucking battleship! Leaf thought as the bamboo crashed down in a monstrous bow wave.

The grasshopper's headplate was smoothly curved and a yard across. The waxy chitinous surface gave no purchase to the hooked foliage, and six powerful legs drove the creature through stems that proved a nearly impassible barrier to humans.

OT Wilding vanished beneath a mat of vegetation that muffled his screams. Yee tried to jump out of the way, but the disaster was too sudden. He got his torso clear, but the stems that cascaded over the trail pinned the gunner's hips and feet to the ground.

Yee lay on his back, yelling as he tried to aim at the behemoth which knocked him down. The muzzle of his rifle was tangled, and its light bullets weren't going to have much effect on the grasshopper anyway.

Leaf's pack held forty pounds of barakite. He had squeezed the doughy explosive into fist-sized balls after he cut it from the second warhead. He reached over his shoulder with his left hand and grabbed a wad; his right thumb poised on his multitool's welding trigger.

He didn't light the explosive. The huge insect was just trying to get away.

The grasshopper's body was much like that of its Earth-born ancestors, but its armored legs were straight and short to carry the mass of its Venus-adapted form. It moved in a succession of tripods: the center leg on the right balancing with the front and back legs on the left while the other three drove forward, then the opposite pattern.

Because the grasshopper was at a full run, the cases of its vestigial wings lifted to uncover the creature's external lungs: fungoid blotches of red, oxygen-absorbent tissue spaced along the midline on both sides of the grasshopper's body. Air diffused through spiracles would not sufficiently fuel the life-processes of so large a body.

The digestive processes in the grasshopper's yellow-striped abdomen rumbled a farewell to K67's crew as the beast vanished again into the bamboo.

Leaf giggled with relief. Then he saw the scorpion.

Yee's heavy pack had prevented him from being thrown flat. "*Somebody fucking help me!*" the gunner bellowed as he used his rifle butt to lever himself upright.

"*Look out!*" Leaf shouted.

Yee rotated his head from Leaf—

To the new track the grasshopper had smashed through the vegetation—

To what had driven the grasshopper off in panic.

The grasshopper had been chewing a path through the bamboo entanglement for days. Leaf and Yee looked down the corridor. New shoots grew from the close-cropped soil at increasing height, in a pattern of pale green/bright green/yellow green.

The scorpion carried its flat belly six feet above the ground. It strode toward the humans with saw-toothed pincers advanced.

Yee screamed and fired the whole magazine of his rifle in a burst that made the barrel glow. Bullets sparkled across the lustrous purple-black head, destroying several of the simple eyes. Jacket fragments clipped tiny holes in the nearest foliage.

"Run!" the gunner shrieked. Bamboo still gripped his legs to the knees. He twisted, then twisted back when he realized he was trapped.

"Geddown!" Leaf bawled. The motorman pressed the stud trigger of his multitool, snapping the arc alight. The scorpion pounced.

Yee dropped the fresh magazine he was trying to insert into the rifle. He thrust the weapon out crosswise as a shield. The scorpion's right pincer gripped the rifle's receiver; its left reached beneath the weapon and caught Yee around the waist. The paired claws were eighteen inches long.

Leaf knew there was no use in running, but he would have run anyway except that the bamboo held him also. He touched the welding arc to his lump of barakite.

He wasn't left-handed. He flung the explosive in a clumsy overhand motion as soon as it started to sputter. Tiny globules flicked his hand and wrist. The intense heat raised blisters instantly.

The scorpion tore Yee out of the bamboo. The gunner was no longer screaming. Blood soaked the waist of his torn uniform and a broad fan across his chest from nose and mouth.

The blob of barakite was softened by its own combustion. It splattered over the arachnid's head instead of flying into the open mouth as Leaf had intended.

The scorpion's pincers thrust the victim between its side-hinged jawplates while the flames roared with blue-white laughter. Sparks flew in all directions. Somebody fired his rifle past the motorman.

Gobbets of burning barakite ignited the load of explosive in Yee's pack.

The spark became the sun—

Became a volcanic pressure—

That shriveled the vegetation gripping Leaf and hurled him back away from its white heart.

September 24, 366 AS. 1050 hours.

"Wait for us!" Peanut Leaf squealed in a voice that hadn't broken by now, his twelfth birthday, and didn't look like it would be getting any longer to try. The oil-drum barricade spouted smoke and orange flame before *any* of the retreating 5th-Level war party reached it, and the Leaf brothers were at the end of the rout.

"Yee-hah!" shrilled a 3rd-Level warrior as he flung a spear made of plastic tubing with a metal head.

The point nicked Leaf's thigh; the thick shaft caught the boy a blow solid enough to stagger him. Peanut would have fallen, but Jacko, fourteen and strong for his age, seized his brother's arm and propelled him like a tractor drawing a cart.

"Don't you fall, you little bastard!" he shouted. "They'll kill you!"

Peanut wasn't in the least doubt about that.

Mongo and Race were already down—which meant dead, unless the 3rd-Level warriors had been in too much of a hurry to make sure by slitting their throats. It had been a ratfuck, an ambush sprung in the air shaft while the 5th-Level war party was just setting out on what was supposed to be a raid.

Now. . . .

Kacentas, War Dragon of the 5th Level, had planned for the possibility of retreat by sliding drums of waste oil across the home corridor. Three hard-faced girls of the Auxiliary were stationed there with torches to ignite the barricade if the raiders were driven back.

The disaster had been so abrupt that the girls lit the drums in the faces of their own warriors, rather than those of the enemy.

The leading warriors cursed and squealed, leaping the drums before the oil was properly alight. The pall of smoke rolled upward and down, following the convection patterns of Block 81's climate control.

An arrow took Kacentas in the air. He tumbled to what would have been the safe side of the barricade.

The Leaf brothers sprinted into the curtain of smoke. Peanut gagged, but the air was clear immediately in front of the barricade. Fuel blasted upward in terrifying columns to mushroom against the corridor ceiling.

The Patrol would arrive within minutes, but within seconds it would be too late.

"Come on!" Jacko cried.

All the other 5th-Level warriors had vanished—except Hurst, who lay at the base of the drums with eyes staring upward from a pool of blood. Hurst had managed to run all the way from the air shaft with his jugular torn open by a spearthrust.

Peanut skidded to a halt. "I can't!" he wailed to the barricade. The heat was a concrete presence.

"Come on!" Jacko repeated shrilly.

He picked up his brother by the throat and the seat of his pants. As he turned to hurl the younger boy to safety, a thrown club rang off Jacko's skull and stunned him.

Peanut fell to the floor. He had lost his steel mace back in the air shaft. There were 3rd-Level warriors all around them. His eyes were open, but his mind refused to accept what he saw.

Jacko was still on his feet. Two of the enemy prodded him with their spears. They didn't drive the points home. Instead, they thrust Jacko backwards, into the oil fires.

Jacko screamed. His arms flailed as if he were trying to swim away from the agony, but there was no way out. For a moment, Jacko's torso forced down the flames, but then the orange-red blanket roared up to cover him again.

And he still screamed.

Sirens and strobe lights flooded the corridor. The 3rd-Level warriors were running away, but Jacko did not move. His black arms lifted from the ebbing flames in a hollow embrace, and his skull greeted the Patrolmen with a lipless grin.

Jacko's throat had shrivelled shut. His brother screamed for both of them.

9

Newton was reloading. Brainard shoved past him and aimed his rifle.

He didn't fire. When the scorpion reared high over the trail it had a face like the heart of the sun and he had to glance away.

The roaring brilliance was barakite burning, not a vision of Hell.

When Brainard looked up again, the scorpion was careening away in a series of spastic convulsions. When its jointed tail straightened, the creature was more than twenty feet long from jaws to stinger . . . but the jaws were gone, the whole head was a blazing ruin, and so long as the decorticated monster continued in the current direction, it was no further danger to K67's crew.

Volleys of shots crackled and whined through the foliage as the ammunition in the backpack went off in the barakite fire. Cartridges without a gun-barrel to direct them weren't particularly dangerous. On a bad day, a bullet or fragment of casing might put an eye out.

That was nothing to worry about, since OT Wilding was gone and they were all dead without his special knowledge.

Just before the scorpion crashed out of sight through a thicket of hundred-foot willows, a human leg fell from the shriveled chitin of its mouth.

Brainard blinked at the purple afterimages of the flame. His ears rang, and his nostrils were numb with the smell of barakite and burning flesh. The suggestion of fried prawns was probably from the scorpion.

He didn't know what to do. He doubted there was anything they *could* do, now.

Leaf lay face down, moaning. Brainard reached out with his left hand and lifted the motorman. The bamboo had withered in the intense heat. It no longer clung to flesh and clothing.

"Good thinking," Brainard said. "With the barakite."

Must have been Leaf who ignited it, though it wasn't his pack because he was still carrying that. Caffey . . . no, Yee had been Number Two. Yee and Wilding were gone, just ahead of the rest of them.

The mat of flame-shrunken stems quivered, then moaned. OT Wilding's slim, aristocratic hand reached out of it.

"God help us!" blurted Caffey.

There was a swollen line across the torpedoman's neck, but he was enough himself again to push his way to the head of the column. He shifted the machine-gun to his left hand and snatched the cutting bar from where Wilding must have dropped it.

"Not that," snapped Brainard. "D'ye want to take his leg off?"

He knelt and began to pry the bamboo upward with one hand and the muzzle of his rifle. The laser communicator flopped awkwardly against his knees. *With Wilding alive, they had a chance.*

The desiccated stems splintered without resistance. *Wilding could save them. . . .*

Wilding was able to sit up by himself when they

cleared the bamboo from his chest. Fresh growth, protected like the officer-trainee by the insulating mat, left nasty sores where it had begun to suck at his back.

"Is he okay?" Bozman called from the back of the line.

Leaf and the cautiously-used blade of his multitool worked Wilding's boots free.

"He's all right," Brainard said. A prayer of exultation danced in his mind as he heard his own flat statement.

"No," said Wilding. "I've sprained my ankle. You're going to have to leave me."

Brainard raised his eyes to the terrain ahead of them. It seemed to plateau, but they would have more climbing to do shortly.

"Who's got the first-aid kit?" he demanded. "Get a pressure bandage on the XO's ankle."

"You can't carry a cripple along with you," Wilding sneered. "Take what you need from my pack and get moving before something worse comes along."

Awareness that the officer-trainee might be right froze Brainard's heart. "Shut up," he snarled.

Wilding's face went blank. Leaf and Caffey, at the edge of Brainard's focused vision, stiffened.

Wheelwright said, "I got the kit," breaking the pulsing silence. "Lemme up to the front."

Men shifted. There was plenty of room in the broader pathway which the grasshopper had chewed through the jointed tangle. Caffey looked at the cutting bar in his hand and said, "Ah, I'll cut him a crutch, okay?"

Yee's rifle lay a few feet away. Brainard picked it up. Shreds of bamboo fiber were stuck to the plastic stock where the barakite had softened it.

"No," said Wilding. He looked at Caffey, purposefully avoiding eye contact with the ensign. "That won't work. The bamboo—any surface vegetation. It'll keep growing after it's cut, and. . . ."

He made a negligent gesture toward the sores on his back. Wheelwright coated them with a clear antiseptic, but the edges were already puckering upward.

The scorpion's pincers had cut the rifle's beryllium receiver almost in half. There were bright gouges through the barrel's weatherproofing and into the steel beneath.

"Right," said Brainard. "We'll use this for a crutch. It's not good for much else." He handed the rifle to Wilding.

Wilding's tongue touched his lips. He looked at the ensign. "Sir?" he said. "I still can't march—"

"I'll help him, sir," said Leaf.

"The junior personnel will assist Mr Wilding in rotation," Brainard said as his mind clicked through the minuscule tasks that he could understand, could deal with. "Newton, Bozman, Wheelwright. Thirty-minute watches."

He'd almost assigned Yee a place in the watch list.

"Leaf, I want you at the end of the column," he continued. He held out his rifle to the motorman. "Take this. Caffey, give me the cutting bar. I'll lead, and I want you and the big gun right behind me."

Leaf turned his head as though he had not seen the proffered weapon. "I don't *want* a fucking gun," he snarled. "Why'n't you let me help the XO? I can do it."

"Newton's carrying the other bar, sir," Wilding said quietly. "You'd better use it. The charge on this one is almost flat."

Brainard slung his rifle. "All right," he said. "Newton, give me the other bar. Wheelwright, take the end slot. *Watch* yourself. Leaf, help Mr Wilding. Stay close. There's a lot of this place that I don't know anything about."

There was damn-all about this place that he *did*
know anything about.

"Sir," offered Caffey. "Ah, d'ye want me to carry the
communicator? It'll get in the way if there's much
cutting to do."

Brainard looked at the torpedoman with a flat
expression which he hoped hid the sudden terror in
his mind. "We'll be following the grasshopper's path,"
he said coldly. "I'll keep the communicator."

*The laser communicator was Brainard's lifeline. Its
hard outlines were all that kept him sane. If he was
still sane. . . .*

July 23, 381 AS. 0301 hours.

The twenty-seven islands on Brainard's navigation
display ranged from mere fangs of rock to a ridged
mass rising to a thousand feet, worthy of a name.

Even the narrower perspective of the console's
central situation display was splotched with islands. But
the natural surroundings didn't matter, because a
Seatiger warship was edging through a channel between
two of the swampy blobs at a charted distance of 5721
yards.

"Ready torpedoes," Lieutenant Tonello rasped over
the interphone. He stood to look over K67's cockpit
coaming, while OT Brainard hid within his holographic
environment. "Flank spee—"

A starshell popped. Tracers snarled overhead mea-
surable seconds before Brainard heard the howl of the
Gatlings that fired them.

"Torpedoes ready," Tech 2 Caffey reported. The
interphone turned his voice into that of a soloist
accompanied by the orchestra of Hell.

"Coxs'n, three degrees starboard."

K67 accelerated like a kicked can. Water slammed upward so near the port side that water drenched Brainard's console. The spout was luminous with the orange flames at its heart. The second shell was dead astern, the third astern to starboard.

Tonello had kept the fans on high, spilling air through the waste slots in the plenum chamber, as the torpedo-craft nosed through the archipelago to find the targets he knew were present. OT Brainard cursed the CO in silent terror because that technique made K67 a sonic beacon. Brainard couldn't help matters at the counter-measures board, though the scattering effect of the islands themselves turned the two-vessel patrol into a flotilla.

It would have taken the fans 90 seconds to spin up from low-signature mode to full power. It took a half-second to slam the waste slots closed and lurch toward the enemy. That was many times the difference between a waterspout astern—and a fireball which scattered indistinguishable bits of crew and vessel after a 5.5-inch shell detonated K67's own torpedoes.

Brainard punched up an identification sidebar on his situation display. When his mind and fingers did *something*, the roar and flashes couldn't drown him in their terror.

The sea was orange with waterspouts; muzzle flashes boiled the whole horizon red and white. K44 vanished from the display. Even the islands blurred and shrank as the shell-storm degraded the data reaching K67's sensors.

Brainard's console told him their opponent was a destroyer-leader with a full-load displacement of 2700 tons and a main armament of six 5.5-inch guns in triple turrets.

He didn't believe it. He was sure from the volume

of fire that they'd jumped a dreadnought. He reached under the panel and switched to the back-up system. The holographic display vanished for a hideous fraction of a second, forcing Brainard to see the carnage around him. Light trembling from flares twisted sea creatures on the surface into shapes still more monstrous than those of nature. Horrors fought and feasted at the banquet laid by bursting shells.

Then the back-up circuits took over. The new display told Brainard the same thing the old one had, that K67 faced a minor fleet element, not a dreadnought. Only a destroyer-leader, only a hundred times the hovercraft's size—

"Launch one!" said Lieutenant Tonello in a voice as clear as glass breaking. K67 shuddered as studs blew open and dropped one of the torpedoes into the sea beneath her plenum chamber.

"Launch two!"

"Tracking!" Caffey reported as he hunched over his guidance controls. The torpedo's own sensors gave the operator a multi-spectral view of the target. If the enemy tried to dodge, Caffey could send steering commands along the cable of optical fiber which connected the weapon to the hovercraft.

The release thump of the second torpedo was lost in the burst of explosive bullets which buzz-sawed across K67.

Lieutenant Tonello's head vanished in a yellow flash. His body hurtled against the back bulkhead. The shatterproof windscreen disintegrated into a dazzle of microscopic beads, and all the cockpit displays went dead. The coxswain screamed and rolled out of his seat. K67 wallowed broadside, still at full power.

Each side-console had an emergency helm and throttle under the middle display. Brainard rotated his unit up and locked it into position. Wind blast through the missing screen hammered him. The destroyer-leader was a Roman candle of muzzle flashes.

A starshell had drifted almost to the surface astern of K67. By its flickering light, Brainard saw another blacked-out hovercraft race across the wave tops toward the target. He hadn't had time to think about K44 since the shooting started.

Brainard spun his miniature helm hard to starboard. The hovercraft did not respond.

A salvo of 5.5-inch shells straddled K67 with a roar louder than Doomsday. Waterspouts lifted the hovercraft and spilled the air out of her plenum chamber. She slammed the surface again with a bone-jarring crash.

The main circuit breakers had tripped. A battery-powered LED marked the breaker box, but Brainard's retinas still flickered with afterimages of the explosive bullets that raked the cockpit. He groped for the box, barked his knuckles on the edge of it, and finally got it open while several rounds of automatic fire slapped K67's skirts.

Brainard snapped the main switch into place. The console displays remained dark, but the hovercraft answered her helm.

The coxswain lay moaning on the deck. "Medic!" Brainard shouted. "Medic!" The interphone wasn't working either.

The circuit breaker overloaded again with a blue flash. K67's fans continued to drive her, but the shell-frothed waves wrenched the vessel into a curve that would end on a rocky islet unless the Seatigers destroyed her first.

Brainard grabbed the circuit breaker with his left hand. He snapped the switch home and held it there. Sparks trembled and his forearm went numb. An overloaded component blew in the coxswain's station, but Brainard had control again.

He overcorrected. K67 reversed her curve as though Brainard intended a figure-8. A three-shell salvo ignited the sea along the hovercraft's previous course.

"Medic!" Brainard cried. He had no feeling on the left side of his body. His left foot thrashed a crazy jig against the cockpit bulkheads.

The sky behind them turned orange.

Brainard looked over his shoulder. Where the destroyer-leader had been, a bubble of light with sharp edges lifted five hundred feet above the horizon. Stark shadows ripped across the neighboring islands as a doughnut-shaped shockwave pushed trees away from the light.

It must have been the target's own munitions, because no torpedo warhead could wreak such destruction.

The destroyer-leader was almost two miles away. The blast made K67 skip like a flung pebble.

Leaf crawled into the cockpit, carrying the first aid kit. He wore gloves.

"Forget that!" Brainard squealed as the motorman crouched over the writhing coxswain. "Hold this breaker closed!"

K67 spewed air through dozens of holes in her skirts, but she would survive until a tender could take her aboard. K67's torpedoes had lost guidance when the system power failed, but her consort had driven in and nailed the Seatiger vessel.

Because of K44, Officer-Trainee Brainard was going to survive this night after all.

10

Leaf heard OT Wilding say, "That's rock, we stop here," as they struggled past a tangle of thorny, interlacing vines.

The words didn't matter to Leaf. Wilding'd been muttering nonsense for . . . a long time, a lot of stumbling steps whatever the clock time might have been. The last time Wheelwright had dressed the bamboo sores on the officer's back, they had scarlet edges and centers of yellow pus.

But they weren't any of them in shape for a dress parade. Leaf saw only blurs because of the sweat in his eyes. He didn't have the energy to wipe his face with his right cuff. The multitool filled Leaf's right hand, and his left arm helped support Wilding . . .

Who was handsome, and rich, and not a pussy after all. During bouts of fever, the officer-trainee couldn't control his tongue—but he kept his feet moving forward. Their route was mostly uphill and the rifle made a bad crutch, but Wilding didn't flop down and die the way Leaf had maybe expected.

Wilding shook himself out of the motorman's grasp. Swaying like a top about to fall over, Wilding said,

341

"We *stop* here," in a voice well accustomed to giving orders.

Leaf realized he was ready to fall down himself. *Fuckin' A.* He rubbed his right eyesocket a little clearer on the point of his shoulder. "Fish!" he shouted to the torpedoman's back. "Get the CO. Mr Wilding wants a word."

And a hell of a bad place to stop for one, but you didn't argue with officers.

There were in a belt of thirty-foot-tall grass which defended its territory against encroaching woody plants by sawing off their stems with glassy nodules along the edges of the narrow grassblades. The competition was as dynamic as that of surf and the shoreline.

Even now in the momentary pause, glitteringly serrated blades twisted close to treat the humans with the same mindless ferocity that would greet an oak or mahogany. All that could be said in favor of going through the grass was that it was possible to cut the stuff. The tangle of thorns to the side was impassible.

Ensign Brainard stepped back from the head of the path he had cleared. His face and hands were smeared with a slick of his own sweat-diluted blood. "What is it?" he asked calmly.

Wilding opened his mouth. He swayed. Leaf reached over to catch him, but the officer-trainee crossed both palms firmly on the butt of his crutch to steady himself.

"That's rock," Wilding said. "Where the berry bush is growing." He gestured with his eyes, but he was clearly afraid that he would topple if so much as nodded his head. "We could rest there. A real rest."

Leaf looked at the tangle. The brambles were woven like a fishnet. Hundreds of small white flowers bloomed among the black stems and foliage, but nothing bigger than a man's arm could penetrate the mass.

A large insect might trust its armor to protect it while browsing on the vines and later berries, but Leaf already had enough experience with surface life to imagine the results. The brambles gave only until the animal was fully within their mass. Then—

Just like a fishnet. A thorn-studded fishnet.

The CO looked at the tangle without expression. "We'll go on," he said flatly. "I can't cut that."

"Hey!" said Caffey. "We can blow it clear! With the barakite."

"No," said Wilding. "We'll use the barakite to burn it. We don't want to pulverize the rock."

Brainard looked from Wilding to Leaf. "All right," he said. "Leaf, you'll lay the charges. All right?"

Leaf nodded. "Yessir."

He shrugged to slide the pack straps off his shoulders. At first his muscles wouldn't respond; then the load slipped abruptly. The straps scraped his arms, and the pack itself bruised the backs of his thighs.

"We'll use portions of the barakite from everybody's pack," the ensign continued. "And *don't* let any ignite that you don't mean to burn."

"Yessir," Leaf muttered. He knelt to begin work.

Brainard turned and cut at the grass rustling lethally closer to the human interlopers. Leaf saw that the CO had difficulty raising the cutting bar enough to use it.

Leaf rolled a ball of explosive between his palms, forming it into a coarse thread. The barakite was tacky in the moist heat, but the plasticizing additive retained its tensile strength so that Leaf could create a creamy white strand as thin as his little finger before the material broke under its own weight.

Caffey began forming a thread of his own when he saw what the motorman was doing. At Brainard's order, the other enlisted men passed blobs of barakite to the chiefs. They were probably glad to be rid of a few pounds of their burdens. . . .

When he had six strands of explosive, each a yard and a half long, the motorman paused. "Okay, that'll do," he muttered to his hands.

Caffey held out a canteen. "Have some water first," he said.

Leaf was too exhausted to argue with any suggestion. "Yeah, sure," he said. He reached for his own canteen.

Water was no problem. The condensing jacket on each crewman's canteen would fill the quart flask within ten minutes in this saturated atmosphere.

"Naw," said the torpedoman. "Use mine."

Leaf took the canteen and drank deeply. His eyes flashed open.

For the first time he noticed that the torpedoman carried two canteens. This one was full of rum.

Caffey grinned. "Essential to life," he said.

"You bet," said Leaf. "Now, everybody keep the hell back."

The brambles trembled softly toward him. He thought for a moment, then said, "Sir, lemme borrow the rifle, okay?"

Brainard handed the weapon over without comment. Leaf set one end of a barakite thread over the flash hider at the rifle's muzzle and used the weapon to feed the explosive through the thorns.

A black twig two feet into the mass suddenly flared its "bark" into a pincushion of spines tipped with brilliant blue. Leaf shouted and jumped backward.

Two black eyes winked at him; a forked tongue dabbed at the air. The tiny lizard folded its scales as suddenly as it had erected them and scurried back into the tangle.

Caffey had his machine-gun leveled.

"What?" Ensign Brainard demanded. "What?"

Leaf took a deep breath. "Nothing," he said. "Stay clear."

He checked around him. Wheelwright supported OT Wilding, and Brainard had dragged Leaf's own pack a safe three yards away. The barakite strands lying on the ground were as good a compromise as Leaf could judge between being out of the way and being ready to use. . . .

He tucked the first thread another inch into the brambles which were already closing on it, withdrew the rifle and tossed it to Brainard, and lit the barakite with his multitool.

Leaf instinctively covered his ears as he ducked away, but the sound was a vicious snarl rather than an explosion. A wave of heat slapped his back.

When the motorman looked around, the half-consumed strand had already fallen to land on rock through the gap its radiance cleared. For several feet to either side, the brambles themselves burned with sullen orange flames, dim by contrast with the blue-white dazzle which had ignited them. Even beyond that range, vines drew back as heat seared away their moisture.

A haze of barakite residues oozed through the tangle. Leaf grabbed a second strand of explosive. He sucked in another deep breath and plunged into the sudden clearing while blobs of barakite still sputtered, cracking rock with the last of their energy.

There was no time for finesse now, but there was less need for it also. The initial blast of heat had stunned the brambles and robbed them of much of their thorn-clawed speed. Leaf tossed his thread of barakite over a slope of vines whose outer surface was already baked brown.

"Here!" shouted Caffey and handed the motorman more barakite.

Leaf laid that strand at an angle to the first, so the near ends were close together. "G' back!" he ordered, but Fish had already skipped to safety. Leaf lighted the explosive.

The barakite hissed forward with teeth of flame. Brambles ignited, roaring in green agony. Rock, calcined and broken, glinted from the drifting ash. The three remaining strands would be enough to clear the outcrop's entire surface.

K67's whole crew was cheering Leaf.

The motorman reached for more barakite by reflex. Screams filled his ears, and his eyes stared at a curtain of rolling oil flames.

July 1, 379 AS. 2355 hours.

Tech 3 Leaf unsealed the front of his clown suit and removed the two-pound strand of barakite which he had wound around his waist. Sweat gave the surface of the explosive a greasy feel. More barakite appeared from beneath the carnival clothing of the other three members of the gang.

Silent fireworks flared above the Commons of Wyoming Keep. Light flickered from the zenith of the impervium dome and reflected even here, to the narrow back alleys of the warehouse district against the dome's outer curve. The air sighed as tens of thousands of throats cheered simultaneously.

"Oh, my god, they're gonna hear this sure," moaned Epling, a hydrofoil gunner now dressed as a cherub. "The Patrol'll be down on us before we even get a drink!"

The buildings were thick ceramic castings. The material was hard as glass and so strong that a warehouse had remained undamaged when an out-of-control truck demolished itself against the structure. Originally the ceramic had a pink tinge, but the grime of centuries had turned everything in the district gray.

"Just button your lip, Epling," Tech 3 Caffey said. "Leaf knows what he's doing. Don't you, Leafie?"

"Who's got the adhesive?" Leaf asked.

Caffey tossed him a finger-sized spray can. Caffey wore a pirate costume, with a broad-brimmed hat over his domino mask.

Leaf spritzed the warehouse wall five feet above the ground and pressed his strand of barakite against it. The adhesive held, despite sweat and the filthy ceramic. Leaf ran the spray down the wall, squeezing the explosive firmly against the surface.

More fireworks went off in sheets of flame. Braudel, dressed as a skeleton, held a tiny infra-red lamp. The goggles beneath Leaf's clown mask filtered out the multicolored splendor of the display.

Leaf began attaching the second strip of barakite parallel to the ground, with one end in contact with the upper end of the first strand. He was outlining a square doorway on the warehouse's featureless back wall.

"My god," Epling muttered, "they'll lock us up 'n throw away the key. They'll give us life sentences to the netters and we'll just cruise up 'n down till something eats us."

Braudel chuckled. "That's better 'n what Cinc Hafner's gonna do if he learns we scooped this shit outa one a' Caffey's torpedoes, hey?"

"Look, cut it out," Caffey growled. "You'll see. It'll go slicker 'n snot. All the Patrol that isn't keeping the lid on parties is off partying themself. And there won't be a sound. Leaf knows what he's doing."

The third strip of barakite formed the other

vertical. Leaf's body trembled. Present reality, his hands forming the explosive against the sheer wall, was a thin overlay to the quivering surface of memory.

In his mind, the distant cheers of the crowd became screams.

"Anyhow," Caffey added defensively, "d'ye think it's going to matter if a warhead weighs a ton or just a ton less spit? And that's only if the fish hits, which they mostly don't."

Leaf set the last stand of barakite where the warehouse wall joined the alley floor in a smooth curve. Pavement and building had been cast as a single unit only a few decades after the dome of Wyoming Keep had been completed.

"Boy, I can taste the booze already!" Braudel said lovingly. "You know, this won't be cheap-ass shit. You 'n' me, we couldn't buy stuff this good if we had all the fuckin' money on Venus! This is Twelve Families booze!"

"Okay," Leaf heard his voice say. "It's ready."

He took out his multitool. The lanyard pulled open the blouse of his clown suit.

Braudel and Epling stepped, then scurried toward opposite ends of the alley.

"No, it's all right!" Caffey growled after them. "I tell you, there won't be a bang!"

"Maybe from the wall, Fish," Leaf said in a distant voice. "Pieces may fly off it."

"Christ!" snarled the torpedoman. "We come this far. Just do it!"

Leaf triggered the multitool's welder. He knelt, then touched the arc to one of the bottom corners of the barakite frame. Coiling fumes as white and solid as bones lifted from the explosive.

Caffey grabbed Leaf's shoulder and dragged him back a few steps. "Not *that* goddam close, for chrissake!" the torpedoman grunted.

The barakite caught with an echoing hiss which gave
the lie to Caffey's promise of silence. Blue-white brilliance flowed up and across the refractory surface. The
flames shivered through curtains of their own smoke.

The ribbons of light joined at the far corner so that
for a moment fire outlined the square of wall. The hiss
built into a snarl like that of a chainsaw, bouncing
between the warehouse and the dome. Epling and
Braudel drew closer again. Their postures indicated the
nervousness which their masks attempted to conceal.

"Christ," Caffey murmured. "Is it going to—"

The outlined square of ceramic shattered.

Intense heat torqued the cast wall. The internal
stresses finally overwhelmed the structure's ability to
withstand them. Twenty-five cubic feet of ceramic
disintegrated into a quivering pile of needles an inch
long or shorter.

Globs of barakite, flung aside by the structure's shrug
of release, vented their last energy up and down the
alley. A dozen speckles of fire smoldered on Leaf's
costume.

"Perfect, Leafie!" Caffey cried as he clapped the
assistant motorman on the back. "Perfect!"

"Right, let's get it!" Braudel said. He stepped
through the opening, ducking to clear the knife-edged
transom. The pile of needles shifted like sand beneath
the mercenary's boots.

Fireworks shimmered above the column, and the
carnival crowd cheered. Leaf's mind echoed with the
screams of his burning brother.

11

Wilding lay on his back, reveling in the pain of his sores because that alone could cut through the veils of fever which otherwise isolated him from the universe. His right leg floated in air, and the jungle canopy wove a slow dance above him.

Venus took 257 Earth-days to rotate on its axis, a period useless for short-term human concerns. Colonists in domes beneath the Venerian seas had no interest in sidereal time anyway. They promptly adopted the Standard Day of Earth—and retained it for all purposes, even after nuclear holocaust had converted Earth into another star glowing in the unseen sky.

For the Free Companies, the conceit meant that four months of daylight followed four months of darkness. Wars continued, driven by imperatives which ignored the calendar as wars commonly ignore all other things.

Bozman, Leaf's striker, moaned beside Wilding in his sleep. The second watch was on duty now.

Everyone was exhausted. Brainard had put half the crew on watch at all times, not so much because that many pairs of eyes were constantly necessary . . . but

350

because that way there were enough waking guards that they could shake alert each of their number when he inevitably dropped off.

Wilding was exempt from the watch list, but he was too feverish to sleep. Wheelwright had sprayed Wilding's ankle with a long-term analgesic before fitting the pressure bandage, so the injury did not hurt.

Wilding's subconscious *knew* that the ankle had swelled to the size of a balloon ascender. It was tugging his whole body upward. The bandaged ankle appeared to be normal size. The back of Wilding's mind told him that was an illusion.

The swollen balloon pulled. Wilding's back twisted queasily against the rock, trying to anchor him.

He stared at the ragged white patch of sky above him. The saw-grass hewed its surroundings clear at ground level, but branches encroached in the third canopy nonetheless. The slight interstices among the high leaves were barely enough to energize the grass for its murderous exertions.

On the other side of Bozman, Ensign Brainard muttered in his sleep. The CO's duties on point had been the most exhausting of all. Despite that, he insisted on adding the weight of the laser communicator to the normal load of pack and rifle.

Flying rays cut through the air 300 feet up, dancing among the knobby branches of a monkey puzzle tree. Each ray was between one and two feet wide across the tips of its wings. The creatures were about as long as they were wide if the length of their slim, ruddering tails were added to that of their bodies.

Though the rays were descended from a purely aquatic species, they carried on an amphibious existence. Their nests were pools in the hollow hearts of mighty trees. Every ten minutes or so, the rays ducked back to wet their gills, but between dips they sailed among the branches and cleared swathes in the flying microlife. Their wings were so diaphanously thin at the edges that the sky glimmered through them.

Wilding watched the rays wheel without slowing. He thought of K67's commanding officer. Brainard went on no matter what, with stolid heroism of a sort that Wilding had thought was only myth.

Nothing fazed Brainard. If he had to carry them all on his shoulders, he would at least try. But the ensign wasn't an inspiration to lesser men like Hal Wilding, because he was too obviously of a different species.

A ray suddenly folded its wings and plummeted toward the ground. Fever sharpened Wilding's sight or else gave him a hallucination of perfect clarity; in his present state, he neither knew nor cared which was the case. A large purple orchid had extended in a sluggish fashion from a monkey puzzle branch. It hung within the circuits the rays were cutting.

The flower's bulbous outline went flaccid when the orchid expelled the bubble of lethal gas which formed within its petals. The stem began to withdraw. The flower's work was done for the time being.

The ray's nervous system was paralyzed. The little creature was dead before it struck the ground. Its body would rot in the damp heat. Some of its matter would be eaten by scavengers. The rest would become a decaying soup, adding its substance to the thin soil at the roots of the monkey puzzle from which the orchid hung.

And the orchid in turn tapped the veins of the tree for part of its sustenance. Life was a chain, and mutual support created the strongest links. Even in a jungle.

Bozman moaned softly. Leaf, Caffey, and Newton were on watch. Good men in their own way, but nothing without Brainard.

Officer-Trainee Hal Wilding was nothing at all, only a burden on the rest of the crew. His leg tried to float him upward, and the stone under his shoulders trembled like a wave trying to lull him to slee—

The rock *was* moving.

Wilding screamed. He lunged into a sitting position. His leg was a pillar of flame without substance.

Bozman cried out beside him. Wilding grabbed the assistant motorman by the shoulders and shouted, "Help! Help! You've got to get me up!"

Everybody was shouting. Brainard lurched to his feet and threatened the jungle with his rifle. A creature in the high canopy hooted in surprise, then hooted again at a greater distance from commotion.

Wilding lifted himself with hysterical strength. Bozman came with him, but Bozman was a dead weight. The hot barakite flames had broken the outcrop as well as clearing it. In the hours that the men had rested, roots crept through the fractures in quest of nutrients.

They had found Bozman.

Blood sprayed from the young technician's mouth, throat, and the dozen wounds in his chest. One thin tendril had broken off. It waggled a grisly come-on from Bozman's left nostril.

Other roots quivered in circles a hand's breadth out of the rock surface, sensing nearby sustenance. Their tips were scarlet for the depth they had burrowed into their victim.

Caffey pointed his machine-gun at the outcrop and fired. Bullets and rock fragments ricocheted in all directions.

A stone snatched at Wilding's left leg. It missed his flesh, but the tug was all the officer-trainee needed to overbalance him.

"Cease fire!" Ensign Brainard roared. "*Cease* fire!"

Bullets had blown flat, pale craters into the rock. The roots still waved in terrible eagerness. Wilding started to fall forward onto them.

Leaf grabbed the officer-trainee from behind. Bozman weighed down Wilding's arms.

"Let him go, for god's sake!" the motorman growled. "We can't help *him*."

Wilding thought the weight had slipped away, but he was no longer conscious of his body. All he could see was the face of Ensign Brainard, surveying the situation with a look of calm control.

June 4, 381 AS. 1147 hours.

Recruit (Officer) Wilding braced in a push-up position as Chief Instructor Calfredi boomed, "Right! Everybody keeps doing push-ups until fatboy gives me twenty more!"

Calfredi's boot probed the ribs of Recruit (Enlisted) Groves, a pudgy youth of sixteen at the oldest. Groves lay blubbering on the ground, unable to rise.

"I want all you guys to know," the instructor continued to the dozen recruits, "that the reason you're still doing push-ups is Groves here is a *pussy*."

Recruit (Officer) was not a rank, it was a statement of intent; but the scion of the Wilding Family did not need formal rank to act as anger dictated.

"No," Wilding said sharply. He would have liked to spring up with only a thrust of his arms, but fifty push-ups in the sun had cramped his muscles too. He rose to his knees, then lifted himself to his feet.

"No," he repeated, noticing that when he was angry his voice sounded thin and supercilious. "We're doing push-ups because you are a sadistic moron, Mr

Calfredi. Except that I'm *not* doing push-ups any more. I'm going to take a shower."

The exercise yard was crushed coral that blazed brighter than the cloud-shrouded sun. Waves of dizziness quivered across Wilding's vision, making the chief instructor shrink and swell.

Calfredi stood motionless beneath his broad-brimmed hat. If there was an expression on his face, Wilding could not read it.

Wilding turned on his heel and strode toward the barracks. He expected an order—*he imagined a plea*—from Calfredi, but there was nothing.

Not a sound from the chief instructor. Gigantic pumps whined from the harbor, refilling a drydock now that repairs to the dreadnought *Mammoth* were complete. A mile away, railguns crashed and snarled at some creature trying to burst through the electrified perimeter of Hafner Base. A public address system croaked information which distance distorted into gibberish.

Just as he opened the door to the recruit barracks, Wilding heard Chief Instructor Calfredi's voice say, "*Down* and up and *down.* . . ."

Wilding slammed the door behind him, shutting out the hot, muggy atmosphere and the sounds of another portion of the universe which had decided it didn't need Hal Wilding.

He'd said he would shower, so he showered. The hot water massaged Wilding's aching muscles, and the dull pressure soothed what it could not wash away: the knowledge that he'd failed again. He had walked away from his commitment to Wysocki's Herd, and nobody even bothered to call him back.

Joining a Free Company had seemed the only way Wilding could express his utter disdain to the Callahan and the whole Twelve Families: disdain for them and

for their entire way of life. But the Twelve Families
didn't care, and now it was evident that Wysocki's Herd
didn't care either.

Wilding supposed he could try to join another mercenary company now that he'd washed out on his first
attempt, but that would be pointless. He hadn't
wanted to *be* a Free Companion, he'd wanted to
make a statement.

Besides, he might fail ignominiously in training with
a second company, just as he had with the first.

It didn't bother Wilding that he wasn't suited to be
a mercenary. The problem was that he wasn't suited
to be *anything* except a drone . . . and if it came to that,
none of the humans surviving on Venus was really more
useful than Wilding was himself. There were ranks and
places, but those were merely means of marking time
until the holders died or the sun grew cold.

Wilding shut off the shower. He would pack his gear
and report to Cinc Wysocki. With luck, the cinc would
send him off immediately to Wyoming Keep. It would
be embarrassing to wait a day or more for a scheduled
run to the keep, sleeping in the recruit barracks with
the men he had turned his back on.

The barracks door opened. It had been about time
for the training cycle to end anyway. If Wilding had
managed to restrain his arrogance for another ten
minutes—twenty push-ups—he might not have expelled
himself from what he had begun to imagine might be
a brotherhood of equals.

The lights went off.

"Hello?" said Wilding.

Boots scuffled on the polished floor. There were several of them. He could hear their nervous breathing.

Calfredi hadn't been ignoring Wilding after all.
He'd just waited to gather a couple of his fellow
instructors.

Now they were going to give the smart-ass recruit a going away present, off the record.

Wilding ran to the side of the bunk room. His bare feet made only a slight squeal on the floor.

The barracks had a single door. If he could avoid the instructors in the dark, he might be able to duck outside. They wouldn't dare attack him in the open. There couldn't be more than three of them, so they might not have left a guard at the—

Wilding's foot slipped. He hit the floor with a thump. Two pairs of hands grabbed him before he could rise. He kicked with his bare feet, stubbing his toe on a booted shin.

More hands seized him. Many more hands. He tried to swing, but his wrists were pinioned.

"What do you bastards think you're doing?" Wilding demanded in a high, clear voice. He would have screamed if he'd thought there was any chance he could be heard outside the concrete walls of the barracks.

"I got the soap!" rasped an eager whisper. A moment after the words, something hard slammed Wilding in the ribs.

The whispering voice had been Groves.

There was a thump and a curse. "Well, back off!" another voice growled through a muffling towel. Panting, sweating bodies shuffled back, but the hands continued to grip Wilding's arms and legs as firmly as if they were preparing to crucify him.

A bar of soap in a sock whistled through the air and cracked against Wilding's right ear. A similar bludgeon caught him on the left side of the jaw as his mouth opened to scream with pain.

"Now listen, you jumped-up pissant," said the voice through the towel. It sounded like Hadion, the tall, intelligent-seeming recruit who bunked next to

Wilding. "Some day we'll have to take orders from you—"

Hadion wasn't wielding one of the socks, because his voice didn't break as two more blows crunched into Wilding's ribs. The soap would deform instead of breaking bones, but the men swinging the bludgeons were putting all their strength into the project.

"—so we're gonna give you a lesson now, before you get somebody killed because you're pissed off."

"Stop, for God's—" Wilding wheezed.

But his fellow recruits didn't stop. Not until they had beaten him senseless.

12

Brainard looked at the body of the man he'd killed by incompetence. Bozman's corpse still writhed, animated by the roots which resumed their meal as soon as Wilding let the dead flesh fall.

Something knocked loudly in the forest: a warning, or perhaps merely an insect driving its sucking mouthparts into the veins of a tree.

Wheelwright knelt on the ground. He put his hands over his face and began to blubber. It must have been a general reaction. He and Bozman had barely been on speaking terms after trouble with a prostitute while they were on leave.

"S-stop . . . ," mumbled OT Wilding.

Leaf held Wilding upright, though the motorman himself was glassy-eyed. Fluids oozing from Wilding's back glued his shirt to the flesh. Rings of fungus—black at the edge, purple closer in, and bright scarlet at the center—were converting the pus-smeared fabric to food.

Brainard understood what Wilding was trying to mumble: *We can't stop now.*

"Right," the ensign said aloud. "Is everybody all right?"

359

Bozman twitched. Brainard's guts roiled. He gestured toward the corpse with his chin and added, "Everybody else."

Caffey wore a stunned expression. He put a hand on his striker's shoulder and said in a gentle voice, "S'okay, Wheelwright, it's all okay. Just put a sock in it, huh, buddy?"

Brainard looked up along his compass line, then back to the men he commanded. He should have known not to stay in one place for more than an hour. No place on Venus was safe if you gave the planet long enough to sight in on you.

"Right," he said aloud. "Fish, break up Bozman's pack and distribute the contents. We've had our rest. It's time to be moving on."

Wilding had saved them. Wilding, so tortured by pain that he could scarcely speak, had noticed the infiltrating roots. Wilding sounded the warning and, despite his injured leg, had tried to drag Bozman to safety.

A born leader. If Brainard were half the man his XO was, they'd have a real chance of survival.

Brainard hefted his pack. The effort made him dizzy. The other men weren't moving.

He would be left alone to die. . . .

"Technician Caffey, what the hell are you waiting for?" Brainard snarled. "An engraved invitation? Wait a few more minutes and I'm sure the jungle 'll send you one. Just the way it did to Bozman."

The torpedoman blinked. He looked around for the dead man's pack. His limbs moved as if he were heavily drugged.

"Now!" Brainard said.

Leaf shook himself like a swimmer emerging from a pool. He bent over, still keeping one hand in contact with the officer-trainee. He groped for Wilding's makeshift crutch with the other.

Wheelwright helped Caffey rummage through Bozman's pack. They threw out the food packets and passed rifle magazines and chunks of barakite to the living personnel. Newton shrugged into his load with the stolid willingness of an ox.

"It's not far to the top, now," Brainard said.

True enough in terms of feet and inches, but the words sounded as flat in Brainard's own ears as they must in those of his subordinates. The peak was very possibly a lifetime away.

"*Stop . . .*" OT Wilding moaned.

Brainard helped Leaf fit the rifle butt into Wilding's hand. They had to wrap the injured man's fingers around the plastic for a moment until he could grip of his own accord.

"Don't worry, Hal," Brainard said. "We're not going to stop."

August 1, 381 AS. 1747 hours.

Officer-Trainee Brainard stared impassively toward the wall behind the table where the members of the Board of Review sat.

The Board was held in a lecture room with full holographic capability. The President of the Board, Captain Glenn, was the Officer in Charge of Screening Forces. He had set the rear-wall projectors to run a reconstruction of the previous week's battle, in which his units had wiped out the Seatiger ambush and set up the Herd's lopsided victory over the Seatiger main body.

Brainard's left arm was bandaged to the shoulder. He wasn't taking in the computer-generated images of heroic battle on the wall toward which his eyes were turned. His mind was too full of remembered terror.

"Though there's no further evidence—" Captain Glenn said.

Lieutenant Cabot Holman started to rise. He sat in the front row—but at the edge of the hall, as far as he could get from OT Brainard's seat in the center.

"Though as I say, there's no further *evidence,*" Glenn continued heavily, "the Board has agreed to recognize Lieutenant Holman for a few remarks. Lieutenant?"

Captain Glenn was bandaged also. Behind the Board, a hologram of the cruiser *Mouflon*, Glenn's flagship, ripped the night with bottle-shaped yellow flashes from her 8-inch guns. The *Mouflon's* superstructure glittered: first with the white sparks of a Seatiger salvo hitting home, then burps of red flame as shells went off within the cruiser's armor.

Glenn was boastful, and he was rumored to have unpleasant sexual tastes; but he had paid his dues.

Cabot Holman saluted the Board, then turned to eye the audience. There were only thirty or thirty-five men within a hall that could have held ten times the number, but thousands of others watched the proceedings in hologram from their quarters.

"You all know what I'm here to say," Holman said. He stared at OT Brainard. Brainard did not turn his head—toward the glare or away from it, though he felt the pressure of Holman's eyes. "You all know what I'm saying is *true.*"

Glenn grimaced. The other Board members were Lieutenant Dabney, from the hydrofoil squadron, and Commander Peewhit, captain of the dreadnought *Buffalo*. Dabney looked at Peewhit. Peewhit, nodding, said, "The Board will be obliged if you just say your piece, then, Lieutenant."

Holman jerked his chin and faced the Board. "Yes sir," he said, clipping the syllables. "The critical

incident of last week's victory occurred when Air-
Cushion Torpedoboat K44 blew up a Seatiger
destroyer-leader, the *Wiesel*. That proved the Seatigers
had divided their fleet to stage an ambush, and so
permitted our forces to defeat the enemy in detail."

Either a director or unlikely chance set the holographic display to the portion of the battle which
Holman described. A close-up of the *Wiesel* filled the
back wall. The patrolling hovercraft had caught its
target at the most inauspicious time possible. The
destroyer-leader was entering the archipelago's main
channel from a shallow cross-channel barely twice the
vessel's own width. The *Wiesel* could not turn to comb
the torpedo tracks.

But she could shoot. The hologram erupted with
salvoes from both triple turrets and from the dozens
of multi-barreled automatic weapons on the destroyer-
leader's port side.

Brainard found the image eerily unreal. There had
been nothing so crisply visible on the morning of July
24; only smoke and glare and the stench of feces
oozing from Lieutenant Tonello's bullet-ripped environmental suit.

"K44 drove in to close range to be sure of her kill,"
Holman said forcefully. "But she had to go it alone!"

The computer-generated hologram illustrated his
words. Hovercraft K44, occasionally masked by crisp,
ideally-cylindrical waterspouts, drove through the
maelstrom from the left foreground.

K44 cut away to the right, pursued by flashing lines
of explosive bullets. The computer drew glowing tracks
to indicate the hovercraft's torpedoes jinking to negate
the *Wiesel*'s attempt to maneuver. There was no
attempt to follow K44 trying vainly to escape.

Nothing was known of K44's end. The computer
could have supplied the single bright flash of a shell,

killing the hovercraft's crew instantly at the moment of victory. But—

All the small-craft men in the audience knew that something more lingering was also the more probable: a bullet-shattered hull sinking slowly in black water, while wounded men screamed and their blood drew the sea's fanged harvesters.

Better to show nothing. . . .

"If K67 had supported Ted—" Holman continued.

He caught himself, swallowed, and resumed, "If K67 had supported K44, the pair of targets might have confused the *Wiesel's* gunners so that they both escaped."

He pointed at Brainard. "Instead, this *trainee*—" Holman's voice made the word a curse "—turned tail and ran, leaving m—k-K44 to take all the fire herself. This *coward* left my brother to die!"

The holographic destroyer-leader expanded into an orange fireball. The glare mounted until its reflection from the cloud layer lighted the night for ten miles in every direction. It was the perfect beacon to summon the Herd's strength against an ambushing squadron that was to have struck from the flank unawares.

But again, the image was too perfect to mesh with Brainard's memory. In his mind's eye:

Objects were outlined against the yellow-orange mushroom. A gun tub. Twenty square yards of decking which fluttered like a bat's wings. A spread-eagled man who burst into flame at the top of his arc and tumbled toward the sea as a human torch. . . .

"Lieutenant Holman," said Captain Glenn, "I promised you an opportunity to speak your mind. I appreciate your personal loss, but—"

Glenn's voice thinned. After the battle, the medics had taken a shell-splinter three inches long from Glenn's shoulder. Its jagged tip had been deep in the bone. His temper, never mild, had stretched as far as it was going to go with the need to show understanding for a junior lieutenant.

"—the Board *will* confer now and determine its findings."

Holman sat down abruptly. He flushed with anger.

"I don't think we need to adjourn, do we?" said Commander Peewhit. "I have an O-Group scheduled aboard the *Buffalo* at nineteen hundred that I'd like to get to."

Captain Glenn glared at the hall. Holman bit his lips but said nothing.

"No," said Glenn. "We'll just talk here for a moment."

The members of the Board of Review slid their chairs into a trefoil. A privacy screen sprang up around them to distort the passage of light and sound waves. Their figures were ghost images on the other side of a gray discontinuity.

The audience began to whisper among itself. Most of those present in the hall had some connection with the proceedings. The other surviving members of K67's crew formed a tight group two rows behind Brainard.

Cabot Holman stared at the officer-trainee with the fixity of a weasel for a rabbit. Brainard looked toward the computer panorama. His mind sorted through disconnected images, all of them terrifying.

The privacy screen dissolved. The Board members faced around. Dabney stifled a yawn. Glenn tried to scratch his bandaged shoulderblade with his good hand, but he couldn't stretch far enough.

"Right," said Glenn, glaring at the audience again.

The wall behind Glenn showed an overhead view of the Gehenna Archipelago as Herd vessels concentrated their fire against the hopelessly outnumbered ambush squadron. Glenn's screening forces were supported by a squadron of dreadnoughts. Every time a Seatiger ship was spotted or revealed itself by firing, salvoes of 18-inch shells blew the victim to scrap.

The holographic screen went gray.

"The Board has reviewed the actions of the officers and men of torpedoboat K67, patrolling against the Seatigers the morning of July 23," said Captain Glenn. "We find the salient points to be as follows."

The face of Tech 2 Leaf appeared on the back wall. The motorman looked even more pugnacious when his features were expanded to the size of monumental sculpture. Leaf had given his evidence with a brutal directness that suggested he was willing to beat the hell out of anybody who doubted him.

"The crew of K67 believed their vessel was making its torpedo run alone," said Captain Glenn.

Leaf's holographic image said, "The target's automatics opened up—that's before the main guns fired. Right then I seen K44 pop all four of her decoys and sheer to port. I had a good place to see 'cause I was checkin' Fan Three and Holman, his boat was on our port quarter."

Leaf's image looked aside. Brainard had expected the motorman to spit, even here in front of the Board of Review. It had probably been a near thing.

Not quite. Leaf stared at the hologram pick-up and said, "I figured they'd cut 'n' run back up the channel we just came out of. I still figure that."

Glenn or a separate director blanked the holographic screen again. The captain resumed, "At the point Officer-Trainee Brainard broke off the action, K67 had received heavy damage."

This time the holographic screen was split. The face of Tech 2 Caffey gave evidence on the left side, while a damage assessment record made after K67 limped back aboard her tender showed to the right.

"I'd got my fish," Caffey said. The torpedoman was a slicker operator than Leaf, but recent memories gave his testimony a punchy credibility Caffey did not always command. "I was tracking. Then *bam*! The console was gone, just gone. Three explosive shells hit it."

The damage-assessment camera tracked over the torpedo station. Wires dangled from the dual-tracking console. What was left of the faceplate lay on the deck, distorted by electrical fires which followed the shell bursts. Blood spattered the deck and bulkheads.

"Wheelwright was hit," said Caffey's image. The torpedoman was trying very hard to sound calm. "He's my striker. Shrapnel in his legs, but he'd fallen down and I thought it was pretty bad. The interphone was out, and my suit lost its air. Turned out the hose was cut. I didn't know."

The other camera shifted aft from the torpedo station. There was a gap on the stern rail so empty that Brainard had to think to remember what should have been in that place.

"A salvo came in, then," the torpedoman continued. "Main gun. I swear I thought they was firing eighteens."

He forced a smile, but the magnified image showed sweat beading at the line of Caffey's close-cropped hair. "Right overhead. There's a flash, just a flash, and the balloon rig's gone. A shell hit it, but it didn't go off till it hit the sea. That's why we're any of us here. They was using armor-piercing shells with time-delay fuzes, so the one that hit us didn't go off till it was in the sea."

The damage-assessment picture switched to a general port-side view of K67. There were more than thirty thumb-sized dimples in the hovercraft's skirts. Each of the explosive bullets had further gashed the flexible fabric with stars of shrapnel around the black central hole.

"I shouted to the cockpit then," Caffey said. "I said, 'Get us the fuck out of here.' I don't know if they could hear me with the interphone shot away. Anyhow, I thought they was all dead."

He took a deep breath. The other camera steadied on the cockpit. Seventeen holes showed in the port-side bulkhead. Only a glittering memory of the shatterproof windscreen clung to its frame.

How did they miss me? Brainard thought. Then he thought, *Why?*

"I felt her take the helm," said the torpedoman's sweating image. "And I prayed to God, because I didn't think anybody else could bring us outa that one. But I was wrong. Mr Brainard could. Mr Brainard brought us out."

The holograms froze, but whoever was directing the display let them hang in the air for several seconds after Caffey ended his testimony.

Captain Glenn cleared his throat. The images vanished into a gray backdrop.

"The findings of the Board are as follows," Glenn said. He glared at the room. "The crew of torpedocraft K67 reasonably believed themselves to be in action alone. The only evidence that their consort did *not* withdraw when the patrol came under heavy fire—"

The captain nodded appreciatively to Lieutenant Cabot Holman.

"—is that the *Wiesel* was destroyed after K67's own torpedo-guidance apparatus had been put out of action. All honor to Ensign Edward Holman and his crew, who attacked from an unexpected angle while the target concentrated its fire on K67."

The change in Captain Glenn's voice as he continued was as slight as the click of a pistol's hammer rising to the half-cock notch. "The first duty of the patrolling hovercraft after they had released their weapons was to report the existence of the Seatiger ambush. Indeed—"

The screen commander's face hardened still further.

"—one might say the duty to report was *more* important than any potential effect four torpedoes could have on the enemy—"

Glenn's visage cleared. "But in any case, Lieutenant Tonello lived and died by his decision, and we do not choose to second-guess him now. When Officer-Trainee Brainard took command, he extricated his vessel from a difficult situation and withdrew at the best possible speed to give his report—in person, since K67's laser communicator had been rendered inoperative by battle damage."

The two junior members of the Board of Review watched Brainard with alert, open faces. Brainard stared past them, toward a wall as gray as his soul.

"Mr Brainard, will you stand," said Glenn.

Brainard wasn't sure his legs would obey, but they did.

"Our recommendation, therefore, is as follows," the captain said: "That Officer-Trainee Brainard be commended for his actions on the night of July 22-23. That Officer-Trainee Brainard be granted a meritorious promotion to the rank of ensign."

Glenn surveyed the hall. "Lastly, that Ensign Brainard be confirmed in command of Air-Cushion Torpedoboat K67 as soon as he has recovered from the injuries he received in action against the enemy."

The audience unexpectedly dissolved into cheers.

Brainard blinked. His skin crawled with hot needles. Men pounded him on the back. The three members of the Board were coming around their table with arms out to shake Brainard's hand.

Across the bobbing faces Brainard saw the glaring eyes of Lieutenant Cabot Holman—the only other man in the hall who knew, as Brainard knew, that Brainard was a coward who had fled from battle with no thought in his mind but of escape.

13

Caffey crushed a three-inch ant against the bark of the cypress with the muzzle of his machine-gun. The insect's needle-sharp mandibles clicked against the muzzle brake, but chitin could not scar the corrosion-proofed steel.

When Caffey lifted the gun, the ant—still thrashing and alive—dropped almost onto Leaf as he squatted.

"You bastard!" the motorman shouted.

He jerked backward, trying to free his hands so that he could grab his multitool. He'd been kneading a lump of barakite into a ribbon, since K67 didn't carry det cord and they needed something to connect nodes of explosive.

The ant twisted toward the motion. Dying or healthy, the insect warrior's only imperative was to attack whatever threatened the colony's tree. Leaf wasn't a member of the colony: that was all that the ant's instincts required in the way of threat definition.

"Are you all right, there?" Ensign Brainard called. "Leaf?"

Leaf slapped the wad of barakite over the squirming

371

insect and squeezed the stiff explosive into a trough in the cypress's bark.

"No problem," Caffey shouted back. "We're fine."

"Just watch what you're fucking doing!" Leaf growled in a low voice.

The two senior enlisted men worked while the remainder of K67's crew guarded them and one another from attack. Leaf squatted among the cypress' gnarled roots. He couldn't see any of the others except the torpedoman.

Like working in a fan nacelle during combat. The job required all your attention, but you knew your life depended on decisions made by people hidden from you. . . .

Another ant warrior jogged swiftly down the trunk toward him. Leaf pulled his multitool down and locked the take-up spool so that the lanyard hung in the extended position.

The island's peak was dominated by a cypress tree over three hundred feet in girth. OT Wilding had mumbled that the monster probably combined the trunks of up to a dozen individual trees which had grown together. The gigantic result had crushed all lesser vegetation in the neighborhood. Its mighty bole added several hundred feet to the island's thousand-foot elevation.

Leaf's present job was to knock the cypress down.

The ant trotted closer, drawn by scent and movement. Leaf held his multitool out. The ant slashed at it. Leaf pressed the stud. The welding arc popped the insect with a stench of formic acid.

"Goddam!" Caffey shouted. "What're you trying to do, kill us both? What if the barakite had lighted, huh?"

"Shut up and gimme some more of it," Leaf said.

The motorman was dizzy with muscle strain and lack

of sleep. There was a rash around the collar of his tunic; the others said it was bright red. The rash itched spasmodically, burning like a ring of fire at the random times something set it off. Leaf's limbs were crisscrossed by grass cuts, some of them poisoned and all of them festering.

He had to keep going with the explosive, because if he stopped for more than a moment, he was going to tear Caffey's throat out.

The torpedoman handed Leaf a wad of barakite, then looked into the knapsack from which it had come. "Not much left," he said.

Leaf grunted. He began to form the explosive into a rope. His hands, particularly the muscles at the base of his thumbs, ached with the effort.

Brainard had led the survivors as high as the ridge would take them. In order to send a laser message, they either had to climb a tree to the top of the canopy— or create a gap where it stood.

"Hang on," the torpedoman muttered. "I'm going to shoot 'em."

"Huh?" said Leaf.

WHAM!

"You fuckin' idiot!" the motorman screamed. He grabbed for Caffey with his left hand. The cutting blade winked from the multitool in his right.

His legs cramped. He fell back as the torpedoman skipped away.

"What is it?" Brainard demanded. His disembodied voice was as harshly emotionless as life in this surface wilderness.

"We're okay," Caffey shouted back. In a lower voice, he snarled, "Look, I *said* what I was gonna do. Fuck off, will you?"

Leaf looked up at the tree trunk. The gun's muzzle blast had driven fragments of three ants into the soft bark. The bullet scar was a white-cored russet dimple in the striated gray surface.

It had been a fucking stupid thing to do.

Leaf opened his mouth to snarl at the torpedoman. Light streaming through interstices in the cypress leaves illuminated Caffey.

The torpedoman's bare skin was blotched with sores. He was allergic to insect bites, and the first-aid cream did him no more good than it did Leaf's own rash. The hard weight of the machine-gun had broken the skin over Caffey's shoulderblades on both sides. The wounds oozed in an atmosphere purulent with fungus spores. His staring eyes were red with pain and fear.

Leaf shivered.

"Don't do it again, huh?" he said. He worked one end of the strand of barakite into the glob of explosive containing the ant. That was the present terminus of the daisy chain he was weaving as far around the tree's circumference as possible.

Climbing a tree was suicide. This particular monster was guarded by a colony of ants which ate fleshy berries the cypress grew for the insects' sustenance. The ants in turn patrolled the vast expanse of bark and foliage, slaughtering interlopers with a catholic abandon.

No life form on the planet could survive the attack of up to ten thousand acid-tipped mandibles. Leaf and Caffey were at risk even on the ground, where they could move easily. Fifty feet up the trunk, with hands and feet constrained and gravity ready to strike the finishing blow, risk became the certainty of death.

The other option was to blow the tree down. That was emotionally satisfying as well as practical.

Leaf waddled two yards further around the trunk, pulling his thin strand of barakite with him. Though the bark had a smooth, glossy tinge, the explosive clung in an adequate fashion to fibrous irregularities in the surface.

"More," the motorman ordered, holding out his left hand. Undergrowth brushed his shoulder, then the back of his neck. Tiny hooks bit in; Leaf's rash flared incandescently. He turned and slashed in fury with the short blade of his multitool.

Caffey waited for the spasm to pass before he dropped a wad of barakite into the motorman's palm. "Just two besides this," he said. "And the one you've got in your pack."

Leaf pressed the barakite against the trunk in contact with the ribbon he had just laid there. "More," he said, and another doughy wad dropped into his hand.

The torpedoman crushed an ant to the bark with his gun muzzle. While the metal held the insect's head, Caffey reached over with his left hand and gripped one of its flailing legs. He moved with care worthy of a man handling white phosphorous.

When Caffey was sure he had the leg, he lifted the gun barrel and flicked the ant over his shoulder. It pattered into the undergrowth.

"Jeez!" Newton shouted from the direction in which the ant had flown.

Leaf and Caffey giggled hysterically.

There was a deep cleft in the cypress's roots. The motorman had to bob to his feet in order to step across it. He continued to feed out the ribbon of barakite.

K67's crew carried about a hundred pounds of barakite among them. They couldn't blow the gigantic cypress *up* with that amount of explosive, but with luck they could knock it down. Leaf and Caffey spaced the charges along one arc of the circumference. When the barakite detonated, it would shatter the tree's root structure and push the trunk toward the steep drop-off on the north side of the ridge.

If the explosive push was hard enough, the toppling cypress would clear a line of sight to the navigational beacon-transponder in the center of Adonis Deep. If the blast didn't topple the tree—

"More," said Leaf, holding out his hand.

—the officers would figure something else out.

Caffey fired a three-second burst from his machine-gun, emptying the ammunition drum.

"*You fucking—*"

And then the motorman saw the land crab which had rushed from the cleft in the roots kicked half-way back by the stream of bullets. Its armor was a deep blue-green. The claw which Caffey shot off was the length of Leaf's forearm. It would have severed the motorman's leg had the pincers closed as they started to do.

"Technician Caffey, report!" Brainard ordered in a voice made tinny by the ringing in Leaf's ears.

"S'okay, sir, we're golden," Caffey shouted.

His face was white. His fingers fumbled as they replaced the empty magazine with a loaded drum.

"Sorry, Fish," Leaf muttered.

The torpedoman had dropped the knapsack. Leaf reached into it and removed the last wad of barakite. He pressed the explosive into the portion already in place instead of stretching it over another yard or two of circumference.

"Now," said the motorman, "let's get the fuck outa this place."

November 12, 378 AS. 1027 hours.

Seaman Mooker sat cross-legged on the upper bunk of the two-man room, wrapped in a sheet like a barbaric

chieftain. His glittering eyes did not quiver when the
two junior noncoms entered the room.

A tribal chant thundered from the recorder lying on
top of one of the lockers. The volume was so high that
the barracks' massive walls had become a sounding
board. The noise was noticeable in the courtyard and
deafening in the corridor; in the room itself, you
couldn't hear yourself think.

Several one-shot drug injectors lay on floor. They
were empty.

Tech 3 Leaf stepped quickly to the locker and
switched the recorder off. The silence was a blow.

"You bastard," Tech 3 Caffey growled. " 'Come help
me get one of my watch up for fatigue duty,' you say.
You didn't tell me he was stoned!"

"Hey, Mookie," Leaf offered cautiously. "We come
to help you."

The seaman sat like a statue. Leaf looked at Caffey
and muttered, "C'mon, you know Mooker as well as
I do. You figured he overslept?"

Caffey grimaced and toed one of the injectors. It
was unmarked, so there was no way to guess what
Mooker had been using.

"Suppose that's all he's got?" Caffey asked. Leaf
shrugged.

The noncoms moved in silent coordination to
either end of the bunk. Its height was a problem.
"Hey, Mookie," Leaf wheedled. "How you feelin',
man?"

Mooker turned his head toward Leaf slowly, as
though he were learning a complex skill. His eyes did
not focus.

Caffey's hand slid out with the speed and grace of
a cat killing.

"*Got*cha!" he said with satisfaction. He flashed Leaf
a peek at the trio of unused drug injectors he'd just

palmed from the mattress. He slipped them into a sidepocket of his tunic.

"Okay," said Leaf, "but how do we sober him up? If an officer sees him, he's fucked."

"*We're* fucked if we don't report this," Caffey grumbled. "Look, Koslowski's running the clinic this morning, and he owes me one. If we—"

"*No!*" Seaman Mooker screamed. "*No!*"

Mooker tried to stand up. His head slammed the ceiling hard enough to stun a shark. He flopped back onto the mattress.

"Now!" said Leaf as he grabbed the seaman's right ankle.

Caffey had Mooker's left wrist. Mooker's right hand came out of the tangled bedding with a powered cutting bar.

The noncoms sprang in opposite directions. Mooker swung the bar at Leaf, but the assistant motorman was already clear. The saw-edged blade struck the bed post and whined as it whacked through the tough plastic without slowing.

A few drops of blood speckled the wall. Mooker had managed to clip the end of his own big toe.

The seaman giggled. He leaped from the bed, spinning and cutting at the air. He had left the bedding behind. Contractions ran across his nude body, sharply defining alternate groups of muscles.

Mooker's skin shone with sweat although the room's environmental system was working normally. Leaf and Caffey backed as far away as they could get in the small room.

The seaman stood against the door, drawing disjointed patterns with the cutting bar. One swipe struck the corner of a locker. The blade caught momentarily. Leaf tensed, but Mooker dragged the weapon clear with a convulsive effort. He waggled it toward the noncom.

Caffey fumbled in his tunic pocket.

The seaman stared fixedly at him. The cutting bar nodded. Its blunt tip was less than a yard from the torpedoman's face.

Mooker slashed behind himself without looking around.

Leaf dodged back, barely in time. He was sweating also.

"Hey, Leaf," said Caffey. He was balancing a drug injector on his thumb. "You want one a these?"

The seaman froze. Behind Mooker's back, Leaf reached to his own collar and ripped off one of the rank insignia studs.

Caffey flipped the drug injector. The cone of gray plastic wobbled over Mooker's head. Leaf caught and palmed it as the seaman turned.

"Give me . . . ," Mooker demanded in a voice that would have sounded unexpectedly bestial even coming from a wolverine. He raised the cutting bar. Blood from his severed toe pooled on the floor around him.

"Sure, Mookie," Leaf said. He flicked his rank insignia onto the upper bunk.

Mooker trembled like a drive motor lugging. Caffey's mouth opened to scream, but at the last instant the seaman leaped for the bed.

Leaf snatched the door open. Both noncoms slipped into the corridor and slammed the door behind them.

The thunderous music resumed almost at once.

"My God," Leaf groaned. His eyes were closed. "My God, I didn't think. . . ."

"Shit," said Caffey. "No choice but the Shore Police now—omigod!"

Lieutenant-Commander Congreve strode down the corridor to them. He wore a dress uniform; his saucer hat was adjusted perfectly to the required tilt.

"What in the *hell* is going on here?" Congreve

demanded. He did not so much shout as raise his cold voice to be heard over the chant booming from Mooker's billet.

Leaf and Caffey snapped to attention. Leaf hoped the other noncom could think of a way to explain—

But Congreve didn't want explanations, he wanted victims. There were a lot of officers like that. . . .

"You! Leaf!" Congreve said. "Open your hands."

"Sir, it's not—" Leaf said as he obeyed. The unused injector dropped to the floor.

Congreve glared at him. "The first thing you can do is take off the *other* rank stud, Seaman Leaf," he said. "You won't be needing it for a long time—if ever. Now, just what is going on here?"

Leaf swallowed. He was braced so stiffly that he was becoming dizzy, as though being rigid would protect him from what was happening.

"Ah, sir," said Caffey. "It's just, you know, a little party."

The lieutenant-commander's face went red, then white. He stared at the name tape on Caffey's tunic. "Well," he said in a voice of dangerous calm, "we'll just see about that."

Congreve pushed open the door of the billet and said, "All right, stand at—"

The scream and the whine of the cutting bar played a descant to the rumbling bass line from the recorder.

Leaf pulled the door closed. "Let's get the fuck outa here," he said.

14

Filters of cyan, magenta, and yellow shifted across Wilding's vision with every beat of his heart. After hundreds of repetitions, the colors locked suddenly into a polychrome whole. The officer-trainee watched Ensign Brainard take a grenade out of his tunic pocket.

A pair of grenades turned up when Wilding searched K67's ammunition locker. Nobody remembered why they were aboard. Maybe to discourage sea life, maybe because somebody had the notion they'd be useful if the hovercraft's crew had to board another vessel—a vanishingly improbable event.

But the survivors needed them now.

Brainard grimaced, tossing the grenade an inch or two on his palm to judge its heft. He stepped toward the giant cedar. Caffey and Leaf fell in beside him. They were trying to look in all directions at once.

"I said, 'Get to cover,'" the ensign ordered harshly.

The torpedoman opened his mouth to protest.

"I'll have five seconds after I pull this," Brainard said. His finger tapped the grenade's safety pin. "I don't intend to spend it tripping over you two. *Get* to cover."

"Yessir," said Leaf. He touched the back of Caffey's

381

hand on the machine-gun grip. Both noncoms shuffled past the roots of the fallen log in whose shelter the remainder of the crew waited.

Brainard disappeared into the sucking undergrowth.

K67's commanding officer was the only reason most of the hovercraft's crew was still alive. Brainard's absolute courage—and his coldly reasoned certainty when anyone else would have been in a blind panic— kept them all going.

"Jeez, I hope this works," Wheelwright muttered.

His hands squeezed the grip and fore-end of his rifle so fiercely that his knuckles were blotched. A grub poked its three-inch head through the bark of the fallen tree and rotated toward the young sailor. "I want to get outa here so bad."

Barakite was extremely stable under most conditions. A bullet impact would only splash a crater in the doughy explosive. Flame would ignite it; but a fire, although intense, would not topple the giant cypress.

To do that, they needed to detonate the barakite— and K67 hadn't carried blasting caps. A grenade placed directly against the explosive might provide the necessary combination of heat and shock to set off the daisy-chain.

The part of Wilding's mind which was not dissociated by pain and fever prayed that it would.

Caffey crushed the grub with the butt of his machine-gun as he slid in beside his striker. "Hell, we got this far, didn't we?" he said. "Now we just sit for an hour or two and let somebody else do all the work."

The log had been the trunk of an ebony ten feet in diameter—a large tree by any standards short of those which included the dominant cypress. Branches of the ebony and cypress had battled for sunlight. Slowly but inexorably, the cypress levered its rival sideways. Finally, aided by a squall, the giant ripped the ebony's roots from the soil and toppled it in splendid ruin.

The dense log was fresh enough to cover the humans as they avenged the ebony's murder.

"Fire in the hole!" Brainard shouted. Foliage muffled his voice and the crashing progress of his run for cover.

Wilding drifted again through pallid filters. Images of Brainard with the grenade merged with his memories of the Board of Review. Then Brainard was an officer-trainee like Wilding, younger by a few years and with only few more months of service in the Herd.

Wilding watched in awe. Brainard never boasted, never grew defensive. He answered questions with such simple precision that it was only in the words of his crewmen that Brainard's icy heroism became apparent.

Wilding had never met a man like that in twenty-five years of living as a prince in Wyoming Keep. As clearly as an epiphany, Wilding knew that he must beg or bribe his way into the executive officer slot aboard Brainard's vessel. That way even Prince Hal might be able to learn the traits of manhood. . . .

A flatworm, mottled and a yard long, rose from the leaf mold as Brainard dodged past the ebony's root ball. The worm fastened momentarily to the laser communicator strapped to the ensign's chest.

Leaf shouted in fury. Brainard crushed the creature against him with a swipe of his rifle butt. It fell writhing. Brainard flung himself down beside the others.

White light flashed across the underside of the leaves. An instant later, the sharp crash of the explosion shocked the jungle to silence.

"Thank God . . ." Caffey murmured.

The blast was over in the split second of a lightning bolt. The following roar seemed to take forever. Over a hundred thousand tons of wood toppled down the island's north slope, carrying all before it.

"Yippee!" cried Newton. He jumped to his feet. Brainard grabbed the coxswain's belt. Newton was too strong for one man to bring down, but Brainard clung for a moment until Leaf and Caffey added their weight.

Newton slammed to the ground with a curse. Dirt, rocks, and chunks of vegetation kicked skyward by the explosion broke like a storm over the humans.

The sudden destruction drove the jungle berserk. Images printed across Wilding's fever in a surreal montage:

A phalanx of three-yard-long katydids crashed through the undergrowth. The flightless insects ran on four legs and scraped the middle pair deafeningly against their modified wing cases.

Caustic green liquid slurped from the hollow core of a cottonwood, then siphoned back into its hiding place. It left smoldering scars across the bark as it withdrew.

A thirty-foot serpent with eyes like fire opals plunged from high in the canopy. As the snake fell, it twisted to strike repeatedly at its own red-banded body.

A hundred other tragedies glimpsed simultaneously. Thousands more hidden in the massive chaos.

The rain of debris pattered to a halt. The noise of the falling tree continued. Ensign Brainard got to his feet and shambled forward. The able-bodied members of the crew followed . . . and Officer-Trainee Wilding rose as well.

The pain in his ankle no longer registered. Wilding drifted on a cloud as pink as sunset. When he rounded the roots of the fallen ebony, the air was thick with the odors of barakite and pulverized dirt.

The explosion had not been enough to destroy the gigantic cypress, but it had caused the tree to destroy itself. Despite its thick trunk, the cypress was as carefully poised as a skyscraper. The blast shattered the support structures on one side while giving the enormous mass a violent shove in the opposite direction.

Gravity did the rest. When the cypress overbalanced, it ripped out the remainder of its roots and slid two thousand feet down an angle-of-repose slope into the bay beneath. The air above the track was gray with dust, pulverized life, and creatures leaping and swooping to gain advantage in the sudden No-man's-land.

The water boiled where cypress branches thrust into the shallows. Sea life was quick to accept the bounty which chance had thrust into its jaws.

"Move," Wilding whispered. "Move. . . ."

Every time Wilding's right foot touched the ground, the world became sepia-toned. Full color returned when he took his weight on his left leg and the makeshift crutch. Still he felt no pain.

The cypress, like most trees growing in thin jungle soils, had wrapped its roots across the surface instead of driving them deep into rock that was bare of nourishment. Even so, the giant took a great bite of ridge line along when it fell. Boulders shook free of the roots which gripped them and bounded in separate arcs through the jungle. The crew of K67 skirted the left side of the crater.

"Hey!" somebody cried. Wilding heard the crewmen's voices shifted up several octaves, by fever or by the ear-punishing blast. "There's a boat down there!"

At first glance, Wilding's heart leaped with hope that gilded what he saw. He shifted the magnifying function of his helmet visor to x20 and looked again.

It was still a boat, a hovercraft. But there was no hope at all.

The vessel was beached—almost beached—several hundred feet west of the seething ruin which the cypress had torn to the bay. It rode very low. Its skirts grounded where the water off the shelving beach was still three feet deep, and the crew had been unable or unwilling to bring their craft ashore.

Instead, the shore had come to them.

Honeysuckle ruled the low ground behind the belt of salt-drenched sand on this side of the island. The foliage moved softly, turning toward the opportunity provided by the cypress' clearing operation. A bridge of vines was arched across the sand to the hovercraft.

The vessel appeared undamaged to the naked eye. Magnification showed that honeysuckle covered all the plastic surfaces in a thin mat. The leaves were brown and shrunken. The colonizing vine had become dormant while it awaited further sustenance.

"Sir, did they come for us?" squealed a foolish, hopeful voice. "Are they going to pick us up?"

Dust settled along the track of the cypress. The flailing roots had dragged torn-up material along, depositing it in a series of clumps and valleys like an oscilloscope pattern. Because the slope still vibrated with the tree's impact, the mounds continued to settle.

Something moved near the bottom of the track. It was big enough to be a shifting mass of vegetation, but it was coming uphill.

"Caffey, set up a tight perimeter," squeaked Ensign Brainard. "We're in the open here, and that's not entirely good. Leaf—"

Wilding stepped closer to the edge. His helmet enhanced as well as magnifying the image. Mimosa fronds waved in the middle of the slope, but Wilding could not see what was beyond them.

No herbivore was likely to be racing to inspect the site of an explosion.

The ridge dropped sharply for a hundred feet, then splayed outward in a marshy knob where water seeped through a fold in rock layers. The cypress had hung there for a moment. When it continued its long slide to the sea, the tree scraped the knob to mud.

Two hundred feet below the smear of flattened marsh, a pile of broken alders shuddered. A forked, black-and-yellow tongue, as long as a man was high, flicked over the wrack to sample the air.

"Get back!" Wilding screamed. His own voice was only the upper sideband of human speech. "Run! Something's coming!"

The head of a monitor lizard, the dominant land predator of the planet, twisted over the alders. The pile of debris scattered beneath the monster's eight-ton weight. Its tongue continued to slip in and out like light quivering over a swordblade.

Wilding stared into the lizard's magnified jaws. The cone-shaped teeth were six inches long, and the yellow gullet was large enough to swallow a man whole.

"Get back!" he screamed, but this time he was speaking to himself. The soil gave way beneath his left foot; his right held for a moment. When the right ankle buckled, the officer-trainee began to float effortlessly, through the air—

Down toward the fifty-foot lizard.

July 23, 382 AS. 0344 hours.

Officer-Trainee Wilding heard the shells howl.

The sound was more penetrating than the crash of the *Mouflon*'s main batteries or even the drumming bass note of 1-inch Gatlings trying to claw the incoming out of the air before it hit the cruiser.

He looked up from his console, trying instinctively to see through the armored ceiling. His mouth was open.

Two Seatiger shells burst in the storm of fire from the automatic weapons. The other four slammed into the *Mouflon*'s bridge and forward hull.

There was a green flash. All the lights went out. Wilding felt his buttocks lift from his chair. He had no sense of direction. The air smelled burned, and the shockwaves of the blast were so severe that he felt them as pressure, not as noise.

Wilding hit his chair again. The emergency lights went on, yellow strips set into the deck and ceiling moldings. Wilding's console hummed and flickered as it re-created the display affected by the power interrupt.

Blue tungsten-sulphide letters on the margin of the display switched from BACK-UP to PRIMARY.

The regular gunnery officer, a senior lieutenant, sprawled at the console beside Wilding's. His face wore a surprised expression. One of the shell impacts had flexed the armored ceiling enough to spall fragments across the bridge. A saucer-sized disk whacked through the lieutenant's neck, then sawed his workstation into sparkling ruin.

Wilding was now gunnery officer for the *Mouflon*'s starboard automatic weapons, though computers would fire the weapons unless Wilding chose to override their electronic decisions.

The *Mouflon* rippled off a salvo from her twelve 8-inch guns. Her hull twisted like a snake from the recoil stresses.

Captain Glenn got to his feet. His left shoulder was bleeding. His good hand pawed aimlessly.

Glenn's eyes focused. He looked down at the deck, picked up his commo helmet, and slapped it back in place over his short-cropped hair. "Damage report," he ordered harshly.

"Hull nominal," said Collor, the *Mouflon*'s executive officer. "Main battery nominal. Fires in three forward compartments, controllable at present." Collor looked up from his holographic display. In the same dry voice as before, he concluded, "Thirty percent damage to bridge command-and-control installations, but back-up systems are in place."

Shock had unbonded a ten-foot swath of sound-deadening foam from the ceiling. Damage-control personnel sawed at the fallen blanket to get it out of the way.

The foam was dense and twelve inches thick. It was supposed to be able to trap spalled fragments. It hadn't done its job well enough for Wilding's immediate superior. . . .

The *Mouflon* writhed with another outgoing salvo. Burning propellant expanded the gun breeches; they rang like huge bells.

Wilding's console indicated that no further Seatiger shells were in the air. The Gatlings were silent for want of targets.

Wilding's mouth was dry. He made an effort of will to close it. For a moment, he couldn't remember why he sat so rigidly in his chair. He was afraid that if he tried to move, his head would slip from his shoulders and bounce to the console, the way the lieutenant's had done. . . .

"Sir," said the lieutenant-commander in charge of communications. He reached over with the sheet of hard copy which his console had just run off.

Captain Glenn bent to take the flimsy. "Wait!" chirped the medic cutting away the back of Glenn's jacket. Glenn shouted a curse, reacting to the pain of the forgotten wound rather than the medic's order.

"First bloody time I wore this uniform," Glenn muttered as he snatched the print-out with his right hand. "*First* bloody time."

The eight-inch guns salvoed again. Each tube fired

a half-second behind the next previous. The firing sequence spaced the shockwaves and avoided a simultaneous recoil which would do more damage to the *Mouflon* than an enemy shell.

Wilding's mind rang with the scream the lieutenant had died too quickly to utter.

"Right," said the screen commander. He keyed his commo helmet with his right hand, still holding the scrap of hard copy. "Cease fire," he ordered. His voice boomed from the bridge tannoy and echoed through every compartment of the cruiser.

"All Root elements," Captain Glenn continued. "Change course to one-one-two degrees and proceed at flank speed."

Wilding was fifteen feet away from the communications console. The red tinge of the characters flickering there indicated the *Mouflon* was now broadcasting to all the screening vessels—code-name Root.

Glenn stood at his console. His broad face wore a cat's grin. He seemed oblivious of the medic working behind him with scissors and a spray can of artificial skin.

"We've finished our job here," Glenn said. "Now we'll join Trunk and finish the rest of it. We can expect to contact—" his voice boomed in exultation "—the Seatiger main body within twenty-five minutes unless they run . . . and they can't run fast enough!"

The *Mouflon* started to answer her helm, but for Wilding the sensation was almost lost in the vessel's pitch and yaw through the wave. A 15,000-ton cruiser requires a great deal of time to change heading by 120°.

"Sir?" said the *Mouflon*'s flag captain. "Should we, ah . . . detach some light craft to tend the vessels that have been disabled?"

"Negative," Captain Glenn snapped. "We have a job

to do. We'll rescue survivors as soon as the Seatigers surrender. Until then, they'll have to fend for themself."

"I'm done, sir," muttered the medic.

Glenn flexed his shoulders and winced. By chance, he was glaring straight at Officer-Trainee Wilding as he concluded, "We're not running a nursery. It's the law of the jungle!"

15

Ensign Brainard looked downslope as the warning rang in his ears. With its keen sense of smell, the reptile would track them as inexorably as the tide came in.

OT Wilding leaped down the steep slope, sacrificing himself to the lizard's jaws in order to save the rest of them. Wilding repeated, "Get back!" even while he slid and tumbled along the track the cypress bulldozed.

It would work. The gift of one life would conceal the existence of five more from the short-sighted reptile.

Brainard opened his mouth to shout, "Back from the edge!" to his remaining crew.

Off the beach far below, the vine-covered torpedo-craft sat like a flaw against the beautiful water surface, which quivered with the thousand colors of a fire opal.

Ted Holman had sacrificed his life to torpedo the Wiesel—and save K67 as it fled under Brainard's command. Brainard wasn't going to abandon Hal Wilding as well.

The monitor lizard lifted onto its clawed toes to scramble over the debris. Its great head swung from side to side, bringing one black eye, then the other, to bear on the officer-trainee. It was the tongue,

392

quivering like a fork-tailed serpent, which would guide the beast to its kill.

"Get back!" Brainard shouted to his crew. He leaped down from the crest to rescue his executive officer.

Brainard stayed upright for half the distance. He was running out of control, but his legs pumped swiftly enough that his boots crashed down each time just ahead of his center of mass.

Wilding lay spread-eagled in the muddy saddle. He rose to his hands and knees, then tried to force himself upright with the chewed rifle which he had somehow managed to grip during his fall. Wilding's back was toward the oncoming monster.

A sprig of running cedar, bruised but not destroyed by the avalanche of timber, lifted a feathery frond at motion and the chance of a meal. The tiny suckers on the underside of its leaves slipped from the ensign's heel, but the touch was enough to cost Brainard his balance. Instinct flung his arms and legs out in a grotesque cartwheel which could do nothing to save him.

Brainard hit on his shoulders. He somersaulted, chance rather than skill, until the roots of a tree demolished by the avalanche flung him into the air. He sailed twenty feet, scraped down on his left hip and arm, and rolled sideways into the man he had come to rescue.

"Come on," Brainard said.

Brainard's voice was a whisper because all the breath had been knocked out of his lungs. He stood up, trying to center himself as the universe spun around him. He had to concentrate on the job. Nothing but the job.

The sun seemed brighter. He'd lost his helmet. His rifle and the pack with his extra ammo had gone too, flung off in his chaotic dance downslope.

The laser communicator was still strapped to his chest. It clacked against Wilding's crutch as Brainard tried to grip the officer-trainee for a packstrap carry. Brainard slapped the quick-release buckle and dropped the communicator to which he had clung with hysterical determination from the time they abandoned K67.

"We can't . . . ," Wilding wheezed.

Brainard took a step. His boot slipped. He had to steady himself with his free hand. A curtain of tears and terror turned the torn slope into a gray-green blur.

Another step. Piled timber crashed nearby. A clod of mud jolted Brainard's back.

The stench of death drove aside every other sensory impression. Wilding twisted out of Brainard's grasp. The ensign turned to seize Wilding again and saw the monitor lizard.

The beast's forelegs and belly glistened with mud, but its hooked claws were clean. The beast's scales were knobby and thick enough, even on the wrinkled skin of its long throat, to shatter a rifle bullet.

Not that either man had a working rifle.

The monitor's open mouth stank with the rotting effluvium of its previous meals. Its tongue flicked out once more and sucked back as the beast struck at Wilding.

Wilding thrust the rifle he used for a crutch into the lizard's mouth, wedging it upright between the upper and lower palates. He clung to the prop. The beast hissed like a boiler venting and reached out with its claws.

Brainard shouted. The laser communicator was at his feet. He picked it up by the strap and swung at the monitor's head.

The heavy mace crunched when it hit. The lizard's right foreleg twisted up and back to probe the point of impact. Wilding lost his grip on the rifle and fell down.

Brainard tottered as he tried to lift the communicator

for another blow. "Geddown!" screamed Caffey from behind him. Brainard lost his footing as he looked back in surprise.

Caffey's machine-gun roared out a fifty-round burst that emptied the drum magazine and heated the barrel white. Blue-gray smoke from the flash suppressant in the gunpowder spurted around the scene in a bitter cloud.

Blood speckled the monitor's yellow maw and the bullet-drilled dimples in its scales. Several rounds sparked as they punched through the alloy receiver of the rifle in the lizard's mouth. The prop folded as the jaws began to close.

Newton and Wheelwright knelt/sprawled beside Caffey. They were firing also, but their shots were lost in the storm of heavier bullets from the machine-gun.

The injuries might be fatal . . . but a lizard this size would take days to die, even if some of the bullets were lucky enough to penetrate the bone-armored brain. Before that happened—

Leaf stepped forward. He thrust, rather than threw, a blob of burning barakite left-handed into the reptile's mouth as the jaws closed. The long, yellow-gray neck spasmed. The lizard's autonomic nervous system caused the throat muscles to squeeze and carry the lethal cargo toward the belly.

Brainard rose into a crouch. He'd lost his pistol, but the butt of Wilding's sidearm still protruded from his holster. Brainard would take that and—

A muffled blast knocked all the humans down.

The monitor lizard's writhing body hurtled downslope in a series of convulsions. The monster's head had vanished. A cloud of liquified blood, bone, and flesh covered everything in a fifty-yard circle with pink slime.

The men roused themselves to sitting positions. Everybody seemed to be all right, even Wilding. *Hell, even Brainard, except for the ringing in his ears.*

Nobody spoke or tried to stand. Below them, the monitor lizard thrashed through the jungle beside the track the cypress had cleared. The beast rolled onto its back repeatedly. The motion flashed its mud-smeared belly scales against the less reflective green-brown mottling of its back and sides.

"I always heard," said Leaf finally, "that if you stepped on barakite while it was burning, it'd blow your goddam foot off. Guess it's not a good idea t' swallow it, neither."

Brainard swallowed. His conscious mind was totally disconnected from his body, but instinct braced him upright and started to bring his feet under him. "I thought I told you to use all the explosive on the cypress," he heard himself say. "So we were sure it went over."

"Sorry sir," the motorman said. "I guess I was in a hurry."

"That's okay," said Brainard.

He stood up and looked toward the top of the ridge. He couldn't imagine how they'd avoided breaking their necks on the steep, muddy slope. There was no way in hell that they could climb it again; nor was there any reason to do so now.

"Right," Brainard said. "We'll head for the other hovercraft now. If we move fast, we ought to be safe enough following where the tree slid."

He eyed a fig that stepped slowly toward them across the cleared swath. The plant tottered forward by extending one slanting root after another, like the legs of a man walking.

"But we better be fast," he added.

"Sir?" asked Wheelwright as he locked a loaded

magazine into his rifle. "Is there going to be crew on the boat?"

"No," said Brainard flatly. "There isn't. The vines got them. There may be a working laser communicator, though."

He toed the unit he had carried from K67. The monitor lizard's claws had punched three finger-deep holes through the unit's tough outer casing.

"The other hovercraft . . . ," the ensign added softly, " . . . is K44."

August 2, 381 AS. 0212 hours.

He was dreaming:

The wand of honeysuckle wavered vertically against the opalescent dawn. A seaman fired at it. Three bullets slapped the tough vines and blew away scraps of foliage.

The bolt locked open. The seaman ejected the spent magazine and reached for a fresh one. His ammunition pouches were empty. He began to cry.

The honeysuckle toppled forward. Its upper end scrunched over the hovercraft's bow, forming a bridge to the great mass of the plant trembling across the narrow stretches of sand and surf.

Leaves uncurled from the tip of the bridge. The speed at which the plant moved when driven by the rising sun was as unexpected as it was horrible.

The coxswain stepped close and slashed with a cutting bar. The multistranded vines resisted, but the shrill whine of the bar laid a swatch of the questing tendrils on the deck.

The bridge hunched as though it had nerves rather than tropisms. The coxswain shouted in triumph and took another cut. A tendril he had missed on the first pass wrapped around his ankle.

The man screamed. He chopped downward. His bar hit the deck short of the vine and howled vainly for a moment. Before he managed to free his ankle, three other tendrils gripped the coxswain's waist, left leg, and the wrist of the hand holding the cutting bar. His environmental suit was no protection. Hollow, inch-long thorns sprouted from the base of every leaf.

The coxswain screamed as though he would never stop. The burgeoning vines crept over him like a blanket drawn up to cover a sleeping infant.

A seaman with a knife lurched forward to help. A tendril lifted toward him. The seaman turned and ran.

The screaming did, of course, stop.

Giant crabs crawled in the surf foaming about the hovercraft. Their claws thumped against the skirts, trying to get a purchase on the tough fabric. Occasionally a crab drew itself halfway out of the water. The crustacean always lost its grip because of the plenum chamber's outward batter.

Honeysuckle fanned in a thin sheet across the deck. There was very little waste motion. Tendrils climbed the gun tub and explored its interior. They quickly realized that the warmth which drew them was that of hot metal rather than a source of nutrients.

The twin seventy-fives had twice blasted off the wand of honeysuckle rising on the shore. The big bullets cratered the beach and jungle beyond. Scavengers, drawn to the commotion, now battled on the torn sand.

But the gunner had fired all his ammunition. Minutes later, the crewmen emptied their personal weapons in a volley at the honeysuckle's third attempt to raise a boarding bridge.

Rifle bullets nibbled at but could not sever the thick strands of the vine's core. . . .

The tendrils which wrapped the breeches of the twin seventy-fives, and other vines that reached a dead end, immediately went dormant as the plant withdrew scarce resources. Leaves withered; the stems themselves went brown and brittle-looking.

Other vines humped and curved themselves more quickly, driven by light and drawn by the surviving crewmen huddled together in the stern. The sun was a ball of white heat shimmering through the clouds of the eastern horizon.

There was a slowly-sinking mound of leaves where the coxswain had been. The epithelial cells carrying nutriment back to the core from that writhing pile had a red tinge.

Tendrils washed toward the hovercraft's stern in a sudden wave. The XO batted at a vine with his empty pistol. Foliage curved around his hand and gun like a green glove. He screamed and threw himself over the rail.

A crab sprang up from the surf. It caught the XO's thigh in pincers eighteen inches long. The honeysuckle did not relinquish its hold.

The young officer hung in the air. Vines wrapped his head and shoulders, muffling and finally choking off his screams. The sea beneath him was a froth of crabs struggling in the blood which poured from his severed femoral artery.

More men cried out. It had the whole crew, all but him. The stern rail pressed the small of his back. He drew himself up on it, raising his feet from the deck across which tendrils swept.

A column of honeysuckle rose from the twitching corpse of his motorman. The tip was as tall as his head. It quivered delicately, absorbing the data from sensors which measured temperature, sound waves, and the moisture content of air exhaled from an animal's lungs.

The vine toppled forward. He screamed as the hollow fangs drove into his face and chest....

The door banged open. "Are you all right? Brainard! Are you all right?"

There was a light on in the hallway of the Junior Officer's Barracks. Brainard didn't at first recognize the speaker silhouetted in the doorway, but the hard, familiar lines of his own room brought him around like a douche of cold water.

He sat up. His sheet tangled him. He flung it off. Despite the room's climate control, his body was clammy with sweat.

"Are you all right?" the other man repeated. Lieutenant Dabney, who'd been on the Board of Review that afternoon.... He had the room across the hall. His voice was more calm now that he saw Brainard was under control.

"Oh, God," Brainard whispered. He covered his eyes with his hands, then realized that darkness was the last thing he wanted. He switched on the bed lamp.

There were more figures in the hallway. He must have let out one hell of a shout when the honeysuckle wrapped him....

Lieutenant Dabney swung the door closed and knelt beside the bed. "Bad dream?" he asked mildly.

"Wasn't a dream," Brainard whispered. "I was aboard K44. I think I was Ted Holman. They all just died. The sun came up, and the honeysuckle got 'em all."

"Hey," said Dabney, "it was a dream. We all have them."

He patted Brainard's knee, but his grip grew momentarily fierce. "Believe me," Dabney rasped in a bleak voice. "We all have them."

"Oh God," Brainard repeated.

The lieutenant twitched. "Look," he went on, his

tone cheerful, reasonable, "don't worry about K44. They took a direct hit. Hell, they probably got caught in the secondary explosions when the *Wiesel* went up. Instantaneous. A lot better than what happens to civilians, dying by inches in a bed while the medics cluck."

He patted Brainard again and stood up.

"Thanks, sir," Brainard said. "I'm fine. But—" He shrugged. "But that isn't what happened to K44's crew," he went on. "They beached their ship. And when the sun came up, the vines got moving."

Brainard smiled. It would have been a friendly expression if his eyes had been focused.

Dabney licked his lips. "Yeah," he said. "Well, if you're okay. . . ."

He reached for the door handle. Before he touched it, he turned and said, "Look, Ensign . . . this isn't exactly my business, but I've been in the Herd longer than you have."

Brainard nodded.

Dabney looked up at the ceiling. He cleared his throat and went on, "Cabot Holman, he's a good officer, don't get me wrong. But he'd always taken care of his kid brother even though there wasn't but three years between them. Ah, nobody's going to think anything's wrong with you if you decided to transfer out of hovercraft. Or. . . ." Dabney met Brainard's eyes. He relaxed visibly to see that the ensign's expression was normal again. "Or look, you could just transfer to some four-boat element besides the one that Holman commands. Okay?"

Brainard stood up. "No, that's okay," he said. "I appreciate what you're saying, but I'll do the job in front of me. Understand?"

Nobody could misunderstand the sudden crispness of Brainard's voice.

"Sure," agreed Dabney with a false smile. He opened

the door, stepped through it, and closed it behind him in the same fluid motion.

Brainard sighed. He turned and unpolarized his outside window.

The sky was opalescent. Hafner Base was to the west of the Gehenna Archipelago. Dawn would have broken over the myriad small islands there half an hour earlier.

16

"Beautiful," said Officer-Trainee Wilding. He balanced cautiously on his left foot so that he could gesture with his new crutch toward the creatures wheeling in the bright sky. "Aren't they the most beautiful things you've ever seen, Mr Leaf? Technician Leaf."

Wilding felt the motorman force down his right arm; gently at first, but with increasing firmness as the officer-trainee resisted. "Come on, sir," Leaf muttered. "We don't wanna stop just yet."

Wilding giggled. "Nope, we can't afford to stop," he said. "We've *got* to keep the common people interested, but we *can't* give them anything real to be interested in. Isn't that right? We can't stop!"

A facet of Wilding's mind knew that he was raving, but that facet was in charge only during brief flashes. The last of the analgesics had worn off hours earlier, but Wilding still felt no pain; only pressure. Pressure that seemed to swell his skin to the bursting point.

"C'mon, sir," said Leaf. "Just a little farther, and it's all on the flat now."

Wilding let himself be guided by the motorman's arm. They were on sand, so it was hard to walk. The

403

muzzle of the rifle Wilding used as a crutch dug into the yielding surface, punching divots and threatening to let him overbalance.

Wheelwright had burned the interior of his rifle barrel smooth with the long bursts he poured into the monitor lizard. Wilding used that weapon as a crutch, and Wheelwright carried the spare that had been Bozman's rifle. . . .

The beach was about fifty feet in width at this stage of the solar tide. The remainder of K67's crew stood in the middle of the strip of sand, staring from a safe distance at the hovercraft and its tracery of honeysuckle.

"I say we just run across it," suggested Caffey. "The vines, they're dead, but they'll hold us till we get to the ship. Just like they was a bridge."

"No," said Ensign Brainard.

The cypress lay in the surf a hundred yards from the humans. A school of flying frogs swept back and forth over the tree's path down the slope.

There were never less than two of the vividly-colored amphibians in the air at any one time. At least a dozen were involved, but after a few passes each frog sailed back to the shadows to wet itself in the pools at the heart of spiky bromeliads. Generally the frogs would not venture into sunlight filtered only by the atmosphere, but the disaster had put up enormous numbers of small insects on which the frogs fed.

"Beautiful . . . ," Wilding murmured again.

"The end shoots will regenerate as soon as we get within fifty feet of them," Brainard said. "Mr Wilding can tell you."

Wilding tittered. His mind did not think that his lips made any sound.

Brainard pointed toward the bridge of honeysuckle with the first and second fingers of his left hand. Fresh leaves gleamed green against the ropes of brown stems. They moved very slowly, as if only the wind animated them.

"Look what's happening already," he said. "We'd get aboard, but we'd never get back. Believe me. To grow, that plant can pump food through its veins at the speed of a firehose."

Leaf looked at the hard-faced ensign. "You seen it, then, sir?" the motorman asked in puzzlement.

Wilding watched the other humans; watched the hovercraft; and watched the frogs overhead. The three images were pallid except where one chanced to encompass part of another. Overlaid viewpoints had rich colors and sharp lines.

"Yeah," said Ensign Brainard. "I've seen it."

The sea's gentle, back-and-forth motion hardened with stalked eyes, then claws stained shades of blue and lavender. Crabs edged sideways onto the sand, skittering a yard forward and half that distance back.

Their spike-edged shells were three feet across. There were already dozens of them on shore. More eyes peeked out of the water.

"Bet it'll burn," suggested Caffey. "The vine, I mean, dry as it is now. The boat, it's fireproof t'anything up to a thousand degrees."

The frogs flew by rhythmic motions of the skin stretched from their wrists to their hind feet. They retained their fore-paddles as canard rudders which allowed them to turn and bank with astonishing quickness in pursuit of their prey.

"You wouldn't think an amphibian could fly without drying out, would you, Leaf?" Wilding heard his voice say. "Even in an atmosphere as saturated as this is. Isn't nature wonderful?"

"If it burns," protested Leaf, "then how do we get aboard? Have *them* carry us?"

He gestured toward the crabs with his multitool.

One of the crustaceans scuttled ten feet closer to the humans, then raced back toward the sea in a spray of sand.

Newton raised his rifle. He fired at the crab. His bullets cracked the carapace and broke the lower jaw of one pincer so that the saw-toothed edge hung askew on its fibers of internal muscle.

"Dumb shit!" Caffey shouted. "How much ammo you think we got left?"

The injured crab reached the edge of the sea before the weight of her fellows brought her down. They flailed the water in their haste to rend the sudden victim. Successful crabs raised long strips of pale meat in their claws, then sidled away to shred their sister further in their swiftly-moving mouth parts.

"Look," growled Newton. "I hate 'em. Okay? Just keep off my back!"

A facet of Wilding's mind giggled at the fire discipline which the trek had hammered into K67's crew; a facet watched the wheeling frogs; and the facet in control of his muscles for the moment said crisply, "No, that was right. They would have rushed us very soon. Newton provided something else to occupy them."

The coxswain looked at Wilding and grinned shyly. Newton's stolid strength was so great, even now, that he hadn't bothered to shrug off his pack while they paused for consideration. "Thanks sir," he said. "Things with claws, I just. . . ."

"Fish is right," said Ensign Brainard, returning to the problem at hand. "The core stems are still full of sap in case there's a chance to grow. They won't burn, so we'll have the bridge to cross on. But all the tendrils will go, and that should slow down the regrowth. A lot. I think enough."

"It's a jungle out there," Officer-Trainee Wilding said

to the crabs furiously demolishing their fellow. "It's a jungle everywhere, did you know?"

This time the laugh was internal but he spoke aloud the words, "It's a jungle in the Keeps, too. Especially in the Keeps."

"Right," said Brainard, putting the cap on his thoughts in his usual, coldly decisive fashion. "To make sure it ignites, we'll need to get a flame into the really dry portion, but it'll blaze back very quickly. What we need is a wad of barakite we can throw. Leaf, do we have any more?"

A machine could act as decisively; but no machine intelligence could process the scraps of available data into the survival of six human beings under the present conditions. . . .

The motorman winced as though he had been struck. "Sir, I'm sorry," he said, "but I cleaned out ever'body else when we blew up the tree, and the last bit. . . ."

"Don't apologize for following my orders, Technician," Brainard snapped.

The sand quivered slowly down the beach toward the humans. If Wilding had been limited to a single viewpoint, he would not have noticed it. When two images merged like a stereo pair, the trembling line was evident.

Brainard ran his fingertip down the front seam of his tunic, unsealing it. "This fabric's processed from cellulose. It should burn well enough."

"Newton," Wilding ordered. "Give me a magazine for this rifle."

"Sir!" said Leaf in concern. "Don't try t'shoot that without we knock the dirt outa the muzzle."

The coxswain handed Wilding a loaded magazine without comment or apparent interest. Wilding locked it home in the receiver well without lifting his "crutch." The muzzle brake was completely buried.

Ensign Brainard took his tunic off. There were dozens of puckered sores on his arms and among the hairs of his chest. "Weighted with a little sand," he said aloud, "we'll be able to throw it aboard K44 from halfway along the honeysuckle bridge. That should do."

Wilding retracted the charging handle and let it clang forward, loading the rifle. "Help me walk," he ordered Leaf curtly.

"Sir . . . ?" pleaded the motorman. He sighed and took his share of Wilding's weight. The officer-trainee stumped toward an event no one else was aware of.

"Better let me handle that, sir," Caffey said to the ensign. "It's going to backfire pretty quick, and—"

"Thank you, Technician," Brainard said, "but it's my job."

Both the thanks and the assertion were as false as a politician's faith. The ensign straightened, knotting the sleeve of his tunic to hold the weight inside. Sand dribbled out through tears in the fabric.

Wilding slanted his rifle outward and drove the muzzle deep in the sand. His surroundings were a montage of images in which nothing was clear. "Is it ready to fire, Leaf?" he demanded. "Is it off safe?"

"Yeah," said the motorman, "but for chrissake, sir—"

"Leaf," Ensign Brainard ordered, "give me your multitool for a—Wilding! What the hell are you doing?"

The line in the beach steadied, then merged with the pimple raised from the sand around the rifle muzzle. The surface mounded as something rose through it, drawn by vibration and pressure which compacted a point of the beach.

Hard chitin clacked against the steel muzzle brake as a shock drove the weapon upward. Wilding pulled the trigger.

The sound of the shot was muffled, but the sand exploded as if a grenade had gone off. Recoil knocked Wilding backward despite the motorman's attempt to hold him.

The magazine flew out. The muzzle brake was gone. Excessive pressure sprayed the cartridge casing in fragments and vapor from the ejection port, but the breech did not rupture.

A hand-sized fragment of bloody chitin lay in the center of the disturbed area. Instead of surfacing, the creature drove down in a series of circles that widened, leaving ever-fainter traces on the beach above. A line shivering toward the humans from the other direction changed course to intercept its injured peer.

Everyone else stared at Wilding. "It's a jungle," he repeated in a high, cheerful voice. "But it's our jungle too."

Leaf bent to help Wilding rise. In the same tone, the officer-trainee added, "There's a hand flare in Newton's pack. I put it there. We'll use that, don't you think. So that we torch the honeysuckle. And not the hero." He chortled.

Brainard shook his head as if to clear cobwebs. "Do you have a flare, Newton?" he asked.

"Huh?" said the coxswain. "I dunno."

Caffey reached into Newton's pack. His hand came out with a short plastic baton: a flare, marked White Star Cluster. "Jeez," the torpedoman said. "We're golden!"

Of course we're golden, said Officer-Trainee Wilding. *We're being led by a hero.*

But no words came out of his mouth, only laughter.

❖   ❖   ❖

Prince Hal's coach, one of less than a hundred private vehicles in Wyoming Keep, bulked in the midst of Patrol scooters like the termite queen in a crowd of her workers.

A score of emergency flashers pulsed nervously. Each light had a different rate and sequence. The combination would drive a saint to fury.

Wilding jumped from his vehicle without waiting for his chauffeur's hand. The warehouse's double doors were flung back. Kenran, the Wilding major domo, stood in the entrance wringing his hands as Patrol personnel walked in and out of the building.

It was a moment before Kenran's eyes registered the arrival of his master. His face wrenched itself into a combination of misery and relief. "Oh, *sir*!" he cried, "it's terrible! Terrible what they did!"

"What *who* did?" Wilding demanded as he strode into the family warehouse. "Just what in heaven's name is going on?"

"Excuse me, sir," said a stocky man with close-cropped gray hair. He stepped between Wilding and the major domo with a studied nonchalance. "I'm Captain Petersen. Would you be the Wilding?"

"My father's indisposed," Wilding snapped. "I'm the family's representative, if that's what you mean. Now, get out of my—"

He put his hand on the stranger's chest to push him aside. The momentary contact shocked Wilding in two ways: Petersen didn't move; and although Petersen wore good-quality—though drab—civilian clothes, there was a pistol in a shoulder holster beneath his tunic.

"I'm in charge of the investigation, sir," said Petersen as he stepped aside so smoothly that he seemed never to have been in the way. "You're welcome to enter, of course; but you'll understand that we don't want a mob of civilians making a bad situation worse."

"Why was it my servants who noticed the damage?" Wilding demanded as he walked into the warehouse. "Isn't that what we pay the Patrol to—good God!"

"Oh, sir!" Kenran wailed. "It's *terrible!*"

"We check the doors of these warehouses every few hours, sir," said Petersen as he followed Wilding into the building. "We don't bother with the back as a general rule, except to run off vagrants. With Carnival, we've been pretty busy, so it was your people who found the trouble when they opened up this morning."

The Patrol had set up additional lights, supplementing those integral to the warehouse. The combined glare turned the interior into a harsh, shadowless pit. It looked like a bomb site. Uniformed personnel recorded the scene and sifted through the debris while Wilding Family servants stood by in shock.

"We didn't think you *could* get through these walls without blowing the whole building to bits," Petersen went on. "Of course, with what they did when they got inside, they might as well have blasted it to smithereens."

Desks of light metal and thermoplastic: hacked or sawn apart, probably with cutting bars. Chairs of similar flimsy construction: smashed, every one of them. Crates with padded interiors: ripped open, and the fixtures they contained hurled onto the floor to be stepped upon.

There was a hole in the back wall of the warehouse, a square so regular that Wilding thought for a moment it was part of the building's design. The edges of cast ceramic were so sharp that they winked in the cruel light. The thieves, the *vandals*, had somehow cut a neat hole in a wall that should have been able to resist cannon fire. . . .

"How?" Wilding whispered. His soul felt empty. The universe had turned to face him, and her face was a skull.

"We're still not sure of that, sir," Petersen said. "'Why' is a bit of a question also, but we think they were looking for valuables, didn't find any, and wrecked what was here out of anger. Are these the normal contents of this warehouse?"

"No!" said Wilding. His face clouded as he tried to think. "But I'm not sure what's usually here, that's not my. . . ."

"Liquor for the party was stored here until the night before last," Kenran said. His voice steadied as it was permitted to deal with normal business matters. "The Family gives a Carnival party in its home, open to everyone in the keep who wishes to come. The quantity of beverages that entails is too great to store on the premises until the event, of course."

Petersen nodded in satisfaction. "Bingo," he said. "They knew about the booze, broke in some damn way, and missed what they were looking for by twenty-four hours."

He surveyed the wreckage again before adding, "So there was nothing left here but this old furniture?"

Wilding went pale. He couldn't speak.

"You, you—" Kenran stammered, "—*idiot*! Don't you know what this was? It was Settlement Period furniture! It came from *Earth*!"

"Oh, my God," Petersen said in a reverent tone. For the first time, the Patrol captain's look of cold propriety gave way to genuine concern.

Wilding stared at the hole in the warehouse wall. "With thousands of common people in the house," he said numbly, "we couldn't have irreplaceable artifacts like these out where they might be broken. We always store them in the warehouse for safekeeping."

Petersen shook his head. "So they could have walked in your front door and drunk themselves silly," he said. "But instead they do this."

He reached down and picked up a shattered tumbler. The scrap was made of plastic derived from petroleum, formed in turn by the bodies of Terran animals hundreds of millions of years in the past.

"Just for kicks," Petersen said. "Just to keep themselves entertained."

17

"When we get onto the honeysuckle, sir," said Leaf, "I'm gonna be holding you from behind. Okay? Like this."

Wilding's rifle was three inches shorter without the muzzle brake. He leaned against the "crutch" with an insouciant grin nonetheless. He made no comment as the motorman stepped around him to grip his left wrist and the tunic over his right shoulder.

Leaf felt Wilding shiver. The officer's wrist was cold and clammy. That was okay, not great but okay. There'd been spells of chills before and Wilding still seemed to be—

Hell, within parameters. Like a drive motor. Nobody expected perfect; just functional, and they were all functional, more or less.

"Right," said Ensign Brainard. "I'll take the flare."

Caffey uncapped the short cylinder instead of handing it to Brainard immediately. He looked at a patch of sky beyond the ensign's right ear and said in a mild voice, "You've got a lot of experience with these, then, sir?"

Brainard chopped out a laugh. "Not as much as you do, Fish," he said. "Sorry."

He surveyed his crew. Leaf straightened instinctively as he met the CO's eyes. Brainard looked back at the torpedoman and said, "Whenever you're ready."

Caffey switched the cap to the back end of the flare, where its firing pin touched the recessed primer. He aimed the tube in his left hand, then rapped the cap sharply. The charge blew the three packets out in a flat arc toward where the bridge of honeysuckle touched the hovercraft's deck.

The magnesium filler ignited while the packets were still in the air. The wavering glare was bright even against the white shimmer of daylight on Venus.

"What do we do if it don't catch the first—" began Wheelwright.

Orange flame overwhelmed the flare's white intensity. The brown, twisted vines blazed up with a roar and a propagation rate just short of that of diesel fuel. The fire's violence threw bits of stem and leaves into the air. The miniature brands were consumed to black ash before they reached the top of their curves.

The hovercraft vanished beneath a curtain of fire. Leaf couldn't believe there'd be anything left when the flames died away. The bridge of honeysuckle became a tube of roaring light. Loud crashing sounds like gunshots blew fragments away when pockets of sap deep in the core vine were heated to steam pressure beyond the strength of cell walls.

The mass of honeysuckle which controlled the shore across the strip of sand was green with nutrients sucked from the soil. The plant trembled and drew back under the stress of heat, but the line of conflagration halted as if the upper edge of the beach were a wall.

The hovercraft re-emerged. Its mottled gray finish was now overpatterned with the black/gray/white of ash. Orange hot-spots continued to dance on the deck, but the stunning roar had ceased.

The bridge still arched across sand and water. When the withered foliage was stripped away, it left a coarsely-woven hawser of interlaced stems. The mass was almost a yard in diameter, but its surface was neither flat nor regular.

"Right," ordered Ensign Brainard. "Caffey, lead Mr Wilding while Leaf follows. Let's go."

When the crew shambled to the bridge at their best possible speed, Leaf realized how badly off they were. He and Caffey carried the officer-trainee by the elbows. Wilding twice had to brace them with his crutch and to keep them all from falling down.

Newton was pretty much okay—maybe having no brains was an advantage in this crap—but the CO wobbled when he reached the top of the core vines. He gave Newton a hand, then stumbled aboard the hovercraft as the coxswain hauled the others up.

A four-foot climb with hand and footholds should have been easy. It wasn't.

The stems had a coating of ash, but the heat-cracked surface kept them from being slippery. Wilding managed to stride across the twisted vines as though he had two good ankles. He was chuckling. Leaf figured that was the fever, but maybe the Founding Families really *were* supermen. . . .

The hovercraft's deck had rippled in the fire, but it was still firm and better 'n' pussy after a week at sea. Close up, the vessel's number was visible on the side of the cockpit. K44, but they'd known that. . . .

Caffey, his escort job done, let go of the officer-trainee. He clamped his machine-gun onto the railing where it covered the shore from which they had just escaped.

"The communicator's here but the ascender's gone!" Brainard shouted from the cockpit. "We've got fuel!"

Honeysuckle aboard the vessel had burned itself into

a slime of ash. Leaf slipped and barely caught himself. Wilding sprawled onto the deck where he'd be fine, just fine, while the motorman did his real job.

They hadn't any of them said it. Maybe they hadn't even admitted it to themselves. But now that K67's crew was back aboard a hovercraft, they were going to sail off this fucking hellhole if they had to paddle with their feet!

Leaf slid into the motorman's scuttle. Ensign Brainard had lighted the auxiliary power unit, so the drive status panel was live. Number Three fan was flatlined.

A glance to the side showed the motorman why: an armor-piercing shell had sledged away the top half of the housing and everything within the nacelle. "Armor-piercing," because HE Common would've detonated on impact, leaving nothing of the hovercraft that you couldn't pack in a shoebox.

But the other three fans would lift a hovercraft with no sweat, so long as the skirts were—

"The skirts're shot to shit," Caffey called. He was in the cockpit with the CO, using the portside console. Nobody needed a torpedoman right now, and OT Wilding was doing good just to sit up straight against a post. "Nothing we can't patch, though."

Caffey opened the repair locker which formed the cockpit's aft bulkhead. Newton and Wheelwright were forward, sawing at the bridge of honeysuckle. The coxswain's cutting bar was out of power, but he still made chips fly with powerful strokes of his arms.

"Caffey," Ensign Brainard ordered. "Shoot that vine apart with the machine-gun. Burned like this, you'll be able to do it."

Leaf got out of his scuttle. After a moment's relaxation, his arms cramped with agony as he forced them to raise part of his weight.

"Sir, we're short of ammo—" the torpedoman said doubtfully.

Leaf started forward to the plenum-chamber access port. Wilding gave the motorman a thumbs-up and chirped something. It sounded like, "Teamwork in the jungle! Keep it up!"

"We're shorter on time!" Brainard snapped. "I've seen what that vine can do when it gets its growth spurt."

Tendrils lifted across the beach. The mass of honeysuckle had begun to recover from its singeing. The blackened core stems showed no sign of life, but nobody was going to press an argument with *this* CO. Caffey stepped to his gun and aimed.

Leaf tugged the screw dog recessed in the center of the access port. The vine that bound it had burned away, but grit and ash clogged the threads. The double handles fought Leaf for a moment, then spun.

Caffey fired a short burst that sent spray back over the rail. The surface of the clear sea multiplied both the muzzle blasts and the *whack* of bullets parting the dry stems. A second burst—then three shots as the machine-gun expended the few rounds remaining in their last drum of ammunition.

Leaf turned the handle to its stop so that it withdrew the dogs in all four sides of the port. He lifted the panel against the friction of its hinges.

"That's got it, sir!" the torpedoman announced.

"Newton," Leaf called. "Cover me with your rifle in case there's something down here who—"

He'd raised the edge of the port about halfway. Because the hovercraft sat on the shelving bottom, not a bubble of air, the water level within was close to the underside of the vessel's deck. Sunlight through the opening showed shapes but not details because the motorman's eyes were adapted to the open sky.

The motion was inhumanly fast, but the storm of cavitation bubbles in the water gave Leaf just enough warning. He threw his weight onto the upper side of the panel before the creature slammed against it from below.

The shock lifted him, but the creature recoiled also. The access port closed. Leaf spun the dogging handle to keep it that way. "Jesus!" he cried. "There's a moray down there longer 'n the boat!"

"I'll take care of it!" said Wheelwright. He reached for his backpack on the deck. "I've got a grenade!"

"Are you crazy?" Leaf demanded. "You'll kill us all!"

The hovercraft shuddered as the eel's sinuous body brushed the skirts from the inside. The creature was agitated with the thought of prey.

Caffey looked at the motorman in surprise. "Hey, it's no sweat, Leafie," he said soothingly. "Concussion'll kill the moray, but the water down there'll stop the shrapnel before it gets to the skirts."

The torpedoman's toe tapped the deck. "Or us. It's no sweat."

"Naw," said Leaf. He'd forgotten that the others hadn't seen what *he* saw when the port was open. "That's not what I mean. The torpedoes are still on their hooks down there. If the grenade sets one of them off—"

Memory strangled his voice.

Leaf didn't have to finish. Caffey knew what a torpedo could do, even to a vessel a thousand times the size of this little hovercraft.

But that's impossible!" the CO blurted.

Leaf looked at him. Ensign Brainard's face was suddenly gray. "This is K44, and they torpedoed the *Wiesel* to save our lives!"

❖   ❖   ❖

August 1, 382 AS. 2215 hours.

Technician 2nd Class Leaf filled his glass from the pitcher and said, "'Bout time you fetch us some more beer, kid," to K67's assistant motorman.

Bozman looked doubtfully at the pitcher, then over his shoulder toward the long, crowded bar of the Dirtside Saloon. "There's plenty left," he said, raising his voice slightly more than the saloon's ambient noise required. "And anyway, I got the last one."

Caffey filled his own glass, then poured the remainder of the pitcher into Bozman's half-full tumbler. He banged the empty pitcher back on the table among its four brethren.

Caffey grinned at Leaf's striker. "You were saying, kid?"

"I was saying," growled Bozman, "that I got the last *two*."

Leaf belched. "That's the price newbies pay for being allowed to sit with vets like me and Fish," he said. "Pay gladly, if they're smart."

The motorman's voice was mellow—for Leaf. The beer had given him enough of a buzz to dull memories the afternoon's Board of Review had churned up. He basked in the glow of being alive.

The Herd, like all the Free Companies, granted its personnel liberal leave to browse the rich entertainments of the keeps. Despite that, men on base duty needed after-hours relaxation; base facilities gave credit against pay; and a certain percentage of mercenaries found they simply didn't like the company of civilians.

The Dirtside Saloon was one of scores of bars within Hafner Base's fortified perimeter. It was full of men, and so were all its sister clubs and saloons.

"Got through another, didn't we, Leafie?" Caffey said in a reflective tone. "Been a few of those."

The Dirtside was lighted by bands of muted green which drifted slowly across the ceiling. The illumination was adequate for the duty squad of Shore Police who kept watch through their image-intensification visors, but Leaf found it hard to be sure of the torpedoman's expression.

"There was a few of them back on Block Eighty-One," Leaf rasped. "Fuck it. Any one you walk away from."

"You two knew each other when you were growing up, didn't you?" Bozman said over the rim of his glass. He was careful not to look at either of the chiefs as he spoke.

"In a manner of speaking, kid," Caffey said.

Leaf laughed without humor. The lights in his mind brightened to billowing red flames for a moment before sinking back into the bar's cool green. "We wasn't friends, if that's what you mean."

"Hell, Leafie," the torpedoman said. "We didn't kill each other. That counts for something on Block Eighty-One." The liquid in Caffey's glass trembled as his fist tightened. His eyes were unfocused. "D'ye ever go back, Leafie?" he asked. All the joking, all the easy fellowship, had been flayed from his voice.

Leaf gulped his beer. "Hell, no," he said. "*Hell*, no."

Caffey looked at the assistant motorman. "Kid," he ordered, "get us another pitcher."

Bozman bobbed his head and scraped his chair back from the table. The noncoms stared at his back as he fought through the press to the bar, but their minds were on other things.

"You're smart," Caffey said. "I went back the once. Half the guys we knew was dead, and the rest of them was in jail. Or on the netters for life, if that counts as life. It's a jungle back there, Leafie. It's worse 'n what's out beyond the perimeter."

The automatic cannon which guarded the electrified frontier of Hafner Base crashed a regular accompaniment to Herd life. It was only by concentrating that the mercenaries noticed them. Leaf's experienced ears could differentiate muzzle blasts from the slightly-sharper counterpoint of shells bursting at the jungle rim. Occasionally, a heavier gun would join in to deal with a particular threat.

"God," Leaf muttered.

Bozman was back with a pticher so full that it sloshed when he set it on the table. The motorman blinked. Caffey looked surprised too. It hadn't seemed there'd been enough time. . . .

"Look," said Bozman as he sat down again, "I got a question. Not—"

Both noncoms jerked their heads around like gun turrets, ready to fire.

"—about any of that," the assistant motorman blurted quickly. "About the Board of Review this afternoon." He forced a smile.

Neither of the chiefs smiled back. "Go ahead," Leaf said.

Bozman licked his lips. "Look," he said. "It's about you guys testifying that K44 sheered off when the shooting started. I didn't say nothing to the Board—"

"Not as dumb as he looks," Caffey said to Leaf. His voice was as playful as a cat killing.

"I didn't say nothing," Bozman continued, staring determinedly at the table, "but I *saw* K44 running in ahead of us all the way."

He swallowed and looked up again, attempting another smile. "I mean, y'know, I thought I did."

Caffey started to laugh. Bozman's expression became so gogglingly silly that the motorman laughed the harder. Leaf leaned over to slap his striker on the back.

"Oh, kid," the motorman chortled. "I forget what a goddam newbie you are!"

Bozman looked as stiff and angry as a whore with a broom stuffed up her backside. "But I *saw*—" he said.

"Our shadow," Leaf interrupted. "You saw our shadow. When the starshells dropped, they threw shadows over the waves ahead of us."

The assistant torpedoman opened his mouth in amazement.

"Don't feel bad," Leaf added. "It happens a lot."

Caffey belched and poured himself another beer. "It happens a lot to *newbies*," he said.

Both noncoms were relaxed and buoyant again. The motorman slid his own glass over to be filled.

"You didn't know Ted Holman, kid," he said, "so I'll tell you: he didn't have any balls. His brother kept pushin' him t'be a hero, but Teddy just wasn't cut out fer that. There's less chance he ran K44 in ahead of us than there is this glass is gonna turn t' gold in my hand."

He raised it, then drank. "Nope, still beer."

Caffey laughed. "I'll tell you something else, kid," he said. "I don't believe K44 circled around and came back, neither."

"But they had to come back," Bozman exclaimed. "They torpedoed the *Wiesel*. I *know* that happened!"

"*We* did for the *Wiesel*," Caffey said.

He raised his left hand to silence Bozman's certain protest. "I know, the console was shot away for our fish lost guidance—but that don't mean they stopped and rolled belly up. Tonello aimed the boat for a hands-off run, and the *Wiesel* wasn't doing any maneuvering the way she was caught in the channel like that."

"Ted Holman's welcome to be a dead hero," the motorman said between swallows, "seeings as he's dead. But I figure K44 took a shell up the ass as she ran."

"You can't outrun a bullet, after all," Caffey agreed philosophically.

"I tell you," said Leaf, watching the patterns his blunt fingertip drew in the condensate on his glass. "I'd sooner have a skipper with the guts to still do the job when the shit hits the fan. It's safer. And sooner or later in this business, the shit always hits the fan."

"Hell, in life," the torpedoman muttered.

"Lieutenant Tonello was a goddam good skipper that way," Leaf said. He slid his empty glass to Caffey.

"And you know?" he continued. "I think this new kid Brainard may be even better."

18

K44 rested in a tidal pool, though the bar a quarter mile to the north was submerged at this stage of solar attraction. Brainard stared over the portside rail. The water was so clear between waves that when he spit, his subconscious expected to see the gobbet dimple the sandy bottom. Instead, there was a splash.

A dozen tiny fish, scarcely more than teeth with fins, converged on the spot. They continued to froth the surface for minutes after they must have been certain there was no prey to justify a battle.

Other iridescent fish prowled among the fragments of crab armor which littered the bottom in a wide fan to seaward. Occasionally a fish found a further scrap of meat to worry from the chitin. Others flashed in to attack their lucky fellow while his jaws were engaged with the scavenged tidbit.

Officer-Trainee Wilding stumped around the cockpit to join Brainard. The enlisted crewmen waited for orders with evident concern.

Brainard knew they were worried. He knew that he *had* to decide what to do . . . but his whole universe had overturned when he learned that the commander

425

of K44 hadn't saved his life. Maybe Fate had done so, maybe there was a friendly God; and maybe the whole universe was a game of chance in which men were chips, not players.

Wilding leaned against the rail and took a deep breath. His face looked pale; cold sweat flecked his skin. He wedged the rifle into the corner where his body met the railing, then gestured at the bottom with his right index finger.

The officer-trainee was doing better since he got a solid plastic deck underneath him. Not physically better. Physically, he looked worse than the rest of them, and they all looked like yesterday's corpses.

The fever had stopped twisting Wilding's mind. Even when he dragged his thoughts through delirious pathways, he still managed to save all their lives, though. . . .

"At least having the moray here limits our problem to one," he said. "Otherwise there'd be hundreds of crabs trying to get at us. That'd be a lot worse."

"Rifle bullets aren't going to kill an eel that big," Brainard said. He turned around and nodded to the men. "Leaf's right, though. I won't chance using the grenade with two torpedoes down in the plenum chamber."

Those were the first words he'd spoken since he learned about the torpedoes. The relief on the faces of his crew was palpable.

"Maybe we could patch the holes from outside the skirts?" Wheelwright offered.

"Don't be a bigger fool 'n God made you, kid," the motorman snapped without real malice. "It's pressure that holds the patching film in place. Stick it on from the outside, and it'll just blow free when we fire up the fans."

"That wouldn't help anyway," said Wilding gently.

"The eel lairs in the plenum chamber, but it hunts outside."

The officer-trainee leaned cautiously over the railing and pointed forward along the hovercraft's side. There was a flared tunnel in the sand where the skirts began to curve in toward the bow. Fragments of crab shell were particularly concentrated near that end of the vessel.

From the size of the opening, the moray was three feet in diameter. That was even bigger than Brainard had thought. A grenade could still do the job.

They couldn't just wait until fresh prey drew the eel away from the torpedoes, though. . . .

"Leaf," the ensign said. "I've seen the damage-control menu, I know what it says. But will K44 really float if we just patch her plenum chamber?"

The motorman frowned as he met Brainard's gaze. "Well, sir," he said, "the one fan's fucked, that's a dockyard job to replace. But three fans 're plenty if you don't need top speed—and if your skirts ain't shot to shit, so they won't hold pressure."

He shrugged. "The read-out says there's nothing so big we can't patch it. Eyeballing the skirts from up here on deck, it looks the same. Lotta little holes, one maybe from a six-inch—but just the hole, it didn't go off. Maybe we get down inside the chamber, there'll be a problem after all. But I don't see bloody why there oughta be."

Caffey, back in the cockpit studying the holographic display Brainard had called up, nodded. "Get rid of the eel, run patching film around the plenum chamber—and we're golden. We can sail the sucker home."

"Then why," said Brainard, "didn't K44's crew do that? They must've known that with their ascender gear shot off, nobody was going to pick up their distress calls more than a few miles away."

His eyes glazed with the vision of spike-thorned honeysuckle, toppling toward him to drain his blood. "Why did they stay here to d-d-die?"

Nobody spoke for a moment. Officer-Trainee Wilding put his hand on Brainard's arm.

"Sir," Wilding said, "I don't think you can understand, because you've never been afraid. But they were just normal men, Holman and his crew. Maybe there wasn't an eel in the plenum chamber, not at first. But something was—crabs, bloodworms. Or it might have been."

"Down there, it gets darker 'n a yard up a hog's ass," Leaf said soberly. "And nobody was gonna risk his life because a chickenshit like Ted Holman told him t' do it."

"Don't tell me about being afraid," Brainard whispered.

A column of spike-thorned honeysuckle toppling forward to drink. . . .

"Right," he said. "We need to bait the eel into the open."

He put his rifle on the deck and bent to unfasten his boots. *Boots and trousers would drag in the water, slowing him down.*

"Caffey and Wheelwright, you'll hold my left wrist and haul me back aboard when Mr Wilding gives the order," Brainard went on. "Leaf and Newton, you're on my right. Mr Wilding, you'll be in charge of the operation—"

The ensign kicked off one boot, then the other. He was afraid to order anybody else to do what had to be done. Ulcers on Brainard's insteps had leaked blood and serum, gluing his socks to his feet.

"—and you'll throw the grenade. Are you up to that?"

"Look, sir," said the motorman, "I can—"

"Shut up," said Brainard. "Are you up to that duty, Mr Wilding?"

The officer-trainee licked his lips. "Yes sir," he said. "Ah, we'll want to—be—here at the stern, as far from the eel's tunnel as we can get."

"Yes," said Brainard. "Yes, of course."

He pulled off his trousers, moving stiffly because of fatigue and injuries . . . and fear.

"Then let's get on with it, shall we?" he said.

Before the jaws of the moray eel in his mind closed and crushed him into a trembling fetal ball.

December 14, 380 AS. 0655 hours.

Brainard and four other youths sat in a circle on the Commons of Iowa Keep, drinking and viewing air-projection holograms.

Commuters watched as they rode to work on the slidewalks surrounding the Commons. There wasn't much entertainment in the gathering, but the youths at least showed some life. They were a relief from the backs of other workers going to empty jobs—or the pensioners hunched on benches beneath the elms, waiting for their empty lives to end.

"See, Brainard?" Rufus said. "It's past time already. They decided they didn't want you—so let's go home, huh?"

He swigged and offered Brainard the bottle. Its original contents had been replaced with a sweet punch made from fruit juice and industrial alcohol.

Brainard waved the bottle away. He looked at the clock on a pole in the middle of the Commons.

"It's not time," he snapped. He was angry that Rufus's gibe took him in for a moment. "Anyway, a few minutes aren't a big deal. Since when did you ever get to your first class on time?"

"We're here now, Brainard, baby," Kohl said in a lugubrious voice. "Seeing our buddy off. Pallbearers at your funeral, that's what we are."

"If he doesn't come to his senses," said Price. "Hey Rufe? Pass me the bottle if soldier boy doesn't want it."

"Hey, look at this one," Lilly said as he switched the chip in his hologram projector.

The image of a tracked vehicle seared the jungle with a rod of flame. As soon as the flamethrower shut off, two armored bulldozers snarled in to clear the gap before it could regrow. Despite the bath of fire, vines lifted and slashed until the dozer blades or crushing treads managed to sever them.

One of the bulldozers broke through the vines into a fifty-foot circle of sand. The driver started to back away. The surface lurched. The bulldozer sank to the top of its treads.

An armored recovery vehicle roared to life. Its path was blocked by the self-propelled plows which tore through the surface layers behind the bulldozers and injected herbicides into the cuts.

The stricken bulldozer lurched again and tilted forward. The engine compartment sank completely beneath the surface. The treads still rotated in reverse, but they could not bite on the loose sand.

The hatch at the rear of the cab flew open. The driver climbed onto the mounting ladder and poised there. Firm ground was twenty feet away.

The bulldozer shuddered. It began to slide downward as swiftly as a submarine which has vented its ballast. Two jointed, hairy arms as thick as treetrunks reached up from the center of the clearing and pulled the vehicle deeper.

The driver leaped desperately. He landed on the

agitated sand. As the bulldozer slipped beneath the surface, its turbulence dragged the man along with it.

The image went blank. Lilly put another chip into the projector. "And that's just land-clearing!" he said gleefully. "You're gonna have people shooting at you besides!"

He'd lifted the chips from the library of Iowa Technical School, where he was completing work in biology. In a year, Lilly would sit glassy-eyed in a chair while his computer plotted plankton patterns onto charts—

Which might be transmitted to the netters—

Which would ignore the charts in favor of continuing their plodding progress across the fishing grounds, stolid in the certainty that any slight gains would be offset by time lost in departing from the preset pattern.

All five of the youths were students . . . except for Rufus and for Brainard, who had just received their two-year degrees.

Brainard swallowed and looked across the slidewalk to the recruiting office. It was still closed, a massively-armored portal as forbidding as a bank vault. Mercenary recruiters were frequent targets of mob violence, both because of what they were and because they were different from the normal round of life in the keeps.

For that matter, the mob didn't need much of a reason to riot.

"Here's one for you, Brainard," Lilly said as he loaded another chip. "Take a look at this!"

Some Free Companies maintained recruiting offices in one or two of the Keeps by whom those companies were frequently hired. Wysocki's Herd, the Seatigers, and the Battlestars shared choice locations on a rotating basis in more than a dozen of the undersea domes. This technique spread the three companies' recruiting base and advertised their wares to the upper levels of keep society: the men who made decisions on war, peace, and hiring.

Brainard thought the recruiter for Wysocki's Herd was on duty in Iowa Keep this week, but he wasn't sure.

And it didn't really matter.

"Back in the Settlement Period, they planned to colonize the surface," said Kline, the other biotechnician. "Nothing came of it."

"Earth came of it," Kohl snorted. "People blowing themselves all up. Hey Rufe—how about some more of that punch."

"Hey, you guys. *Look* at this. It's a neat one."

"Dead soldier," said Rufus, turning the bottle upside down. The drop that formed on the rim did not fall.

"We got beer left in the cooler," Kohl offered. He spun the lid open.

The hologram hanging above the middle of the circle was of a lifeboat, bright yellow and seemingly empty. It bobbed as the sea's glassy surface swelled slowly, then subsided. The boat's image enlarged as the camera closed in.

"That didn't really affect things," Kline said. "The Holocaust, I mean. The surface colonies were supposed to be sent from the Keeps, not Earth. They just weren't. Too big an effort, I guess."

The lifeboat filled the holographic field. The camera was positioned above the little vessel, looking straight down. It seemed to be empty until the cameraman increased magnification still further.

A few quarts of water sloshed in the lifeboat's bilges. Tiny toothed things flashed and quivered there. They were fighting over the disarticulated bones of a human hand.

"C'mon, Brainard," Kohl said. "Have a beer at least. Keep your strength up."

Rufus chuckled. "The condemned man drank a hearty meal," he said.

"Want to see what happens when stinging nettles get through a Free Company's perimeter?" Lilly said with enthusiasm as he changed chips.

A tall, fit-looking man in a blue-and-silver uniform stepped off the slidewalk in front of the recruiting office. His exposed skin had the mahogany tan of surface radiation. He reached toward the door with a chip-coded key in his hand.

Brainard stood up.

"Aw, c'mon, Brainard," said Rufus as he struggled to rise also. "You don't really wanna do this."

When the mercenary saw the group of young men, he shifted the key to his left hand and did not unlock the door. "Yes?" he called across the slidewalk.

His right hand hovered at waist level, almost innocently. His little finger carefully teased open the flap of the pistol holster which completed his uniform.

"I've come to enlist," Brainard said loudly as he strode toward the slidewalk.

"Aw, Brainard," Kohl muttered.

A professional smile brightened the recruiter's face. "Then you've come to the right place," he said as he reached toward the door again.

"And why spend the effort to die on the surface?" said Kline rhetorically as he sucked on the bottle he had already emptied. "Life in the Keeps is just fine the way it is!"

The slidewalk carried Brainard sideways, though he crossed it in two quick strides. He walked back along the berm.

In the center of Iowa Keep and every other domed city beneath the seas of Venus was the Earth Memorial.

An image of Mankind's home blazed, representing the white light of the self-sustaining silicon reaction in the rocks of the actual planet. A wreath of black crepe encircled the display.

The armored doors of the recruiting office spread before Brainard like the jaws of death.

19

Wilding hallucinated.

He sensed his environment as if every detail were engraved in crystal. He had infinite time to pore over his surroundings and rotate them through his viewpoint.

Pores on Brainard's cold face as the ensign knelt with his back to the water.

Pressure blotches where the enlisted men gripped Brainard, four scarred hands holding each of his.

Individual scales jeweling the sides of fish. Sunlight shone through clouds and clear water to turn fanged horrors into things of miniature beauty.

Wisps of sand drifting in vortices near the mouth of the tunnel fifty feet away, marking movements of the monster within the plenum chamber.

"Right," said Brainard. "Is everybody ready?"

Yessir/Yeah/Uh-huh/Yessir

A wide variety of syllables, timbres, volume—and it all had the same meaning. *You are willing to die for us, so we will stand by you.* A computer would not understand, but men understood.

Hal Wilding understood for the first time how Nature ordered the jungle—and what it meant to be a man.

435

"Mr Wilding," said Brainard. His voice trembled minusculely with fear and anticipation. "Are you ready?"

Wilding nodded. "I'm ready," his voice said. His mind marveled at the precise normality of the words. "I understand."

Doubt flecked the corners of Brainard's eyes, briefly there—and gone. No use worrying, and no time for it either.

"All right," the ensign said. "I'm going in." He lurched backward into the glassy water.

Large fish swirled shadows at the limits of visibility. They were drawn by sound and movement aboard the hovercraft, but they sensed also the huge moray which laired beneath the vessel. They would not attack—unless enough blood scented the water to overwhelm their instinct for self-preservation with the desire to kill.

Crabs marched closer in the shallows. Their legs stirred the fine sand of the bottom into a smoky ambiance through which the flat, spike-armored carapaces drifted sideways. The crabs' outstretched fighting claws scissored open and closed, for the moment cutting only water.

The moray's tunnel was still and dark. The hovercraft shivered as a slimy body brushed its underside.

Ensign Brainard kicked, stirring the surface.

The four enlisted men looked more like corpses than they did able-bodied humans. The cuts, scrapes and sores that covered their bodies were individually minor, but the cumulative effect would have sapped the will of the strongest of men. Their faces were stark. They knew that they would have to pull their commander out of the water more swiftly than the moray could strike; and all of them doubted their ability to succeed.

"Has the eel . . . ," Brainard asked, pausing to kick again. His exhausted muscles trembled with the effort of keeping his head out of water, but his eyes were indomitable. " . . . shown itself?"

"It's moving inside the plenum chamber," Wilding said. His tone was calm, soothing. He was a part of Nature. "It'll come soon."

All of their clothing was in rags. Leaf knelt beside the officer-trainee. His feet were turned outward. The soles of his seaboots were a synthetic which combined a gummy grip with the toughness of mild steel and stability at temperatures up to 880°.

A purple fungus had devoured half the thickness of the right sole and was sucking a dimple from the heel of the left boot as well.

"Do you know what we're fighting for?" Wilding asked softly.

A twenty-foot shark curled in toward the hovercraft. A rifle on the deck beside Wilding pointed out over the sea. He knew the weapon was unnecessary at the moment.

The shark banked and fled toward the safety of its distant fellows, showing its pale belly. Its pectoral fins were spread like wings.

"For our lives, you bloody fool!" Leaf gasped. "That's what we're fighting for!"

Sweat blinded the motorman. He was desperately afraid that the sweat sliming his palms would cause his hands to slip when Ensign Brainard's life depended on him.

"No," explained Wilding, "that isn't why we're still fighting, still here."

His fingertips knew the surface of the grenade. On the deck lay the safety pin. The grenade's spoon handle pressed upward against Wilding's palm, straining to ignite the fuze train. The safety pin could be reinserted if the moray refused the bait . . . but Wilding knew that the beast would come.

Soon.

"Any one of us would have given up long ago if he'd been alone," he said aloud. "Even you, sir. Even you."

It was a wonder the way his tongue shaped to the words.

"For God's sake, man!" Caffey snarled. "Are you watching for the fucking eel?"

"I'm ready," Wilding said. "I understand."

Brainard's face lifted toward the officer-trainee. The ensign's face showed no concern; no expectation, even. Only the physical strain of making his wracked muscles kick the water to bring the jaws of a multi-ton monster down on him. . . .

Miniature fish darted in and out, confused by the thrashing. One of them snatched at the pus-soaked fabric of Brainard's sock. The scavenger's jaws stayed clamped although a kick lifted it from the water. When the fish splashed down again, one of its fellows sheared through its body just behind the head.

The torpedoman muttered a curse or a prayer.

"We're fighting for each other," Wilding said. "That's good, but it's not good enough. When we get back, we have to fight for all Mankind."

The crabs scurried away like a mob fleeing a madman with an axe when Brainard started to kick. They resumed their sidelong advance, each moving individually but marching in lock-step because identical imperatives ruled their rudimentary minds.

The crustaceans pulsed forward and dashed back; but a little closer with every cycle. Soon one of them would spring from the sea floor with its claws wide to seize the man in the water. . . .

"Otherwise we're part of the jungle," Wilding said. "And the jungle will win."

"Oh God!" Leaf cried in despair. "I can't hold—"

It was the moment.

"Now!" shouted the officer-trainee. As the word came from his mouth, electric motion slid out of the tunnel.

The moray was green. Its jaws were open. The ragged fangs were up to ten inches long.

The sharks and lesser fish at the edge of vision vanished. The ranked crabs exploded backward behind a curtain of sand, tumbling over one another in their haste to escape nemesis.

The moray struck through the sea more swiftly than gravity could have pulled a boulder in thin air. The undulant movement slapped water violently against the hovercraft.

The grenade left Wilding's fingers as if it were playing its part in a marionette show in which strings connected all existence.

"Hah!" shouted one of the enlisted men as the four straightened and lunged backward in unison. Ensign Brainard lifted toward the shell-torn gap in K44's railing.

Brainard was still in the air. His head and shoulders were over the deck, but his legs flailed above the sea.

The moray's head slid out of the water. Its palate was a cottony white. Leaf threw himself forward to block the monster's spearpoint teeth with his body. Wilding *knew* what was about to happen. He held the motorman's shoulders with the strength of a madman.

The grenade went off in the moray's throat. The creature's head flew apart. The thick slime coating its body was bright yellow, and the scales beneath were blue.

The spray of the moray's blood in the air was red, and the spreading red blur in Wilding's mind overwhelmed his consciousness.

❖   ❖   ❖

July 2, 379 AS. 0101 hours.

Wilding watched Francine's coiffure echo the fire-works with increased intensity. Charged strands woven among the hairs trapped and re-emitted the light a band higher on the spectrum.

When the fireworks flashed silver, Francine's hair sparkled with all the colors of the rainbow.

She turned to face him. Her body moved against the balcony rail like that of a cat rubbing itself, and the smile on her broad lips was feline as well.

"What are you thinking about, Prince Hal?" she asked in a purring chuckle which admitted she knew what any man was thinking about when he looked at her.

She was here with Tootles. Neither she nor Wilding wanted to arouse the hostility of the Callahan Family; but she would flirt and he—

He had invited her out on the roof of his penthouse.

Members of the Twelve Families and their entourage partied two levels below. A drunken mob of common people spilled onto the street from the ground floor of Wilding House, keeping Carnival in their own way.

More fireworks burst against the dome. Sparks spun down in varicolored corkscrews, and the crowd howled.

Wilding grinned, cat-smooth himself. He pointed a languid finger toward the boulevard. "Oh," he said, "I was thinking about them, Francine. What is it that they really want?"

The woman's stance did not change, but all the softness went out of her features. "Why ask me?" she said in a brittle voice. "How would I know?"

They were no longer flirting.

"Because you should know," he said. "Because I *want* to know."

Since he was host, he had not drunk heavily. There was enough alcohol in his brain to free the sharp-edged knowledge that he usually hid under an urbane exterior: he was a Wilding. For all practical purposes, he was *the* Wilding.

While Francine was a tart whom Tootles, Chauncey Callahan, had lifted from the gutter.

Her dress was a metallic sheath. It fitted Francine's hard curves as a scabbard of hammered silver would fit a scimitar. The natural color of her hair was black, and she wore it black tonight. It formed a pair of shoulder-length curls to frame her face, heart-shaped and carefully expressionless at this moment.

A door opened onto the balcony below. Half a dozen slurred, cheerful voices prattled merrily. "And *then*," Glory McLain trilled, "he wanted her to lie in cold water, I mean *really* cold, before she came to bed, and—"

The McLain girl's voice lowered into the general babble. The balcony was thirty feet below the penthouse roof; the partiers were unaware that there was anyone above them.

Francine moved away from the railing with a sinuous motion. She did not glance down to betray her concern about being seen—by Tootles, by someone who would mention the fact to Tootles.

Wilding stepped to the side also. "Don't they ever want a better life, Francine?" he said softly.

Fireworks began to spell letters across the dome: W-Y-O. . . .

Common people cheered and drank, while aristocrats gossiped about necrophilia.

The penthouse roof was planted with grass and palmettoes. The seedstock had come to Venus in the colony ships rather than being packed into terraforming capsules. It had not been exposed to the actinic radiation and adaptive pressures which turned the Earth-sprung surface life into a purulent hell.

Francine spread the fingers of one hand and held them out against a palmetto frond, as if to compare her delicacy against the green coarseness.

"They don't want anything better," she said. She turned to look at Wilding. "They don't deserve anything better," she added fiercely. "If they did, they'd have it, wouldn't they? *I* bettered myself!"

There was a pause in the fireworks and the sound of the crowd in the street. " . . . and I don't mean young girls, either . . ." drifted up from the balcony.

Wilding turned to look out over the railing. He stayed back from the edge so that he could see the half the width of the boulevard while remaining hidden from the partiers on the balcony. In the boulevard women who might have been prostitutes danced a clog-step with partners of all ages, accompanied by a hand-held sound system.

"They've got energy," Wilding said. "They could do. . . . *something*. Instead, what they get is a constant round of shortages and carouses."

He felt the warmth of Francine's body. When he turned, she was standing next to him again.

"Artificial hatred of neighboring Keeps," he went on, astounded at the harshness in his own voice. "Artificial wars, fought by mercenaries—"

Francine's dress had a high neck and covered her ankles. The fabric was opaque but so thin and tight that the shimmering fireworks displayed her nipples with nude clarity. She was breathing rapidly.

"—under artificial conditions," Wilding said, "so that war can be entertainment but not destroy the planet the way Earth was destroyed. But that's not the only way Mankind can die, is it?"

"Prince Hal," the woman said in whispered

desperation. She took his hands in hers. Her palms were clammy.

He'd drunk too much, or—

But he must have drunk too much. "Those people down there could colonize the surface some day," Wilding said. He enfolded the woman's tiny hands in his own, trying instinctively to warm her. "They could colonize the stars. All they need are leaders."

"Prince Hal," Francine begged, "don't *talk* like this. Please? You're scaring me."

"You're afraid of change," Wilding said. "The mob's afraid of change, *everybody's* afraid of change. So Wyoming Keep has the Twelve Families, and all the other Keeps have their equivalents. Comfortable oligarchies determined to preserve the status quo until the whole system runs down. And no leaders!"

Francine lifted Wilding's hand to her mouth. She pressed it with her teeth and lips, an action somewhere between a kiss and a nibble. He could feel her heart beating.

More fireworks went off to amuse the Carnival crowd.

"It's nothing but a jungle life," Wilding whispered.

The woman stepped back and raised her hands to her neckline. There was hard decision in her eyes. "All right, Prince Hal," she said. "You want a leader? Then I'll lead you!"

Francine touched a catch. Her garment slid away to become a pool at her feet. She was nude beneath it. Her body was hairless and perfect.

"And you'll like where I take you, honey," she added with practiced enthusiasm.

EPILOGUE

"Here ye go, buddy," said the short, grinning thug with the scarred face. He tapped on the door marked CHIEF OF STAFF. "Mr Brainard'll fix you up just fine, I'll bet."

The Callahan kept his face impassive, though a vein stood out from his neck. He never lost his temper in front of underlings.

The man who had brought him from the guarded entrance to here, when he had demanded to be taken directly to the Wilding, was named Leaf. The Callahan knew him by reputation—rather better than he wished were the case.

The Chief of Staff's office was opened from the inside by another thug. This one was named Caffey, and the Callahan knew of him also.

"Gen'leman to see Mr Brainard, Fish," Leaf said with a broad smile.

He was play-acting; both of them were. This was nothing but a show, with the Callahan forming both the straight man and the audience.

Caffey raised an eyebrow. "Alone?" he said.

He was a marginally smoother character than Leaf.

At any rate, the muted beige tunic and trousers affected by all the Association functionaries had a civilian appearance on Caffey, while the garments seemed to be a prison uniform when Leaf wore them.

Looks were immaterial. Leaf and Caffey had equal authority as the Association's Commissioners of Security. They were equally brutal, equally ruthless; and equally dedicated to their job.

"There's half a dozen more come with him," Leaf said, "but one at a time seemed safer. The rest 're cooling their heels in the guardroom. Unless they got smart with Newton, in which case they're just cooling."

Caffey chuckled. "Takes a real direct view of doing his job, that boy. Too dumb to get tricky, I s'pose."

"The men you're talking about are the Council of the Twelve Families," said the Callahan, finally stung to a response. "*Not* a street gang! We're here to meet with the Wilding."

Leaf grinned. "Not a *street* gang, I guess," he said. The soft change of emphasis made his words a threat.

Caffey looked over his shoulder. His stocky body still blocked the doorway. "D'ye want to see Mr Callahan, sir?" he called, proving he had known perfectly well from the beginning who he was dealing with.

"Of course, Fish," answered the unseen within. "I'd be delighted."

Caffey stepped aside, gestured the Callahan mockingly forward, and closed the door behind himself.

Brainard sat behind a desk which was large and expensively outfitted, but cluttered with hard copy. He had the tired, worn appearance of a man older than his chronological age. His face and hands were flecked with minute dimples. Plastic surgery had not quite restored the texture Brainard's skin had had before jungle sores ate into it.

The Wilding's chief of staff looked hard and

dangerous. The Callahan had reason to know that Brainard was both those things, and more.

"I didn't come to talk with you, Brainard," the Callahan said. "My business—*our* business—is with the Wilding."

Brainard shrugged. "Have a seat," he said, gesturing the Callahan to one of the comfortable chairs facing the desk. "Since you're going to talk to me anyway."

He smiled at his visitor. The expression was as precise as the click of a gunlock. "And as a suggestion, Mr Callahan . . . unless you refer to him as Director Wilding, I'm the only one you *are* going to talk to this afternoon."

The walls of the Chief of Staff's office were decorated with holographic projections of the surface of Venus. The images were not retouched for propaganda purposes.

To the Callahan's right, huge land-clearing equipment tore at the jungle. On the wall over the door, other machinery formed barracks blocks and small bungalows from stabilized earth. On the visitor's left, humans of both sexes inspected an experimental plot of vegetables growing beneath an ultraviolet screen.

The wall behind Brainard did not carry a hologram. An automatic rifle hung there in a horizontal rack. To even the Callahan's inexperienced eye, the weapon was in poor condition. The metal surfaces were scarred, and fungus had pitted the plastic stock and fore-end.

The Callahan grimaced, then sat down. Forcing himself to look Brainard in the eyes, he said, "All right. What is it that he really wants?"

Brainard smiled. This time the expression was almost gentle. "Just what he says he wants, Mr Callahan," he said.

The Council had—the Callahan had; he was the Council and they all knew it—offered Brainard a bribe early on in the process. Brainard had sent back a polite note with the money—enough money to have set him up for life in any Keep on Venus.

The next night, a mob of thousands of Association supporters had sacked and burned Callahan House. A Patrol detachment stood by and watched. They were outnumbered fifty to one by the rioters.

Patrol Headquarters directed the detachment to open fire. The on-site Patrol commander countermanded the order immediately. He realized that the men on the mob's fringes had the deeply-tanned skin of Free Companions—and that the objects outlined against their cloaks were surely automatic weapons.

"Listen, Brainard," the Callahan snarled, "the time for playing games is over! You're a practical man. *You* know that the notion is impossibly expensive."

"Expensive, of course," Brainard said. "And while we pay Free Companions to defend large surface settlements, neighboring Keeps will raid our fishing grounds." He leaned forward. His tunic touched the papers on his desk and made them rustle. "But the fishing grounds are played out, and the settlements will be exporting protein in a few years." Brainard's eyes were hard and empty, like a pair of gun muzzles.

"It's not impossible, Mr Callahan," he said. "And it's not expensive at all, compared to the centuries of phony war that you and yours have kept going!"

The Council made approaches to Leaf and Caffey after the attempt to subvert Brainard failed. This time the money did not come back—but neither did the agents carrying it.

Three days later, one male member of each of the Twelve Families was kidnapped. The operations were simultaneous and went off flawlessly, though several guards were killed in vain attempts to interfere.

The victims were dumped in front of the Council

Building the next morning. They were alive, but they
had been shaved bald and their skin was dyed a bright
blue.

After that debacle, the Callahan shelved what he had
thought of as his final contingency plan. He was afraid
to think about what would happen if he attempted
assassination—and failed.

"Phony wars, Brainard?" the Callahan sneered. "It's
real lives your master's scheme will cost, and there'll
be a lot of them. Has he thought of *that*?"

Brainard's fingers gently explored the dimples on his
cheek. It was a habitual gesture, an unconscious one.
"We've seen death before, Mr Callahan," he said tone-
lessly. "People die no matter what. This way—" His
eyes had gone unfocused. Now they locked on the
Callahan. "This way they have a chance to die for
something. And they're willing to. By *God* they're
willing to!"

"Yes, because you've stirred them up!" the Callahan
shouted. He gripped the arms of his chair fiercely, as
if to hold himself down.

Brainard chuckled unexpectedly. He slid his chair
back and stood up with an easy motion. "That's right,
Mr Callahan," he said. "Because we stirred them up.
Because we're leading them. But—" The relaxed voice
and posture vanished as suddenly as it had appeared.
Brainard pointed his index finger at his visitor and went
on, "—the common people *are* willing to go. And
they're going to go. The only choice the Twelve
Families have now is to support the process." Brainard's features changed. For the first time, the Callahan
saw the face of the man who directed the activities of
killers like Lea and Caffey. "Or be burned out of the
way," Brainard said, voice husky. "Like so much honeysuckle."

The Callahan stared across the desk at Brainard. He

had never before in his life hated a human being as much as he hated this one—and his master.

But he had not ruled Wyoming Keep for twenty years by being a fool.

The Callahan stood up. "All right," he said quietly. "Then I suppose we'd better support the process, hadn't we? May I see Director Wilding now?"

The two men walked down the hallway together, toward the office of the Director of the Surface Settlement Association.

THE REAL JUNGLE:
Belize, 2001

My wife Jo and I got up at 4:30 AM on July 13 and drove to our son and daughter-in-law's (Jonathan and April) house in Burlington, where we loaded all the luggage into April's Rodeo and went to RDU airport. The flight to Miami was on a full 727 (no problems, though I hadn't realized American still operated 727s) and the flight to Belize a 757 with lots of empty seats. International flights (which I take rarely) are strikingly upscale, providing cooked food on china with steel flatware instead of plastic containers and utensils.

International Expeditions, the tour organizer, provided a guide in Miami to make sure we got from one flight to the other. That gave me a correct notion of how careful they are with their clients.

Our first guide in Belize, Martin, had come to there as a mahogany company executive in 1975. He took us through Belize City (the capital and largest city with 70–80 thousand people in a country of 250–260 thousand total) while we waited for the other six of our party (who were flying in through Dallas). The houses reminded me of older Brunswick County (NC) beach houses: colorful, run-down, and frequently on stilts because of hurricanes. Some of the oldest places in the city are built of bricks carried over in the 19th century as ballast for mahogany ships. There are also "drowned cayes" in the bay where ships dumped ballast on which mangroves then took root, though they're underwater at high tide. (The lift is only 18 inches in Belize.)

The educational system works very well. The churches build the schools and choose the teachers, but the government pays those teachers. People whose faith doesn't have schools of its own (the big ones are Roman Catholic, Anglican, and Baptist) send their kids to some other church's school, but the kids aren't required to take the religious instruction. Literacy was 96% until the recent influx of refugees from El Salvador and Guatemala (some 80 thousand illiterate Spanish speakers) dropped it to 64%.

Twenty-five percent of the country's Gross Domestic Product comes from tourism, and they really do care about visitors. There are "Have you hugged a tourist today?" posters and tourist police to make sure only licensed guides are operating (we ran into a checkpoint of tourist police later in the afternoon).

Most cars are used sub-compacts from the U.S., generally from Texas and California. Used tires are imported from the U.S. also. Gas is about twice the U.S. price.

Then back to the airport, where there's a Harrier GR.3 on static display. The British sent a squadron of Harriers to Belize in 1976 when Guatemala was threatening to invade. They flew non-stop from Britain, refueling repeatedly. Castro allowed them to overfly Cuba: nobody but CIA likes Guatemala. (I will have more bad things to say about Guatemala in the course of this account, I suspect.)

We were switched to a different guide—Edd, a Creole who'd been an officer in the defense forces—and separate driver, Peter, also a Creole who'd been in the defense forces. Peter drove us from the airport in a Toyota Coaster, a 28-seat diesel bus with a five-speed manual transmission. It was a very rugged and satisfactory vehicle with two seats to the left and one to the right of a center aisle which could be filled by jump seats. It was comfortable, holding ten tourists, the guide and driver, and all our luggage without crowding. Peter took us places on it that I'd have wondered if a jeep could get through.

After his stint in the defense forces, Peter had worked for many years with ornithological projects. He was a really exceptional birder and communicated his enthusiasm to me.

At the New River we boarded a boat while Peter took the bus on to Lamanai by road. The boatman, Ruben, was also a birder. As with every part of this trip, getting there was part of the experience—not just travel. IE packed us full of information.

A word on my equipment. For the trip I'd gotten the recommended packet of background books, which included one on the wildlife of Belize. In addition I'd gotten a specialist birdbook (*A Field Guide to the Birds of Mexico and Adjacent Areas*, by Edwards) which proved very handy: full, but small enough to carry in a cargo pocket. Peter praised it, though he had a massive volume of his own in his backpack.

I'd also gotten a pair of military specification Steiner 8x30 binoculars. They have great depth of field, so by setting them for 30 feet they're effective from 20 feet to infinity. That permitted me to follow flying birds, but birds are so close in Belize that often I could only use my glasses by increasing the eye relief. A standard pair might have been more useful in the circumstances that obtained.

I'd planned to carry my Minox 35-millimeter camera, but I'd dropped it while practicing and didn't get it back from the shop in time. I used instead an old

Nikon point-and-shoot with a 35-70 mm zoom. I took 200 ASA film, thinking that was the choice for outdoors in the tropic sun; 400 or faster would've been a much better idea in the rain forest. Jonathan's new Fuji digital proved excellent, and he had no difficulty downloading from his card to his laptop.

The boatride—a river through the rainforest in late afternoon—was a remarkable experience. I won't try to list all the wildlife, particularly birds, we saw, but it was a wonderful harbinger of things to come. Two Morelet's crocodiles (a freshwater croc unique to Belize, coming back from the verge of extinction) approached. Every stretch of river had a ringed kingfisher, a territorial bird patterned like the much smaller belted kingfisher of the U.S. Raptors were frequent and unconcerned by our presence. The snail-eating kite (a.k.a. Everglades kite) is still common here because the apple snail (its sole item of diet) remains abundant. A fork-tailed flycatcher, 5 inches of bird followed by 9 inches of tail, overflew us.

The sun was low as we approached Lamanai Outpost Lodge. Directly beneath it, rising from the solid forest, was the top of the High Pyramid at Lamanai—at 33 meters, the tallest pre-classical Mayan structure known. This day alone was worth the price of the trip, so far as I was concerned.

On the morning of July 14th we got a better view of the site. Lamanai Outpost Lodge has a small number (maybe 12?) of individual bungalows and a restaurant with excellent food. The roofs are thatched with boton palm fronds, as were those of all the dwellings we stayed in during the trip (including those of Victoria House in San Pedro, which was air conditioned). In the landscaped grounds are many birds and various lizards, particularly the crested basilisk which has a very long tail (twice the body length). It's also known as the Jesus Christ lizard because younger (lighter) individuals can run across the surface of water.

After breakfast we—the ten tourists under the tutelage of Edd and Peter—went on a nature walk to the ruins. I was particularly struck by the chachalacas, chicken-sized birds which were hopping around in trees like finches, and the fact that the flycatchers range upward to 9" in overall length. Down from us along the river was a treeful of neotropical cormorants, and across the river a flock of woods storks clustered in a small pond where presumably something tasty had hatched or was swarming.

We passed a family of black howler monkeys, dozing in the trees. They took little notice of us. The infants were more active than the adults, but it was a hot day and leaves aren't a high-energy diet. None of the howlers we saw during the trip were calling, but we heard howlers in the morning and evening at Tikal.

Palm trees are more varied and interesting than I'd realized before the trip. Both the cohune palm and the boton palm begin as clusters of huge leaves sprouting from the ground, but they grow impressive trunks if the surrounding forest is thick enough to require them to do so to reach the light. The give-and-take palm is a relatively slender tree, but its trunk is covered by a hedge of downward pointing needles which induce fever in those they prick. The bark, however, is a specific against the tree's own poison (thus the name, give-and-take) and that of other vegetable irritants including the white poisonwood.

Most trees in the forest are covered by epiphytes growing on their bark and branches, but the allspice stays clean by shedding its bark twice a year. The bark itself is aromatic, but the spice is made from the berries.

In the trees at the river landing where we had lunch

before entering the ruins were several raptors and some strikingly colorful birds including blackheaded trogons and the oriole-like Montezuma oropendula—brilliant and 20" long. I repeat: I didn't come to Belize as a birder, but I became one while I was there.

In the museum were flint and pottery objects found at the Lamanai site. The Spanish forced the local people to build a Catholic church. Archeological investigation of the ruins (the locals burned the church during a 17th-century revolt against the Spanish) turned up a multiform monster of pottery which the builders had buried when they built the church, apparently as a curse.

The Pre-Classic temples here at Lamanai were my first experience of Mayan ruins. The first we saw was the Mask Temple, so called because of a huge face sculpted in the side. Most of the Mayan sites are built of very soft laterite limestone and weather quickly when exposed. The face is being reconstructed (the archeological term appears to be "consolidated") because it's deteriorated badly in the past few years. The Mayans themselves had the same problem and are now known to have kept carvings under thatched roofs at least during the rainy season.

We were able to climb this temple. It's not as impressive as others we saw later in the trip, but it was a wonderful experience.

The Mayans constantly rebuilt on the same sites, so while the Mask is from ca. 500 AD, Classic Period, the foundations of the pyramid date well back into Pre-Classic times. The reconstruction of a site requires a decision as to what time horizon the reconstruction is to represent. (This is as serious a problem in Rome or London as it is in Mayan country, of course.)

Breadnut trees are common around former Mayan sites and were presumably a cultivated species. Their hickory-nut sized fruit matures in July, before maize, and can be ground with slaked lime into flour to make bread. This is the sort of datum which I find fascinating, although I don't expect it to ever enter my fiction directly. The fact that it made my mind kick over in a new direction—*that's* the value of it to me.

At the site were a number of striking birds, including a huge Pale-Billed Woodpecker. I thought of my parents and how much they'd have loved the birds of Belize. Maybe more of their interests rubbed off on me than I'd realized.

There was a ball court at Lamanai. The games, a feature throughout Mayan history, were played with a solid rubber ball slightly smaller than a soccer ball. Reliefs indicate that one of the two players was executed after the game; our guide, Edd, noted that there was argument as to whether it was the winner or the loser who was beheaded.

This puzzled me, because I knew Mayan script had been largely deciphered. There should've been an answer to the question. To get ahead of my account by a little, Foster (our specialist guide at Tikal) had a degree in archeology. I asked him and got the following explanation:

1) In the Pre-Classic Period the games were used to choose a courier to take a message to the gods. The players were all highly-trained members of the nobility. The winner had proved himself the most fit. He was beheaded as a matter of honor and sent with the message.

2) In the Classic Period the games (still a noble prerogative) were used as a means of ordeal to decide matters at issue (much like the Mediaeval European trial by battle). In addition, conquering kings arranged fixed matches with prisoners. In this period the loser would be executed.

3) In the Post-Classic Period, ball games were a sport. Kings had teams which played for entertainment.

This was interesting in itself and a useful reminder that no culture is static for millennia. It irritates me when people talk about "what the Romans did" when Roman history covers thousands of years with sharp differences in all aspects of life within that general flow. I'd just made the same mistake about Mayan history.

It also reminded me that "popular information" generally prefers mystification to later-learned facts. There may be more of this regarding the Mayans than some other peoples, because archeologists had invented a mythical gentle Mayan culture and decipherment of the Mayan texts was somewhat of an embarrassment to them. Throughout Mayan history, victims were publicly tortured to death as a regular part of any festival. A portion of the archeological establishment consciously suppressed this information until quite recently.

We weren't able to climb the two other major temples at Lamanai—the 33-meter High Temple and the Jaguar Temple, so called from the stylized jaguar face created in blocks (sort of crocheting in stone) on one side. The modern concrete staircase built up the back of the High Temple had collapsed during Hurricane Keith last year, doing considerable damage to the original structure.

I noted here and at other Mayan sites that the authorities frequently make steel and ferroconcrete additions—and that these regularly do serious damage by concentrating the stresses of storms and earthquakes that the original structure had survived for the preceding millennia. This is as true at European and Asian sites as it is here. You wouldn't think it took a rocket scientist to look at, say, the Parthenon or Sphinx "repairs" and decide not to repeat the mistakes of past centuries of would-be conservators.

The back of the Jaguar Temple hasn't been excavated. It faces the landing site and museum. Neither

I nor any other member of our group had been aware that it was a temple until we came back around from the other side and found ourselves where we'd started.

Lamanai is a zoological study area as well as an archeological site and an ecotourist destination. In the afternoon we had a description of the zoological mission by the director of the project, then talks by two of the researchers—a woman whose specialty was bats (she brought in a yellow-throated bat for us to view and gently pet) and the man who was researching the diet of Morelet's crocodiles in the New River. The most striking bat datum that I picked up was that tent-making bats roost by day under large leaves whose support veins they clip so that the leaf folds over a clutch of bats. The crocodile man doubles as a herpetologist and brought in a small green iguana (the lecture room has dark cubicles in the walls where specimens can be kept quietly against need) and a garden snake. Save for the boa in the zoo, this was the only live snake I saw in Belize; my dreams of seeing a fer-de-lance in the wild were therefore dashed.

Following the lectures, we went on what was billed as a Mayan Medicine Trail, a nature walk focusing on the botanical uses of the forest. I learned to distinguish various standard palms. Palm trees are the most striking portion of the forest in much of the region that we visited. This surprised me, as I'd not really thought of palms as forest trees but rather as lone images on sandy beaches. There were those too—Jonathan got some lovely pictures of palms on the beach at San Pedro— but when one views Lamanai from the river, one sees an expanse of broad cohune palm fronds with only occasional other admixtures.

Another common aspect of the forest are leaf-cutter ants. These make 6-inch-wide trails, occasionally merging into much wider boulevards, which are easily distinguished from the trails of larger animals by being completely clear of vegetable material. The ants drop formic acid and completely destroy the leaf and twig litter that is found everywhere else. Once you've learned to identify them, you can see ant trails snaking across all the archeological sites—I took a picture of one across the main plaza at Tikal from the top of the palace.

Along the trail was a fallen tree which (by permission) locals had started to turn into a dugout canoe; they'd abandoned the project because the trunk was rotten at one end. It was a good view of how the process was carried out: the exterior had been rough-shaped and the interior was excavated with fire, adze, and apparently saw cuts.

In the Lamanai property is a sugar mill which was operated in the period 1860-75. (I'm told it figured in the Harrison Ford movie *The Mosquito Coast*, which was filmed in Belize.) Massive iron gears on equally massive brick foundations stand in the midst of jungle.

Also on the property (though some distance from the mill) is a brick storage cistern, apparently for grain. It's 19 feet deep, with no sign of other construction nearby.

At night we went out on a spotlight boat tour of the New River and its lagoon. We viewed bird life, but the crocodile researcher was along hoping to capture crocodiles for his diet study. For the most part the birds remained resting as we passed, though several big boat-billed herons flew away when struck by the spotlight. Fishing bats worked the lagoon in considerable numbers, pretty much ignoring us. There were many 3-inch fish in the shallow water, probably the right size for the bats.

The northern potoo, a relative of the whippoorwill, is famous for its ability to look like a branch. At night, however, its huge eyes glow like beacons when the light catches them.

There were many crocodiles out in the night, but for the most part they sank out of sight when the boat got near. They're opportunistic feeders, eating among other things the large apple snails. This can cause a skewing of diet data because though the snail shell quickly dissolves in the gut, the trapdoor (operculum) that closes the shell over the snail survives for a very considerable period.

The researcher finally caught a 5-foot croc by wading under the branch where it lay and looping it with a cord on a pole. Landing the critter was a lengthy business, though the outcome was never really in doubt. When the croc was aboard, the researcher and the boatman duct taped shut his jaws and then eyes, quieting him immediately.

Somebody asked whether it was a male or female. "Let's see," said the researcher, pulling on a latex glove and sticking a finger up the croc's vent. He was male.

Because the crocodiles are territorial, the last thing the researcher did before we set off for the lodge was to take a GPS reading of the exact location. The following night (after stomach pumping) the croc would be returned to the same spot.

Thence to the bungalow and to bed, utterly exhausted but full of amazing memories.

July 15 started in a relaxed fashion—IE is good about not overstressing clients, though believe me you don't get bored. We watched the lizards and hummingbirds in the gardens, and I got a picture of the chiclero kettle placed there as an accent. The sap of the chicle tree was gathered and boiled down much like natural rubber (or for that matter, maple syrup). Until 1975 chicle for chewing gum provided 25% of the Belize Gross Domestic Product. Then the Japanese found a way to process a synthetic out of petroleum, and the market for real chicle collapsed.

Chicle wood—zapodilla—is very dense and resistant to decay, by the way. The Mayans used it for lintels in their structures; at Tikal we saw beams that've survived well over a thousand years.

We then took the bus to the Belize Zoo, quite a long trip. The local people practice slash-and-burn agriculture. Land that has been abandoned after a few seasons grows back first in guinea grass and tall cecropia trees; there were many such stretches along the way. There were also orchards and coconut groves, most of the latter dying of the virus that is sweeping Belize. People are now planting resistant varieties, but what had been the standard Belize coconut tree is going the way of the elm and chestnut in North America.

The local subsistence farmers plant corn, squash and beans in the same hole as the Mayans did. The squash grows along the ground and the beans use the cornstalk for support. Ninety percent of the grain in Belize, however, is grown by a small number of Mennonite immigrants (who left Germany for the U.S., then moved to Mexico, and in the 1950s settled in Belize) who by dint of hard work and Western agricultural methods are hugely more productive than the locals.

Because the Mennonites (some of whom eschew internal combustion machinery; others use tractors and outboard motors for their fishing boats) keep to themselves, there's been relatively little ethnic tension, but their *per capita* income is much higher than that of any other group in the country. One can hope—I hope—that envy won't drive these productive people out of Belize as has happened to them so often in the past.

We stopped en route at an anomaly, a Belizeian winery. The owner, a Creole about 60 years old, developed gardens and a winery on the 20 acres the government granted his father for being a veteran of World War II. So far as I could tell there was no difference between him and his neighbors, save that he was much harder working and imaginative. (There was a wall around the property to keep the garden furniture from going missing; before that he'd chained it down.)

The wines were local recipes for local fruits, among them orange, grapefruit, "blackberry" (a tree; not what we know as blackberry in the U.S.), cashew (from the fruit, not the nut), tamarind, and sorrell. Tourists had sent him books on winemaking after they got home— he'd been working without any help whatever before then. His bottles were liquor bottles from El Salvador, his corks from Canada (a visitor had found him a source), the plastic caps from Mexico, and his bottling machinery was British. He was selling the product for $3.50 U.S./bottle or three for $10. Heaven knows what it tastes like (I'm teetotal), but we brought some back for friends.

Thence to the zoo, a recovery operation stocked solely with injured animals and those released from poachers. The cages are very large and incorporate the vegetation that was on the site before it was fenced, so it can be quite difficult to find even good-sized animals. There was a lot of, "Is that it up there?" and the like. The facilities have largely been built by the Royal Engineers. The British army keeps a jungle training site in Belize and pays for the use of it by carrying out infrastructure projects within the country. The zoo was a beneficiary of this policy.

The woman who founded and runs it (she'd come to Belize 20 years ago to shoot a documentary and stayed) came by with some chicken scraps while we were there, so we got to watch the jaguars gambolling. Even I got good pictures of the friendly tapir, and the tamandua (lesser anteater) was an absolute ham.

Tapirs follow regular trails through the jungle and are therefore easy to shoot, but they—like jaguars and most other native animals in Belize—are making a comeback during the past decade or more. Belizeans have taken readily to the notion of the natural world as a tourist resource and a subject of national pride.

In the macaw cage was a clay-colored robin which had managed to squirm in through the mesh and was frantically trying to find a way out. The macaws watched it with mild interest.

It was an extremely hot day, and we were all wilting after the combination of the winery, a patio diner en route (it was called *Cheers*), and the zoo. The air-conditioned bus was a pleasure on the long trip to Pook's Hill, and I say that as one who normally dislikes and avoids air conditioning.

When we left the main road, the going became extremely bad. Here above all I was impressed by the Toyota and by Peter's skill. We were on a narrow rutted track, steep both up and down. The diesel and 5-speed manual transmission were more than adequate; Peter only rarely dropped into compound low. (My year driving a city bus allows me to appreciate excellence in this aspect of the trip.)

At one point Peter stopped and pointed out a pair of collared aracaris eating the fruit from a rubber tree. Aracaris are a form of toucan—smaller than the keel-billed, but big by almost any other standards—and brilliantly colored. They were just another of the striking species of birds we saw at every stage of the trip.

Pook's Hill is a nature reserve with a bush-hogged "lawn" on the slope beneath the lodge, an open-sided building with a thatch roof. The lower story (ground level at the back as the upper floor is at the front) is a common dining area, enclosed against the bugs. The individual bungalows have whitewashed walls of cast concrete and thatch roofs with a ceiling fan. The baths were large tiled rooms with a shower at one end and the toilet and washstand at the other; the water was drinkable (I did) though there was bottled water as elsewhere in Belize for those who didn't want to trust the taps.

The generator ran till bedtime, 10 PM or so, and then a battery bank kept the fans running till about three in the morning. It was in all respects a lovely location.

Here as later at the Victoria House we ran into a minor glitch: IE thought the Drake party was father, mother, brother and sister—and carefully arranged separate beds for Jonathan and April. (The two other parties with us were couples with a teenaged female dependent.) It was easily solved in both cases.

Vickie, who runs Pook's Hill with her husband, is English by birth and a fabric designer by former trade. She in a very nice way is a rabid naturalist as well as a thoroughly decent and interesting person. I noted that there were (seriously poisonous) give-and-take palms growing beside the bungalows and asked about them. She explained that two had been there but she'd transplanted the others because she'd noticed that the collared aracaris liked them. She then paused and said, "I guess they do send an odd message to guests, don't they?" But they didn't, not really.

Edd suggested a dip in the stream running through the property. The four Drakes took him up on it; the others, somewhat to my surprise did not (one family had a stomach bug; the daughter had been barfing on the extremely rough road and the father wasn't feeling great). It was a quarter mile away through rain forest, a neat walk in itself which involved crossing the stream on a rope bridge with a log floor.

And the stream was magnificent. It was broad but fairly shallow—chest deep or less throughout most of its width, but a trifle over six feet on the outside of the curve. Two-inch-long fish nibbled our body hair as soon as we got in the water; they were harmless but utterly unafraid. A solid wall of jungle rose above the bank. A large antnest of mud sat on the crotch of a branch hanging over the water; and from it grew a rare orchid which was in bloom. The orchid's seeds have a gelatine coating which the ants like. They carry the seeds to their nests, where they may germinate—as this one had.

There were many high points to our trip. Swimming in this jungle stream the two nights we were at Pook's Hill was one of them.

After dinner we got out our flashlights and Edd led us on a walk around one of the circular jungle trails in the darkness. It was an interesting experience, though wildlife itself was sparse. There was a coatimundi (an elongated raccoon), a large frog, and most strikingly a bat flying down the trail at head height with something in its talons. It may have been a fishing bat like the many we saw at Lamanai; alternatively, the prey may have been a large cicada.

Thence back to the bungalows and to bed, the close of another day of amazing experiences.

On July 16 I got up early for birds. We were handicapped by the fact that Peter had cut himself shaving (his scalp) and wasn't able to join us till late. Edd is a very good field naturalist, but Peter's knowledge of birds borders on the supernatural.

Fortunately, the birds made it easy. There was a cecropia tree just down from the lodge. A pair of crimson-collared tanagers were eating seeds in it and carrying them back to their nest in a nearby palm. They're striking birds, and indeed had pride of place as the back-cover illustration on my field guide.

Thence to Barton Creek Caves. The slightly sickly

family remained behind, which is probably good because the road this morning was if anything worse than that which brought us to Pook's Hill (which we retravelled as well, of course). At one point we backed up to allow an old Toyota minivan to get around us in the other direction; the driver must have been a local guide, because he swept his minivan through ruts that I was sure would bog him. Further on, we forded a creek.

This is a good time to mention the weather, a factor in any trip to the region. The rainy season should've started at the beginning of June, but no significant rains had fallen by the middle of July; the scattered nighttime showers while we were there didn't mark a change. Central America is undergoing a drought, and BBC noted that within a month a million people in the region would be in need of food aid.

I greatly regret the drought (human environmental changes—global warming and the destruction of rain forest over much of the region, particularly Guatemala— may be at least partially responsible, though droughts are believed to have brought down the Mayan civilization as I'll mention later). So far as we were concerned as tourists, the lack of rain made the trip much more pleasant. (I know what monsoon rains are like.)

Barton Creek Caves is privately owned (like Pook's Hill and Lamanai), but it serves backpackers and budget tourists as well as coddled ecotourists like ourselves. There's a large thatched marquee under which more than a hundred people could shelter (and scores did), with picnic tables and a bar. A number of family groups were swimming in the stream outside the entrance to the caves.

We rented canoes and entered the caves, three per canoe including a local guide who joined us. Whoever was in the back paddled, and the person in the middle was responsible for the light: an automobile headlight in a handgrip, attached to a truck battery by a length of flex with alligator clips. To turn the light on, you clipped both leads to the battery posts.

The ceiling rose in some places to 105 feet. There were striking stalactites and blooms of flow rock, though relatively few stalagmites. Several bridges crossed the cave, and occasionally the passage was low and narrow enough that the canoe scraped.

The Mayans regarded caves as sacred space. There are burials and grave goods in the caves, some of them (jugs set in niches) visible from the canoe. They've been studied by archeologists but not removed, which I think is a reasonable compromise. (Mind, I'm neither an Amerind nor an archeologist.)

Bats roost on the cave roofs. Fruit bat excrement is acid, so over the years they've dissolved conical pits as much as a foot into the limestone. They huddle there in their little burrows and flutter away if the light stays on them too long (which I tried to avoid).

Algae grows hundreds of feet deep into the caves. That nearest the entrance is greenish; farther in the growth is white; and a pinkish algae remains on the walls even very deep into the caves.

The algae surprised me, but not nearly as much as the plants did. Fruit bats sometimes excrete intact seeds, which won't be a surprise to anybody who's gardened with cow manure. The seeds sprout in the blob of fertilizer, also no surprise. But they continue to grow to over 4" high with deep green leaves, photosynthesizing from the light brought into the caves by tourists like us.

I didn't get any worthwhile pictures of the interior, but Jonathan's digital camera and Jo using faster film did. The caves impressed me in many ways, and my neck ached a trifle for weeks after from the amount of time I spent looking up.

I was struck during the tour that the unsophisticated commercialism of the site harked back to an earlier age in the U.S., for example the Black Hills in 1940 when my folks honeymooned there. Nowadays the volume of tourists, governmental involvement to protect a natural resource, and sophisticated marketing have changed things back home. (This is an observation, not a complaint in either direction.)

From the caves we went to Green Hills Butterfly Farm where the mistress—co-owner with her husband, both of them Dutch by birth—had lunch laid out for us on tables under the usual thatched marquee. As elsewhere the food was prepared by local servants and (as more often than not) it was chicken with a variety of rice, beans and vegetables. The concession to . . . hmm, I started to say Western tastes, but that would be pretty silly . . . First World tastes was a garden salad which is foreign everywhere in the region. She suggested we throw the scraps, including the chicken bones, over the fence to the chickens and guinea fowl, as that's what she would do afterwards if we didn't. (I did.)

A foot-long, brilliantly-colored lizard ran under the tables as we were eating. "What's that?" I said. The lady looked at me oddly and said, "That's my helper George"; meaning, I realized after a moment, the local man who'd just come over to ask her a question. Jonathan and I laughed in our usual fashion, while people looked at both of us oddly. (The lizard turned out to be a barred whiptail, a male in breeding colors.)

We then got a tour of one of the breeding greenhouses. The farm raises five kinds of butterflies; the caterpillar of one variety has extremely poisonous spines, so they're segregated in a separate greenhouse for safety. The plants within are chosen for for their blooms. There are also dropper bottles with sugar water (rather like hummingbird feeders; and washed with bleach every week, just as we do at home with our hummingbird feeders) and leafed twigs of chosen types in vases for the butterflies to lay eggs on. The blue morphos refuse to lay eggs on anything but living plants, so there are also a number of tiny saplings in pots.

Leaves with eggs on them are transferred in the evening to plastic containers like those you'd get deli coleslaw in, segregated by species. The containers are opened daily and a fresh leaf dropped in (this also changes the air; the containers aren't vented). When (as usually happens) multiple eggs hatch on one leaf, the leaf is cut with scissors and part goes into a new separate container with its crop. The process continues day by day until there's one caterpillar in each container. (The woman doing this with blue morphos had the quick efficiency I've seen in other highly-skilled workers doing a repetitive task.)

When the caterpillars pupate they're transferred to a screened box, still segregated by species. Green Hills supplies a number of butterfly houses in Europe and the U.S., including that of the Durham Science Museum which Jo and I saw last year. (They can only be transported as pupas.) To be honest, I'm not certain what happens to the other butterflies as there must be more than're necessary for breeding purposes; perhaps they're simply released into the wild.

This is a very large-scale, labor-intensive project; I was thoroughly impressed. (I was thoroughly impressed by an awful lot of what I saw during this trip.)

Thence back to Pook's Hill in the evening for dinner and a chance to relax, which I very much needed. I managed to turn my notes for the day into journal entries; there was so much going on every day that finding time for that necessary task was frequently difficult.

✦   ✦   ✦

We got up early in the morning of July 17 for another look at the birds of Pook's Hill before we left. I'd seen keel-billed toucans silhouetted in flight the afternoon we arrived in Belize, but this morning we got good views of them in all their size and color. They're the national bird of Belize—and a good choice therefor among many striking alternatives.

We went by bus to our second significant Mayan site, Xunantunich. On the way we paused in San Ignacio, the second city of Belize. The houses again reminded me of older dwellings in Brunswick County, NC, where we go to the beach every summer: smallish, generally shabby, often on stilts against flooding during hurricanes, and frequently brightly colored. There were many Internet cafes, many travel bureaus, and many shops with tourist wares.

The road passed two cemeteries here and another at San Jose Succotz. The graves in the region are mostly above ground because of the high water table. The stones and slabs are generally painted in bright pastels. The look and feel of these cemeteries is quite different from those of the parts of the U.S. where I've visited cemeteries.

At Succotz there's a hand-worked ferry (the operator cranks his raft along a cable) crossing a tributary of the Belize River to get to Xunantunich. There are three very large green iguanas (one was over 5 feet long) wandering around the ferry site; none of our group fed them, but I presume there's some reason they live in this location.

The raft wouldn't take the weight of the Coaster, so we loaded onto one of a pair of old blue Ford vans (the other passed us going the other way) that carry tourists to the site a mile upslope. The ride was hot (there was a little fan whirring in the back, but most of the windows didn't open), cramped, and extremely rough, but it sure beat walking.

Xunantunich was built to tax river traffic during the Classic period; it had only about 7–10 thousand people (as opposed to Tikal, one of some thirty known Mayan sites which probably had some 175 thousand residents at their peak). It's relatively small, so you can get a feel for the whole site from the restored pyramids unlike Lamanai and particularly Tikal.

During the late '70s while Belize was still British Honduras, the brutal military dictatorship in Guatemala threatened to take over the country by force. The British moved in troops and aircraft. Xunantunich became a British army observation post with concrete stairs to the top. Not surprisingly there's been earthquake damage since then.

One of the mounds visible from the main pyramid is cratered. An archeologist blew it open with dynamite and announced that there was nothing inside . . . which was certainly true after he got done with it. Any Iowa farmer with an Indian mound on his property could've told him that's not how you find burials and grave goods. (I'm not saying I condone the practice; just that my in-laws used dynamite for stumping, not grave robbing.)

We drove from Succotz to the Guatemalan border, where there was considerable bureaucracy and (especially since I'm slightly agoraphobic) discomfort. I read a book as I stood in line with a great crowd of other people, waiting for petty officials to stamp forms and take money. (Belize and Guatemala charge people who are leaving the country, $20 and $30 per head, respectively.) I found the whole business unpleasant and—it seemed to me—unnecessary.

Thence back on the bus and a long drive to Tikal. The road is now quite good, becoming paved a few miles from the border. Apparently the road had been awful but the complaints of tour operators forced the government to act—though I gather "act" in this case means spend aid money on construction instead of using it to line the pockets of officials. The aid ran out a distance short of the border, but the gravel portion is drivable.

A line of poles—like telephone poles but without wires—parallels the road. Jo later learned the poles were set up to prevent people from landing light planes on the concrete highway. There's very little traffic, even less than in Belize.

Jonathan noticed that we were being followed by a blue Toyota pickup with two men in it. I asked Edd, who said with obvious embarrassment, "They're friends." It appears that IE provides armed guards for its groups while they're in Guatemala, but they want to keep the fact quiet so as not to spook clients. The trucks carrying cases of Pepsi and Coca-Cola also have armed guards: anyone in the country with cash has to be guarded, because thirteen families control all Guatemala's wealth. Grinding poverty turns most of the population into potential bandits.

Our hotel, the Tikal Inn, is one of the three within the park site. They're private property, remaining under a grandfather clause when the rest of the large tract became public. I assume the Tikal Inn was the best because IE did an excellent job in all the other arrangements, but the place wasn't prepossessing. None of our party were willing to swim in the pool; the restaurant was dirty (food that dropped on the floor would still be there at the next meal) and the staff sparse and untrained. (The waiters couldn't take an order for soft drinks and water in English, for example.) Our room and that of Jonathan and April beside us had cross draft and were reasonably comfortable. The other rooms had windows only on one side, and when the electricity went off at 10 PM, the ceiling fans stopped also.

After settling into our rooms we walked through forest to the archeological site a quarter mile away. There are many armed police throughout the site, up on the pyramids as well as lounging in guard posts at intersections on the ground. Coatimundis, spider monkeys, ocellated turkeys, and crested guans (a larger version of the chacalaca) are as common throughout the site as pigeons are in downtown Chapel Hill.

The site, which the Canadians cleared to its present extent in 1975, is huge. The population during its long *fluit* was about 175,000, far beyond what the region's present slash-and-burn agriculture could support. The Mayan kingdoms use raised-bed agriculture in the swamps around the city, forming "paddies" with three-foot-high walls and filling the interior with rich muck from farther out in the swamps. Raised bed agriculture can feed 1000 people/acre against 65/acre for slash-and-burn.

During the dry summer months the paddies were watered from the reservoirs on high ground in the city. The great causeways of the city were designed not only for pedestrian traffic but also to channel water (along the plastered gutters to either side) into the reservoirs for later distribution.

The region is subject to periodic droughts; recently one lasted for sixteen years, dropping the annual rainfall from 100 inches to 45 inches. A similar drought struck toward the end of the 6th century AD. The reservoirs didn't fill, so the crops on the raised beds would've shrivelled before becoming ripe. This in turn ended the Classic Mayan period. Tikal remained an important site, but the nature of warfare changed from war for the sake of honor, to war in which the conquered city was annihilated to gain its territory to support the victor.

We entered the Great Plaza past a shrine house, where the king would talk to his ancestors. Temple 1, the tallest surviving pre-Columbian structure in the New World, was closed to tourists but we climbed Temple 2 across from it and also Temple 5 to the south. The acoustics are such that you can easily talk to someone on the opposite pyramid about 200 feet away. Originally Temple 1 was an astronomical observatory, but the ruler who built Temple 2 converted Temple 1 to a tomb for the body of his father, killed in war but later recovered.

Reuse, cannibalization of building materials, and overbuilding are characteristics of all Mayan sites. There are now 16 small temples on the North Acropolis, but they're built on at least 150 earlier temples. The palace on the south side had rooms on five levels. There are steps up to the top, but there are also bleacher seats in the form of broad steps where the court would sit facing the populace gathered in the plaza. The higher a noble's rank, the higher his seat. The king on top would be comfortably ensconced on pillows of jaguar skins stuffed with feathers and kapok from the ceiba tree.

We went from the Main Plaza to the much older Temple of the Lost World, which we climbed with the intention of watching sunset from the top. I was in pretty rocky condition by this point, mostly as a result of descending Temple 2 sideways with my right leg leading the whole way. My left leg started to cramp. There'd been a lot of riding followed by a lot of physical exertion, and that stupid mistake had cost me much of my normal capacity for physical exertion.

The Temple of the Lost World was worth the effort. At 130 feet it's by no means the tallest structure at Tikal, but you can climb to the very top whereas much of the height of the higher temples is in combs which weren't ever meant to be climbed. The view of the jungle below us was marvelous: a bat falcon was making circular passes from a ceiba tree nearby; two birds of prey—they may have been hook-billed kites, but Foster and Edd were uncertain and Peter didn't come with us—were perched in plain sight a quarter mile away. Toucans were hopping among the treetops at the foot of the pyramid.

With us on top of the pyramid were three backpackers. They became excited when our guides pointed out the toucans, and we let them borrow our binoculars to watch those huge, brilliant birds. It struck me that though they were travelling to the same places as we were, they'd have seen nothing but jungle from here, if it hadn't been that we—with Edd and Foster—were present at the same time. I greatly respect what the backpackers were doing on their own, but I'm glad for myself that I waited to go until I had enough money to hire expertise that would enrich the trip beyond anything I personally brought to it.

Because the sky was cloudy, we came down from the pyramid before it was full dark (which would've made the descent really tricky, given the shape I at least was in). It'd been quite a day.

At dinner, Edd and two members of the hotel staff played the marimba. I was struck by how much reverb the instrument had.

I got up early on July 18 and went out birding with Pete as I usually did. Jo and Edd joined us. We got a good view of a blue-crowned motmot which has two long tailfeathers that're bare shafts save for a tuft at the end. While I wasn't pleased with the Hotel Tikal Inn generally, I've got to give some credit to any place which has these analogues to the birds of paradise living on the grounds.

There was also a bat falcon sitting on top of a high bare limb, picking apart something with a long tail (possibly a snake). It was a lengthy process. Throughout our stay in Central America I was pleased and surprised by the way birds of prey lived near humans without concern. The family of marsh hawks with which we've shared our property for the eight years we've been in the present house would never let me get as close as this falcon and many other raptors did.

We returned to Tikal with Foster, starting this time with Complex Q, one of a series built over the course of Mayan civilization to mark a 20-year cycle. Each complex has pyramids to east and west, with a nine-door palace to the south (symbolizing the Underworld) and a corbelled arch to the north (symbolizing Paradise) opening to an engraved stela and altar which recount the ruler's achievements.

The carved altars weren't functional. The altars in the plaza on which prisoners were tortured to death in odd numbers—three, five, or seven at a time generally—and their associated stelai weren't carved, though they probably had painted legends when they were new. The altar in the north archway is carved with a full description of the dedication ceremonies for the complex, including the names and means of torture by which the victims were sacrificed.

Later generations overbuilt previous monuments. What kept Q more or less intact was that it was built in 771 AD, just before the final collapse of the Mayan Kingdom. Complex R followed it, but R was heavily cannibalized centuries later by a successor group, the Mopan Maya.

Toucans and oropendulas—big, brilliant orioles—flew among the trees throughout the site. I truly was able to live my dream, to stand in ancient stone cities buried in the jungle.

We curved back to the five-story palace on one side of the Main Plaza (there was quite a lot of walking on this trip, even without climbing pyramids at intervals). The Mayans claimed (perhaps correctly) to be Olmecs who migrated from homes along the coast. Throughout Mayan history, seashells and mother of pearl were luxury items because they were reminders of the national past.

There was trade with the Toltecs of Teotihuacan (the region of Mexico City) but the route is difficult (the Spanish administered Yucatan from Peru, not Mexico City). In 300 AD the ruler of Tikal made a personal journey to Teotihuacan and returned with a wonder-weapon—the atlatl, the spearthrower—and two Toltec warriors skilled in atlatl tactics.

This revolutionized regional warfare, turning Tikal into a superpower before rival cities were able to adopt the new weapon. When the king died without blood heirs, he appointed as his successors the Toltec warriors who'd come south with him. From one of these (the other died of lingering injuries incurred in the climactic battle) the royal line of Tikal continued through the Classic period. Architectural themes from Teotihuacan appear at Tikal thereafter.

Foster says that in the lower levels of the palace (closed to tourists) pale orange plaster still covers the walls, picked out by a red understripe and paintings of prisoners in black. Construction was by small stone blocks, more or less the size of bricks, rather than the sort of multi-ton ashlars the Egyptians used.

The public portion of the palace has expanses of white plaster, in some cases with graffiti made by 11th-century Mopan Mayans as well as by 20th-century tourists (mostly Spanish speaking, I noticed). People are people.

We went from the palace to Temple 4; it's 215 feet high but the ladder to the top of the comb (which the guidebooks mention) is no longer there; we reached only the level of the chamber at least 30 feet lower. Only the top portion of the pyramid has been cleared, so access is by a pair of wooden ladderways up the side. This is a very practical addition which doesn't harm the original structure. It seemed to me that the ladder was less tiring than climbing the original stone steps of other pyramids.

From the top there's a striking view of the peaks of other pyramids rising above the treetops, but the jungle is so thick that one doesn't have an overview of the site or any real awareness of its extent.

On the way back to the hotel for lunch, we passed a huge Spanish (also called hardwood) cedar. I got pictures of the buttress roots spreading from the base. That's another of the trip highlights for me.

There was also a line of army ants passing alongside our trail. On the other side I noticed a number of bright orange (probably poisonous) millipedes which weren't being harmed by the ants but which seemed to be unable or unwilling to cross the ant trail. If I'd seen them a year ago, the giant millipede of *Mistress of the Catacombs* would've been orange . . . but if I live, there'll be other books.

Jo and I got up early on July 19 and did the usual nature walk with Edd and Peter, around the hotel grounds. This morning we didn't see coatimundis, but there was a herd—flock? covey?—of agoutis, which you can think of as large guinea pigs. (The paca, a truly giant guinea pig, we saw only in the zoo.) A flock of white-fronted parrots passed over so low that for a change I actually saw them as parrots rather than parrot-shaped silhouettes.

I asked Peter, by the way, how he could say with such assurance (for example), "Those are red-lored parrots," or, "Those are brown-hooded parrots," when the birds were high overhead against a bright sky and the identification marks are the color of the small patch of feathers between their eyes. "By their calls," he said; which was obvious after he said it, but still quite remarkable.

Edd pointed out 4-inch-long caterpillars which lay on trunks and branches in groups of twenty or more, tight together like swatches of brown velvet with thin white stripes. These were the caterpillars of the Banana Owl moths, one of the species Green Hills Butterfly Farm raises. As adults they're huge and rather attractive, but the masses of caterpillars are pretty disgusting.

Near the museum was a slough covered with water hyacinths. A limpkin—a wading bird with a curved beak—walked over the hyacinths, dipping down and finally coming up with a 4-inch apple snail. (Everything from hook-billed kites to Morolet's crocodiles seems to eat them; I'd never thought of snails as a major item of diet, but I was wrong.) It held the snail in one foot, popped the hinge with its beak a couple times, and winkled out the meat to swallow.

Immature purple gallinules (visualize a colorful chicken) were walking on the hyacinths also. I don't know what they were eating, but an adult minced out on a drooping banana stem and ate one of the ripe bananas with deliberate pecks.

Thence back to the room to pack. Jo went walking and didn't come back till well after they'd collected the bags, so I had the nervous task of hoping I'd finished packing all her stuff. I checked three times and had April go over the room also; we seem to have succeeded.

I was wearing the Old Iowa tee-shirt my webmaster had sent me. In the lobby a couple from Cedar Rapids saw the shirt and struck up a conversation. The wife was originally from Guatemala. "I tell my family," she said, "how hot it gets in Iowa in the summer and how cold it gets in the winter, and they look at me and say, 'Why do you live in such a terrible place?'" Given that I moved to North Carolina myself when I learned how much milder the winters were, that's a fair question; but there's a lot about Iowa that I miss, and the conversation reminded me of that.

We ate lunch, still in Guatemala, at a hamlet called El Renata overlooking the river. There were dugout canoes pulled up on the bank; women washed their clothes in the stream. A huge brindled mastiff slept in the roofed patio where we ate, and another dog lay in the screened bathhouse.

We proceeded to Flores, a good-sized city with the regional airport. Every other shop in the business area appeared to be a travel agency; there were also bars with brightly (and often imaginatively) painted exteriors, and souvenir shops where the staff was more aggressive than I was comfortable with. To be honest, the whole country of Guatemala gave me the creeps; that mastiff wasn't "just a pet," nor were the guards following our bus "just friends" as Edd put it.

Thence to the airport, where we said goodby to Peter (who would drive the bus back to Belize City) and outprocessed. I had my usual trouble with forms, but we made it and boarded a Tropicair Cessna Grand Caravan (15 seats including the pilot, and a single turboprop engine). The flight to Belize airport was smooth. We inprocessed (having just come from a foreign country) and flew back in the same plane to San Pedro on Ambergris Caye.

A very battered Ford van carried the luggage and some of our group to the Victoria House where we were staying. The rest followed in a four-seat golf cart, the standard transportation in San Pedro for those who don't want to walk. The town is of about 3,000 people, strung out along the beach with basically just one long central street.

The Victoria House is very plush, with air conditioning even in our individual thatch-roofed cabanas (with the sea breeze, we didn't use the air conditioning except for the first night). By this point I was pretty thoroughly wrecked, but a shower perked me up. Dinner was ample and excellent.

And to bed, where I slept like a rock.

We were up early on July 20th to go birding with Edd. We didn't see either the roseate spoonbills or the American crocodiles (which live in salt water, unlike the Morolets) which are supposed to be present on Ambergris Caye, but there was a flock of white ibis and many egrets. There were also Great Blue Herons, which I'm used to from NC but which are impressive birds nonetheless.

We then went snorkeling; the first time for the four Drakes, though the other two families were experienced. The initial practice session off the end of the dock went well enough. I managed to control my breathing, and because the flippers provided positive buoyancy I was just about able to float. (For those of you who don't know: when I blow my lungs out, I sink even in salt water. This is one reason I never got far in Boy Scouts, as to pass the swimming test you had to float for ten minutes without paddling. Because of the laws of physics, I could no more do that than I could fly.)

There were schools of fingerlings near the dock, and I even saw an immature barracuda. So far, so good.

We then went out to the barrier reef (the second longest—Australia's is the longest—in the world). I was struck on the way out (an impression reinforced by later experiences) that most of the shallow-water sea is utterly barren. There are stands of manatee grass and turtle grass, their leaves pale from the fine sand lying over them. There are no visible fish in the grass, and most of the seafloor is *just* sand or mud. The wreck of a fishing schooner was an oasis of fish and other life in the middle of this wasteland. Clearly artificial reefs *do* work, and having seen the natural condition— a submerged desert—I'm puzzled that there's not a lot more lobbying for them. This would be something positive for Greenpeace and similar outfits to do, as opposed to creating television opportunities for their activists.

The snorkeling itself was one of those interesting experiences, like a few I had in Southeast Asia a long time ago. I could get along all right so long as I was floating face down and paddling just a little (otherwise my legs would slowly sink). The problem was that I couldn't get anywhere in particular without expending a great deal of clumsy effort, and there was a slight current.

At one point I drifted into the boat channel and Edd had to drag me back. (A tourist had recently been killed there.) In my struggles I got water in my mask and had to empty it while thrashing uncomfortably. I managed to swallow a bit of sea water in the course of things, and I became so physically exhausted that I was afraid I was going to throw up after the effort of getting back aboard the boat.

That's the downside: my own physical incapacity and lack of skill. The vivid life on and around the coral heads was quite marvelous during the times I wasn't drifting away on the verge of drowning, however. Edd enticed a 5-foot green moray eel out of the coral, giving me a real-life glimpse of one of the critters I used in *The Jungle*. (Come to think, I believe there was a giant iguana in *The Jungle* also. As well as grasshoppers and murderous honeysuckle.)

The boat moved to another part of the reef, Shark and Ray Alley. The nurse sharks and sting rays are used to being handled. Edd and the captain horsed them around freely, feeding them bits of fish. Touristy stuff, but they were quite real nonetheless.

Jo had even worse problems than I did: she simply couldn't get used to the mask. Jonathan and April did better, but not well enough that they wanted to go out again in the afternoon with the rest of the group.

Jo and I went instead on a glass-bottomed boat with an eclectic group of tourists from other hotels. Most were Spanish speaking, but there was a young Italian couple and a pair of American women in their late 20s with the 6-year-old daughter of one.

The clear panels weren't large and a crack had been repaired with plywood. When there might be something to see below us, the owner splashed water on the panels to compensate for the scratches, but for the most part there was nothing to see so this wasn't a problem.

In the course of the three-hour ride we saw a sea turtle (underwater and off the side of the boat; there was no way to tell which species) and a very striking rainbow parrotfish. By tossing out chum the owner brought shoals of blue tang as well as gray and yellowtail snapper around us.

The American women rode on the upper deck of the boat where the choppiness was amplified. They went into the water with others when the boat anchored. The mother immediately came back with her daughter and began retching while the daughter whimpered that she had to go to the bathroom really, really bad. Mother, between fits of nausea, tried to shut the child up or alternatively to get her friend over to take the child back into the saltwater rest room. It was, in its way, an entertaining episode.

We got back in late afternoon and relaxed. I even ate dinner, which wouldn't have been my bet while I was out with the snorkel.

On July 21 we went snorkeling again. One of our fellows had bought Jo a pair of goggles which worked for her (as the mask had not). Another explained to me that using my arms was counter-productive; I should simply kick. I found that really did work, though there were still problems.

The main one was that I had to keep moving, at least slowly, or my legs would sink. The other members of the party were good swimmers and—particularly the women—had positive buoyancy; they simply didn't understand that if they zoomed in front of me to look at something of particular interest, I was either going to bump them or my legs would sink. The water over coral heads was often very shallow, so I was in a constant state of agitation lest I inadvertently kick and damage some delicate structure.

Having said that, the amount and brilliant variety of life around the corals was fascinating and lovely. I'd brought the guide to reef life which IE suggested but (unlike the other guidebooks in the package) it was almost useless: there was simply too much there. (I did identify a dusky squirrelfish which looped out of his crevice and back; but compared to the fun I had identifying birds, fish were rather disappointing.)

There were several shoals of 6-inch reef squid. Their half-transparent bodies are flattened in a horizontal plane, and I saw no signs of two tentacles being longer than the rest. Edd and the captain assured me that they were squid, not cuttlefish, however.

Several of the party had disposable underwater cameras. They worked, but at least Jonathan's and April's pictures were of no particular merit in contrast to what they did with digital and film cameras on the surface. The images were blurred and washed out, even in the very clear water where we were.

My second attempt at snorkeling was much better than the first—I wasn't in fear of my life, nor on the verge of barfing—but it still falls into the category of educational rather than delightful. I might go snorkeling again if I were in a place that offered the opportunity, but I would never go somewhere in order to snorkel. It's one of those things I'm glad to have done—once.

The afternoon was free time. I simply relaxed, read, wrote up my notes into proper journal form, and chatted.

I've listened to BBC News on short wave for twenty years and had brought my current radio (a Sony ICF-7600 about the size of a trade paperback) along. While demonstrating it to Edd, I stumbled onto a favorite program (programme, I suppose I should say: *From Our Own Correspondent*) at an unexpected time. It was a small serendipitous pleasure, one of many on the trip. It made me think of Dad, a short wave enthusiast all his life, and how much he and Mom would've loved the trip themselves. I wish they were still around so I could tell them about it.

A low-key day and a good way to unwind before the grueling trip home.

On July 22 we were up early and did another little nature walk with Edd. San Pedro didn't have the natural interest of other places we'd been—it was a town, after all—though the young iguanas on the trees were of note. Because we'd walked the same route each morning, it was obvious that the lizards were very territorial—but even their postures seemed to be the same from day to day.

We chatted with Edd, who wanted to know about

writing. (People tend to think being a writer is a more exotic business than I find it to be.) He's had two (English language) poetry collections published in Belize and promised to send a copy to me in return for *Mistress of the Catacombs*, which I'll mail him as soon as I have copies myself.

We flew from San Pedro to Belize City in another Grand Caravan, outprocessed (bureaucracy was the least pleasant part of the trip, though it wasn't horrible or I suppose even unreasonable), and boarded an Airbus for Miami.

U.S. Customs wasn't a problem either, though the sheer scale of the operation was daunting. A DC-9 to Raleigh-Durham, where we picked up April's Rodeo. Jonathan drove us back to their house; we transferred our luggage to our car and Jo drove us home.

The house and animals were clean and happy.

It was an amazing and wonderful trip. It wasn't a vacation—it'll be years before I'm ready to do anything like this again—but for the rest of my life I'll be processing what I saw and learned.

Got questions? We've got answers at
BAEN'S BAR!

Here's what some of our members have to say:

"Ever wanted to get involved in a newsgroup but were frightened off by rude know-it-alls? Stop by Baen's Bar. Our know-it-alls are the friendly, helpful type—and some write the hottest SF around."
> —**Melody L** *melodyl@ccnmail.com*

"Baen's Bar . . . where you just might find people who understand what you are talking about!"
> —**Tom Perry** *perry@airswitch.net*

"Lots of gentle teasing and numerous puns, mixed with various recipes for food and fun."
> —**Ginger Tansey** *makautz@prodigy.net*

"Join the fun at Baen's Bar, where you can discuss the latest in books, Treecat Sign Language, ramifications of cloning, how military uniforms have changed, help an author do research, fuss about differences between American and European measurements—and top it off with being able to talk to the people who write and publish what you love."
> —**Sun Shadow** *sun2shadow@hotmail.com*

"Thanks for a lovely first year at the Bar, where the only thing that's been intoxicating is conversation."
> —**Al Jorgensen** *awjorgen@wolf.co.net*

Join BAEN'S BAR at
WWW.BAEN.COM
"Bring your brain!"